THE
CHOCOLATE
THIEVES

Ian Hudson

Elaine

Jilli

ISBN: 9798630215345

Thank you...

A Chocolate Thieves 100% Cocoa Truffle of appreciation to
Lizzie, Helen, Chris B., Peter D., Bex, James, Ben, Lucy, Polly,
Ashley, Dave J., Paul, Mina, Mandy, Sally, Gub, Guy,
Tamsin and Christine for listening to and reading drafts of
this story, and for answering research and technical questions.

&

To the ensemble of eccentric rogues I've met along the
chocolate road for their kindness and encouragement.

Copy-edit by Hannah
at Black Cat Editorial Services.

PART ONE

THE CHOCOLATE THIEVES

He takes a moment to inhale deeply through his nose the exquisite scent of Mrs Hoddinot's finely crafted artisan chocolates. 'Bloody delightful.'

In the light of his head torch, with a gloved hand, he grabs a handful of chocolates from the nearest box, putting one in his mouth – a Wild Blackberry Compote encased in a gloriously rich dark chocolate. Its intense flavour tendrils seductively creeping over his taste buds send a shiver of elation through him. 'Delicious.'

'Get to it, Dunstan,' comes the hushed impatient command from just outside the window.

Dunstan drops the rest of the chocolates in his hand into the jacket pocket of his suit, selects a stack of boxes and passes them to the waiting gloved hands of Furness expectantly hanging in the air at the window. In turn Furness takes a step back and passes the boxes to the gloved hands of Savage who puts them into CHOC 4 – the black London taxi that is the preferred mode of transport of The Chocolate Thieves.

Box after box goes into CHOC 4 until there is the sound of a door opening and closing somewhere in the building above them. There are breathless moments of listening. Then there comes the relieving flush of a toilet. And the chocolate-box-loading system resumes until there is the unmistakable creak of a footfall on stairs just outside the storeroom door.

Dunstan freezes mid-step.

There is the sound of a key being put into the lock, the click of the unlocking of the lock, and now there is the turning of the door handle.

The door quietly opens and into the storeroom, in his navy pyjamas, blue plaid dressing gown and matching slippers, creeps the chocolatier's husband, a sensitive, forty-seven-year-old man with allergies and thinning mousy hair – known locally as Mr Hoddinot despite this being his wife's family name. Watching and listening for someone outside of the storeroom, he quietly closes the door and tiptoes backwards away from it.

Dunstan surreptitiously lifts the lid of the top box of chocolates on the stack he is holding and slips his hand inside. At the same time Furness sticks his head through the window to see what is going on. 'Oh fuck' forms a silent expression in his eyes and on his lips on seeing Mr Hoddinot creeping backwards towards his friend.

Realising he is walking through a torch beam Mr Hoddinot slowly turns round and comes face to face with the balaclava-wearing Chocolate Thief. He goes to cry out but before he can expel a sound Dunstan's hand retracts from the top box of chocolates and shoves a handful of the man's wife's artisan chocolates into his mouth.

There is a moment of stunned silence and chewing.

Dunstan casually pops a chocolate into his own mouth – a tinglingly earthy Ginger Beer.

The alarmed Mr Hoddinot goes from inert surprise and chewing to panic. Hand to throat he points frantically at the boxes of chocolates Dunstan is holding.

'What?' The Chocolate Thief looks at the box he took the chocolates from that he shoved into Mr Hoddinot's mouth, that he watched him chew and then swallow. *CONTAINS NUTS* is written in bold font across the lid. 'Oh fuck.'

2

Discarding the chocolates Dunstan goes over to Mr Hoddinot who is now writhing on the floor, tries to assist him, but can offer little of any help.

'What's he doing?' asks Furness.

'He's gone into anaphylactic shock,' comes Dunstan's concerned response.

'Why?'

'Nuts! He's fucking allergic to nuts.'

'Why did you give him nuts?'

'Well I didn't exactly have time to show him the fucking selection menu and discuss allergies.'

Savage appears next to Furness at the window. 'What the fuck is going on?' He sees the choking Mr Hoddinot. 'Oh dear. This does not look good. Is it nuts?'

'Yes,' confirms Furness.

'Yes – thought so. Not good at all. The symptoms are unmistakable – the mouth and lips tingling, face swelling, a feeling of tightness around the throat, difficulty breathing due to an asthma-like attack, dilation of the blood vessels causing general redness of your skin and hives. There will be nausea, a fast heart rate, low blood pressure, so feeling faint or ready to collapse and a sense of impending doom.'

Mr Hoddinot points a trembling finger at Savage, barely able to speak, his voice a strangled shriek, 'What he said.'

'He's going to die,' offers Savage matter-of-factly.

The choking Mr Hoddinot is now desperately scratching at the door and trying to reach up to the handle to open it to get out of the room.

'Where's he trying to get to?' wonders Dunstan.

'You'd think he'd be happy to die in the scent of all these exquisite chocolates,' ponders Savage.

A saving-the-dying-man thought occurs to Furness. 'Has he got an epinephrine pen?'

Mr Hoddinot stops scratching at the door and starts

nodding frantically and pointing upstairs.

Dunstan looks up as if seeing through the ceiling. 'Oh bloody hell.' He pulls the dying man away from the door, opens it, runs out of the storeroom and up the stairs.

Off the landing he finds the bathroom. He hurriedly searches through the toiletries and medicines in the mirrored bathroom-cabinet on the wall above the sink – eventually finding the epinephrine pen on the top shelf.

Turning round he is face to face with a sleepy Mrs Hoddinot, a forty-four-year-old woman not to be trifled with, even dressed, as she is, in her blue nightshirt with *Hoddinot's Hot Chocolate* emblazoned in cocoa-shaded lettering across it. 'Who the f—' she begins to exclaim but Dunstan is too quick for her – he pulls a chocolate out of his pocket and shoves it into her mouth.

He pushes past her, then stops mid-stride and turns back to look at the chewing face of the artisan chocolatier. 'You're not allergic as well are you?' She shakes her head. 'No. You're okay. Good. Right. Bye.'

Dunstan runs down the stairs, pursued by a now-very-awake-and-determined-to-catch-him Mrs Hoddinot. He dashes through the storeroom – stabbing the choking Mr Hoddinot in his thigh with the epinephrine pen as he does so. Furness and Savage run from the window to CHOC 4. Grabbing one last box of chocolates, Dunstan dives out of the window, roles into a run and jumps into the waiting taxi. Savage thrusts CHOC 4 into gear, floors the accelerator and they wheelspin away from the scene of their thievery.

The kitchen, like the rest of The Chocolate Thieves' run-down Georgian house, has an environment of habitable decay. Shafts of winter sunshine coming through the window cut through the wood smoke lingering in the room from the cosying fire in the grate. The kitchen table is laid for three – a pot of tea steeping in the centre of it.

Furness is serving up a full English breakfast – luxurious slices of fried black pudding, runny-yoked poached eggs, sizzling venison sausages, juicy field mushrooms, plump grilled tomatoes and thickly sliced buttered toast.

Dunstan is sitting at the table, with a direct line of sight through the house to the front door, reading a newspaper.

Savage walks into the kitchen. 'Good morning, my fellow rogues.' He takes his chair at the table with a view of the garden through the kitchen window. 'It's a bright start to another day out of the cold shadow of the hangman's noose.'

Furness and Dunstan both greet him with a preoccupied, 'Good morning.'

Savage cups his hands around the teapot to check its temperature and pours some milk into the three cups on the table. 'What ails the world on this blue-skied winter's morning, Dunstan?'

'The usual economy of war and poverty, Savage,' reports Dunstan, adding, 'Cocoa price is at a five year high.'

'Testing times,' proffers Savage.

Furness places three wonderful plates of food on the table. Dunstan discards the newspaper and Savage stirs the tea in the pot. Furness watches with familiar bewilderment as Savage and Dunstan admire the food in front of them as if he doesn't produce a fine breakfast every morning – which he does.

'Excellent work, Furness,' offers Dunstan as he inhales the multiple scents emanating from his plate.

'Indeed,' affirms Savage. He goes to pick up the teapot but the handle comes off in his hand. The other two ignore this as if it is a common occurrence – which it is.

Furness passes Savage a tea towel as he sits down in his chair at the end of the table. 'Make the most of enjoying every mouthful – the restaurant's running out of suppliers not to pay.'

Savage uses the tea towel to pick up the teapot and pour cups of strong tea for each of them. 'Testing times indeed.'

Dunstan picks up a bottle of Furness's homemade hot-and-spiced chocolate breakfast sauce off the table and liberally douses his breakfast with it before passing it to Furness who does the same before passing it to Savage who does likewise.

They simultaneously tuck into their delicious breakfast.

'Last night was a close call and for what?' proffers Furness with a hint of irritation.

'Ninety-two boxes of Mrs Hoddinot's assorted handcrafted artisan chocolate treats,' teases Dunstan.

Savage smiles with delight as he looks towards the boxes of chocolates from last night's heist stacked in the corner of the room. 'I've been salivating at the prospect of trying her new range of chocolates this last month. Such silkiness with decisive floral and earthy cocoa notes to the chocolate. And what robust flavours: Apple & Cinnamon, Rhubarb Delight, Blackcurrant, Gooseberry Tart, Caramel Cup, Salted Nutty Whip, Morning Espresso, Citrus Crush, Wild Honey…'

Dunstan nods enthusiastically. 'They're bloody delicious.'

'And they're fair trade organic,' adds Savage.

Furness is frustrated at them missing, if not blatantly ignoring, his point. 'Well, that's okay then, we don't want to steal bloody delicious non-ethical chocolates do we.'

'If we show restraint in our indulgence it's just enough to keep us going for the month,' suggests Savage.

This last comment gets sceptical glances from Furness and Dunstan.

'This level of crime doesn't pay. It's a fucking hobby,' says Furness feeling the need to point out the obvious.

'Accepted, it is small fare for the effort,' agrees Savage.

'And good work in nearly killing Mr Hoddinot,' Furness taunts Dunstan.

Dunstan defends himself. 'Who the fuck creeps around their own shop in the middle of the night to steal their own chocolates? Allergic to nuts! Probably a fucking diabetic as well with artery-clotting levels of cholesterol. Fucking idiot!'

'He did puff up,' observes Savage.

Dunstan does an impression of Mr Hoddinot puffing up and choking which gets smirks off the other two.

Savage drinks his tea and finds himself looking at the framed black-and-white photograph of a police line-up standing on the mantelpiece – it could be the three of them a hundred years ago. Savage's imagination takes him into a 1920s silent film with the title *The Chocolate Thieves* emblazoned across the screen…

The original Chocolate Thieves arrive outside the Midas Chocolate Company in a London taxi with the registration CHOC 1. They run in, grab as many boxes of chocolates as they can each carry and run out again, pursued by the proprietor, one Alfred Midas. The Chocolate Thieves jump into CHOC 1, Savage takes the wheel, Furness and Dunstan in the back, and they speed away.

An intertitle appears on screen of Alfred Midas shouting, 'Stop! Thieves!'

The police arrive and are sent in pursuit of The Chocolate Thieves by the irate chocolatier.

A frantic car chase ensues through the traffic and

pedestrian-filled roads – cars shunt, horses bolt with their carts and baskets of shopping fly through the air as pedestrians dive out of the way. Suddenly the engine of CHOC 1 explodes in a cloud of steam and the taxi grinds to a halt. Savage and Furness jump out and get into an arm-waving altercation about the engine. When the police arrive on the scene The Chocolate Thieves try to run for it but are quickly caught. Savage trying to steal a horse-drawn brewery dray – the old nag harnessed to it refusing to take even one step until it has eaten the contents of its nosebag. And Furness trying to ride a tram without paying.

Dunstan has remained seated in the back of CHOC 1 and when a police officer looks into the taxi at him The Chocolate Thief shrugs his shoulders as if he has no idea as to what is going on and points to his wristwatch pretending he is late to arrive somewhere.

The three of them are charged with stealing chocolates and sent to trial. There appears on screen an intertitle of the judge's sentencing: 'Mr Savage and Mr Furness, you have been found guilty of the crime of larceny and causing distress to a decent hard-working entrepreneur. So, I have no hesitation in sentencing you both to twelve months' imprisonment. We can but hope the time you will spend incarcerated teaches you the error of your ways. And as for you, Mr Dunstan, you are free to go. Just be of care whose taxi you get into in the future.'

Savage and Furness glare at the judge as Dunstan winces at the disproportionate length of their sentences.

Back in the present, Savage looks at the other two busily eating, oblivious to his journey into the past. 'What is the date?'

Dunstan consults the newspaper as he takes in a mouthful of field mushroom and grilled tomato, and says,

'1st March.'

Furness butters himself some more toast.

A hundred years,' says Savage, standing up. He walks over to the photograph, picks it up, and studies it. 'It's a hundred years since this photograph was taken.' He has their attention. 'A hundred years since our great-grandfathers raided the Midas Chocolate Company and began this chocolate odyssey.'

'Bloody hell!' is Dunstan's surprised response.

'What's your point?' asks Furness.

'My point is, gentlemen, that this is an anniversary that cannot go unnoted. My point is, gentlemen, there can be no more petty pickpocketing of confectionary. No more petty pilfering of Apple & Cinnamon and the like.' A large bluebottle buzzes around the table, annoying Furness and Dunstan. 'It's time that every chocolate-craving, tingling, taste bud in the world knew the name, The Chocolate Thieves.' Unnoticed by Savage, lost as he is in his reverie of the photograph, the bluebottle lands on his backside. 'Why do we do this? It is not a hobby.' Furness passes the tea towel to Dunstan. 'It is a way of life. And it is time we became more than a confectionary folk tale. It is time we became legends.' Dunstan flicks the tea towel at the bluebottle, misses it, and with a loud slap connects with Savage's rear. 'Ow! You absolute rotter!'

At New Scotland Yard the detective knocks twice on the door of her senior officer and walks into his office.

DI Gloom looks up at her from his laptop. 'There's been another one, DS Silky.'

'Another what, sir?'

Turning the laptop round so she can see the screen, DI Gloom points to a news feed – the headline reads, *HODDINOT'S CHOCOLATE HEIST*. 'They took nearly a hundred boxes of her handcrafted artisan chocolates with a street value of just under £2,500.'

'Chocolates? I'm your leading murder detective.'

'Yes – you are. And well done on solving the Microwaved Russian Bride case.'

'Thank you, sir.'

'Insightful deduction that she'd been dissected, cooked and served up as ready meals at the Belgravia Baby Boomer's Day Centre – is there anyone that generation won't eat?'

'It seems not, sir.'

'A man nearly died last night of a nut allergy. So, it's kind of a murder case.' DI Gloom picks up a thick case file off his desk and hands it to DS Silky.

Written across the front of the file are the words *THE CHOCOLATE THIEVES*.

DS Silky flicks through the file. The first chocolate theft case, titled *Midas Chocolate Company*, has a copy of the police's black-and-white line-up photograph of the original Chocolate Thieves attached to it – the names Savage, Furness and Dunstan written in white ink above their heads.

'This case needs your highly tuned detective's brain,' encourages DI Gloom.

'These cases go back a hundred years. You can't arrest ghosts,' protests DS Silky.

'This may well be a fondant-centred crime, Sergeant, but this is clearly a long-standing family firm that we have never got close to catching more than once and know not the identity of apart from their names and what they might look like.'

'We have their names and what they look like, yet we don't have them in custody?'

'No evidence.'

'What?'

'Ever since they got caught on that first heist they always turn up in suits, balaclavas and gloves, commit a chocolate heist, leave no forensics and vanish again. Every report on a chocolate theft in that file ends with ...*and they got away in a London taxi with the registration CHOC 1 or CHOC 2 or CHOC 3 or CHOC,* bloody, *4!*'

'We have their names. Have you tried the electoral register?'

'No idea. What does it say in the file?'

DS Silky flicks to a page in the file and reads aloud the attached note, '*Whereabouts unknown. Yes, I've checked the electoral register and every other way we have of tracing people, come on, I'm a detective, I know what I'm doing – these people don't exist. Signed, DS Popper.*'

'Ah, yes, DS Popper – he's transferred to vice.'

A business card drops out of the file onto DI Gloom's desk. DS Silky picks it up and reads it. '*Dorothea's Rare Vintage.*'

'Ah, yes, that's my niece. Into this kind of thing – you know folklore, history of crime and cold cases. She's got a whole incident room on The Chocolate Thieves. In fact, it's probably a good place for you to start. Her number is on the card.'

DS Silky tries to hand the case file back to DI Gloom. He ignores it. 'Sir, I investigate bodies. Where are the bodies?'

'Think of the kudos, DS Silky, of being the detective to finally apprehend the notorious and elusive Chocolate Thieves.' His sergeant sighs. 'Think headlines!' DI Gloom does the conventional newspaper headline gesture with his right hand and says, '*A HUNDRED YEARS OF CHOCOLATE CRIME ENDS.*'

'*STICKY END FOR THE CHOCOLATE THIEVES*

DETECTIVE,' mimics DS Silky.

'Now, that tickles my taste buds,' he chuckles mischievously.

Selecting a Rhubarb Delight for himself, DI Gloom offers his sergeant a chocolate from the box of Mrs Hoddinot's chocolates he has on his desk.

DS Silky selects a Wild Honey, pops it into her mouth and quivers at the quality of the flavours, offering an involuntary 'Bloody lovely.'

In her first-floor studio, resident artist at the Dunstan Gallery, Soho, Kyoko Kurokawa is discussing with Dunstan the quality of the Eliot Hodgkin still life painting of a sliced-open cocoa pod with raw cocoa beans on the table between them.

'When was the last time we sold one of my paintings as genuine?' she both questions and protests.

'Kyoko, just look at what you've painted – it is as good as anything Hodgkin did.'

The artist runs her hands through her black hair to diffuse her frustration then returns them to her hips. 'Just sell it as in the school of Hodgkin.'

'It's going to sell as genuine,' decides Dunstan and he takes the painting downstairs into the gallery and stands it on the display easel just as the door of the gallery opens and in walks the potential buyer.

Lawrence Smythe is a man with the demeanour of someone trying to make a decision about something of which he has very little knowledge. With him is an older man carrying about him a learned air of scepticism laced with an unsettling self-confidence.

'Mr Smythe, good to see you again.' Dunstan greets him with a deceptive air of pleasure and self-assurance.

They shake hands.

'Mr Dunstan, this is a friend of mine, Charles Rutter. He's going to take a look at the painting for me. Help me make up my mind. Reassure me I'm buying a genuine… I mean, the right painting.'

'I see.' Dunstan holds out his hand. Rutter shakes it as if it doesn't really matter if he does or not. 'Well, here it is, an original Eliot Hodgkin.'

Smythe looks expectantly at his friend for his approval of the artist's work.

Charles Rutter stands back to take in the composition of the painting – pausing in its execution. Then the art expert steps forwards to closely examine the brushwork – seeing every detail. He examines the construction of the frame, the original sales label on the back – *The Royal Academy Summer Exhibition 1962* – and the quality of the board and the paint to see if it is of the correct period. He steps away from the painting, taking a moment to once again consider the realisation of the still life – too quickly coming to his conclusion.

'It is not genuine,' the art expert curtly pronounces.

'I think you'll find it is,' asserts Dunstan. 'Look, it's signed, *Eliot Hodgkin.*'

'It is a good effort at a Hodgkin – I'll grant you.'

Dunstan persists. 'Look again. See how the flow of the brushstrokes is perfect. The full, yet truthful, colour variations.'

Charles Rutter is unmoved. 'The paint and board are genuine. The inspiration is not.'

Determined to sell the painting, Dunstan continues, 'Can you not see how he has infused the work with realism, mystery and poetry, as the objects of study, the freshly opened cocoa pod and the beans, are seen for the first time?'

Charles Rutter shakes his head. 'The only mystery is

how you cannot see that this painting is out of time. The shades of tempera are too young, the hand of the artist – gifted as they are – is yet too unrefined for this period of Hodgkin's work.'

Dunstan turns his attention to Lawrence Smythe. 'You can't deny it is in the school of Hodgkin.'

'I do not want a likeness, Mr Dunstan, I want an original Eliot Hodgkin,' insists Smythe with the indignity of the wounded party.

Charles Rutter surveys the gallery of forgeries of British painters. 'The artist who painted these for you – if they ever do any original work, do call me,' he hands Dunstan his card, 'they are hiding their talent in simulacra.'

Dunstan reads the card, '*The Courtauld Institute of Art* – what are you, a mature student?'

The art expert is unimpressed. 'I am a leading authority on British twentieth-century painting.'

And with those last words Lawrence Smythe and Charles Rutter exit the gallery.

Kyoko, brush in hand, appears in the doorway at the back of the gallery and gives Dunstan a look of 'I told you so.'

'Damn it!' Dunstan reaches into his jacket pocket, retrieves a chocolate and pops it into his mouth – the Mulled Winter Spices having a soothing effect on his disappointment.

Savage wanders through the market at Covent Garden filling, with sleight of hand, his mouth and pockets with chocolates from the confectionary stalls he passes. At a stall of eccentric tat he ponders the purchase of a new teapot.

'Your finest and rare, vintage, 1960s, chocolate brown, mirror glaze, English teapot,' the enchanting woman behind the stall informs him, adding, 'It makes a lovely cuppa, well, four lovely cuppas in fact, or three stronger ones, or two very strong ones depending on the quantity and quality of the tea used – as I'm sure you are aware.' And with a not-so-subtle flirtation she hands Savage her business card.

Savage glances at it, *Dorothea's Rare Vintage*, then tucks the card into his pocket. He studies the teapot from all angles, like a connoisseur. Assessing the quality of the glaze – it is even and uncracked. Lifting the lid and looking into it for staining or the lack thereof – it has been well looked after. Then sniffing the inside of the pot – satisfied with the appropriate level of quality tea odour. He does a pouring action assessing the balance of the pot. 'Has it a strong handle?'

'Indeed it has,' Dorothea assures him. 'Designed for a man with strong hands but with sensitive taste buds.'

'And what about the spout?' He runs his finger along it – there are no imperfections. He puts the end to one eye to look down it, lifting the lid to let in some light – it is clean and well formed.

'I think you will find it's always at the correct angle to pour perfectly.'

'How much is it?'

'Well, your finest and rare, vintage, 1960s, chocolate brown, mirror glaze, English teapot capable of making four lovely cuppas, £50.'

'Try again.'

'£45?'

'And again.'

'£35?'

'Once again.'

'£25?'

'Will you wrap it?'

Dorothea proceeds to carefully wrap the teapot in tissue paper and put it in a bag which she exchanges for Savage's cash. 'Would you like me to carry it home for you?' she hears herself say.

'I'm sorry?'

'I mean to say – do be careful carrying it home.'

'I will be,' says Savage, lingering longer than he needs to in the moment. Then with a light smile he walks away.

Dorothea pulls out her research file from her satchel tucked beneath the stall, opens it and studies the original photograph of The Chocolate Thieves. 'Savage, that was bloody Savage!' She watches The Chocolate Thief disappearing into the flow of people making their way through the market.

Dorothea abandons her stall and stalks Savage all the way to his home. Which to her surprise is situated in a quiet street a short distance from the British Museum. She watches Savage produce a door key and enter the fourth house in the street through its paint-cracked black door. Above the door is a weathered sign, *The Black Truffle Hotel* – the picture on the sign being, as expected, a black chocolate truffle on a cream background.

She looks for the street name. The sign is above her head on the wall of the first house – *Truffle Street*. 'You're kidding me.' How the hell did she not know this street was here? How many times has she walked past it, mapping The Chocolate Thieves' heists or on her way to the museum?

Her heart pounding and her fingers trembling with excitement she takes a photograph of the house with her phone then walks around the end of the street to the back of the houses. Here is a mews of what would have once been stables. Most of which are now small houses – a few are garages. Counting the doors she comes to the double garage stretching the width of the end of The Chocolate Thieves' garden. Unfortunately the garage and well-established trees in their garden obscure her view of the back of the house.

Dorothea takes more photographs of the location. At home she'll add them to her research file and work on an access strategy – determined, with lustful excitement, to one day see inside Savage's home. Then the bloody obvious dawns on her. 'It's called The Black Truffle Hotel – I could just book a room as a guest. Perfect.'

Sitting at her desk, DS Silky is reading through the crime report of the Mrs Hoddinot heist – concluding the obvious that it was a straightforward act of larceny. The near-death experience of Mr Hoddinot being accidental. Although no doubt an experienced prosecuting barrister would argue that it was a case of grievous bodily harm just short of being manslaughter.

Next she goes through the CCTV footage, watching the black London taxi, with the registration CHOC 4, slow down as it quietly drives along the cold, rain-washed, Islington street past Mrs Hoddinot's chocolate shop. Under the elegant cocoa-shaded lettering of her name, boldly signed above the door of the blue Victorian frontage, is written *Artisan Chocolatier since 1880*. All the lights are out in the shop and in the flat above. After driving around the end of the street, headlights switched off, the taxi pulls up at the rear of the building. Out of the taxi get three suited, balaclava and glove-wearing men. The first produces a short-bladed knife and skilfully unlatches the lock of a sash window, quietly slides the window open and enters the building.

'So you are The Chocolate Thieves.'

The taxi is expertly loaded with boxes of chocolates

until they have to make their quick getaway upon discovery of their presence inside the chocolatier's shop.

The detective watches The Chocolate Thieves driving away from the scene of the crime through the London traffic. The time code confirms that the heist took place from 1.02 to 1.22am – allowing CHOC 4 to lose itself in the late-night traffic of taxis and buses in central London.

The detective shakes her head. 'Very clever.' There are just too many options for direction of travel. It will take her days to trawl through all the possible routes they may have driven and she has no doubt that The Chocolate Thieves are smart enough to know, and make use of, the camera blind spots.

She tries retracing the direction of travel of CHOC 4 prior to the heist – again they evade detection, appearing on camera just before their destination.

'They've a hundred years of plying their trade,' she reminds herself.

Avoiding arrest by using basic evasion techniques and by keeping their faces covered with the balaclavas – all very simple and effective. If she did trace them to a specific destination she has no facial identification of them committing the crime. 'The vehicle was stolen, Detective,' and, 'Used in a crime, you say, Detective – how unfortunate.'

Watching the hours of footage to spot any reappearances of the taxi on the security cameras across London really isn't an option. The digital crime baskets of the team of detectives she supervises are full with their own cases of larceny, violence and curious deaths – all are too busy to help her on this ridiculous investigation. Not that she would waste any other detective's time on it. Something DI Gloom is well aware of – she wishes he'd find some other way of entertaining himself other than testing her determination to solve any crime she is handed.

It being evident that these criminals know how to disappear, for now, she takes the expedient course of action and makes a call to the security camera control centre and asks to be notified of any sightings of a taxi with the registration plate CHOC 4.

This done, DS Silky opens The Chocolate Thieves file and begins to read. Culturally significant heists through their criminal history stand out: *Midas Chocolate Company* in 1920, *International Chocolate Fair* in 1934, *Regent Street Sweet Shop* in 1941, *White's Chocolate House* in 1953, *Soho Delicatessen* in 1969, *New Rose Cocoa Den* in 1976, *Capital Chocolate Vaults* in 1986, *Brit-Choc-Art exhibition* in 1994 and the *Millennium Cocoa Jewels* stolen from Somerset House in the early hours of New Year's Day 2000.

Hours later, she is now alone in the office – her desk lamp the only light on the whole floor. Even the agoraphobic DI Gloom has made it out of his office to go home.

And as she suspected the moment she was handed the case, DI Gloom's name is listed as an investigating officer along with a roll call of legendary detectives – Doyle, Wyndham and Garner who failed to stop the activities of The Chocolate Thieves. He's using her skills to close a file that he has so far failed to close himself. Wanting his name as senior ranking officer with *solved by* written next to it in the file before he retires. Knowing she isn't going to willingly add the name DS Silky to the list of failed investigations.

'A hundred years – this is just the chocolate heists that were reported or made headline-worthy news.' DS Silky picks up Dorothea's business card. 'You have an incident room, do you?' She calls the antiquarian's number.

Dorothea answers on the second ring as if expecting someone else. 'Dorothea's Rare Vintage – the past before your eyes.'

'Hello, this is DS Silky. I'm investigating The Chocolate Thieves.'

'Are you – really?'

'Yes. Your uncle suggested I give you a call.'

'Dear old Uncle Gloom.'

'He said you have done extensive research on The Chocolate Thieves.'

'Indeed – I have done some investigating. If truth be told it was me who compiled the file you no doubt have in front of you. I've continued documenting their activities from the local news reports, online crime forums and social media sites, recording the word on the street, the mapping out of their heists…'

'You've a map of their heists?'

'Yes. From the very first – in fact I've just added Mrs Hoddinot's.'

'Could I call on you to have a look at your map?'

'Of course you can – have you my address?'

'Yes – it's written on the back of your card.'

'When were you thinking?'

'I'll see you in twenty minutes.'

A violent storm has blown in across the city – scurrying its inhabitants through doorways into bars and restaurants as they run with inverted umbrellas for cover. Trees are bent double, bins tumble along streets scattering pedestrians, cars and buses swerve about in gusts of howling wind and the blinding blades of rain. There is not a building that doesn't rattle in fright of the storm's pending violation.

The Furness restaurant, Soho, with its stripped-back decor of aged raw-plaster walls, bare floor boards, exposed steel joists, subdued lighting from low-hanging bare bulbs, reclaimed wooden tables and leather upholstered chairs and 6 Music playlist, has an atmosphere of contemporary urban retro-dystopian cool that should ensure it is never not fully booked – but it never is.

This evening's chalkboard menu of reclaimed traditional British dishes reads, Furness Mains: *Venison in a Seductive Blackcurrant & Chocolate Sauce with Parsnip Mash*; *Duck in a Rich Plum & Chocolate Sauce*; *Pheasant in a Delicate Redcurrant & Chocolate sauce*; *Fish & Rustic Chips with the Furness Fiery Chocolate Sauce*; *Fish Pie of Salmon, Smoked Haddock & Prawns in a White Chocolate Sauce topped with a Cheese Mash* and the Chef's Dish of the Day – *Pan Fried Cod in Cheddar Cheese & White Chocolate Sauce with Rustic Potatoes, Spinach & Peas*.

Furness Desserts: *Apple & Blackberry Crumble*; *Plum & Ginger Crumble*; *Cherry & Honey Crumble – all served with White Chocolate Custard*, or, *Two Scoops of Sheep's Milk Ice Cream – Raspberry & 80% Cocoa Chocolate*.

The restaurant is empty but for one couple waiting impatiently for their meal – two Chef's Dish of the Day.

The cooking starts going wrong when Furness can't decide which two of the four cod fillets he has to cook – after wasted minutes he eventually decides which two look like they should be served in the same meal. As the cod pan-fries he fusses for an age over the right blend of chocolate, milk, butter, flour, cheese and seasoning to create the perfect sauce. By the time the sauce is ready the plated fish is looking rather forlorn – as are the sides of rustic potatoes, spinach and peas. To finish with, Furness fusses over the presentation of the two plates of food.

Afia Lowe, the assistant chef and waitress at The Furness, apologetically tops up the couple's glasses of white wine then heads into the kitchen to see where their dinner has got to.

Furness is now staring at the two plates of food. He sniffs them, dips his finger in the pan of leftover sauce on the hob next to him and tastes it – he's unimpressed.

'They're about to leave,' Afia curtly informs him.

Furness shakes his head in self-disappointment. 'It looks shit and that sauce lacks salt or something?'

Afia stares at him in disbelief. 'Not again. Please. Don't do this again. These are the first customers we've had this week.'

'Is the fish too dry?' Furness asks her. 'I'm not sure it can go out.'

'Every fucking dish! It's perfectly acceptable dried cod in chokeable under-salted cheese and chocolate sauce – which is getting cold.' Afia grabs the two plates and heads into the restaurant, leaving Furness in silent protest.

She arrives at the diners' table just as the restaurant door closes on the couple, who, having downed their glasses of wine, have decided to eat where they can get served. Through the closing door the wind gusts rain into the waitress's face as she stands there with the unwanted plates of dinner.

Raging, Afia strides back into the kitchen, throws the two plates of food at Furness, who just about ducks out of their path, and storms out of the kitchen door slamming it shut behind her. Furness listens to her angry footsteps stomping up the external stairs to her flat above the restaurant. Its door is slammed shut behind her too.

Furness sighs at himself and takes a chocolate from the box of Mrs Hoddinot's on the counter next to him and pops it in his mouth – almost immediately he pulls the expression of a man eating something foul-tasting. He looks at the chocolate menu. 'Gooseberry! What a stupid idea!'

Dorothea opens the door to DS Silky, who holds up her ID, and invites her in out of the storm. 'Welcome, Detective Sergeant Silky – wonderful name.'

'Thank you.'

The antiquarian's Highgate flat is stylishly decorated with twentieth-century vintage furnishings. She directs the detective through to a small study, the shelves of which are full of books on antiques and history – with a section dedicated to the history of British crime. One wall is given over to a large-scale map of London with an incomprehensible tangle of coloured strings pinned to it.

Dorothea offers DS Silky a chocolate from a box of Mrs Hoddinot's; the detective looks at her quizzically. 'Oh, no, Detective, they're not illicit. I bought these. I always like to eat the chocolates from The Chocolate Thieves' latest heist. It gets me closer to their palate.'

DS Silky selects a Wild Elderflower Cordial and Dorothea a Lemonade for herself. Both chocolates reveal expressions of how delicious they are on the faces of the two women.

'How the hell does she make these chocolates so good?' asks DS Silky.

'I know, giddying isn't it.'

After a shared moment of distracted flavour appreciation it is Dorothea who gathers herself first. 'So, a murder detective on the hunt for The Chocolate Thieves. How exciting.'

'You've been reading my press clippings.'

'Yes, your reputation precedes you – the detective who solved The Mudlark Murders.' Dorothea waves her mobile phone at her. 'And I called dear old Uncle Gloom.'

'Of course you did.'

'Are you expecting bodies?'

'I hope so.' DS Silky checks herself. 'Of course not.

23

Though from the report last night they came close to ending the life of Mr Hoddinot.'

'But they saved him. In your experience how many criminals do you know would do that?'

'Not many – if any.'

'And how are they supposed to predict the nut allergy of the proprietor's husband? Who, by all accounts, was stealing his wife's chocolates. Serves him right, really.'

'So this is the map.'

'Indeed it is, Detective Sergeant Silky.' Dorothea admires her own work and takes the opportunity of the company of a stranger to explain her mapping. 'The white pins are the locations of the heists and the black pins the points of last witness of CHOC 1, 2, 3 and 4. The coloured strings refer to both the number of the taxi and the era of The Chocolate Thieves. CHOC 1 is white wrapped in black for the 1920s and white wrapped in yellow for the 1930s. With the change of generation CHOC 2 is black wrapped in blue for the 1940s, black wrapped in brown for the 1950s, and black wrapped in white for the first half of the 1960s. With the next change of generation CHOC 3 is yellow wrapped in white for the second half of the 1960s, yellow wrapped in red for the 1970s, yellow wrapped in orange for the 1980s and yellow wrapped in teal for the 1990s. A change in generation again and CHOC 4 is green wrapped in silver for the 2000s, and green wrapped in blue for this decade.'

DS Silky is speechless.

'I have synaesthesia,' Dorothea confesses.

'Yes, I can see that.'

'Helpful? You're welcome to photograph it.'

DS Silky takes a photograph of the incomprehensible map with her phone to humour Dorothea. 'So, who do you think these men are?'

Dorothea sits on the edge of her desk, eager to tell her new friend the history of The Chocolate Thieves. 'They've always been Robin Hood figures robbing chocolate for the poor. In the depression of the 1930s they raided the top-end hotels of London, distributing their bounty to those in the slums. In the Blitz of the forties they fed the bombed-out families. The ongoing rationing of the fifties created a black market in which they thrived. In the swinging sixties hash cocoa was all the rage so they got everyone stoned. In the seventies they were icons of anarchy in the UK. In the eighties they exploited the era of greed trading chocolates in the financial district. In the nineties they supplied the sugar rush of the Britpop generation. In the new millennium, as wars rage and economies crash, they have become part of our fading heritage – the arcane idea of the folklore criminals. And yet, they are still romantic.' Dorothea drifts into reverie.

'Have you ever encountered any of The Chocolate Thieves?' the detective enquires and Dorothea pauses long enough for DS Silky to become suspicious. 'Have you met any of them?'

'Possibly,' Dorothea hesitantly answers.

'Go on,' prompts DS Silky.

'A man who bought a teapot from me today, well, he looked like Savage.'

'He bought a teapot from you?'

'Yes, a lovely rare, vintage, 1960s…'

'And you didn't think to report this to dear old Uncle Gloom?'

'Well, I wasn't sure.'

'Yes, you were.'

'Yes, I was.'

'You didn't follow him?'

'I'm not a stalker.'

'Yes, you are.'

'Yes, I am. But I lost sight of him in the market.'

DS Silky sighs. 'Not helpful, Dorothea.' The detective takes a moment to gather her thoughts. 'He paid you in cash?'

'Yes. But I gave him my card. So when he calls me…'

'When he calls you?'

'Yes, when he calls me, I will call you.'

'And how do you know he will call you?'

With a rakish smile, Dorothea says, 'Oh, he'll call me.'

'Oh. Good.' DS Silky hands Dorothea her card, selects a Dandelion and Burdock from the box of Mrs Hoddinot's chocolates and leaves.

The Sleight Of Hand in Whitechapel first opened its doors in 1716. The flailing-in-the-wind old sign hanging over the door depicts a nimble-fingered eighteenth-century rogue relieving a gent's coat pocket of its coin. Telling any visitor of sound mind to the public house all they need to know about the establishment.

Opened by black marketeer Stanley Oak, The Sleight Of Hand has been in the same family ever since. With the first child, always named Stanley – whether male or female, inheriting the right to run the pub as custodian of its heritage.

The architecturally unchanged dark-cornered, smoke-aged, oak-panelled, multi-roomed interior evokes the very definition of the word 'secrecy'. Breathing in the air is taking in the history of the villainy that stalks the city's streets. It is where you drink through the years in the company of the city's finest rogues, highwaymen, pickpockets and whores – the highwaymen John Rann, Captain James MacLaine and William Plunkett, thief-taker Jonathan Wild, the thief Jack Sheppard and prostitute

Mary Milliner were just a few of the early infamous patrons. And whose patronage helped give The Sleight Of Hand its reputation as a safe haven for the city's underworld – a place to spend stolen coin and fence a loot of jewels and other objects of desire.

Alongside the portraits of previous patrons, many of whom had their lives ended on the gallows, are illustrated techniques of sleight of hand and the pickpockets' trade, folklore ballads and cases holding artefacts of criminality and illusions.

The first three generations of The Chocolate Thieves family have sketches of their likeness hanging in a room known as the Rogues Gallery.

Successive Stanley Oaks fence any specialist goods The Chocolate Thieves acquire that need the illusion of disappearing out of the time in which they exist. It is through the hands of the present landlord's father they passed the last significant illicit trade of The Chocolate Thieves family – the *Millennium Cocoa Jewels.*

The storm throws itself at the windows, desperate to get inside. The fire gutters with the rain and wind coming down the chimney – the flames defiantly flickering back to life in the grate. The fifty or so evening drinkers and diners shiver as the door is blown open and more people are scuttled into the pub.

Dunstan counts out the last of the money in his pocket onto the bar to buy three bottles of The Sleight Of Hand Chocolate Stout.

'So, the art trade going well, Dunstan?' teases Oak.

'Thriving, Stanley,' replies Dunstan with a wry smile, picking up the bottles and carrying them over to where The Chocolate Thieves have sat themselves at a table near the open fire. Taking his seat he passes around the drinks and rejoins the conversation.

'We are not. No. We are never going to sell our home,' commands Savage.

'The house is worth at least six million,' challenges Furness.

'If it doesn't fall down in this storm,' points out Dunstan.

Savage is not going to yield. 'The Black Truffle Hotel has been our place of refuge for four generations! It was acquired through justifiably nefarious means to give our family a home. And always will it be such!'

The Chocolate Thieves remember the story of the acquisition of their home. A story they'd been told many times by their parents as a lesson in friendship and of loyalty – an old black-and-white film plays in each of their minds' eyes…

While they languish in prison Savage and Furness's wives and children are being evicted from their rooms at The Liquorice Hostel for not having enough money to pay the rent.

Dunstan and his wife, their baby son in her arms, now with penniless pockets – having handed over the last of their coins to the proprietor to stay in their room for another week – are watching the eviction. 'Please don't send them out onto the street. I will find the money they owe you,' pleads Dunstan.

But the rancid hostel proprietor, Algernon Liquorice, is unmoved. 'I've told you before, I mind not if the beds in this establishment aren't just used for sleeping in. In fact I expect it. If they knew what their bodies were for they'd have the money for the rent and they wouldn't be homeless.' The proprietor points a bony finger at Dunstan and his wife. 'Pay your rent on time or you are out on the street too. Mind you, your wife is the prettiest of the three, you should have no trouble getting the money to pay me what's owed.'

Anger flares in Dunstan and he puts a protective arm around his wife and child. Homeless Savage and Furness's wives, carrying their children and their few bags of possessions, forlornly walk away along the street into a life of destitution.

One week later.

In Dunstan's room his wife, holding their distressed baby, worriedly paces up and down awaiting the return of her husband. Dunstan enters the room carrying a box of Black Truffles. She stares at him in disbelief. 'We cannot pay the rent with chocolates.'

At the bottom of the stairs Liquorice shouts up to them, 'It's rent day, Dunstan!'

Dunstan looks at his wife and child, the thought of them living on the streets terrifies him. 'It's worth a try.'

Downstairs he knocks on the door of the proprietor's room, handing him the Black Truffles when he opens it.

'Paying the rent with chocolates?' snarls Liquorice.

'It's all we have to give you.'

He selects one of the truffles and sniffs it, his expression shifting from suspicion to greed. 'It buys you one more night. Then I want you gone.' He retreats into his room, slamming the door in Dunstan's face.

The next morning.

Dunstan, bags packed, without knocking on the door, angrily enters the proprietor's room to return his key. He finds the vile old man dead on the rug in front of the fire having choked from gluttonously scoffing and swallowing without chewing properly, the now-spilled half-eaten box of truffles on the floor next to him.

The Chocolate Thief smiles at nature's justice. 'That's put an end to your cruelty.'

The Dunstans secretly bury the body of Algernon

Liquorice in an unmarked grave in an overgrown corner of the garden. Then seeking out and finding the deeds to the property in a drawer full of papers in the deceased proprietor's room, Dunstan transfers the ownership of the hostel, by forging the dead man's signature, into the names of Savage, Furness and Dunstan.

Finally, the Dunstans change the name of the hostel to The Black Truffle Hotel – both welcoming Savage and Furness, newly released from prison, and their families into their home.

Dunstan's voice brings them back to the present. 'Look at us, we're three single men rattling around in that house stealing chocolates with no one to give them to.'

'Tell Kyoko you are in love with her. Tell Afia you love her too. Give them both a box of chocolates each. Then they can come and live with us,' retorts Savage.

'And you?' asks Furness.

'I am the custodian of our heritage. I haven't time for love.' This nonsense gets raised eyebrows of incredulity off Furness and Dunstan. 'Besides,' Savage continues, 'I've started a new monograph today, *The History of The Chocolate Thieves* – and it's going to need a final chapter.'

'The final chapter is us decaying in that house as it falls down around us,' taunts Furness.

'So what do you suggest we do to get some money, Savage?' asks Dunstan.

'Sell your gallery. Sell your restaurant.' This suggestion is greeted with stares of disbelief from his two friends. 'I know. I know. Who'd want to buy them?'

Furness glares at Savage as if he's contemplating doing him some serious harm. He catches Dunstan's eye who scowls at him and Furness forgets the idea.

Dunstan takes the opportunity to state the bloody obvious to his friends. 'It's a hotel – we could always rent out some rooms.'

Savage and Furness's response is explosively swift. 'Fuck off!'

Savage elaborates. 'Are we skivvies? Do we toil? No! We are thinkers and artisans.' He begins to get upset. 'We are not selling, nor opening up our home to strangers. Never!'

'Okay, no selling of the house,' Furness reassures him.

'And no strangers in our rooms,' adds Dunstan disappointedly.

'Next you'll be suggesting I take fares in CHOC 4. Ply my trade at the train stations of the capital. Chipperly dispatching tourists to the sights of interest in this great city. Criss-crossing the capital ferrying politicians, bankers, celebrities and swollen-ankled shoppers to their destinations of pleasure.'

Furness smiles. 'That's actually a good idea.'

'Yes,' agrees Dunstan, 'I can see you doing that. You have the Knowledge.'

'Fuck off!'

Furness and Dunstan laughing at the image of Savage the cabbie actually draws a smile from man too.

The storm violently rattles The Sleight Of Hand, desperately trying to get into the building.

'What about selling some of the contents of the house?' suggests Dunstan.

'Good idea, some of the furniture and whatever antiques are in the attic must be worth enough to get the roof done,' says Furness.

'Gentlemen, what is the point in having a house if it is emptied of its soul,' stalls Savage.

'It's always been the people in the place that have given it life,' counters Dunstan.

'I know, agreed, but as custodian of our home, I tell

you, our family still live in those rooms. So we are not selling anything,' defends Savage.

'They're all dead. They don't need anything to sit on,' Furness sarcastically retorts.

'Our home has become a dust-sheet-covered museum,' growls Dunstan.

'And what are we contributing to this museum?' asks Furness.

'Love and continuity,' Savage informs them. 'We value the cultural significance of what we have. We are men of the analogue world in a digital age.'

Dunstan looks at Savage in disbelief. 'We've all got iPhones, iPads and Wi-Fi-enabled televisions in our rooms.'

'If we are to continue the tradition of The Chocolate Thieves we've got to make it pay. We can't keep stealing chocolate for pleasure. Our lives are stagnant,' argues Furness.

'We need to create a future for ourselves. We need to fund a future. The haul is getting smaller as the paying customers' demand for chocolate is getting higher. Every heist there are fewer and fewer chocolates in the storerooms of the chocolatiers,' says Dunstan – hoping Savage will listen to this truth for once.

But Savage is deaf to their words. 'Nothing else matters but our duty to the name, The Chocolate Thieves. And saving our home from the ravages of time. So let's be realistic. What would our great-grandfathers, our grandfathers, our fathers do? They created a folklore but a hundred years requires legendary status. We need to think. What is the ultimate chocolate crime?'

They each take a drink of stout and sit in silence – their minds completely blank.

At The Black Truffle Hotel slates are being blown off the roof. In the attic rooms bowls and buckets fill and spill over with rainwater. All the single-glazed sash windows and the doors rattle and whistle with draughts as the storm attacks the building.

Savage, Furness and Dunstan pull each other along the street and in through the front door – it takes the three of them to shut it. Suddenly the storm breaks in through the back door. Dunstan, closely followed by Savage and Furness, runs against the wind into the kitchen and tries to shut the door but to no avail. The sash window shoots up and Furness fails to close it. Savage is trying to hold down the table and chairs. The photograph of The Chocolate Thieves' great-grandfathers is blown off the mantelpiece – the glass in the frame shattering as it hits the floor. The contents of the kitchen – utensils, pans, crockery and knives – flies at them, desperately trying to decapitate them.

Finally, as the storm takes a breath, the door is returned to its frame, the window shut and the scene momentarily becalmed.

But all too soon the untamed forces of nature return to the kitchen with terrifying ferocity.

The Chocolate Thieves dive out of the room to find shelter somewhere in the house. Each grabbing as many boxes of Mrs Hoddinot's chocolates as they can carry. Savage taking the old photograph of the original Chocolate Thieves with him.

The storm is raging chaos throughout the house. Rotten window frames are blown out – showering the air with shards of glass. And doors are taken off their hinges. Pictures fly in all directions. Dust-sheeted items of furniture in unused rooms hover like ghosts then crash against the walls falling dead onto the floor only to be reanimated moments later.

Trapped in the house by the dangers outside The Chocolate Thieves are trying to secure the windows and patch with old blankets and mattresses the holes being ripped in the roof. Savage is lifted off his feet and sucked halfway out of a hole that appears just above his head – rescued just in time by Dunstan who pulls him back into the attic.

'It's too dangerous,' shouts Dunstan. 'The best we can do is secure the doors.'

'We have to save our home,' shouts back Savage.

Dunstan drags him out of the room and together they pull the door shut and lock it.

On the lower landing a two-pronged torn off tree branch comes crashing through the window he has just secured, straight at Furness. 'Oh, hell!' The branch pins The Chocolate Thief to the wall.

Savage and Dunstan arrive to free him.

'It seems nature has it in for us too,' observes Dunstan.

Furness, bruised but not seriously injured, says, 'This really is the end of us.'

The three of them dive into their respective suites – locking and barricading their doors.

Savage collapses into a chair and eats a handful of Mrs Hoddinot's chocolates without a care for the flavours. He picks up the storm-damaged old photograph of their ancestors. 'This is not the end of The Chocolate Thieves.'

DS Silky exasperatedly knocks on the door to DI Gloom's office and walks in. 'They really do not officially exist anywhere. I've checked every record there is. There isn't a birth, marriage or death certificate anywhere for the Savage, Furness and Dunstan we are looking for. No medical records, no school registrations, no registered phones, broadband or TV licences, no utilities, no pensions, no national insurance numbers, no war records, no registered businesses, no property on the land registry, no cremations and no graves. Just that one criminal record a hundred years ago.'

DI Gloom doesn't look up from his paperwork. 'Keep looking.'

DS Silky eyes the box of Reaper's Raspberry Fingers on his desk. He does not offer her one. So, with a frustrated shake of her head, DS Silky leaves the office.

A Machiavellian smile ripples over DI Gloom's expression and he indulges in another chocolate.

Having spent the morning tidying up after the storm, doing what repairs they can in an attempt to keep the house weatherproof, their home more than ever looking like a derelict house inhabited by opportunist squatters, The Chocolate Thieves have returned to their daily routines.

Savage is sitting at the kitchen table – an open box of Mrs Hoddinot's chocolates and pot of tea to hand. A headline in the newspaper he is reading catches his eye: *RARE COCOA TREE FRUITS AT KEW.*

Furness is at the restaurant leaning against the kitchen counter, an open box of Mrs Hoddinot's chocolates beside him, reading a different article: *THAT MIDAS TASTE – THE MOST EXPENSIVE CHOCOLATE IN THE WORLD.*

Dunstan is sitting at the gallery's reception desk, an open box of Mrs Hoddinot's chocolates within easy reach, reading the headline, *THE END OF CHOCOLATE.*

Savage's taste buds tingle as he reads. *A rare cocoa tree housed in the Palm House at Kew Gardens has produced fruit for the first time in 100 years.* He touches the photograph of the evergreen tree – four metres tall with yellow and orange cocoa pods hanging from its trunk and branches.

Furness's eyes widen. *Master chocolatier Midas, of Covent Garden, is to launch his new luxury chocolate range – That Midas Taste, in time for Easter*. He sneers at the photographs of the sickeningly opulent chocolates placed alluringly throughout the article.

Dunstan trembles with excitement. *The world's supply of chocolate is running out. The £100billion global industry is down to its last six million tonnes of cocoa beans. An amount equal to only one year's supply*. He stares in shock at the accompanying graph, with its red line depicting the cocoa harvest's tragic decline and its blue line depicting the indulgent rise in global demand for cocoa, dramatically illustrating the problem facing the chocolate industry.

Savage reads on. *Found in the hidden mountain valley of the Marañón River in Peru, this tree was gifted to Kew by the ancestors of gentleman explorer and botanist Sir Rory Risker*.

A deep-seated rage stirs in Furness as he reads. *Those lucky enough to afford these luxury delights will be able to gorge on the That Midas Taste Easter Truffle – made with 90% rare organic Ecuadorian Nacional Arriba cocoa, English black truffles, Capet Roi de Chocolat champagne and infused with edible twenty-four-carat gold. The silky, smoky, luxurious flavours will be as rich as the price at £20,000 per box of four truffles*.

Dunstan is astounded by what he is reading. *The worldwide shortage of chocolate is due to cocoa tree disease. Destroying 90% of crops is the fruit-rotting witches' broom – a virulent fungal disease that threatens to completely wipe out the once resilient Forastero variety from which the majority of the world's chocolate is derived*.

Savage is salivating. *A sample taken has revealed the DNA of the beans to be pure Nacional. This strain of cocoa is thought to have been completely wiped out in its native Peru – having succumbed to sweet-toothed explorers, environmental conditions and disease.*

Furness's rage is simmering. *Also on the chocolate menu will be individually wrapped jewel-adorned English Fruit Chocolates of organic blackcurrant, raspberry, apple, pear, plum and gooseberry fruit creme coated in a delicate 70% Porcelana chocolate at £10,000 a box.*

Dunstan is calculating the deals to be done. *The shortage has led to prices of cocoa beans rising four fold in the last three years from £2,000 to £8,000 per tonne.*

Savage is in full cocoa arousal. *Rugby-ball-size pods grow out of the trunk of the tree, in which are housed the cocoa beans. There are sixteen pods growing on the Kew Gardens tree, each containing 20–60 cocoa beans, estimated to produce 900 grams of chocolate – enough to make one very special Easter egg.*

Furness's rage is now reaching boiling point. *Silver bars of fruit and nut made with organic Dates and Walnuts, Apricots and Hazelnuts, Raisins and Chestnuts in 75% Criollo cocoa and adorned with one-carat diamonds at £7,000 each; 60% cocoa chocolate-coated Elvish Wild Honey Drops at £1,000 each and 50% cocoa dark chocolate English Wild Mint Leaves at £450 each.*

Savage is seeing his chocolate future. *But you will have to wait. The country's leading cocoa scientist, Dr Rikard Linnaeus, said yesterday, 'As tempting as it is we have decided that the cocoa beans from this rare tree are too important to be made into chocolate and will be used to propagate new trees from this unique variety of cocoa for future generations of chocolate lovers.' So, for now, no one will know what this unique chocolate tastes like.*

Furness is shaking with contempt. *Speaking about his new range Midas said, 'Yes, these will be the most expensive chocolates in the world. They will be chocolates for the palates of the elite. People who have earned the right and deserve to indulge in That Midas Taste, wherever, whenever.'*

'Elitist bastard!' rages Furness.

Scarlett Vamp the Chair of the Association of Artisan Chocolatiers of London said last night, 'The result of our disregard for nature means cocoa is facing extinction. The very existence of chocolate is under threat.' Dunstan gives an intrigued smile at the opportunity he sees before him. 'Bloody hell.'

'Truly a gift of the chocolate gods,' says Savage in wonderment just as the handle of the new teapot breaks off in his hand as he distractedly picks it up. 'Why?' he pleads.

Three newspapers land on the kitchen table at the same time. 'Got it!' The Chocolate Thieves say in unison. They pass round the articles – taking the time to read every word.

'Now all we need is a plan,' says Savage.

The three of them look at each other – thinking.

They each take a chocolate from the open box of Mrs Hoddinot's on the table – Savage selects a Hazelnut Bite, Furness a Mint Cream and Dunstan a Blackcurrant Delight. Letting the flavours caress their palates and stimulate their roguish minds. Time silently ticks by on the clock on the wall above the fireplace. Then they begin to smile at each other – realising they have come to the same conclusion. Smiles that break into laughter at the brilliance of their plan.

DS Silky thrusts the *That Midas Taste – the most expensive chocolate in the world* article in front of DI Gloom. 'This is how we catch them.' DI Gloom reads the article. 'Forget the file and history. Forget who they were. We can only catch The Chocolate Thieves in the present.'

'You're right, DS Silky. You'll have whatever you need to catch these sticky-fingered trufflers.'

This time DI Gloom offers DS Silky one of his Reaper's Raspberry Fingers and the detective pops one into her mouth with a wicked smile.

The next two days are spent raising the money needed to undertake the planned heists – primarily being able to put some fuel into CHOC 4 and feeding themselves. Savage cannot bring himself to sell any of the house's contents and Furness has no ingredients left to cook for any potential diners – of which there are none anyway. But good fortune arrives when Dunstan actually manages to sell one of Kyoko's paintings, titled *Nude Eating Chocolate* by Bernard Dunstan, no relation, for £4,500 cash.

When offered her cut Kyoko only takes £500 with the words, 'Invest it unwisely for me.'

Dunstan splits the rest of the cash between himself, Savage and Furness. 'There's nothing to stop us now.'

DS Silky walks into the first-floor room of the unoccupied out-of-lease shop opposite the Midas Boutique in Covent Garden. It's the perfect position to see all the activity during the day and at night taking place where she believes The Chocolate Thieves' next heist will happen.

At present all is as you would expect at a high-end chocolatier's. The self-aggrandising Midas, in too-clean-to-have-done-any-chocolate-making all-white chef's clothing, his Midas logo embroidered in gold thread on his left breast, is impatiently overseeing the display of the chocolates.

The cloned all-female boutique staff, in white logo-emblazoned T-shirts, cropped trousers and heels, and who are too thin to look like they've ever eaten a chocolate, cater to the whims of the wealthy and the tourists who walk into the sterile environment empty-handed beneath the bold gold lettering of the Midas name on its spotless white background. The clientele sample and select chocolates, pay by card or with phones without asking the price of their indulgences and walk out again clutching white and gold Midas-branded gift bags.

Settled comfortably in for her uneventful evening shift in the high-tech control room at Kew Gardens, the attendant security guard dunks her chocolate biscuit into her mug of 'This will keep me awake' coffee and savours its flavours.

Looking up, the mug of coffee at her lips, she watches, enthralled, the surreal and quite frankly absurd scenario, streamed via the night-vision security cameras to the fourth screen in the bank of ten high-definition monitors across the wall in front of her, of a London taxi driving through the now inexplicably open Marianne North Gallery gate.

Frozen in the moment she watches the taxi turn right and drive at speed across Kew Gardens, pull up at the Palm House, drop off two passengers and proceed on its way.

The security guard's lips are burning from the coffee and it is now she remembers it is her who has the responsibility to raise the alarm – which she does.

Furness and Dunstan, both carrying hessian sacks, run up to the door of the Palm House – Dunstan picks the lock and he and Furness walk inside. They switch on their head torches and Dunstan leads the way to the cocoa tree.

Once at the tree they quickly harvest the sixteen cocoa pods – Furness climbing up the tree to reach the higher-growing pods, dropping them down to Dunstan to put in the sacks.

Circling the Palm House in CHOC 4, Savage takes a mouthful of delicious hot chocolate from the cup he has in the taxi's cup holder. 'Oh dear – that was quick,' he says to himself on seeing the arrival on the scene of the gang of security guards.

Finding the open door the guards pour into the Palm House. Picking up their full sacks Furness and Dunstan hear the approaching footsteps. 'Run for it!' they tell each other in unison and head off in different directions.

Savage watches the ensuing chase of torch beams. 'Not good. Not good at all.'

Furness is rugby tackled by a security guard – his hessian sack spilling cocoa pods across the floor. He eels his way out of the guard's grip and as the man goes to stand up he gives him a hard kick to his groin. 'Ow!… really no need for that,' the man whimpers onto his knees. His straight-ahead path blocked by more guards, Furness picks up his sack and the loose cocoa pods and runs up the stairs to the raised walkway that runs around the inside of the Palm House. Seeing the headlights of the approaching Savage in CHOC 4, he drop kicks, in quick succession, the two cocoa pods he's carrying under his arm – the pods break through panes of the glass roof and fly through the air. Savage opens the left passenger-door window and the pods land in the back of the taxi.

Dunstan charges down two security guards that stand between him and the door, shoulder barging them out of the way, knocking them winded to the floor. But as he reaches the door he is grabbed and thrown down by another guard. Quickly getting to his feet he picks up a spilled cocoa pod and throws it to the guard standing between him and the door. The guard catches the pod with a surprised look, as he is wondering what The Chocolate Thief is up to; Dunstan promptly kicks him in the shin. 'Ow! That really fucking hurts!' the guard cries out as he hops about, releasing the cocoa pod. Which Dunstan catches and, after picking up his sack, he runs out of the Palm House.

Having run completely around the walkway and down the second flight of stairs Furness joins his friend outside.

They both look about for Savage.

'Where the hell is he?' demands Dunstan.

Around the corner comes CHOC 4 pursued on foot by more security guards.

'Bloody hell!' exclaims Furness.

Running up to CHOC 4 Furness and Dunstan throw both sacks of cocoa pods through the open windows into the back of the taxi but cannot make it into CHOC 4 themselves. A guard rugby tackles Dunstan for the cocoa pod he is still holding – Dunstan throws it to Furness who runs with it, defiantly elbowing guards out of his way. Dunstan dismisses his assailant with a kick to the bridge of her nose as he scrambles away. Back on his feet he takes a pass from Furness and rolls across the bonnet of CHOC 4 as Savage scatters the uniformed men and women. Taking sips of his hot chocolate as he drives, Savage does a continuous figure of eight around and through the melee, sideswiping guards with the wings of CHOC 4 and knocking them down with his expertly thrown open driver's door. Dunstan stealthily hands the cocoa pod back to Furness as they pass each other, then lifts a guard off their feet and plants them into a flower bed face first.

Furness drops to his knees and a high tackle flies over the top of him. Springing into a run he dummy passes the cocoa pod to Dunstan running beside him and both sidestep a slow-reacting burly guard. Reaching CHOC 4 they dive into the back of the taxi and Savage speeds them away to safety. Leaving behind them an exhausted, bruised and bloodied group of security guards collapsing onto the ground.

DI Gloom is not a happy man. This is obvious by the volume of the shouting he is doing at DS Silky. 'I said catch them! Look at these headlines!' He points to the morning's streaming news-feeds on his laptop: *KEW RUGBY, COCO POD COPS*. 'Look! It's gone viral!'

DI Gloom shows DS Silky the CCTV footage of the Palm House break-in and the game of cocoa pod rugby, to which she feels the need to point out the obvious. 'They're not police officers, they're private security guards.'

'I know they're not police officers. But the media-believing general public don't care about the truth. And nor does the Mayor!'

'This doesn't make sense. All past heists have been of chocolates not the ingredients. They were supposed to be raiding the Midas Boutique.'

'So why did they raid the Palm House at Kew Gardens?'

'They have stolen a rare variety of cocoa which suggests they intend to make some unique chocolate.'

'I can see why you've got the reputation for incisive deductive reasoning you have.'

'My point is this isn't their normal modus operandi. They steal chocolates and by all accounts these chocolates are not seen again. They must just eat them.'

'That is what you do with chocolates.'

'So do they know how to make chocolate from raw

cocoa?'

'You're asking who's making the chocolate?'

'Yes. If they can't make the chocolate themselves who are they selling this rare and no doubt very expensive raw cocoa too?'

'A wealthy chocolatier.'

'Yes. It has to be someone with money and chocolatier skills. Someone who is about to launch the most expensive and exclusive chocolates in the world.'

DI Gloom frowns at her as he tries to get to the name she is yet to say.

DS Silky gives her DI the answer. 'Midas.'

'Midas?'

'According to what I've read, and been told, no chocolatier in the city is more exclusive.'

'Yes – that does makes sense.'

'Of course it could be a client paying a high-class chocolatier to make the chocolate for them.'

'But someone with the arrogance of Midas would be the alchemist.'

'We are already watching his boutique in anticipation of The Chocolate Thieves targeting his new range of That Midas Taste chocolates, so we'll see if the stolen Kew Gardens cocoa pods end up in his hands.'

'His chocolate-coated prints are all over this crime.'

'We will of course select other chocolatiers to watch. But my detective's instinct tells me Midas is involved in this heist.'

'Fine deduction, DS Silky.' DI Gloom offers his sergeant a chocolate from his box of Featherlight's Fruit Fondants.

DS Silky smiles with satisfaction and selects a Red Grape.

In the kitchen of The Furness restaurant The Chocolate Thieves, each wielding a large-bladed knife, are cutting open the Kew Gardens cocoa pods, extracting the dark brown and purple cocoa beans from the white mucilaginous pulp and putting them into a fermentation box – the pods yielding 900 beans.

'The cocoa beans have to ferment for a week or so before we dry them and then roast them in preparation for the making of the chocolate,' instructs Furness.

'Pure Nacional Forastero – the rarest cocoa in the world.' Dunstan grins.

'You will make the finest of chocolate, Furness,' announces Savage, 'my palate salivates at imagining the complexity of flavours.'

The cocoa pod husks are collected up, bagged and thrown into the back of a passing rubbish lorry by Savage and Dunstan as they leave. This is happening just as Afia comes out of her flat – what are they doing here at this time of day? As she walks into the kitchen Furness is coming out of the cellar.

He locks the door and puts the key into the pocket of his chef's trousers. 'Good morning, Afia – what shall we cook for today's special?'

Afia is instantly suspicious of his good mood. 'Good morning to you too.'

Furness opens the fridge door, picks up a steak and sniffs it. Afia leans against the counter watching him – she idly pops a Mrs Hoddinot's Caramel Cup into her mouth.

'How about steak and rustic chips with The Furness Fiery Sauce?' he asks her.

'Okay. Sounds suspiciously delicious.'

Standing at the first-floor window, camera to hand, the police officer looks across the street into the Midas

Boutique where the master chocolatier is curtly conducting his staff to fulfil the needs of his elite clientele. 'Just a normal trading day, Sergeant,' he says into his phone.

DS Silky hangs up and turns her attention to the CCTV footage on her computer of The Chocolate Thieves' raid of the Palm House at Kew Gardens. It is comical viewing. Being opportunistic and artfully professional. And yet again a demonstration that these men do not lose their heads in the ensuing chaos of the discovery of their in-progress heist.

She rewinds to the day before.

Visitor after visitor stops and photographs the cocoa tree – everyone spending more time looking at the tree via their camera phone screens and taking selfies than looking at the remarkable act of nature in front of them. Then DS Silky spots a face she thinks she recognises and stops the footage. Referring back to The Chocolate Thieves case file she searches out the photograph of the original Chocolate Thieves and holds it up next to the freeze-framed image of Dunstan on her computer screen.

'Is it you?'

DS Silky sits back and ponders what to do next. She opens Google and types in the name 'Dunstan' followed by the word 'chocolate'.

The first thing to catch her eye is a tweet by Tallulah Conche dated the 3rd March. *Just bought a lovely painting, Nude Eating Chocolate by Bernard Dunstan from his namesake at the Dunstan Gallery, Soho*. Attached to it is a photograph of the painting; it is a self-portrait by Kyoko – reflected in a mirror she is lying on her bed eating a chocolate in the light of the evening sunshine streaming through the window.

There is no website for the gallery so the detective grabs her jacket and heads out the door.

Savage takes the card for Dorothea's Rare Vintage out of his pocket and dials the number. As he waits for Dorothea to answer her phone Savage takes a moment to select a Salted Nutty Whip from the box of Mrs Hoddinot's chocolates on the kitchen table.

'Dorothea's Rare Vintage, relics to relish, tat for all tastes,' comes the cheerful voice over the sound of the market.

'Hello, I bought a teapot off you a few days ago.'

Dorothea's knees twitch with excitement at hearing Savage's voice. 'I remember. The rare, vintage, 1960s, chocolate brown, mirror glaze, English teapot capable of making four lovely cuppas.'

'That's the one.'

'Are you phoning to tell me how wonderfully it steeps the leaves?'

'No.'

'How wonderfully it pours?'

'No.'

'Oh?'

'The handle has broken off.'

'Really?'

'Yes – the first time I used it.'

'Oh dear – that's unfortunate! How firmly did you grip it?'

'The usual required grip for a teapot handle.'

'I see. Would you like it replaced?'

'If you would be so kind.'

'Not a problem. I've got another one here – somewhere. I'll deliver it to you in person – for no extra charge.'

Dorothea hangs up before Savage can say he would prefer to collect the teapot or to give Dorothea his address – The Chocolate Thief smiles to himself, amused at the possibilities of what will happen next.

The steaks rest on a plate ready to fry, The Furness Fiery Sauce simmers on the stove, the rustic chips are cut, parboiled and oiled ready for the oven – but there are no diners.

Having checked to see if anyone has walked into the restaurant Afia returns to leaning on the prep table with Furness and their discussion on their favourite flavoured Mrs Hoddinot's chocolates.

Furness inspects a Gooseberry Tart. 'Why would you think gooseberry would make a good flavour for a chocolate. It tastes like a worn sock. Try it.'

'Fuck off!' Afia plucks a Morning Espresso from the box and pops it into her mouth. 'Wow! Now – that is a hit!'

Furness samples a Citrus Crush – uncontrollably screwing up his face. 'Blimey. That's limey.'

Spiced Rum – in her mouth it goes. 'Hmm – that is good. It makes me want to dance.' Afia turns up the radio; 6 Music is throwing out 'High' by The Cure. 'It's my childhood song.' She steps into the tempo of the music and pops a Spiced Rum into Furness's mouth. He nods and groans with approval and begins to dance with her around the kitchen.

DS Silky walks into the Dunstan Gallery and begins to look at the paintings as if she is a potential customer.

Dunstan approaches her, picking up on her genuine curiosity at the art hanging on the walls. 'Good afternoon.'

'Hello.' Her eyes scan every detail of his features and relaxed demeanour – the ancestral DNA is uncannily strong.

'Looking for anything in particular?'

'A still life.'

'I see. Flowers, fruit, leaves?'

'Cocoa beans.'

'Have you seen our Eliot Hodgkin?'

'No.'

Dunstan draws DS Silky's attention to the painting of the cocoa pod and beans now hanging on the gallery wall. 'A brilliant twentieth-century painter of still life who never failed to capture nature's beauty.'

DS Silky steps towards the painting. 'It's remarkable.'

'He had an acute eye and a sophisticated touch.'

'Have you seen the cocoa tree at Kew Gardens?'

'Yes – I was there two days ago. It's not until you see the real thing do you realise how good he was. I thought I might write an article comparing reality with his work. So I went to Kew to photograph the cocoa pods – how often do you get to see chocolate on its tree?'

'You've seen the news that someone has stolen the cocoa pods?'

'Yes – hell of a game of rugby.' Dunstan absentmindedly rubs his bruised ribs.

'You come from a family of chocolate thieves.' DS Silky holds up her ID.

'Do I? Have you been doing my family tree, Detective? Thought I might do that myself once I retire. But if you've made a start I'd be grateful to have what you've found out. But why the interest in me?'

'You said you were at Kew the day before the robbery.'

'Like many other people – it's a very enjoyable day out. Maybe you should take a day off and pay a visit yourself. Fresh air does wonders for the mind and the skin.'

'Your name came up in connection with a crime linked to chocolate.'

'Not in my lifetime it hasn't.'

DS Silky shows Dunstan the original Chocolate Thieves photograph.

Dunstan laughs. 'That's a hundred years old.'

They stand eye to eye.

'Did you steal the cocoa pods?'

'DS Silky, I sell paintings of still life not the real thing.'

'Are you in contact with the descendants of Savage and Furness?'

'More genealogy, Detective? Are there any descendants?'

DS Silky spots the box of Mrs Hoddinot's chocolates on the reception desk. 'Do you like chocolate, Mr Dunstan?'

'I do. And please – do help yourself. A gift from a grateful client.'

DS Silky takes a Poached Plum – the perfect blend of the naturally sweet fruit with the earthy cocoa distracting her from her questioning.

'Detective, the people in that photograph are dead. Shouldn't you be at the cemetery if you want to question them? Or possibly consult a medium,' teases Dunstan.

DS Silky hands Dunstan her card. 'In case you remember anything suspicious from Kew. And if you find yourself in possession of an exceptionally realistic still life of cocoa pods.'

'So you're looking for a sweet-toothed artist?'

'I'm looking for a sweet-toothed villain.'

'Have you questioned the local dentists?'

'Goodbye, Mr Dunstan.'

'Goodbye, DS Silky.'

Having watched the detective exit the gallery Dunstan turns round to see Kyoko looking at him, suspicion written across her eyes, from the doorway at the back of the gallery. He tries to smile reassuringly at her – it doesn't work. Dunstan selects a Sloe Gin from the box of Mrs Hoddinot's chocolates and ponders DS Silky's visit. How long will it be before she finds Savage and Furness? No detective has got this close to them in two decades. But what have The Chocolate Thieves done of any significance since New Year's Day 2000?

It is now late evening and Savage sends a text to Furness and Dunstan. *I'm on my way.*

Savage leaves the house through the kitchen door, walks the length of the garden to a barely visible, overgrown with ivy, door in the wall through which he enters the garage where CHOC 4 is parked alongside three other cars hidden under tarpaulin. Savage opens the garage doors, quietly pulls CHOC 4 out of the garage, gets out of the taxi, closes and locks the garage doors, then gets back into CHOC 4 and drives out into the night.

At the restaurant Furness reads Savage's text, leaves his opened chocolate recipe books scattered across the prep table, changes out of his chef's clothes, turns off the lights and heads out of the kitchen door just as Savage pulls up in CHOC 4.

After watching from the window of her flat, waiting for Furness to leave, Afia heads downstairs to the restaurant. She walks into the kitchen – observing the opened recipe books and what Furness is researching. In the staff changing area Afia goes through the pockets of Furness's chef's trousers to retrieve the cellar door key. Afia unlocks the door to the cellar, switches on the light and heads cautiously down the stairs, keeping a watchful eye out for spiders and opportunist rodents. The fermentation box is on a table in the centre of the cellar. Afia peers inside taking in the sight of the fermenting cocoa beans. She pulls a puzzled expression – then there is realisation. 'No bloody way!'

Dunstan reads the text from Savage. Through the gallery window he checks for the presence of an unmarked police car with DS Silky inside. There she is – parked down the street with a clear view of the door to the gallery. Dunstan goes through the door at the back of the gallery, heads upstairs, walks through Kyoko's studio, where she is painting, up another flight of stairs to the second floor, through Kyoko's living space, up into the attic rooms, out of a window onto the roof, over the roof to a fire escape attached to the back of the adjacent building, down the fire escape and along the street to the waiting CHOC 4.

The Chocolate Thieves arrive at the loading bay door of the Capital Catering Company – wholesale suppliers to catering firms. Dunstan sets to work gaining access through a window. From inside the building he opens the loading bay door, Savage reverses CHOC 4 inside and Dunstan closes the door again.

Savage, Furness and Dunstan switch on their head torches and set about loading CHOC 4 with bags of cocoa powder, bars of cocoa butter, vanilla extract, cane sugar, bottles of every possible colour of food colouring for chocolate, edible diamonds, sapphires, emeralds and rubies, edible gold and silver – on rolls, in books of leaf, in jars of flakes and dust.

Once they have all that they have come for Savage and Furness get in CHOC 4, Dunstan opens the bay door, Savage drives out, Dunstan presses the close button, ducks under the closing door, joins the other two in CHOC 4 and they drive away into the night just as the building's alarm goes off.

'I've done some asking around about DS Silky,' Dunstan informs the other two at breakfast, 'she's the real deal, a highly regarded murder detective, intelligent with an eye for detail that others don't see. She's on to me and she'll soon find you two. Stanley Oak informed me she's the detective who solved the Automaton Killings.'

'A murder detective?' questions Furness.

'A different way of thinking,' suggests Savage.

'She's showing around that photograph of our great-grandfathers,' adds Dunstan.

'Really?' Savage is intrigued. 'That is interesting.'

As Dunstan is busy eating his breakfast the habitual bluebottle, having survived the house-wrecking storm, lands on the back of his head. Furness picks up the newspaper lying on the table, roles it up and takes a fast hard swipe at the fly, missing it and whacking Dunstan across the head with such force he spits out the mouthful of egg and sausage he is eating and falls off his chair onto the floor.

'You fucking idiot!'

Enjoying her morning coffee Kyoko looks out of her studio window at the still present, asleep in her car, DS Silky.

The detective is woken by her phone ringing. It is DI Gloom. She ignores it. She checks the time: 9am. It is now she notices the fresh cup of coffee with the chocolate on top in the car's cup holder. Written on the cup is *Good morning, DS Silky*. She looks about her to see if anyone is watching her – there is no one. Then she sees Kyoko stepping away from the gallery's first-floor window.

DS Silky picks up the chocolate and sniffs it – it smells okay. She licks it – it tastes okay, so, with a shrug, she pops it in her mouth. It's a Mrs Hoddinot's Double Chocolate Wake-Up. Her eyes go wide – very wide. 'Fuck!' She takes the lid off the coffee and sniffs it – it smells okay. She takes a mouthful and groans with relief. It is now she realises her bladder is fit to burst – time to find a toilet and quickly.

Afia is watching Furness making chocolate out of the stolen ingredients. There is an expression of curiosity across her face that Furness knows is leading up to a question.

'You're one of them, aren't you?'

'I am?'

'How else do you explain the cocoa beans fermenting in the basement?' Furness continues blending the ingredients into a pan on the stove. 'And the chocolate and edible jewellery ingredients that have suddenly appeared.' Furness stirs the chocolate. 'It's you. You're one of The Chocolate Thieves.'

Furness stops what he is doing and looks at her. 'Yes, I am. It's a family tradition.'

'That's why you're always eating boxes of chocolates. I thought you were just comfort spending what little cash you had on treats.'

'No, they're all pilfered.'

'Savage and Dunstan too?'

'Yes.'

'Bloody brilliant.' Afia grabs his face with both hands and kisses him on the lips. 'I bloody love you.'

She pulls Furness into a joyous hug and he quietly replies, 'I love you too.'

Afia steps back and looks expectantly at him. 'So, what are we making?'

Furness grins mischievously at her. 'I need you to procure some fresh cherries, ginseng, stout, valerian root, fresh prunes and some mint.'

DI Gloom points at the headline, *CAPITAL CATERING COMPANY RAIDED – WHAT ARE THE CHOCOLATE THIEVES MAKING?* 'Do you know what they are making?'

DS Silky looks at the article. 'An Easter egg made from the rarest chocolate on earth. Adorned with edible gems, silver and gold.'

'How do you know that?' asks a surprised DI Gloom.

'It's Easter soon – what do you think they'll be making?' she replies incredulously.

'Yes, well, Detective, you have been outside Midas's boutique and Dunstan's gallery for days. What have you found out?' DS Silky does not have anything to say. 'As I thought. Get yourself to the scene of the crime. And get some evidence to arrest the bloody Chocolate Thieves.'

DI Gloom throws a Barge's Barnacle into his mouth from the open box on his desk. Dismissed without being offered a chocolate DS Silky disappointedly leaves her superior's office.

The artist is sitting at her easel painting a Picasso-inspired portrait of Dunstan when he delivers into the studio sacks of cocoa powder, bars of cocoa butter, vanilla extract, sugar and the bottles of chocolate colouring. 'I've got a new commission for you. I want you to produce some original work. Your own work. In chocolate.'

Kyoko, without looking at him, smiles enigmatically and carries on painting.

'Good.' And with that The Chocolate Thief leaves her to her work.

Tommy, the owner of the Capital Catering Company, is talking enthusiastically about the heist as DS Silky has a look around the wholesalers. 'They knew what they were doing. There was no sign of them breaking in. I only knew stock was missing when I went to put together an order.'

'Didn't the alarm go off?'

'Yeah, but it's always doing that. I've got a remote

switch. Glanced at the live feed of the security cameras on my phone. It looked okay. So I just turned it off and went back to sleep.'

'I see. So you saw stock was missing…'

'That's when I checked the footage again. Let me show you.' Tommy shows DS Silky the recording of the burglary on his phone. 'You've got to hand it to them. They're smooth.'

'You're covered by insurance?'

'Of course. But you know what? Orders have gone up. Best publicity ever. People want to buy from where The Chocolate Thieves steal. I'm thinking of getting a plaque: *The Chocolate Thieves stole from here. These premises were raided as part of the great chocolate heists of…*'

'Edible gold and silver was taken,' DS Silky reads off the printed-out inventory of what was stolen she has in her hand. 'How much is the stock worth?'

'Not that much – about £2,000. It's what you create with it and the attitude you put into the chocolate that gives it value – just ask Midas.'

'What do you mean?'

'Being a successful chocolatier to the rich is all about attitude and exclusivity. Is there anyone more arrogant, self-publicising and elitist in the chocolate world than Midas?'

'So are The Chocolate Thieves in competition against Midas or in league with him?'

'They haven't raided his boutique yet, have they?'

'No.'

Tommy smiles. 'They will.'

'That amuses you?'

'Midas has cancelled orders with us at the last minute and returned stock more than once – saying it's inferior. It's not. If it was The Chocolate Thieves wouldn't have stolen it.'

'Do you recognise any of these men?' She holds up the original photograph of The Chocolate Thieves.

'I'm only forty-four.'

'What about the names Savage, Furness or Dunstan?'

'Let me introduce you to Gene in accounts.'

They walk into Gene's office.

'Did I hear you say the name Furness?'

'Yes, you did,' answers DS Silky.

'We put him on stop a year ago for failing to pay his bills – he still owes £5,000.'

'Did he look like this man?' DS Silky holds up the photograph for Gene to view.

'I'm only fifty-two. They were online orders. Here's the restaurant's address.' Gene shows DS Silky her computer screen. 'It's called The Furness – get it?'

Furness and Afia have been busy making three flavour types of 70%-cocoa chocolate truffles.

'The Cherry and Ginseng is an aphrodisiac,' Furness informs Afia.

'Really?'

'Tradition has it that the sweet flesh of the cherry combined with the blood-warming ginseng, well, they're supposed to give freedom to the desires of the individual who eats them.'

'I hope you've made enough.'

'The Stout and Valerian is a sleep inducer guaranteed to send to sleep the most ardent insomniac. And the Prune and Mint will help one go.'

'One go where?'

'No. Go.'

'Oh. Go.'

There is a determined knock on the kitchen door. Then,

without being invited, DS Silky opens the door, walks in, holds up her ID and smiles at them both – particularly Afia. 'Hello.'

Afia pops a Cherry and Ginseng Truffle into her mouth.

'Hello,' replies Furness, 'we're closed today.'

'Yes, the sign on the front door said so, yet here you are making chocolates.'

'A private catering contract. How can we help you?'

'Where were you two nights ago?'

'Afia and I were here in the throes of conception.'

'Yes, that's true, we were conceiving,' confirms Afia.

'Chocolate recipes?' asks DS Silky referring to the three trays of truffles on the prep table.

'Yes,' answers Furness.

'Would you like to try one?' Afia offers the detective a Cherry and Ginseng Truffle.

DS Silky, not breaking eye contact with Afia, flirtatiously pops one into her mouth. Furness rolls his eyes at them. The detective quivers in delight at the delicious flavours of the robust, rich chocolate, poached fruit and spice. It takes an effort but DS Silky manages to refocus on her questioning. 'So you didn't go shoplifting at the Capital Catering Company?'

'We order online.' Furness politely deflects the question.

'Not from there, you don't.'

'We recently changed suppliers.'

'They'd like you to pay your outstanding bills. You have receipts for all your stock?'

'Do you have a warrant for your curiosity?'

'Tell me – how long does it take to make chocolate?'

'Flavour knowledge takes years of experimentation.'

'We made these this afternoon,' Afia tells her.

'And from raw cocoa beans?'

There is a flicker of concern across Afia's face.

Furness smiles. 'Weeks of controlled environmental preparation.'

DS Silky looks around at the empty restaurant. 'Somewhere secluded, somewhere away from prying eyes.'

'What does the chocolate you are looking for taste like?' challenges Furness.

'No one knows – yet,' replies DS Silky pointedly.

'How do you find a chocolate no one has ever tasted?' enquires Afia.

'Protein and DNA molecular marker analyses of the cocoa beans.' DS Silky makes it sound like she knows how this works.

'So you have less than two weeks to find the cocoa beans before they are chocolate,' Furness informs the detective.

'It would seem so.' DS Silky produces the photograph of The Chocolate Thieves and hands it to Furness.

On seeing it Afia snatches it out of Furness's hand to look more closely at it. 'Bloody hell. That looks just like you and…'

'You really are the DNA police, DS Silky,' says Furness cutting across anything Afia might let slip.

'Is it worth me asking if you know the descendants of the other two in the photograph?' enquires the detective.

'No,' is Furness's blunt reply.

DS Silky takes back the photograph. 'Okay. Goodbye. For now.' And giving them both a knowing smile the detective leaves.

Afia stares wide-eyed at Furness. 'It really is a family tradition.'

'Let's get these chocolates boxed up. We need to test them.'

That evening Savage walks into his suite carrying a cup of tea and a box of chocolates labelled *Furness and Afia S & V*. Setting the tea and chocolates down on a table next to his armchair, he stokes the fire, then settles down for the evening to read his signed, well-thumbed, first edition copy of *How Chocolate Changed The World* by the rare-cocoa hunter Marcus Nibs.

In the storeroom at the back of the gallery Dunstan is sitting in a well-used leather armchair, surrounded by forged works of art, enjoying a bottle of chocolate stout and eating from a box of chocolates labelled *Furness and Afia P & M* as he reads a magazine article titled *THE LOST ART OF LONDON*. His attention is on *The London Chocolate Time Piece* – a hundred-year-old gold, diamond and sapphire, civil and solar, four-hundred-part, encased in chocolate-tinted glass, pocket watch.

At the restaurant Furness opens the box labelled *Furness and Afia C & G* and eats one – noticing that they have significantly reduced in number. 'Afia, how many of these Cherry and Ginseng Truffles have you eaten?'

Afia appears in the doorway of the staff changing area in figure-accentuating teal lingerie and provocatively hangs on the door frame. 'Enough.'

Furness smiles with lascivious pleasure and lets his lustful eyes drop down over her taut body – knee-weakening, pulse-quickening, desire takes away any words he might have wanted to speak.

Afia takes a feline step towards him, revealing that she has a riding crop in her hand that she cracks across the palm of her other hand with alarming relish.

Furness takes a nervous step backwards. 'Ah!'

At The Black Truffle Hotel Savage is fast asleep in his armchair, head tilted back, open book on his lap, snoring loudly.

Dunstan's stomach rumbles, he instinctively rubs it, then a crease of urgent concern appears across his brow. He leaps up out of his chair, trips over a Grayson Perry vase depicting The Chocolate Thieves' *New Rose Cocoa Den Heist*, desperately gets to his feet and darts out of the storeroom, up the stairs, past the painting Kyoko in her studio, up the second flight of stairs and into the toilet. Desperately unfastening his trousers and rapidly pulling them, along with his underwear, down to his ankles. Once seated Dunstan groans with tear-inducing relief as his bowels empty and empty and empty.

Bent over the prep table Furness cries out in the pleasure of the stinging pain as Afia repeatedly whips his bare behind. Crack! 'Who's a naughty Chocolate Thief?'

'Ow! I am.'

'Who is?'

Crack!

'Ow! I am.'

'Yes – you are. And I love it.'

Crack!

Afia pulls him up, spins him round and throws him onto his back on the prep table and jumps on him, drinks from a bottle of red wine then pours some into his mouth. She discards the wine, grabs his face in her hands and bites his lips. 'You might just die tonight with a smile of agony on your face.'

At breakfast the following morning Furness stands pale and trembly behind his chair at the end of the table, quietly drinking a fortifying cup of tea.

Dunstan, his stomach empty, scoffs his cooked breakfast.

Savage walks into the kitchen. 'Good morning, good morning. I must say I feel wonderful. I had the most restful sleep I've had in years last night. Wonderful chocolates, Furness.' He sits down, pours himself a cup of tea from the tea-towel-wrapped teapot and tucks into his cooked breakfast.

Dunstan, through a mouthful of food, complains, 'You clearly weren't given the same chocolates I was. Fucking prunes...' He scowls at Furness.

'So, what adventures await us upon this bright early spring day?' There is no reply from Furness who is staring thoughtfully into the air in front of him, sipping his tea. Nor from Dunstan who is now eating Furness's breakfast, but he does, with the jab of his knife, refer Savage to an article in the newspaper.

Savage reads the headline and opening paragraph. *AFRICAN COCOA DEVASTATED. The resurgence of black pod disease has claimed all the cocoa plantations in Ivory Coast and Ghana. It is now feared all of the cocoa trees on the African continent face extinction.* With a shake of his head, Savage says, 'This is grave indeed.'

The house bluebottle swoops in front of Savage and he follows its flight to where it lands on the flies of Furness's trousers. In a swift movement Savage picks up Furness's unused fork and decisively attempts to impale the fly with it. Missing the fly he stabs Furness in the testicles.

Furness showers the table in spat-out tea and crumples to the floor. 'Fucking hell!'

From her vantage point in the police surveillance room DS Silky watches the black SUV with tinted windows drive into the mews alongside the Midas Boutique and pull up at the side entrance. Two men wearing black suits and sunglasses get out of the front of the car – one scans the area to make sure it is secure while the other rings the doorbell. The door is opened by Jennifer, the underappreciated boutique manager. There follows a brief conversation after which, with a nod of approval between the two men that all is as it should be, the rear passenger door of the car is opened and out steps a black-suited woman with a briefcase handcuffed to her wrist, who walks briskly into the boutique.

DS Silky decides to take a closer look.

On entering the boutique the detective is hit by the intoxicating scent of freshly made chocolates lacing the air. She observes the comprehensive security camera coverage of the minimalist interior design. As she goes to walk into the back of the boutique a sales assistant with a too-helpful lipstick smile asks if she can assist her. DS Silky shows her ID to the young woman and walks past her.

In the back of the boutique is a busy kitchen, an office and storeroom. Outside the office stand the two black-suited men guarding the meeting. DS Silky walks over to them and shows her ID. They step aside, one of them knocking on the door, the other one opening it for her.

Stepping into the office the detective walks into a precious gems deal. On the desk is a black cloth upon which are small piles of diamonds, sapphires, emeralds and rubies.

The black-suited woman is patiently indulging Midas as he pretends to know what he is looking for in the diamonds.

'They must be perfect. Each one the same size,' demands the chocolatier.

'I assure you they are all, as requested, near identical, one carat and colourless,' she replies.

DS Silky holds up her ID as she enters the room. Jennifer and the black-suited woman look at her with curiosity. Midas ignores her and concludes his assessment of the gemstones. 'Yes, these are perfect for my work.' He signs the paperwork headed *Van Bloed Gemstones International* and the black-suited woman and her two security men exit the boutique.

Jennifer locks the gems in a safe and leaves the office.

Midas looks at DS Silky, sizing her up. 'The Chocolate Thieves?'

'Yes.'

'You think I need to steal cocoa pods from Kew Gardens?'

'Did you?'

'No. If I had wanted them I would have asked for them.'

'Did you ask for them?'

'Yes – I did. Out of the curiosity of an artist to create something original.'

'For a unique profit?'

Midas guides DS Silky out of his office through the kitchen to the front of the boutique, speaking with the grandeur and self-confidence that success brings. 'Detective, I have the finest cocoa sent to me from all over the world. Tell me, have you tasted the rarest of Criollo from the Caribbean? With its delicate yet complex chocolate flavour – rich in long secondary notes. It is the princess of cocoas. And I have the wealthiest people you can imagine hungry for my creations. More than enough to make a "unique" profit.'

Midas gives a discreet nod to one of the sales assistants who proceeds to pour a takeaway hot chocolate and prepare a small gift box of Midas Gold Chocolates for the detective.

DS Silky holds up the photograph of The Chocolate Thieves. 'Are you acquainted with the contemporary versions of these men?'

'Of course not.'

'Your great-grandfather Alfred Midas knew them. In fact I'm sure your families would have crossed paths more than once in the last century.'

Midas bristles. 'I deal in chocolate not corpses, Detective.'

DS Silky knows he is not telling her something – actually she is sure he is not telling her about a whole family history of encounters with the descendants of the men in the photograph. 'You are a likely target for The Chocolate Thieves.'

'Let them try. We have adequate security. And a client list who know how to deal with lowlifes.'

'We will keep a surveillance team watching the premises until after your launch of That Midas Taste.'

The young woman hands DS Silky the takeaway cup of hot chocolate and box of chocolates and Midas concludes their conversation. 'Please, indulge yourself.'

'So you're rich, great, good for you. But what Midas represents is self-congratulating narcissism and the celebration of the exploitation of others. "Chocolates for the palates of the elite. People who have earned the right, and deserve, to indulge in That Midas Taste, wherever, whenever." Wanker!' Furness furiously stirs a pan of low cocoa, high in sugar, chocolate. 'And his chocolate is so bloody ordinary – too coarse, too sweet and with a weird bitter aftertaste. There is no sophistication or complexity of flavours. He is simply an overhyped amateur.'

'So what does that say about his rich clients' taste buds?' asks Afia as she goes outside.

'Ignorance of experience,' says Furness raising his voice so she can still hear him. 'Chocolate flavours are supposed to seduce you.'

'And there's his name,' Afia calls back with a chuckle –

deliberately enticing Furness to rant some more.

'Yes,' agrees Furness. 'All the cocoa he touches turns to gold. I repeat – wanker!'

Afia, holding her nose, walks back into the kitchen carrying a bag of rotting fish. Putting it down in front of Furness who enthusiastically opens it – the stench of the decaying cod, trout and salmon is terrible.

Afia wretches with repulsion.

Furness smiles a full Machiavellian smile. 'Excellent.'

At the Kensington Auction House Dunstan is looking through a collection of pocket watches when he hears a woman exclaim, 'Oh – how disappointing!', from where the lots of paintings are displayed.

'Not what you are looking for, Ms Crystal?' the auctioneer assisting her enquires.

'No. As lovely as it is – this is not it. I'm looking for a genuine Lowry titled *The Easter Fair*, from 1938. This is *The Summer Parade*, inspired by him most certainly but I think not by his hand. It's important to me that I find the right painting because my mother is in it as a little girl and I want to reconnect with her child spirit. Thank you for calling me but I will just have to keep looking.'

Leaving the auctioneer to his work Ms Crystal wanders over to the astronomy and astrological items up for auction but dismisses them as being of little interest.

Dunstan follows Ms Crystal out of the auction house, keeping her in sight as she drifts through the area buying a lunch of fruit and cheese from a deli and stopping to engage in familiar conversations with the friends and acquaintances she meets in the street. Eventually they arrive at her shop; *Ms Crystal and Daughter Antiques* declares the silver on ink-blue sign. Beneath the name is written *The Past Is Your Future. Established 1960*. Ms

Crystal lets herself in and turns the sign hanging inside the door from closed to open.

Dunstan doesn't go in but surveys the interior through the shop window – the antiques within are astronomical in nature along with curiosities from the practice of astrology. Looking at the items displayed in the shop window his eyes rest on an object in an open box of blue silk sitting between a turn-of-the-last-century sextant and a nineteenth-century ship's telescope – it is *The London Chocolate Time Piece*. Its exquisite bejewelled mechanism quietly ticking away time.

'Bloody hell!'

He slowly reaches out a hand to try to touch it through the glass of the shop window.

Afia comes out of the storeroom with a box of rotting blackcurrants, raspberries, apples, pears, plums and gooseberries. Furness inspects the fruit and smiles the same Machiavellian smile as before.

Afia proceeds to blend the bitter-smelling fruit into a pulp as Furness prepares another pan of low cocoa, high in sugar, chocolate.

Savage appears at the kitchen door and raises an eyebrow of curiosity at the antiquarian who is making a pot of tea.

'Hello,' says Dorothea brightly. 'The front door was open. Well, no, it wasn't. But I let myself in anyway. I thought we could try out your new teapot.'

'How do you know where I live?' enquires Savage.

'You let me follow you home after you bought the first teapot.' Dorothea gives the tea another stir and replaces the lid.

Smiling, enjoying her forthrightness, Savage takes his chair at the table and goes to pick up the teapot. Dorothea slaps his hand to stop him, sits down, and pours two cups of perfectly steeped tea. Savage takes an approving sip.

'You live in a hotel with two other guests.' She points to the three sets of crockery and cutlery on the draining board.

'The sign is historical – it is our home.'

'I was thinking of asking to book a room.'

'There's no need for you to do that.'

Dorothea looks at the boxes of Mrs Hoddinot's chocolates and at the photograph of their great-grandfathers standing on the mantelpiece. 'You really are Savage – one of The Chocolate Thieves.'

Savage reaches for a box of chocolates and offers one to Dorothea. She takes a Sweet Chestnut, Savage a Pure Cocoa Truffle. 'Yes.'

'Cool.'

Afia puts a container of pig's blood and fat down in front of Furness who opens it to inspect the putrid liquid and once again smiles his Machiavellian smile.

'We still need coarse marmalade and a bunch of nettles,' he instructs her.

Interestingly there is only one clock in The Chocolate Thieves' house. It is hanging on the wall above the fireplace in the kitchen, silently depicting the passing of time.

'It's because successive generations have hated the sound of a ticking clock,' Savage tells her.

'The fear of time passing – what is that called?'

'Chronophobia.'

Disappointingly the expansive multi-roomed cellar is empty of anything but firewood and coal. In the lounge Dorothea relaxes in one of the armchairs. In here, beneath the dust sheets, are a collection of comfortable worn-leather, velvet-cushioned, sofas and armchairs and occasional tables. Hanging on the walls are historical maps of London, portraits, still lifes and cityscape paintings by forgotten artists.

In all the rooms the faded wallpaper dates from the 1930s and mirrors hang over unlit fireplaces. Large rugs cover the floors. The lighting is period chandeliers and wall lamps.

In the dining room she sits on one of the chairs at the table and imagines the conversations over dinner. The room holds a table and nine chairs, a pristine *TCT*-marked bespoke white dinner service and bone-handled silver cutlery, an art deco cocktail shaker with glasses, an ice bucket and wine and spirit glasses – all waiting for use at an intimate party or a family celebration.

On the stair walls and along the landings hang photographic family portraits.

'Each generation of Chocolate Thieves decade by decade,' Savage informs her.

Dorothea intensely studies the photographs, fascinated by the lineage of their DNA and the succession of beautiful, fully of character, women marrying into each generation – appearing every inch the equal of the men in stature. The family genes are so strong that it is only the clothes and the taxi they are driving that give away which generation of Chocolate Thieves is which.

'How wonderful,' she gasps.

Savage points at a photograph. 'CHOC 1, all died in the bombing of London during World War Two.'

'Tragic.'

'CHOC 2, Savage succumbed to diabetes, Furness drowned in a vat of 90% cocoa chocolate, Dunstan died from heart disease induced by rotten teeth.'

'Rotten teeth kill you?'

'Apparently so – the gum disease periodontitis and the vascular nature of gums leads to bacteria spreading through the body and there ends the heart.'

'Crikey!'

'CHOC 3, Savage, again, diabetes – blind and missing a leg. Furness choked on just one more before-bed homemade chocolate-coated English Butter Toffee. Dunstan heart attack – arteries were as clotted as a fish and chip shop drain.'

'Bloody hell! What about their wives?'

'Lovely and toothless. Equals in wit and cunning – do you think these men could have committed their eighty years of chocolate heists without them?'

'And here are the three of you standing next to CHOC 4. No wives?'

'Not yet.'

Dorothea lies on a bed in one of the unused rooms. All the dust-sheeted bedrooms are simply decorated and furnished with a bed, bedside table with lamp, a writing table and armchair, wardrobes of period suits and dresses and more family photos.

Furness's suite is white and tidy – meditative with a library of recipe books.

Dunstan's suite is tranquil blue – it holds a library of art history books. A lot of which are left open and scattered around the room.

Dorothea looks out of one of the windows onto the quiet hidden street. 'The people who live in the other houses – do they have any idea how infamous their neighbours are in The Black Truffle Hotel?'

'I don't believe they've been curious enough to ask. People rarely see what is under their nose.'

Returning her attention to the interior, she says, 'They

are still here, aren't they? The generations that lived here. I mean they are in the hand-and-foot-worn varnish of the stairs. In the chairs where they relaxed and at the table where they dined. In the beds where they slept. And in the wood smoke and chocolate scent of the house. Having now seen their photographs and their rooms – I can hear their voices.'

Savage smiles and nods in agreement and appreciation of her sensitivity for the home he loves so dearly. 'Yes they are and always will be.'

In the attic rooms the cold breeze billows the tarpaulin covering the holes in the roof. Dorothea has uncovered a 1930s Bristol Chocolate Company slot machine. In the drawer at its base is a collection of King George VI pennies. She puts one in the slot and pulls the arm, the reels spin, the colours blur, stopping with a jolting clank on a bell, a cherry and one bar of chocolate. She pulls the arm again and watches the reels spin – this time she gets three chocolate bars and with a clunk a small bar of chocolate drops into the winner's tray on the front of the machine.

'No way!' exclaims Dorothea. 'It's a genuine 1939 bar of Bristol's chocolate.'

'It has never done that for anyone else,' an amazed Savage tells her.

Should she eat it? Dorothea sniffs it. It has the odour of dry dark chocolate and machine. She drops it back into the tray.

'My suite is dedicated to the study of chocolate,' Savage tells her. Green-walled and the most lived-in with its library on the history of chocolate, writing desk and constantly burning fire in the grate it has a homely warmth with the alluring musk scent of the man fused with the seductive nature of old books and chocolate. 'The history of Theobroma, the food of the gods, or chocolate, is one of wisdom, desire, lust, vice, gratification, conquest and of course addiction. I've written a number of monographs on the subject.' Savage waves his hand at the shelf of self-published writing.

Dorothea scans the titles – *A History of the Flavours of Chocolate, From Pod to Palate; How Cocoa Became Chocolate; The English Chocolate Houses; Cocoa Conquistadors; Chocolate and the Industrial Revolution* and *Chocolate in the New Millennium*. 'So much to savour,' she enthuses.

'My latest is *The History of The Chocolate Thieves*.' He nods towards his laptop on the writing desk.

'Really!'

'Just the final chapter to live.'

Dorothea sees Savage's balaclava and gloves resting on a table and looks lustfully into his eyes. 'Put on the balaclava.'

Savage offers Dorothea a chocolate from a box of Mrs Hoddinot's he has on his desk. Dorothea selects an Apple & Cinnamon, Savage a Wild Honey.

'Just the balaclava?'

'And the gloves.'

After a day of intense chocolate-making, Furness and Afia stand back and admire their work.

'And on the chocolate menu tonight, miss, we have edible-diamond-adorned silver bars of rotten fish coated with a 25% cocoa chocolate laced with fish oil at £7,000 each.'

'Or, sir, if you'd prefer, 10% dark chocolate devilishly sour marmalade drops at £1,000 and 5% cocoa milk-chocolate-coated English roadside nettle leaves at £450 each.'

'And what have we here, miss?'

'Well, sir, these are individually wrapped edible-gem-adorned rotten English fruit fondant chocolates coated in an anaemic 10% cocoa chocolate at £10,000 a box.'

'And for the ultimate indulgence, miss, I offer you the That Midas Taste Black Pudding Easter Truffle – made with 90% non-organic pig's blood and fat coated in a blend of 25% cocoa and 75% aniseed chocolate infused with four-carat edible gold. Yours to delight in for a mere £20,000 a box.'

'Oh! How lovely, sir!'

'Our pleasure, miss.'

They both chuckle with malicious delight.

Reflected in the full-length mirror in his suite Dunstan surveys his disguise – blue pinstripe suit, aged skin, a grey wig of shoulder-length hair, equally grey facial hair and eyebrows, and a pair of wire-framed glasses. 'Good morning, Mr Garrick.' The tone of his voice higher than normal and cracked to imply age and eccentricity.

Satisfied with his disguise he takes down Kyoko's painting of Lowry's *The Easter Fair*, from above the fireplace, puts it very carefully – for fear of smudging the still-drying oil paint – into a carrying case, exits the house and gets into the waiting CHOC 4.

Four days earlier he'd run into Kyoko's workshop demanding she stop what she was doing and that she paint him one of Lowry's rare London scenes.

'The commission you gave me to do my own work has lasted twenty-two hours,' she pointed out to him.

To which he'd smiled, shrugged and added the word, 'Please.'

For *The Easter Fair* she chose a 1930s piece of board from the storeroom, then selected the artist's favoured palette of five oil paints from the racks at the back of the studio – flake white, scarlet vermilion, yellow ochre, Prussian blue and ivory black from the Winsor & Newton company.

Painting from her mind's eye at the speed and with the energy and flare of the artist she is emulating she began the forgery by coating the board with flake white. Once this was dry enough to work on she sketched out the desired scene in pencil and painted in the backdrop that the characters in the painting inhabit – the London skyline, the stalls and rides of the fair. In the foreground she populates the scene with quirky stick-like figures wrapped in coats, scarfs and hats. Remembering to include the ubiquitous black dogs that appear in so many of the artist's paintings. All the characters in the scene carry expressions of happiness as they enjoy the entertainment of the fair. Finally Kyoko painted in the smiling little girl in her yellow coat and scarlet hat that will be Ms Crystal's mother. The composition is one of era-defining joy.

With the title and signature applied to the bottom left corner Dunstan had taken the painting home to dry and smoke-age above the open fire in his suite.

Mr Garrick walks into Ms Crystal and Daughter Antiques with a confidence and smile befitting the theatre of his disguise. 'Ms Crystal. I am Mr Garrick. And according to our mutual friends at the Kensington Auction House I have something in my possession that will enchant you.'

Ms Crystal, full of sceptical curiosity, gets up from behind her desk to greet him.

Mr Garrick, carefully and suspensefully, slowly takes the Lowry out of the carrying case and stands it on a chair.

'You have found it!' Ms Crystal shrieks, clapping her hands to her face, eyes bulging out of their sockets, as she looks at the painting in wonderment. 'I thought it lost forever. I thought never to see it in my lifetime.'

'Well, it has remained uncatalogued all these years having been kept in the same family.'

'Where did it come from?'

'The wall of the home of a Mrs Veigel of Adelphi Terrace, where it has hung above the mantelpiece all these years since it was purchased by her ancestor when the paint was still wet in 1938.'

'Why did she sell it to you?'

'The usual reasons – inheritance tax, addiction, greed.'

'Is it genuine?'

Mr Garrick, ignoring the question, takes Ms Crystal by the arm. 'It's important to find the perfect viewing point. Now, stand here. Yes, that's right. Now, it looks good, doesn't it? But let's take a step back. And let's try a step to the left. And now two to the right. And back to the centre. Take one step forwards. And three steps backwards. And two steps forwards. Now, you see how these simple changes of viewing position give you a variant of perspective of the events depicted and the unique place to stand to truly see the painting.'

'So revealing, Mr Garrick.'

'Indeed, Ms Crystal. Now, let's walk past it, back and forth, viewing it out of our peripheral vision. That's it – back and forth we go. You see the way the figures move as if we are walking with them through this wonderful scene and the excitement of the Easter Fair is happening all around us. Do you see it?'

'I do! I do! It's incredible! It's like I am actually there!'

'Now, let us step into the painting. Breathe in the scent, that's it, sniff it, smell the scent of that exciting spring day in the aged paint. Are we time-travelling? Back to that day. Yes! I think we are there.'

'I can hear the sounds of the fair and their voices chattering and laughter. What fun they are having, Mr Garrick!'

'It's a classic Lowry.'

'You know, I think that's her, my mother, the girl in the yellow coat and scarlet hat. So cute – isn't she? It is her, isn't it?'

'I'm sure it is.'

Ms Crystal steps back to view the whole painting and smiles with satisfaction. 'Payment, Mr Garrick?'

Mr Garrick smiles and looks towards *The London Chocolate Time Piece* in the shop window.

An entwined Savage, in balaclava and gloves, and a trouserless Dorothea fall into the fourth bedroom on the first floor and proceed to writhe on a squeaky metal-sprung bed amongst the dust-sheeted furniture.

'Tradition has it that cocoa was first consumed as a drink in Mesoamerica as far back as 1900 BCE. Though new archaeological evidence suggests it was consumed a thousand years before that in the Amazon rainforest of modern day Ecuador,' Savage informs her. 'The Mayans believed the pods of the cocoa tree were an offering from the gods to man. The formal classification *Theobroma cacao* means "Food of the gods", from the Greek "theos" for god and "broma" for food. The origins of the word "chocolate" are lost to history. But it is thought by some that it derives from the "Nahuatl" word "xocolatl", made up from the words "xococ" meaning sour or bitter, and "atl" meaning water or drink.'

'Fascinating – go on.'

'Until the sixteenth century, chocolate was unknown to Europeans. But through the explorations of the Conquistadors came assimilation of the culinary habits of the Native Americans.'

'Assimilation – wonderful.'

'Cometh the Industrial Revolution cometh the revolution in the production of chocolate from a drink to an edible solid state and by 1847 we had our first eating chocolate.'

'A glorious time – tell me more.'

'The marketing of chocolate was cunning and appealed to the narcissism of the vain. And chocolate has always been said to be an aphrodisiac. It is believed to boost your fertility and reverse ageing. A mere lick, it was said, would "Make old young and fresh, create new motions of the flesh." Ow! Ow! Bloody cramp in my foot!' Savage falls off the bed.

'Eleven rooms to go,' gasps an exhausted, dishevelled Dorothea.

The gloved hand of Savage reaches up, takes hold of her shirt tail and pulls her onto the floor. 'I've not finished with you yet.'

In her studio Kyoko has melted the cocoa butter and added food colouring, cocoa powder, sugar and vanilla extract in various quantities – making bowls of blue, red, green, purple, yellow, orange, brown and black chocolate paint.

Artist, brush in hand, looks into the clean white surface of the edible sugar paste canvass.

Waiting.

Stillness descends.

She dips the brush into the blue chocolate paint and sweeps it across the canvass. Staining the canvass with layer upon layer of blocks of paint so thinly the colours shimmer through each other. The finished chocolate panels offer a beautiful experience – one that affords the viewer the tangible illusion of an eternal journey through the passing of time.

Late that evening DS Silky turns the handle of the unlocked door and quietly pushes it open. Stepping into the kitchen of The Furness restaurant she begins searching for evidence to support what she knows to be true – that Furness is one of The Chocolate Thieves.

Beneath her, in the cellar, inspecting the now-on-drying-trays Kew Gardens cocoa beans, Afia hears the detective's footsteps above her. She stealthily ascends the cellar stairs to the kitchen.

DS Silky takes one of the Cherry and Ginseng chocolates from the open box on the counter. The moment she pops it in her mouth her face expresses sheer delight at the scintillating flavours – she grips the edge of the prep table with both hands as her whole body quivers.

Afia appears in front of her. 'Breaking and entering, DS Silky?' She eats one of the Cherry and Ginseng chocolates.

'I just called by and saw the back door was open.'

'Unlocked when you turned the handle.'

'I was investigating the possibility of there being a crime in progress.'

'Is there?'

'What's in the cellar?'

'You know only a warrant gets you an answer to that question.' Afia takes a bottle of house red off the wine rack and opens it.

'Your boss, Furness…'

'Not here.'

'Where?'

Afia just smiles.

If Furness was at Midas's boutique DS Silky's phone would have rung. 'Tell me about him.'

'Be specific.' Afia pours two glasses of wine.

'I know he's one of The Chocolate Thieves.'

Afia hands DS Silky one of the glasses of wine – they drink. 'A heroic, masked, outlaw stalking the moonlit night to pilfer chocolates for the sweet-toothed poor and disregarded of our fair city.'

'You think their crimes romantic?'

'I think it's what we, the people, need.'

'Victims of crime?'

'Folklore. Outlaws taking on the establishment's way of life. The excitement of their derring-do. Just staying out of reach of the law.'

'Until one day they are betrayed for a reward by the whispers of a confidant. And the people see their outlaws, their heroes, swing by the neck from the gallows at Newgate.'

Afia puts her wine down and takes another Cherry and Ginseng chocolate – she bites and swallows half of it. She puts the second half of the chocolate into DS Silky's mouth. 'They're rogues – what real harm are they doing?' DS Silky chews and swallows the chocolate. Afia takes the wine glass out of the detective's hand and puts it down on the counter. 'You can have whatever you desire.' Afia kisses and bites on DS Silky's lips. Lingers in the moment looking into the detective's eyes for reciprocated desire. Then, with unconstrained lust, DS Silky pushes Afia against a fridge as she kisses her. Entwined they bounce around the kitchen – pulling each other's clothes open to get at the flesh within. DS Silky, with nimble fingers, expertly searching Afia for the cellar key – which she doesn't find.

'All you desire – but not me.' Afia opens the kitchen door and pushes DS Silky out into the night – slamming it shut and locking the door on her.

Standing in a doorway a short distance away Dunstan is discreetly observing the morning's comings and goings of the set-up for the That Midas Taste chocolate launch at the Midas Boutique. The chocolatier continuously barking orders at his scurrying staff.

He also observes the presence of a police officer in the window of the surveillance room opposite the boutique.

Turning the page of the newspaper he is pretending to read he is distracted by an article with the headline *FEARS FOR GLOBAL COCOA SUPPLY* and the sentence *Cocoa price reaches a world record high of £10,000 a tonne*. It is now obvious to Dunstan that whoever controls the supply of the global demand for the last of the world's cocoa, and the chocolate made from it, is going to become very wealthy. And the chocolatier he is looking at knows how to exploit every opportunity to fleece his patrons.

Kyoko adds gold leaf to a delicately painted scene of a man and woman wrapped in each other's arms sharing a kiss that communicates both intimacy and eternity – expressing the truth that in these moments of true pleasure only these two people exist. Completed portraits of people, similar in appearance to The Chocolate Thieves and the women in their lives – including DS Silky – stand drying around the studio. All of the scenes depicted exploring the transcendental sensuality of human interaction.

Savage and Dorothea step out of the kitchen door into the wild garden that is slowly creeping into spring at The Black Truffle Hotel. The sky is blue and the sun teases warmth through the crisp air. Halfway along the path Dorothea spots a headstone against the wall to her left with the epitaph *CHOC 1 SAMUEL SAVAGE 1892–1940 & KATHERINE SAVAGE 1895–1941, IN LOVING*

MEMORY, TCT. It is now Dorothea sees the other gravestones alongside it – each with the same style of epitaph, naming The Chocolate Thief and their wife. *CHOC 1 WILLIAM FURNESS 1894–1940 & ANNA FURNESS 1897–1941, CHOC 1 TRISTAN DUNSTAN 1896–1940 & CELIA DUNSTAN 1899–1942. CHOC 2 MARTIN SAVAGE 1918–1970 & DORA SAVAGE 1918– 1973, CHOC 2 VICTOR FURNESS 1919–1967 & SARAH FURNESS 1920–1976, CHOC 2 EDWIN DUNSTAN 1920–1974 & CONSTANCE DUNSTAN 1922–1975. CHOC 3 TERENCE SAVAGE 1951–2001 & PATRICIA SAVAGE 1952–2003, CHOC 3 JONATHAN FURNESS 1952–2004 & JOSEPHINE FURNESS 1956–2007, CHOC 3 GLEN DUNSTAN 1950–2006 & LYDIA DUNSTAN 1954–2008.*

'They're all here,' she says.

'Where else would they be buried? This is their home,' replies Savage.

Walking into the garage, with the flickering-on of the lights, Savage pulls the tarpaulins off the vehicles. 'Let me introduce you to CHOC 1 – our great-grandfathers' *1919 Beardmore MK1*. Alongside it we have CHOC 2 – our grandfathers' *1948 Austin FX3*. This is CHOC 3 – our fathers' *1965 Austin FX4*. And here we have CHOC 4 – our very own *2002 London Taxi International TXII*.'

Dorothea's eyes go wide in awe at the sight of the four London taxis and she explores the cars with unrestrained excitement. Opening the doors of each vehicle – getting behind the wheel and sitting in the rear passenger seats. Inhaling the atmosphere of each one. 'The scent of history – a wonderful cocktail of machine, leather and chocolate.'

Savage is pulling on overalls. 'Our task today is to give these beauties a tuning. As their speed and reliability will, I believe, be vital in saving our skins in the coming days.'

At the end of the trading day DS Silky walks into the police surveillance room opposite the Midas Boutique. Waiting for her on a table near the window, along with a camera, in Midas packaging, is a cup of steaming hot chocolate and a box of chocolates. The gift card reads, *Indulge yourself, wherever, whenever. M.* DS Silky removes the lid of the hot chocolate and takes a sip – it tastes wondrously good. She also eats one of the chocolates – which is sublime. But it seems different in taste and characteristics than the chocolates Midas had gifted her on her visit to the boutique. This is smoother, silkier, with a more defined cocoa resonance – more like Mrs Hoddinot's or even Furness's chocolate. More robust in flavour with a deeper unknown earthier flavour. Should she be suspicious? But of what? It is interesting that she has begun to notice the subtle differences between the chocolatiers' creations.

She looks out of the window at the boutique. Its windows are now blacked out with *That Midas Taste–*emblazoned drapes in anticipation of tomorrow's launch. She watches as the arrogant chocolatier leaves the premises with his arm around a woman still young enough to be impressed by his inflated sense of cultural standing. Jennifer the manager, still inside the boutique, locks the front door behind them.

Afia, carrying a tray of hot chocolates and a selection box of chocolates in Midas packaging, approaches an unmarked van full of police officers parked discreetly out of view of the boutique.

In the van one of the officers is on the phone to DS Silky. 'Yes, Detective, we are in position – awaiting your orders.'

An officer opens the van's front passenger window with an expression of undisguised appreciation of Afia and curiosity at her intentions.

'Thank you for keeping our chocolates safe. I thought you would like a treat,' she says sweetly.

'Thank you – that's very kind of you,' the police officers say to her with admiring smiles as they enthusiastically share out the drinks and chocolates.

Afia walks away and quietly, with a malicious smile, says to herself, 'Enjoy.'

Jennifer, making sure the side door is securely locked, heads out of the mews and walks in the direction of the Underground station. Out of DS Silky's line of sight Dunstan appears out of the shadow of a doorway and follows the manager.

At the Underground station Furness appears in front of Jennifer, blocking her way and gently holding her by each hand. 'Jennifer! How wonderful to see you.' The manager is completely taken aback – who the hell is this person? 'You look so well,' continues Furness. 'Still grinding cocoa beans for that outrageously egotistical fuck Midas?' Dunstan approaches Jennifer from behind and relieves her bag of her keys to the Midas Boutique. 'My palate pessimistically salivates at the prospect of his ludicrously indulgent new range.' Furness abruptly ends the conversation and walks on leaving the bemused Jennifer to continue her journey home.

A few streets away Furness and Dunstan get into CHOC 4 where Savage has parked out of sight of unwanted eyes.

An hour later, having drunk her comforting hot chocolate and devoured the box of chocolates, DS Silky is now asleep – standing up, head resting against the window, her breath steaming up the glass.

And half of the van of police officers have also drifted off to sleep. While the other half have jumped out of the vehicle desperately in search of toilets.

The Chocolate Thieves pull on their balaclavas and gloves and Savage quietly drives past the van of out-for-the-count police officers and the sleeping DS Silky into the mews alongside the Midas Boutique.

Dunstan gets out of CHOC 4 and goes through the stolen set of keys until he finds the right one to open the side door. Savage and Furness join him, carrying the containers of fake Midas chocolates. The three of them enter the building, close the door behind them and switch on their head torches. Dunstan grabs a handful of cocoa powder from a nearby sack and blows it onto the security alarm keypad – the powder sticks to the four digits used to set and to turn off the alarm: one, four, five and nine. But the powder has gone up his nose and he begins to sneeze. Furness grabs Dunstan's head and shoves it into the sack of cocoa powder from which comes a muffled sneeze and the puffing-up of powder. Standing up, the face of his balaclava covered in powder, Dunstan glares at Furness, who shrugs. 'What else was I supposed to do?' Then Dunstan begins to sneeze again and Furness repeats the shoving of his head into the sack – again there comes the muffled sound of a sneeze and the puffing-up of powder. With a tut Savage steps towards the keypad and inputs a code which switches off the alarm within two seconds of it going off. The other two stare at him wondering how he knew the code.

'The date his grandfather opened the shop – 1945,' whispers Savage.

Finding a stack of empty Midas presentation boxes The Chocolate Thieves set about filling them with the fakes. Once this is done they swap them with the boxes of That Midas Taste chocolates already on display in the shop.

The stolen Midas chocolates are put into CHOC 4 as

Dunstan resets the alarm and locks the door – leaving the keys on the ground a few feet away. And Savage quietly drives them away past the still-asleep detective.

Down at Embankment station The Chocolate Thieves distribute the That Midas Taste chocolates amongst the homeless bedding down there for the night. Dunstan taking photographs with his phone of them gratefully eating the most expensive chocolates in the world.

The following evening suited private security personnel open the door of the Midas Boutique for the exclusively invited guests – chocolate-addicted billionaires from every sphere of global trading, supermodels, musicians, actors, sports people and influencers from across the world arrive for the launch of That Midas Taste.

The paparazzi surround the red-carpeted entrance, filling the air with camera flashes. Lifestyle journalists talk overexcitedly into microphones and cameras – telling their viewers how excited they are to be there and grabbing quick interviews with the elite guests.

Midas is in his element sycophantically smiling as he welcomes his wealthy patrons. The brightly sparkling gold and silver bejewelled chocolates are all eyed with glutinous desire.

Iced 75% Haitian cocoa chocolate champagne in flute glasses is handed out. And lines of 100% pure Columbian cocoa powder laid out on tablets of slate are snorted through chocolate straws. Soon the whole boutique is buzzing on a chocolate high.

Midas silences the room. 'My friends.' His hands are held out like those of a cocoa messiah. 'Welcome to the launch of the exclusive That Midas Taste range of the most expensive and luxurious chocolates in the world.'

His captivated audience applaud.

'I have travelled to far flung parts of the world and selected the finest, rarest, most potent cocoa growing on the planet to create these tantalising delights. The like of which, I assure you, your palates have never before tasted.

'Silver Bars of Fruit and Nut – made with organic dates and walnuts, apricots and hazelnuts, raisins and chestnuts enveloped in 75% Wild Amazonian Criollo cocoa chocolate and adorned with one-carat diamonds.'

Tongues tingle.

'The 60% Sri Lankan cocoa chocolate-coated Elvish Wild Honey Drops. And 50% Cuban cocoa chocolate-enveloped English Wild Mint Leaves.'

Lips are licked.

'The jewel-adorned English Fruit Chocolates of organic blackcurrant, raspberry, apple, pear and gooseberry fruit creme coated in a delicate 70% Porcelana chocolate.'

They are wide-eyed and salivating.

'And, I present to you my exquisite, unique, creation – the silky, smoky, luxurious flavours of the exclusively handcrafted That Midas Taste Easter Truffle made with 90% rare organic Ecuadorian Nacional Arriba cocoa, English black truffles, Capet Roi de Chocolat champagne and infused with twenty-four-carat edible gold.'

There are gasps of appreciation and anticipation.

'These chocolates are created for your sophisticated elite palates.'

The sound of flattered giggles.

'It is an honour to sate all your chocolate desires. Indulge yourselves, wherever, whenever. I present to you, That Midas Taste.'

The guests applaud loudly and begin to gorge on the proffered indulgences.

The realisation that something is wrong is swift.

And the orgy of earthly delights soon turns to chaos as

the mouths of the skeletal vegan lifestyle influencers are stung on the nettle leaves and the sour marmalade drops make gargoyles of the faces of the at-the-top-of-their-sport athletes.

Supermodels and musicians well practised in stomach evacuation spray putrid puke over each other as the rotten fish fingers and decaying fruit chocolates induce collective vomiting.

Pig's blood and fat is expelled out of the mouths of the truffle scoffers – running down the jowls of the traders, future tech CEOs and making dribbling fools of the critically acclaimed leading actors.

Dresses and suits are ruined and egos are violated.

Midas is unable to comprehend what is happening around him – how dare they reject his chocolate mastery.

There is a pause in the mayhem.

Then, as one, the enraged elite guests pelt Midas with the monstrous chocolates they have been served. The chocolatier cowers in fear for his life. Every moment of this is captured on camera by the feral paparazzi and reported via live news-streams by the clamouring lifestyle journalists.

Furness is cooking breakfast. The headline of the newspaper article Dunstan is reading exclaims, *WORLD COCOA SUPPLY AT ALL TIME LOW*. The first line of the article stating all that needs to be said: *There is only two million tonnes of cocoa left in the world.*

Dorothea hesitantly walks into the kitchen.

Furness and Dunstan stare at her for a short time then say in unison, 'Who the hell are you?'

Savage appears behind her. 'Dorothea is my house guest.'

'About bloody time,' reply Furness and Dunstan.

'Dorothea, these rogues are…'

'Furness and Dunstan. I recognise you from your DNA.' She points at the photo of their great-grandfathers. 'What an honour,' she enthusiastically shakes their hands, 'to be here with the three of you – The Chocolate Thieves.'

Savage gives his friends a satisfied smile.

Furness serves up four plates of breakfast.

Savage goes to pick up the teapot but Dorothea slaps his hand away and pours out four cups of perfectly steeped tea.

'What do you do, Dorothea?' asks Dunstan.

'I'm into relics.'

Furness and Dunstan giggle childishly.

Savage frowns at them. 'Dorothea redistributes the junk,' he corrects himself, 'the neglected artefacts of the past that others would carelessly landfill.'

'We call it vintage in the trade. I sold him your new teapot.'

Dunstan's phone, lying on the table, flashes up a news feed.

'We don't do phones at the breakfast table,' scolds Savage.

Ignoring him Dunstan picks up his phone and accesses the article. 'Bloody Hell!' The others stare at him expectantly. 'Midas has put up a £1,000,000 reward on us!'

The other three, as one, take out their phones.

Dorothea plays a news report of an angry and defiant Midas standing on the steps outside his closed boutique talking to the gathered media. 'My work, my art, has been polluted by pettiness. But I will not be deterred. I am the greatest living chocolatier and I will relaunch That Midas Taste. And in pursuit of justice I offer a reward of £100,000 for the arrest and successful prosecution of The Chocolate Thieves.'

'Is that all?' shouts a heckler.

'You want more. Fine. £500,000!'

'You can afford more than that,' goads another heckler.

'Alright – £1,000,000! Yes! £1,000,000 for the arrest and successful prosecution of The Chocolate Thieves,' rages the chocolatier.

The news report cuts to footage of the chaos of the That Midas Taste launch the previous evening.

Dunstan anonymously uploads the photographs of the homeless eating the most expensive chocolates in the world, with the tagline *The homeless say, 'Thank you, Midas'*, signing it *TCT*, to all online news and social media sites.

The photographs instantly go viral.

Follow-up reports depict the homeless cashing in the jewels from the chocolates to buy food and clothes for themselves and other homeless people. Those with bank accounts save the money and some take the opportunity for a few nights in a hotel – to take a bath and sleep in a bed.

When asked what he thought of the most expensive chocolates in the world a homeless man known as George The Teeth – a former pastry chef – responds by saying, 'We're all very grateful for them of course, but as one professional to another, I would say, the chocolatier lacked the skills to truly temper a smooth chocolate therefore inhibiting the true flavours of the cocoa. And the fruit creme was unbalanced leaving a bittersweet aftertaste. But thanks for the new filling.' And George The Teeth smiles a diamond-toothed smile.

When shown who his chocolates have been eaten by and hearing the homeless man's review of his creations Midas cannot control his rage. 'It's a waste of my artistry. How can these people appreciate the subtleties, the nuances, of my chocolate with such ignorant mouths.'

His arrogance and insensitivity towards the homeless people gifted his chocolates and generally his absence of humour at the stunt pulled by The Chocolate Thieves stirs up a social media storm of anti-Midas sentiment in praise of The Chocolate Thieves – with calls for no one to claim the reward offered for their arrest and prosecution.

DI Gloom and DS Silky are arguing – again.

'Under our fucking noses! They swapped the chocolates under our fucking nose! It's like you want to make us look like idiots. Don't you want to work here anymore?'

'They drugged us with cups of hot chocolate and the most exquisite confectionary, sir.'

'Drugged you with hot chocolate! Tucked you up in bed with your teddy too? Sang you a fucking lullaby as well, did they?'

'I'm a murder detective not a fucking sweet-shop monitor! You want me to solve crimes, give me a body. I don't care whose – a trussed-up lingerie-wearing politician, a prostitute strangled by a metallic hand, mudlarks washed up on the shore of the Thames, a bludgeoned environmental activist in possession of state secrets, a man lost in time, an SVR spy poisoned by polonium. I don't fucking care! Just give me a fucking body to investigate.'

'Have I seen that film?'

'Don't you understand? I'm up against every chocolate addict's Robin, fucking, Hoods! Which is everyone in the fucking city! No one is going to give up The Chocolate Thieves.'

'But they're criminals! They're breaking the law!'

'Nobody cares. They hate the Midases of the world. He's a chocolate banker.'

'Is that rhyming slang?'

'Aaaahhhh!' DS Silky steals one of DI Gloom's Rusty's Nut and Raisin chocolates and storms out of the office, slamming the door behind her.

Kyoko, paintbrush in hand, is putting the final touches to one of a series of chocolate paintings of London. They are an exploration of the urban landscape that the viewer observes and interacts with daily. A series of paintings about the contradiction of city life – a representation of the seeking out of anonymity and exhibition. She has used the silver leaf to simulate dappling light on the river, the rain and birds. The edible gold leaf for sunsets and apartment lights. And she has depicted the recent storm that raged through their lives in dynamic swirling colours.

Dunstan walks into the studio carrying a bottle of wine and two glasses. He looks closely at every painting – in awe at what Kyoko has created. His eyes well with tears and he looks with admiration at the artist. 'They're beautiful. Truly beautiful.'

Kyoko smiles and daubs the end of his nose with blue chocolate paint. 'Open the wine.'

They sit on stools and Dunstan pours out two glasses, distracted by Kyoko's work. 'I've wasted your talent getting you to work as a forger.'

'I've learned how to paint from the masters.'

'Chocolate is your medium.'

'It would seem so.'

'To a discovered artist.'

They touch glasses and drink.

'Is this going to work?' she asks him.

'It has to. Anyway – why would we stop now? What we are doing – it's beautifully ridiculous. And so far we are getting away with it.'

'The legend of The Chocolate Thieves.'

'It's all illusion – but isn't everyone's life? That said – this feels real. This is success at our fingertips. You know my life is all about the deal – I'm addicted to the performance and the deception. But this is bigger than getting cash in my pocket. It's the imagining, the audacity, and the realisation of the plan. Look at this wonderful city – the way everyone lives their lives. We all need the absurdity of what The Chocolate Thieves are doing.'

Kyoko holds up her glass of wine. 'To the illusion, the plan and the absurdity of life.'

They touch glasses again and drink.

'So – what about you? What does this all mean to you?'

'For me life is very simple. Every morning when I open my eyes the first thing I think is, "What am I going to paint today?" It has always been this way – since I was very small I have painted. There is nothing else I have ever wanted to do – it's the way I talk to the world.'

'Which is your favourite? Which one don't you want to sell?'

Kyoko smiles and looks towards a painting of two lovers entwined. 'That one. I think, no, I know I have captured what it will feel like to be those people.'

'What is it titled?'

'*Us.*'

Across the city, across the country, across the world people are reading newspaper articles, listening to the radio and watching streaming news about the global cocoa crisis.

In the hands of an investor the financial newspaper reports *COCOA THE PRICE OF GOLD*. An environmentalist sighs with resigned inevitability on reading *FAIR TRADE ABANDONED*. A global commodities trader calculates the black market deals still to be done on hearing *STOCKPILES OF COCOA HIDDEN ACROSS GLOBE*. A spokesperson for the Food and Agriculture Organization of the United Nations is interviewed under the headline *AFRICAN COCOA FARMERS STARVING*. The cynical eye of an Interpol agent sceptically watches the television report of what is supposedly the drifting wreck of a cargo ship beneath the headline *THE LAST OF THE SRI LANKAN CRIOLLO LOST AT SEA*. A botanist shakes their head when informed *WITCHES' BROOM SWEEPS ACROSS ECUADOR*. Footage of a despondent cocoa farmer with a devastated harvest is shown under the words *FROSTY POD ROT CREEPS THROUGH SOUTH AMERICA*. Over footage of Mrs Hoddinot's shop window are the words *THE LAST EASTER EGGS*. And tears run from the eyes of chocolate addicts, young and old, on reading the words *RIP CHOCOLATE*.

It's 2am. CHOC 2 driven by Savage with Dorothea, CHOC 3 driven by Furness with Afia, and CHOC 4 driven by Dunstan with Kyoko pull up outside the Global Cocoa warehouse at the Port of Tilbury. All disguised in balaclavas and wearing gloves, they get out of the taxis.

'Where's all the security?' asks Afia.

'They don't believe they're a target yet. It's still easier for people to buy or pinch the ready-made chocolate that's left on the shelves of the shops,' answers Furness.

Dunstan takes the lead. 'We need to get enough cocoa to make our point and encourage others to take action.' He picks the lock of the staff entrance to the warehouse and the others follow him inside.

The warehouse is stacked high with sacks of cocoa.

Dunstan directs their attention to a pile of empty sacks and coils of rope as they make their way to the centre of the warehouse. He walks out into clear view, while the others hide behind sacks of cocoa, and awaits the arrival of the few security guards that are on duty, who he hopes are watching him on the monitor attached to the other end of the CCTV camera of which he is looking down the lens.

Eventually three security guards appear – their torches flashing over Dunstan. They are immediately jumped by all six of The Chocolate Thieves – a sack pulled over each of their heads, the guards are bound with rope and left tied up in a corner of the warehouse.

After opening the loading bay doors and reversing the taxis inside The Chocolate Thieves load them with sacks of South American Criollo and West African Forastero cocoa and drive away.

They spend the rest of the night delivering the sacks of cocoa to artisan chocolatiers across London – Mrs Hoddinot's, Barge's, Featherlight's, Reaper's, Rusty's and Vamp's. Pinned to one of the sacks left at their door is a note from The Chocolate Thieves: *Make chocolate for the people – 21st March is Chocolate Liberation Day. TCT.*

'Dunstan!'

The Chocolate Thief walks into the studio to be confronted by a naked Kyoko standing in the centre of a large canvass covering the studio floor holding a bowl of orange chocolate paint.

'Take off your clothes,' she instructs him. 'One more painting.'

Moments later a laughing Dunstan and Kyoko are having the time of their lives – playfully pouring all the colours of edible chocolate paint over each other and rolling around on the canvass to create prints of their bodies.

Once the intoxicating aroma of cocoa fills the kitchen, the trays of roasted Kew Gardens cocoa beans are pulled out of the oven. When the beans are cooled, Furness pours them into a food bag then bashes them with a rolling pin.

Afia goes outside with the broken cocoa beans, in a bowl, and her hair dryer and blows away the crushed shells leaving a bowl full of cocoa nibs.

Back in the kitchen Furness puts the nibs through a juicer, collecting the cocoa liquor in a bowl at the juice port. At the pulp port they collect the residue cocoa pulp and send this back through the juicer – this action is repeated until all the pulp is reduced to a cocoa liquor.

'Chocolate is addictive because it contains tryptophan – an essential amino acid that is a precursor to serotonin which produces feelings of elation. And phenylethylamine, nicknamed, "chocolate amphetamine", which causes the feelings of excitement and attraction.' Furness pauses for a moment looking at the rich deep-brown cocoa liquor.

'What is it?' asks Afia.

'We are the first people to make chocolate from these cocoa beans in a hundred years.' He puts his finger into the cocoa liquor and tastes it – letting the flavours reveal themselves. 'Fuck! That's so chocolatey. The raw bitterness evaporates off your tongue leaving a wonderful pure cocoa flavour.'

Afia dips her finger in the liquor then tastes it. 'Hmm! I've never tasted anything like it. The way the chocolate flavour sits on the palate – it tastes strangely old and new.'

They both dip their fingers in again to taste more of the liquor. Furness plays with the flavours in his mouth, considering what to do with the chocolate recipe. 'Okay, we don't want to get in the way of the natural flavour of the chocolate – let's make it 80%.'

Furness weighs the liquor and does some calculations

on a piece of paper. Weighs out the required amount of organic sugar and grinds it to create a fine powder. At the same time Afia melts a small amount of organic cocoa butter.

Then Furness pours the cocoa liquor into a grinding mill and adds in the sugar and melted cocoa butter. He also adds in some organic vanilla. 'We leave the grinding mill running for twenty-four hours to smooth out the chocolate.'

Dorothea runs into one of the attic rooms of The Black Truffle Hotel – frantically locking the door behind her. She runs to the window but no one in the street below looks up at her pounding on the glass of the nailed-shut sash window. Footsteps approach. She hides under the bed and watches black leather brogues walk around the room. How did he get through the locked door? The suited figure drops to his knees to look for her under the bed and she rolls out from her hiding place. With desperate fumbling fingers she unlocks the door and runs down the stairs – but they won't reach the lower landing. She takes step after step on the never-ending stairs. Until she jumps. The stairs falling away from her, she floats in the air past portrait after portrait of The Chocolate Thieves. Finally, she lands in the hallway. Footsteps come from three directions – the lounge, dining room and down the stairs. The front door is locked and bolted – so no escape out into the street. They are getting closer. Into the kitchen. Again, the door into the garden is locked and bolted – terrified, she desperately pulls on the bolts but they won't draw back so she tries turning the unturnable handle.

A gloved hand grabs her shoulder and she screams.

She is tied to a chair.

An intense light flares in her eyes.

The Chocolate Thieves appear before her.

Savage raises his hands in which he is holding a pair of pliers and a scalpel. 'You know I can't let you leave if you can speak. Now – open wide.' He leans in towards Dorothea. Dunstan holds her nose to get her to open her mouth so she can breathe. Savage clamps the pliers onto the end of her tongue, pulls it out to its full length and proceeds to cut it out of her mouth. Waving it at her before throwing it into Furness's frying pan where it sizzles and smells like bacon.

Next, Furness pushes a chocolate tongue into her mouth. 'A perfect fit.'

Now, Dunstan throws her out into the street. 'Enjoy talking to DS Silky and dear old Uncle Gloom.'

Dorothea staggers through the streets, trying to ask strangers for help – all back away from her in fear or brush her aside in irritation.

Two faces she recognises appear in front of her.

'Tell us where they are,' demands DS Silky.

'Speak up, Dorothea – where are The Chocolate Thieves?' implores DI Gloom.

Through tears of desperation Dorothea tries to talk but her words are merely gurgles as her tongue melts – the chocolate running out of her mouth, down her chin.

The antiquarian wakes up in a sweat barely able to breathe. She scrambles out of bed and slowly gets her breath back at the window – checking her tongue is still there.

From the bed comes Savage's voice. 'Is there something you wish to tell me?'

All news-streaming services are covering the Chocolate Liberation Day impromptu street parties across London. Entertained by music and circus acts the partygoers are getting high on the best of the city's artisan chocolates.

Banners are displayed emblazoned with the slogans: *THIS IS CHOCOLATE LIBERATION DAY; CHOCOLATE FOR THE PEOPLE*; *CHOCOLATE IS A HUMAN RIGHT*; *END COCOA SLAVERY*; *FAIR TRADE FOR COCOA FARMERS*; *SAVE COCOA – SAVE THE PLANET*.

Mrs Hoddinot is being interviewed. 'It's incredible. What a joyful day.'

'Is it true you've made the chocolates you are giving away from stolen cocoa?' asks the journalist.

'The cocoa was gifted to us by The Chocolate Thieves. We, the artisan chocolatiers of London, are making and giving away our chocolates in defiance of the globally inflated pricing by the greedy cocoa conglomerates who are stockpiling what is left of the world's cocoa with the intention of exploiting for profit the chocolate needs of the people.'

'Weren't you a victim of The Chocolate Thieves?'

'Best publicity I ever had. But let me tell you this: The Chocolate Thieves have asked us to share our love of chocolate, our love of people and love of life and that is what we are doing.'

Scarlett Vamp steps into shot. 'Cocoa is the food of the people. It has given us vitality of life for thousands of years. We must find a way to stop its extinction.'

The interview is drowned out by the chants of partygoers. 'Chocolate is a human right! Chocolate is a human right! Chocolate is a human right! Chocolate is a human right!'

The news-stream cuts to an interview with the Home Secretary, Robina Head. 'This is anarchy. And I have instructed the Commissioner of Police to bring order to our streets.'

The political journalist is unimpressed by this statement.

'Is it true that the Prime Minister, the Chancellor and yourself, Home Secretary, all have shares in Global Cocoa whose warehouse The Chocolate Thieves raided?'

Ruffled, the Home Secretary intends to stand her ground. 'My concern today is the restoring of our share price, I mean, restoring law and order to the streets of London.'

'It's just a party,' the journalist goads.

'But it's the wrong kind of party,' insists the Home Secretary.

A stressed DI Gloom, surrounded by newspaper cocoa crisis headlines and streaming news-feeds, is shouting at DS Silky – who is shouting back.

'What the fuck is happening to the world?'

'I told you – to the people, The Chocolate Thieves are folklore heroes!'

'The PM wants them arrested and the Mayor wants to give them the Freedom of the City!'

'And the people?'

'They just want free chocolate!'

'Then let the voice of the people be heard – it's only chocolate!'

'No. We are servants of the law. There must be chocolate order. Find the fucking Chocolate Thieves and fucking arrest them!'

DS Silky's eyes fall on the box of Vamp's Naughty Day Dreams chocolates on DI Gloom's desk – he warns her off with a fierce glare.

Furness pours the chocolate out of the grinding mill into a bowl and gently heats the chocolate over a pan of hot water until it reaches fifty-five degrees centigrade – at the point Furness is satisfied, it has reached a full crystal melt.

He pours two thirds of the chocolate onto a flat rectangular marble stone lying on the prep table. With two palette knives, one wide and one narrow-bladed, he begins to spread out the chocolate and then scrape it back together, folding the chocolate over and over. He encourages Afia to take over and she tempers the chocolate as he has shown her. When it drops to twenty-seven degrees centigrade, the point at which dark chocolate begins to thicken to become a solid, Furness scrapes the chocolate off the marble slab back into the bowl with the rest of the chocolate and stirs the two together.

'Good quality, properly tempered chocolate has the right clean sound to the snap when you bite into it and a consistency of melting when it warms up in your mouth. The melting is especially important because it controls how well the chocolate releases the flavours onto your tongue.'

Furness dips the end of the narrow palette knife into the chocolate and they watch it set with a smooth satin sheen – the chocolate is tempered to his satisfaction.

They both taste the chocolate again.

'Perfect!'

'Bloody lovely!'

'Now – we create.'

Afia fetches two large, cocoa-pod-sized, Easter egg moulds – the moulds are lined with chocolate and left to set. This process is repeated four times until there is a thick layer of chocolate in each mould.

Once set, each half of the egg is coated and lined with twenty-four-carat edible gold leaf. Next, Furness gently opens the case to study the intricate workings of *The London Chocolate Time Piece* – cutting out of a tray of set Kew Gardens chocolate the delicate and sophisticated interior mechanism of a pocket watch which he then assembles in one half of the egg.

In the second half of the egg he writes *The Chocolate Thieves 2020* – using melted chocolate as ink embossed with edible gold dust.

The two halves of the egg are hinged together with layers of gold leaf to create the watchcase.

DS Silky is wandering through Soho deciding what to do next to get her desired result in this ridiculous investigation. Which is simply to put an end to her trip into the chocolate underworld and get back to solving murders. She stops to purchase a hot chocolate from a street vendor. She has never eaten or drunk so much chocolate in her life before this case. How addicted is she becoming? Ironically, just as The Chocolate Apocalypse has arrived.

The sign on the gallery door reads *Closed for hanging of exhibition.* From across the street, sipping her hot chocolate, the detective watches Dunstan and Kyoko decisively hang one of the artist's paintings, step back, then swap it with another painting until one of them intervenes and makes a final decision on the hanging and they move on to the positioning of the next piece of art.

So what is she to do about The Chocolate Thieves?

Afia is right – people want their rogues. All evidence of any chocolate heists they've committed will have been eaten by now. As for the stolen Kew Gardens cocoa – it's gone. They'll just have to accept that it has been turned into untraceable, soon to be eaten, chocolate. And with chocolate coming to an end, isn't it simpler to leave The Chocolate Thieves to the world of Dorothea's folklore? But if she is to get back to her own reality she needs to satisfy DI Gloom that this case and The Chocolate Thieves crime file is closed for good. Which means despite the lack of Kew Gardens cocoa evidence, if she can create the opportunity, she will have to arrest the people who she knows stole it.

So what to do?

DS Silky takes out her phone and calls Midas – the solution is possibly really quite a simple one.

Midas answers his phone in his usual curt manner – the world is subservient to him, after all. 'Yes?'

'Midas, I suggest you pay a visit to a restaurant called The Furness.'

As she walks out of the kitchen door, Afia is passed by a man in a flat cap, with the collar of his coat turned up, on his way into The Furness restaurant. Savage and Dorothea pull up in CHOC 4 and Afia hands over a stack of small gift boxes – each containing a single Kew Gardens Chocolate Black Truffle. As Savage drives off Afia realises who the man who walked past her is. 'Midas!'

In the kitchen Midas is glaring at Furness. 'You fucking amateur! You recipe-following cook! What is this place? This empty soulless place? This is not a restaurant. Where are your diners? I've learned about you, Furness – the cook who can't cook to order. Pathetic!'

'And yet – I taught you a lesson.' Furness smiles.

'Oh yes – what lesson is that?'

'Be humble with your talent.'

'And live down here with you? Be a Chocolate Thief?'

'I'd prefer you to keep well away from me. But yes – try living a real life.'

'I am Midas, the king of chocolate gold, and I will rise again higher and even more successful.'

'I can smell rotten fish. Is that you?'

'What do you know about chocolate – eh? You do nothing but steal others' creations like all the generations of your family before you.'

'They were poor and hungry.'

'Survival of the fittest.'

'You arrogant fool. You've no understanding how people have to live. Open your eyes. Learn your own history. Generation after generation of Midases let their ego get in the way of them seeing the impact of their actions on the people around them. Don't you see what you and your clients are doing to the world?'

'Our wealth keeps the global capitalist digestion active. We live the meritocracy of which you only dream – my elite clients created their wealth.'

'Through the exploitation of the poor.'

'We create the world that we all deserve. A truth you are unwilling to accept. You will not be liberated by the pleasure we take in our success because you don't know how good it tastes.'

'It's not jealousy, it's a hatred of cruelty, of arrogance, of your celebration of inequality as a right of success. But most of all – it's that your chocolate is fucking shit.'

'Why you…' Midas spots the tray of remaining Black Truffles. 'Is this the Kew Gardens chocolate?' Unable to resist he takes a truffle and eats it. His eyes go wide as the exquisitely smooth and perfectly balanced chocolate releases its flavours – both ancient and new they ripple over his taste buds. 'You made this chocolate?'

'We did.' Furness nods towards Afia who is standing at the kitchen door listening to their exchange.

'This is beautiful! It is perfection! Work for me.'

Furness looks at Midas in total disbelief. 'What?'

Midas is insistent. 'Yes. You must. Forget everything – all the wrong that has been said and done. You will work for Midas – both of you.'

Furness shakes his head. 'That's not going to happen.'

Midas has no way of comprehending Furness's

response. 'Why not? What have you got here? You're a nobody.'

'Fuck off!'

Midas turns to Afia. 'Just you then, my chocolate princess. Bring your talent to my court. Forget this culinary loser.'

Afia is not impressed – which isn't a good thing for Midas. Something he is about to become very aware of. 'You arrogant, narcissistic, piece of faeces. This man has more talent, more heart than anyone I've ever met.' Afia, with speed and precision, punches Midas in the face and he falls, out cold, to the floor.

Furness looks down at the knocked-out Midas then at Afia's still-clenched fist. 'Bloody hell!'

'How did he find us?'

'DS Silky must have told him of her suspicions.'

'That's disappointing.'

Furness and Afia dump the unconscious chocolatier on a bench in Soho Square. Afia produces a bottle of whisky from her coat pocket and pours it over him. She puts the half-empty bottle into his hand, steps back and takes a photograph of Midas with her phone. Posting it online with the tagline *Midas down amongst the people* – it instantly goes viral.

A youthful-for-his-age, symmetrically featured man, standing in front of a tailor's mirror being fitted for a suit, reads the card that came with the Black Truffle: *Dorian, still salivating for the food of the gods? TCT*. He eats the truffle with seduced appreciation.

In a grand hotel a sophisticated woman is enjoying a very civilised afternoon tea. On the table is a newspaper reporting the sexually explicit photographs of a British politician and Chinese spy operating in London. The waiter arrives with the Black Truffle and card. *Irene, an opportunity that eclipses all others. TCT.* She eats the truffle and licks her lips with delicious delight.

A curious-looking man, sat at a workbench upon which a hare is being taxidermied, reads the card that came with the Black Truffle: *William, there is something incubating that will be of interest to you. TCT.* He licks the truffle with sceptical curiosity.

At a florist's, a charmingly delicate woman is arranging an elaborate display of flowers. She is handed the Black Truffle and card by an assistant. *Elizabeth, something with an extraordinary fragrance. TCT.* She breathes in the aroma of the truffle and breaks the stem of a rose she is holding between her fingers.

An adventurer author is signing copies of his international best seller, *The Cocoa Winds*. He is handed the Black Truffle and card by the bookshop manager. *Marcus, it's the taste of the exotic. TCT.* He eats the truffle and pulls an expression of craven delight at the taste of the hunt.

A pale man dressed all in black, sitting by a fire in a low-lit room of morbid anatomy drinking a glass of rich blood-red wine, reads the card that came with the Black Truffle. *Stoker, we have the taste of the night for you. TCT.* He bites into the Black Truffle with sharp, pointy teeth and with the darkest of desires savours the life-giving flavours.

In a private booth of an underground strip club a large, brown-suited, unappealing sweating man being given a glittery feigned-erotic lap dance is distracted by the card that came with the Black Truffle. *Henry, something to make the ladies love you. TCT.* He eats the truffle with sleazy gluttony.

A woman in a catsuit is stealing bars of gold from a vault in Bond Street. Her rucksack full, she exits the building into a quiet side street and gets into her BRG Mini Cooper. On the dashboard is a gift box with a Black Truffle in it and a card. *Gilda, it's pure gold. TCT.* She grins a flash of gold-capped pearl white teeth, throws the truffle in her mouth and speeds away.

DS Silky, sitting at her desk reviewing what evidence she has on The Chocolate Thieves and thinking about how to convince DI Gloom that her phone call to Midas is the most elegantly effective way of disrupting their lifestyle, answers the ring of her mobile phone.

'I want The Chocolate Thieves reward,' says the whispered conspiratorial voice.

'Dorothea, where the fuck have you been?'

'Call me Chocolate Teapot.'

'Why?'

'I want a cool codename.'

'What do you know? And do I really want you to tell me?' The answer to this question is 'No' but the detective feels duty bound to listen to any information Dorothea has to tell her.

'Dunstan's gallery tonight – that's where and when they're auctioning the *Kew Gardens Easter Egg.*'

'And you know this how?'

'He called me back.'

'You're sure it's tonight?'

'The egg is in the cup.'

The line goes dead.

DS Silky absorbs the information she's just been given. The detective knows the only way to identify that this Easter egg is made of the Kew Gardens cocoa beans is a confession from Dunstan. And that is very unlikely to happen. But if a raid stops The Chocolate Thieves financially gaining from their crimes at least she's achieved something. And, if nothing else, she'll possibly get to eat some very rare chocolate.

DS Silky bursts into DI Gloom's office, making him jump and spill hot chocolate over himself. 'They're auctioning the *Kew Gardens Easter Egg* tonight!'

'By cocoa! How do you know this sweet truffle of a treat?'

'Dorothea's charm got it laid.'

'What a truffler! Cancel everyone's night off. Round up as many officers as you need. A hundred years of chocolate thievery ends tonight!'

The gallery is full of people buzzing with enthusiasm for Kyoko's work. Dunstan has phoned his client list along with inviting fellow artists and art critics to the private view. On a plinth in the centre of the room in a large silver egg cup is a gold Easter egg.

Dunstan, standing next to Kyoko, addresses the guests. 'Ladies and gentlemen, welcome to this exhibition of *The City In Chocolate* by Kyoko Kurokawa. I think you will agree with me that this collection of paintings is some of the most beautiful and original work we have had on the walls of this gallery. It is, to my eye, quite an exceptional achievement to produce such truthful work of sensitivity, desire and passion – evoking all that we experience in chocolate…'

DS Silky and six uniformed officers come through the gallery door. 'Police! Everyone stay where they are.'

'What are you looking for, DS Silky?' enquires Dunstan.

'I thought I'd pick up a Kew Gardens original,' replies the detective, walking towards the Easter egg.

Dunstan looks at Kyoko, gently holds her hand and smiles a rakish smile. Realisation of his intentions ripples across her eyes and she can't help but smile as she conspiratorially mouths the words, 'I dare you.'

Dunstan looks at DS Silky then at the expectant guests and instructs them to 'Eat everything!'

Chaos ensues as the buyers, artists and critics dive at the paintings – frenziedly pulling them off the walls and like feral animals biting into them and breaking chunks off to devour.

The uniformed officers go into a panic trying to stop the riot – but to no avail.

Dunstan stands in the middle of the anarchy laughing.

DS Silky gets to the egg and holding it with both hands she gives Dunstan a look of triumph. He shakes his head at her. At which point DS Silky is rugby tackled to the floor by the art critic from *Chocolate Addicts Magazine* and the egg flies through the air and is kicked about the room by the dozens of scuffling feet.

Kyoko grabs her favourite painting, *Us*, off the wall – punching a surrealist artist in the eye who tries to get to it first and kicking a woman, who's bought six of her forgeries in the last four years, in the shin when she tries to take it off her.

Dunstan takes Kyoko's hand and they run upstairs, through her studio and living space, up into the attic rooms, out of the window, onto and across the roof and climb down the fire escape.

In the street Savage pulls up in CHOC 4, they jump in and Savage speeds away. 'Good evening. I trust the private view went according to plan?'

'Perfectly,' Dunstan assures him.

'That was fucking wild!' Kyoko laughs.

Referring to the painting, Dunstan says, 'You saved it.'

'This is for us to eat.'

They kiss. Then pull on their balaclavas and gloves.

Bruised and bloodied DS Silky has secured the Easter egg. She sniffs it – it smells wonderful. She rattles it next to her ear – there is something inside. The detective looks around her at the destruction of evidence and gives in to her cravings. 'What the hell.' She bites the top off the egg. It tastes so organic. So bloody wonderful. And she bites off another chunk. Her reward for being forced to take on this ridiculous case.

Inside the egg she finds a Chocolate Thief figurine wearing a badge on the lapel of its suit, upon which are written the words *I Am A Chocolate Thief.* DS Silky begins to laugh, the sort of light laugh that convulses spontaneously from the very core of one's being – the sort of truthful laugh that cowers all lies of civility.

The flashing blue lights of police cars appear in the rear-view mirror of CHOC 4 and the sound of sirens reaches The Chocolate Thieves. Savage increases speed, cutting in and out of the slower-moving traffic. After turning down several side streets he pulls up at the back of The Furness restaurant where Furness and Afia, already in balaclavas and gloves, are waiting with a box containing the authentic *Kew Gardens Easter Egg.*

They get into CHOC 4 and Savage pulls away just as the police come around the corner. 'Where is it to tonight, ladies and gentlemen?'

'A gallery of London's finest rogues if you please, driver,' requests Dunstan.

'Right you are. I may have to take the scenic route.' Savage turns sharply to the right, sending the four in the back tumbling onto each other.

'Careful, Savage – you'll break the bloody egg,' pleads Furness.

'I've got to lose them,' he says with a gleeful glint in his eye.

Pulling alongside a delivery bike Dunstan opens his window and helps himself to a spinach and ricotta pizza from the box on the back of the bike – sharing it between the five of them.

Screeching to a halt to avoid hitting pedestrians crossing the road, the police emergency stop next to them and there is a tense moment of revving of engines as they wait for the road to clear.

Savage pulls away first, beating the police in a drag race through the next junction. At Cambridge Circus he slides into a space in a row of stationary taxis and the police fly past. He turns CHOC 4 around and shoots off in the opposite direction.

A police helicopter joins the pursuit – its searchlight picking CHOC 4 out of the diverging traffic.

Down through Covent Garden where Furness leans out of his window and snatches a bottle of white wine off a waiter's tray to wash down the pizza as they pass the street tables of a restaurant. A living statue of a Victorian fruit and veg porter is sent into a spin as they fly past – turning his thrown-into-the-air produce into a performance of erratic juggling. Driving quietly around the market, they pass a busker singing an impassioned rendition of David Bowie's 'Heroes' – Kyoko takes twenty quid from Dunstan's pocket and drops it into the young woman's hat. All eyes of the tourists and revellers seem to be on them – pointing and saying, 'Look – it's The Chocolate Thieves.' The police vehicles converge on the market. But the curious selfie-takers have formed a protective cordon.

It is cat and mouse.

Seeing an opportunity, Savage politely gestures for the crowd to part – which they do. He floors the accelerator and to the cheers of their audience they swiftly depart the scene.

The police catch up with them and they drive a ballet through the fountains of Somerset House.

Out onto and along the Strand.

At Trafalgar Square they join the swarm of taxis and night buses. Savage going from high momentum to a crawl in what seems like a fraction of a second to his passengers in the back of CHOC 4.

Looking like every other taxi from above, CHOC 4 stays with the flow of traffic and the helicopter searchlight loses them. And the progress of the pursuing police cars is halted by belligerent cabbies and bus drivers determined to deposit and pick up their fares.

At last, in the melee of taxis, buses, cars and people that is central London, The Chocolate Thieves are free to quietly drive away east into Whitechapel.

In the Rogues Gallery, Dorothea, dressed in suit, gloves and balaclava, is serving the masked guests – The Seducer, The Seductress, The Hare, The Flower Woman, The Hunter, The Vampire, The Glutton and The Cat – glasses of The Chocolate Thieves cocktail: Criollo cocoa rum, ginger beer, a squeeze of lime and mint leaves chilled over crushed ice.

Savage drives CHOC 4 into the lock-up at the back of The Sleight Of Hand – Stanley Oak closing the door on them. From inside they exit through a discreet door into the public house.

The guests go quiet when The Chocolate Thieves walk into the gathering.

Stanley Oak locks the door on the proceedings.

Savage walks to a lectern at the far end of the room, Dorothea stands next to him. Furness to his right with Afia – putting the *Kew Gardens Easter Egg* on a plinth. Dunstan, with Kyoko to Savage's left, presses the live stream activation button on his phone – filmed through multiple discreetly placed cameras the auction is now being broadcast via a VPN to the world.

Savage commands the room from the lectern. 'We are The Chocolate Thieves.' The room erupts into applause. 'Thank you.'

Furness opens the *Kew Gardens Easter Egg* to reveal the intricate pocket watch mechanism in which sits *The London Chocolate Time Piece*.

The room gasps in awe and wonder and applauds again.

Savage continues, 'This unique, beautifully sculptured Easter egg, wrapped in twenty-four-carat edible gold leaf, is made with 80% cocoa from the rarest of pure Nacional harvested from Kew Gardens. This variety of cocoa has been completely wiped out in its native Peru – having succumbed to sweet-toothed explorers, environmental conditions and disease. This is the first cocoa harvested from this tree in over a hundred years. And one of you here this evening, this Easter, will lose yourself in the enchanting ecstasy of its mysterious and exotic flavours.'

Tense excitement envelops the room.

'The sculptured chocolate watch mechanism houses *The London Chocolate Time Piece* – an exquisite hundred-year-old gold, diamond and sapphire, civil and solar, four-hundred-part, encased in chocolate-tinted glass, pocket watch. The only one of its kind in the world. The name of its master craftsman unknown. It too was thought lost in the cocoa dust of time.'

Dare they to breath in the presence of such artistry?

Savage smiles at his audience. 'Shall we start the bidding at £1,000,000?'

The Seducer smiles.

'£1,000,000 I am bid.'

The Flower Woman excitedly raises her hand.

'£1,250,000.'

The Hare glances furtively towards Savage.

'£1,500,000.'

The Vampire gives a grave nod.

'£1,750,000.'

The Cat grins and winks.

'£2,000,000.'

The Glutton mops his sweating brow.

'£2,250,000.'

The Hunter glances towards The Seductress, who has yet to bid, as if she is the one to conquer. He now directs a look of determination at Savage.

'£2,500,000.'

It is now The Seductress gently raises a finger of her gloved hand.

'£2,750,000.'

The auction continues with involuntary giggles, furtive glances, intimidating stares and malevolent grins – every one of these chocolate addicts determined to outbid the others.

The illustrated rogues hanging on the walls watch on with eager mischief in their eyes.

Time hangs surreptitiously in the air.

Until the price is pushed as far as the room can take it.

'£10,000,000 I am bid, going once, going twice. Last chance.' Savage pauses – he makes eye contact with each of the masked faces. Then hits the gavel on the lectern. 'Sold! For £10,000,000.'

The Seductress takes the room's applause.

Newspaper headlines, news channels and streaming news-feeds all report with fevered excitement on The Chocolate Thieves' secret auction with images of *THE MOST EXPENSIVE CHOCOLATE EASTER EGG IN THE*

WORLD.

DI Gloom chokes with anger while eating a soothing 50% cocoa Ealing's Green Tea Infusion on reading The Chocolate Thieves being called *THE PEOPLE'S VILLAINS*, and what they have achieved described as *THE CHOCOLATE CRIME OF THE CENTURY*.

Scarlett Vamp smiles with relief at reading *MONEY FROM SECRET EASTER EGG AUCTION GOING TO HELP SAVE CHOCOLATE SAY THE CHOCOLATE THIEVES*.

DS Silky sits back in her chair, eating the last piece of her appropriated Easter egg, and nods in agreement when reading the auction described as *THE MOST AUDACIOUS ART CRIME EVER*.

Leaning on the bar of The Sleight Of Hand Stanley Oak distractedly eats a 60% cocoa Gallows Cry and reads the in-depth analysis headlined *CRIME, ART AND CULTURAL REVOLUTION – THE 21ST-CENTURY VILLAIN*.

In the Palm House at Kew Gardens, standing in front of the stripped-of-its-pods cocoa tree, Dr Rikard Linnaeus looks down at the three potted cocoa tree saplings – a tree labelled *Savage*, *Furness* and *Dunstan* after each one of The Chocolate Thieves.

He picks up the chocolate gift box resting against Furness's tree, opens it and takes a sniff – his senses filling with a rich earthy aroma. Then he gently picks up the Black Truffle and takes a bite. The cocoa scientist shivers with pleasure and smiles at the release of the liberty-inducing flavours. 'Bloody rogues.'

In the kitchen of The Black Truffle Hotel, Furness and Afia serve up six full plates of breakfast that everyone thinks is very good – enthusiastically congratulating them both on their efforts. Dorothea makes the tea – slapping Savage's hand away to stop him picking up the teapot. Kyoko opens the kitchen door to let the buzzing bluebottle out. And Dunstan folds his newspaper from reading an article with the headline *A LIFE WITHOUT CHOCOLATE*. The bottle of Furness's homemade hot-and-spiced chocolate breakfast sauce liberally douses the six plates of food and they all tuck in.

Savage, Furness and Dunstan find themselves looking at the black-and-white photograph of the first generation of The Chocolate Thieves standing on the mantelpiece.

Dunstan speaks first. 'A hundred years.'

'Generations of this family living on chocolates,' adds Furness.

Savage's smile is the broadest of the three. 'We are legends.'

PART TWO
THE CHOCOLATE APOCALYPSE

Late evening and it is the end of another day of shops
being looted for their stock of chocolate bars, biscuits,
cakes, ice creams, breakfast cereals and drinks – literally
anything edible containing chocolate is taken. Flashing
blue lights and sirens of emergency response vehicles give
chase to smash-and-grab getaway cars that screech into
life as loot-laden hooded figures jump into them. Gangs of
moped-mounted teenage muggers ride in all directions
snatching booty out of the hands of the chocolate pilferers.
Lovers shout at each other – they shove, throw punches
and kick over which one of them gets to eat the last piece
of the bar of chocolate liberated from broken-into vending
machines. Shaking addicts scurry into shadowed doorways
desperate to devour their last-ever fix. The shattering of
shop windows, the kicking-in of doors, the screams of
alarms, the cries of cruelty and the wailing of sirens is the
soundscape of the city. Molotov cocktails set shops and
vehicles ablaze – the heat of flames, the choking acrid
smoke, the scent of burning lives. Music of every genre
cascades through the air as bars spill into the streets – the
beats and rhythms of every culture's end. Sex is currency
as the facade of personal morality is discarded along with
any pretence of dignity. And everyone watches themselves
on the twenty-four seven news-streams continuously
broadcast on the capital city's digital billboards with the
ever-present headline *THE END OF CHOCOLATE*.

The Chocolate Thieves drive slowly past the boarded-up front of Lullaby's in Mayfair. Notices declaring the chocolatier is no longer trading are pasted across the door and where the display window should be. Beneath the multicoloured, playful font of the shop sign is written *Chocolate For Dreamers Established 1890*. There is no sign of life from within the shop or in the flats above. Savage drives around to the rear of the building.

The three of them alight CHOC 4 and Dunstan makes entrance through the kitchen door.

Savage deals with the alarm: one, nine, six, zero. 'The year of the man's birth.'

Once inside they seek out the storeroom where, after Dunstan picks the double-locked door, they find the shelves are full of boxes of Lullaby's English Fairy Tale and Folklore Chocolates.

Savage samples a Herne The Hunter. 'Delightful. The rich chocolate positively shimmers off the taste buds.'

Furness a Merlin: 'Brilliantly made – full of complex yet delicate flavours.'

Dunstan a Will-O'-The-Wisp: 'Addictively lovely.' Then after a moment more of flavour appreciation, 'Well?' he asks of Furness.

Furness shakes his head. 'These chocolates aren't made with the Forastero Amelonado for which Lullaby is renowned.'

'So Scarlett's information is correct,' confirms Dunstan.

'All is not as it seems in dreamland,' adds Savage.

'So what is it?' wonders Dunstan.

'It's a South American Criollo variety,' Furness tells them.

Savage eats another chocolate, a Jack's Gold. 'A prince of cocoas.'

'But there's no Criollo being imported under licence

into the country,' says Dunstan as he seeks out a sack of cocoa. The label reads *Forastero Amelonado product of Ivory Coast imported by Global Cocoa.*

'It is definitely not that – I'm sure it's a South American Criollo,' insists Furness. 'Probably Peru, going on the cocoa's lightness on the palate – but there is something mysterious in the base notes.'

Dunstan looks into what remains of the looted shop – there are discarded, smashed and ignored jars of all varieties of traditional sweets: fudge, fruit bonbons, pineapple chunks, lemon sherbets, rhubarb and custards, jelly babies, ginger creams, and so on. 'These chocolates are definitely for private clients,' he tells the other two.

'Wealthy patrons with elite palates,' comments Savage.

'Sounds very familiar – doesn't it?' says Dunstan.

'Indeed it does,' says an unimpressed Furness.

After filling their pockets with chocolates they begin loading CHOC 4 with the boxes of Lullaby's English Fairy Tale and Folklore Chocolates.

On his last trip, as Savage reaches the taxi, a post-pee-behind-the-bins drunk staggers over to him and stares at him as if trying to recognise the balaclava-wearing Chocolate Thief. Keeping his eyes on the man, Savage slips his hand into the top box of chocolates he is holding. The drunk points at him as if he's finally realised who Savage is and is about to say so. So Savage extracts his hand and puts a chocolate into the drunk's mouth. For himself he selects and eats a deeply mysterious Druid's Stone. The drunk chews, sways, his face lighting up in satisfaction at the well-made chocolate, and goes to stagger away. Stops. Turns back towards The Chocolate Thief and holds out his hand. Savage puts the box of chocolates into it. And drunkenly smiling in appreciation of the gift, the man wonders off into the night.

Furness and Dunstan load the four remaining sacks of the mystery cocoa into CHOC 4. Driving around to the front of the shop, Dunstan jumps out and sprays the words *CHOCOLATE FOR THE PEOPLE* in chocolate-coloured spray paint across the boarded-up windows. And The Chocolate Thieves drive home through the dystopian landscape that is the city.

DS Silky looks out of a window on the sixth floor of New Scotland Yard with fascination at the ridiculous city. The detective had spent the summer quietly avoiding DI Gloom who seemed to be enjoying his extended sulk on not being the senior police officer to apprehend and prosecute The Chocolate Thieves on their hundredth anniversary of chocolate crime.

With The Chocolate Apocalypse, murder cases have been replaced with a succession of ever more serious complaints of person-on-person violence. But she knows it is only a matter of time before someone takes advantage of the chaos running through the streets to end a few lives.

The detective's attention is drawn to the office television where the self-satisfied, overpaid, under-comprehending, always on dumbed-down editorial message, striving-for-the-most-extreme-and-simplistic-of-replies journalist Callum Cawte, host of the late news review programme, introduces his guests.

'So, as the country and the wider world descends deeper into The Chocolate Apocalypse, what does the end of chocolate mean for humanity? With me to discuss this are: Seb Lilburne, spokesperson for Chocolate For The People.' A kind-faced, long skeleton of a man shifting about in urban eco-warrior combats. 'Bill Whittaker, CEO of Global Cocoa – the leading cocoa traders and an advocate of the creation of homogenised disease-resistant cocoa varieties.' A middle-aged man with swept back greying hair in a tailored charcoal pinstripe suit – still alive despite an unsated taste for all forms of the most expensive indulgences. 'And live-streamed from Scotland is Professor Duncan Forest, expert in global environmental economics at Stirling University.' An eccentric of statistics with thinning wild white hair and piecing blue eyes – who, if asked, probably wouldn't remember what he is wearing.

Cawte turns away from the camera to the recipient of his first question. 'Seb Lilburne, is Chocolate For The People a serious political movement or just a bunch of chocolate addicts lobbying for unrealistic outcomes?'

'CFTP is a movement centred on the liberation of cocoa production. The only way to save chocolate is for all cocoa to be independently fairly traded native varieties and not a vulnerable homogenised single high-yield crop.'

Whittaker interrupts with a laugh. 'Your ideas go against the rules of our capitalist social order. Globalisation necessitates the homogenisation of all crops to generate the highest yields to feed the ever-increasing population of the world.'

'But why can't the cocoa farmers be paid a fair price?' Cawte asks him.

'We drive the price of cocoa down to maximise our profits.'

'And cocoa farmers starve and pure cocoa dies out,' responds Lilburne.

'Your thinking is primitive. Capitalism is both elitist and libertarian – you get the society that you pay for and Global Cocoa supply the marketplace we have created with the most efficiently grown cost-effective varieties of cocoa,' the CEO says, using the brutality of his version of the truth with the ease of a man who knows he's going to get rich out of The Chocolate Apocalypse.

'That's a fair analysis, is it not?' asks Cawte of Lilburne.

'It is global enslavement to an elitist ideology that is literally creating a food apocalypse. It is not just cocoa that is endangered. Other popular foods such as honey, bananas, apples and coffee, to name but a few, are too. We are truly entering a period where only the wealthy will be able to afford to eat.'

'So you're saying the plight of cocoa is an allegory for global food supply,' overexplains Cawte.

'Of course it is,' responds Lilburne already frustrated with the presenter insisting on explaining the bloody obvious. 'Your viewers aren't stupid, they know this is happening.'

'These are the same viewers raiding their neighbours' cupboards for chocolate,' taunts Whittaker. 'Listen, what you're saying is fiction. We are at the cutting edge of agricultural science – the food chain will survive. If we do what you say with cocoa then it will become more elitist. Global Cocoa are trying to grow chocolate for everyone, not just the ideological environmentalist middle classes who can afford to pay more for their chocolate.'

'Nonsense,' exclaims Lilburne. 'The chocolatiers want a fair trade in cocoa.'

'A few artisan metropolitan chocolate-makers but not the person in the street,' adds Cawte, wanting to keep his voice in the argument.

Whittaker sighs, as if tired of having to explain the obvious to a child. 'Global manufacturers want a global trade in chocolate which means a fair marketplace and price for cocoa. Commercial chocolate-makers use the least amount of cocoa in their chocolates to maximise their profits. And no one in the street cares. It's just like your low-end clothes – cheap mass-produced materials, cheap garment-manufacturing, cheap retail – queues in the shops.'

Lilburne sees an opportunity to get angry. 'And we end up in a world of child slave labour and where people buy clothes, wear them once and throw them away as they would a sweet wrapper. We have to make capitalism ethical.'

Whittaker laughs again. 'Good luck with that when prices rise.'

'Then pay your workers more. Give them a share of the profits – share out your wealth.'

Whittaker is incredulous at the implausibility of this suggestion. 'If we do that prices will rise even higher and less money will circulate around the economy which defeats the purpose of the pay rise – you really don't understand free market economics, do you.'

'I understand what it is to be poor.'

'Do you?' asks Cawte. 'We live in a country with a functioning welfare state. Have any of us ever gone without food?'

'Have you seen the food banks? Are you aware of the uninhabitable life-threatening overpriced privately rented living conditions the generational poor of this country have to live in?'

'Yet they can still afford commercially popular chocolate brands – or could when there was some to buy,' goads Whittaker.

'The point Chocolate For The People is making is that with The Chocolate Apocalypse we have an opportunity to evolve our capitalism to a re-imagined kinder global economic system – for the benefit of all people.'

'That is a fair point – in this crisis why don't we evaluate the social and environmental cost of our economy?' asks Cawte of Whittaker – changing sides in the argument for fear of the audience perception of lack of balance.

'Success necessitates an economic and social hierarchy,' replies Whittaker, pointing a fat finger at Lilburne. 'You're just a bloody leftie dressed in a smock of political and social ignorance. Or worse – denial.'

'And you're an elitist boor,' counters Lilburne.

'Elitist glutton, if you don't mind. And in fact I'm a pragmatist just like everyone watching this debate who wants to secure our way of life.'

'Gentlemen, let's concentrate on cocoa if it is, as you say, an allegory for the wider problems of the world's food supply.' Cawte tries to sound cheery and reassuring.

'Don't you see what is happening in the world?' Lilburne glares at Whittaker. 'Cocoa is dying. People are dying. Just so you can turn a profit. Creating one super-cocoa to supply the world will not work – it's too late. The only way to ensure our ecosystem is to sustain a diversity of plant life and cultures.'

'You make everything so emotional – people only want one culture,' counters Whittaker. 'This homogeneous world is the legitimate child of capitalism that allows us not to have to think about what we eat and how we travel, the cities we live in, the language we speak and the technology we all rely upon. You're fighting against the reality of human progress.'

'What progress? Where have you been?' asks Lilburne, stunned at what he sees as his opponent's blindness. 'People have been resisting the world you describe for centuries.'

'Well they haven't been fighting hard enough – it's here and happening all around us,' scoffs Whittaker. 'Which suggests the people didn't really want the romantic vision of socialism you're offering. For one simple reason – it's regressive.'

Realising his key point, Lilburne attacks. 'This isn't about the old world view of capitalism versus communism, conservatism versus socialism – it's about the creation of a future society that works for all peoples. You and your elite are out of date. The enslavement to your destructive ideology is at an end. The planet is resisting your dystopia – climate change is real and the end of cocoa is only the start of the food apocalypse that will necessitate a new way of life.'

Whittaker belligerently dismisses the truth: 'Best we eat as much chocolate as possible while we still can then.'

Cawte brings the patient, amused, expert into the debate. 'Professor Forest, what's your scientific take on all this – is the demise of cocoa the start of the food apocalypse?'

'Good evening. Cocoa cultivation has for years contributed to deforestation and the endangerment of the natural habitat of the species therein. But we do all just love our chocolate. The end of cocoa is not the start of the food apocalypse – it is, in fact, just one symptom of it. But to argue that the likes of Global Cocoa shouldn't continue to exploit the planet's resources under the licence granted them is futile. As I told the Prime Minister and the Environmental Audit Committee a year ago – humanity will not change its behaviour.'

'Excuse me, Professor,' interrupts Cawte, 'people are very aware of the environmental damage being done to our planet and have been driving forward international climate agreements.'

'Ideological sticking plasters.' Professor Forest curtly dismisses the interruption. 'The riotous self-serving behaviour of our fellow citizens, from every socio-economic group and political ideology, seeking out one last fix of chocolate on the streets of the towns and cities across the world on this very evening informs you of that. The facts of our food apocalypse speak for themselves. There are an estimated 400,000 known plant species. Of which, 31,000 have a documented use. More than 6,000 plant species have been cultivated for food. Although, fewer than 200 make major contributions to food production globally, regionally or nationally. And only nine account for 66% of total crop production. One in five plant species is under threat of extinction. Agrobiodiversity is a concern as plant genetic diversity has been lost as farmers worldwide cultivate genetically uniform, high-yielding varieties. Twelve plants and five animal species provide 75% of the world's food. Any species extinction from our global food chain is catastrophic for global food consumption. This clearly puts doubts on human survival. But it's all too abstract a threat when the supermarket shelves are still full of food. To be fair most people did buy into our global food economy in good faith – but we failed to read, and take the time to consider, what was written in the small print or keep the receipt. To conclude, unless we wake up from our global consumerist stupor, unless we all rebel against our extinction – we, the human race as we are today, are doomed. Just take consolation in the fact that the elitist Whittakers will die of starvation or of the ensuing war for what nutrition is left to be had alongside the proletariat Lilburnes of this world. And the planet will slowly recover from our existence and keep orbiting the sun long after we are gone. Now, if you'll excuse me, it's past my hot chocolate and bedtime.' And with that Professor Duncan Forest gets up out of his chair and walks off camera.

Whittaker laughs as one who's going to continue to enjoy the party until the end of his time. Lilburne has the demeanour of a man with the determination for the fight to save the world. And the stunned Cawte looks into the camera. 'Well, that just leaves me time to say good night and sleep well – if you can.'

The credits role.

'Well done, Professor Forest,' DS Silky thinks out loud. At last someone telling the truth. But, if anyone is listening, it is a truth that will make The Chocolate Apocalypse, even more so, a very unsafe time to live in.

The September sun's warmth hasn't reached the morning's news headlines the detective encounters on her way to the mortuary: *FINAL YEAR'S SUPPLY OF COCOA GONE IN SIX MONTHS*; *NO CHOCOLATE FOR CHRISTMAS* and *COCOA TWICE THE PRICE OF GOLD*.

DS Silky walks into the sterile autopsy room. 'You have a body for me, Dr MacCarrion.' The excitement at the prospect of a new murder case is written across her face.

'Indeed I do, Detective.'

MacCarrion pulls back the sheet covering a corpse with inappropriate gusto. 'I give you the late Leonard Piper.' The deceased is a man of average height and build, in his late forties, with greying black hair and lived-in features.

DS Silky looks at the dead man, fascinated by what she is seeing on his face – it is an expression of pure joy. She tries not to laugh. 'Bloody hell! What did you see?' Looking down his torso, but for the autopsy incisions, there is not a mark on him.

'My esoteric theory is he glimpsed the true mortality of the self and the eternity of love,' pronounces MacCarrion.

DS Silky frowns at him. 'And your actual medical findings, Doctor?'

'The actual cause of death was inhalation of unpurified Thames water,' he prosaically informs her.

'So why call me? He drowned. There's not a mark on

him. What's suspicious? Something he ate?'

'Analysis of stomach contents confirm the consumption of the gastro-delighting pub grub of steak and ale pie with rustic chips. Washed down with four pints of chocolate stout. Chased with four single-malt chocolates – the chocolate being 45% cocoa with the other ingredients being cocoa butter, sugar and vanilla.'

'That's extravagant.'

'Indeed. Clearly Mr Piper was a man wanting to relieve himself of his cash.'

'And toxicology?'

'This is where we find the mystery.'

He gives DS Silky an opportunity to guess at what he found in Piper's system.

DS Silky chooses not to guess. 'Go on.'

'TCP.'

'The antiseptic?'

'No, this TCP is tenocyclidine – PCP's psychotic lover. It dates from the labs of the late 1950s. It is a dissociative anaesthetic drug with psychostimulant and hallucinogenic effects.'

'What dosage?'

'For the full effect – 10mg.'

'So what would he have experienced?'

'Effects may begin within minutes of ingestion and last up to twenty-four hours – if not longer. The high dissociative drugs create is due to stimulation in glutamate at NMDA receptors and of the neurotransmitter dopamine.'

'Like chocolate.'

'Yes. But instead of the delight of tingling taste buds and a quiver of gratification Mr Piper would have experienced extreme alterations in sensory perception of light, sound and time. Hallucinations both hearing and visual. Feeling separated from the self and his environment leading to a sense of floating and drifting. But any pleasure or fascination with this altered state would have most likely been short-lived. Physical changes would have been increased blood pressure, heart rate, breathing rate and body temperature. Along with psychological distress – anxiety, extreme panic, fear and paranoia that could lead to exaggerated strength and aggressiveness. Ironically – if he hadn't have drowned the combination of that dosage of TCP with the consumption of alcohol on the central nervous system means he'd have likely died from respiratory arrest.'

'How was it ingested?'

'As a fluid – the concentration of TCP within his system suggests the stout or the chocolates were laced.'

DS Silky can't help but smile at the mystery before her. 'But did he take it deliberately?'

With an indulgent smile Midas pops the Gold Nib, a 75% Mexican cocoa chocolate, into the mouth of the Ukrainian fourth ex-wife of a very wealthy shipping magnate client he is conjoined with in bed. What better way for her to spend the millions of pounds received in her divorce settlement than on the most expensive chocolates left on the planet – and fuck their creator. The name Lullaby flashes on the chocolatier's phone lying on the bedside table.

Midas answers the call mid-thrust. 'Yes.'

'Don't you dare FaceTime,' panics the woman.

Midas puts his finger to her lips to silence her.

Lullaby's excitable voice shouts down the phone. 'Midas – they've taken all of them. Every box of English Fairy Tale and Folklore Chocolates is gone. Along with the rest of the sacks of cocoa.'

Enraged, Midas withdraws from the woman leaving her

stranded and unsatisfied on the bed as he paces the room. 'Fucking hell! The bloody Chocolate Thieves!'

'They would seem the likely culprits.'

'That's two million pounds' worth of chocolates gone into their mouths,' Midas rubs his chest in distress, 'the loss of such artistry.'

'Indeed. So what are we going to do? They've potentially enough evidence to incriminate – if The Chocolate Thieves know what they have.'

'I assure you their thieving palates will know they're enjoying something unique.'

'But tasting and identifying are two different things. Aren't they? There is no one else in the city who knows what the chocolate tastes like. No one who can identify it for them – is there?'

'True.' But then a blood-chilling realisation courses through Midas's veins. 'Except…'

'Who?'

'I'll deal with her.'

The glittery silver lettering on a purple background above the door of the chocolatier's in Fitzrovia reads *VAMP*, beneath which is written *Cocoa is seduction by London's leading sensuality chocolatier. Established 2000.*

Dunstan, carrying a sample from one of the sacks of cocoa taken from Lullaby's, holds the door open for a blushing customer scurrying out of the shop – a Vamp gift bag gripped in his hand.

'Enjoy your anniversary – you naughty boy,' Scarlett calls after the man in her finest smoky tones. 'Hello, darling,' she says on seeing Dunstan walk in, 'let's go through to the tasting room.'

The chocolate scent of Vamp is intoxicating – its warmth and sensory curiosity evoking that of a perfumery.

The decor suggests he's in the suite of a high-class mistress. The chocolates are displayed on glass trays on round tables: The Blue Garter, Gingerly Whipped, A Hard Spanking, Moonlight Fondant, The Dance Burlesque, Peekaboo, Oh You Naughty Girl, Something For The Lady In You, On The Tip Of My Tongue, Pierced Nipple, A Blush Of Rouge, and so on. Dunstan helps himself to A Glint In The Eye – a subtle passion fruit jelly wrapped in secretive 80% cocoa.

In her room of chocolate alchemy Scarlett dips her long slender finger into the sample of cocoa Dunstan has brought with him and sucks the powder off it. 'Tell Furness he's correct – it is a Criollo.'

'From where?'

Scarlett dips and sucks her finger again. An expression of realisation, surprise and concern ripples across her face as she explores the flavours on her palate. She darts over to her Book of Cocoa – her bible of tasting notes. 'It can't be?' she says with a tone of fascination as she furiously flicks through the pages of the book.

'Can't be what?'

'How would they have found it?'

'Found what?'

Scarlett is now an expression of horror and fear as she reads out her flavour notes. '*Red in colour, a deep chocolate aroma, a copper earthiness, immediate intense flavours of a natural, wild complexity that dance violently on the tongue with gentle fruity top notes. An exciting yet soothing, pure, life-giving chocolate.*'

'That's a bloody accurate description,' comments Dunstan having tasted the cocoa again.

'What have they done to get their hands on it? Dunstan, this really is wrong. And, I mean, really wrong.'

'Scarlett – what have you tasted?'

'Blood Cocoa.'

'And what is Blood Cocoa?'

'It is a lost Peruvian cocoa. Legend has it, no, I know it as a fact, that it is derived from the cultivation of the cocoa rations of the slaves on the first plantations. Its life-sustaining properties are legendary and wrapped in superstition.'

'The food of the gods.'

'That's what the slaves believed. They found that they had inadvertently cultivated a cocoa of extraordinary life-enhancing properties – it kept them alive and healthy through the daily brutality of their lives and the waves of disease.'

'So why is it so rare?'

'The story goes that the plantation owners, curious at the vitality of their slaves, discovered what they had grown and demanded that they cultivate it for them so to profit from its potency. So the slaves burned all the trees and refused to grow any more of the cocoa while they wore the shackles of their masters. They were massacred for this act of defiance – hundreds of people were butchered. But the surviving children of the butchered slaves saw that the blood of their parents rejuvenated the destroyed cocoa trees. That's why it is known as Blood Cocoa. The children escaped, taking the new cocoa trees into the forest with them. Never to be heard of again.'

'How do you know what it tastes like?'

'In my twenties I went on the cocoa trail. I travelled down through Ecuador and arrived in a tiny Peruvian village called Cacao de Sangre in the Piura region. Where a very old man, at least 100 years old, told me the story of the slaves and let me taste the gift of the Blood Cocoa Tree. Secretly grown in the wild it kept alive the escaped slave children. The old man was a direct descendant from the first slaves brought to the plantations.'

'But why share his secret with you?'

'He'd seen me taking detailed flavour notes of the cocoa varieties – he understood I was genuine in my respect for their culture and told me the story to record its flavours as part of our chocolate history. And, I suppose, to keep the mystery of Blood Cocoa alive.'

The Chocolate Thief takes a moment to absorb the story.

'I've never tasted such beautiful, pure, cocoa since. Until now. I'm telling you, Dunstan, this is definitely Blood Cocoa.'

'How did it get into Lullaby's?'

'I wasn't alone on the cocoa trail. Many fascinated by chocolate took the journey. Not long after my encounter with the old man was the first time I met Midas.'

'And you told him the story?'

'No. No way. I knew who his family were and what their arrogance and greed had long done to the very taste of chocolate. But one day I lost this book – thought it had gone for good. Until I found Midas sat in a cafe reading it. He claimed he'd found it in the street. But I know he'd taken it from my bag. I have no doubt that Midas has paid the right people, the right amount of money, to point their guns at the heads of the children of the descendants of the slaves to force them to divulge where the Blood Cocoa is growing.'

'And seduced Lullaby to use it to make folklore chocolates.'

'At a time he can extract the ultimate price for the rarest of experiences.'

'He really is an evil bastard.'

DS Silky knocks two sharp knocks on the door of DI Gloom's office and walks in. 'I've got a curious death.'

She holds out the autopsy report on Leonard Piper.

DI Gloom reluctantly takes the report out of the detective's hand. He quickly scans Dr MacCarrion's findings and hands it back to her without comment.

DS Silky continues, 'It could simply be death by misadventure while hallucinating due to the high dosage of TCP. An eyewitness standing on Westminster Bridge described Piper as simply walking into the river until he was submerged and not reappearing until he was pulled out of the water two hours later. But I'd like to find out where he acquired the TCP.'

DI Gloom opens a drawer in his desk, takes out a case file and hands it to DS Silky. 'You'll need this.'

Written across the front of the file are the words *THE CHOCOLATE POISONER*.

DS Silky flicks through the file. The first chocolate poisoning case was reported in 1968. The close-up photographs of the face of each successive victim depict a variety of horror-film expressions: ghastly gargoyled, comically vein-popping bulging wide-open eyes, spine-chilling dread and the silent scream. Along with the Piper variety of peacefully sleeping in euphoria.

As she reads, DS Silky absentmindedly reaches out a hand for one of DI Gloom's chocolates. He moves the box of Lullaby's London Myths out of her reach. 'These cases go back decades.'

DI Gloom tells her what she is on the way to deducing, 'The description of your victim's demise matches the true cause of each death in that file.'

'So all the victims were poisoned with, or had coincidentally taken, TCP and eaten chocolates. A serial poisoner?'

'With the cultural diversity of victims. The lapses of time between deaths. There's no definitive pattern.'

'Just random chance.' The detective flicks through more of the file – a *Dorothea's Rare Vintage* card drops out onto DI Gloom's desk. She picks it up. 'Seriously – not again.'

'Dorothea's the best chocolate-crime researcher we know.'

DS Silky inappropriately smiles excitedly. 'A real murder case.'

'In this instance, Detective – don't eat the evidence,' advises DI Gloom.

'The purity of the cocoa flavour is sublime,' says Savage as he eats a Flibbertigibbet selected from the box of Lullaby's English Fairy Tale and Folklore Chocolates in the centre of the kitchen table.

'Wonderful,' says Afia enjoying a Guinevere.

'Exquisite,' declares Kyoko savouring a Lancelot.

'Really quite charming,' proffers Dorothea as she eats a King Arthur.

'So elusive,' says an intrigued Furness eating a Florimonde's Bead.

'Intriguing,' is Dunstan's opinion on the Celtic Knot.

'Very unusual – the way the chocolate perfectly delivers the flavours across the taste buds,' comments Savage.

'And lingers,' adds Afia, 'drifting into an echo of the cocoa.'

'There's a red colour to the flavours,' ponders Dorothea.

'And a copper quality beneath the cocoa,' describes Kyoko.

'It's the perfect balance of the 70% wild cocoa flavours, fruits and spices and Lullaby's very unique conching and tempering technique – secret only to himself,' Furness tells them.

'This is what chocolate has always been – an elixir,' remarks Savage.

They sit in silence for a moment in contemplation.

'Well – now we know what a £100,000 box of chocolates made with a cocoa cultivated with the blood of slaves taste like,' concludes Dunstan.

'Is there a more Faustian chocolatier in the world than Midas?' asks Afia.

'No and it's time to put a stop to his grotesque practices,' instructs Furness.

'All we need is a plan,' says Savage.

Silence as the six of them think on the different ways to deal with Midas.

After a time Savage, Furness and Dunstan share a glance and a malicious smile. Dorothea, Afia and Kyoko look at each other in bemusement. 'What are they planning?'

The walls of Delilah's, a private members' chocolate house in St James that first opened its doors in 1715, are lined with portrait after portrait of self-aggrandising cocoa dealers and chocolatiers. All the gaunt men of the Midas lineage are immortalised from Jeremiah in 1718 through the generations to the present day vessel of their DNA. The plump Whittaker's are here too – from Thomas in 1717, the first CEO of Global Cocoa, to today's example of gourmandism. Maps of plantation empires hang between the portraits, depicting the history of cocoa fortunes gained and cocoa fortunes lost.

The centrepiece of wonder in Delilah's dining room is the ornate silver chocolate fountain out of which every variety and flavour of chocolate the world has to offer continuously flows. But the most important artefact in Delilah's is the large, gilded Cocoa Clock hanging on the wall of the bar – a wonderfully intricate eighteenth-century time piece that simultaneously tells the time across all cocoa-trading continents. It is witness to every cocoa deal and gamble taken with the shake of hands – by its time all are accountable.

Beneath the Cocoa Clock Midas is having a drink and a private conversation with his partner in crime in the illegal cocoa trade. 'Bill, this is our sweet spot – the time is right for us to make a killing.'

'Agreed. The truth is Global Cocoa can't publicly do any more than we have. We're stockpiling the last of the known cocoa on the open market. And once this is achieved the board have agreed the company will cease to exist as a trader and concentrate on cultivating disease-resistant plantations of homogenised cocoa until such time that we can trade its yield – guaranteeing our continued cocoa fortunes.'

'In the meantime we've got to get our hands on the last shipments of every rare variety of cocoa we can procure – and turned into chocolate just as cocoa becomes extinct,' enthuses Midas.

'To that end I've just got my hands, free of any personal cost to us, on ten sacks of wild Sri Lankan Criollo. Market value £250,000 a sack – 100% pure profit, my friend.'

'How have you done that?'

'I sent company-paid armed mercenaries hired as security at our plantations on a trip into the forest where they relieved the natives of their harvest. Admittedly, with some resistance and a little blood shed – the pointing and firing of guns does cut out any needless profit-denting outlay.'

'Well done. Deliver the cocoa to my boutique.'

'I thought Reaper was taking the next shipment? Arm's length and all that.'

'The bloody Chocolate Thieves stripped Lullaby's last night.'

'What!?' The ice in his cocoa whisky rattles as Midas's casually delivered revelation sinks in. 'You're telling me I've just lost out on a £1,000,000 dividend, aren't you?'

'It's the game we play.'

'I don't want to play a fucking game. I want to make a lot of money while there's still cocoa in the world to get a return on my investment.'

'To which end – I am dealing with The Chocolate Thieves.'

'You'd better be.'

'I think it's time our leashed detective inspector be let off for a run.'

Whittaker angrily nods his approval. 'Yes, well – just do it.'

'And in the meantime I'll be making all the chocolate and selling it direct to my exclusive client list. As you've demonstrated – let's cut out any more complications and maximise our profit.'

Delilah, a redheaded woman of sensual mystique known only by that single name bestowed upon all the women who have been the chocolate house's guardian over the centuries, approaches them.

'Gentlemen, I have the most delightfully decadent chocolate proposition for you.' She radiates naughtiness.

'You have us held in anticipation,' replies Midas at his most lizardly.

Having been through the personal effects found on Leonard Piper's body, DS Silky finds herself at the University College London English Faculty, walking through the door, left open for her by a hurriedly exiting creased-of-brow student, of Professor Yvonne Stance's office – the head of English Literature.

'Professor Stance?'

'Yes,' comes the curt authoritarian answer.

DS Silky holds up her ID. 'I'm here about your colleague, Professor Leonard Piper.'

'His office is four doors down,' says Stance returning to her annotation of a manuscript after the merest glance at the detective.

'He is dead.'

'Have you shaken him? He could just be asleep. He's an insomniac by night, narcoleptic by day. He once fell asleep during one of his own lectures – storytelling through osmosis. Completely above the first-year students' heads – they very sweetly put his jacket over him as if it were a blanket, switched off the lights and quietly left for the bar.'

'No – he drowned.'

'Oh, dead dead,' she realises, looking up from her work.

'Yes.'

'Murdered?'

'Why do you ask?'

'Morbid curiosity. He specialised in London detective fiction – he'd have appreciated the poetic nature of it.'

'Would someone have wanted to kill him?'

'No idea. Want to see his office?'

'Please.'

'I'll need to call for a master key.'

DS Silky holds up Leonard Piper's bunch of keys.

'What about a wife or a lover?' the detective enquires as they walk along the corridor.

'Did he have a private life? I've never taken the time to think about it. Here you are.'

The white writing on the black sign on the door of the deceased academic's office simply reads, *Professor Leonard Piper*. On the wall next to the door is a notice board with a tutorial and lecture timetable pinned to it.

'Being dead meant Professor Piper would have missed

six tutorial sessions and two lectures – the students didn't report him missing when he wasn't in attendance?'

'Detective, most of the students are themselves missing.'

DS Silky opens the door. Professor Stance lingers in the doorway watching as the detective has a look around her dead colleague's office. An unremarkable small room of mostly fiction books and academic papers. DS Silky sits in his chair and sees the academic's lair from the late man's point of view. The room is tidy and disciplined – evidence of an ordered mind. Suggesting every action, every enquiry, was considered and deliberate. The drawers of the desk hold a hidden-away neat arrangement of pens and stationery. There is no sign of a box of chocolates. The bin is empty – the college cleaners have done their job. The only notable item on his desk is a framed photograph of a smiling woman in her mid-thirties carrying the air of a partner in crime – it's a face DS Silky has seen before. In the man's wallet, yes, but also somewhere else – it will come back to her.

Referring to the photograph, she says, 'Who is this?'

'No idea. I never asked him.'

'Will there be a next of kin in his personnel files?'

'Possibly. Truth is, I only knew him as the man who walked these corridors – the story goes he came here in 1988 to study and never left.'

'How good an academic was he?'

'He was brilliant – that is the one thing I do know about him. Stories were his DNA. He had an instinct for their language and structure – and the truth they convey.'

The continuous news-stream on Dunstan's iPad announces the devastating news that African cocoa plantations have officially been wiped out by the cocoa tree disease known as black pod rot. The sombre-faced journalist reports, 'After years of neglect through the cocoa conglomerates' exploitation of farmers and intensive farming techniques the soil is dead and black pod rot has spread across the key cocoa countries of Cameroon, Nigeria, Ghana, Ivory Coast and Togo. Another factor has been the demise of traditional cocoa-cultivation skills as the unfair trade practices of conglomerates lead to generations of independent farmers diversifying away from their traditional crops. And now African cocoa is extinct.'

A video call flashes on the screen and Dunstan touches the answer icon.

'Hello, Ekow – how is life with you?'

'Good afternoon, Dunstan. Life is good today.' The plantation owner pans his phone over drying racks covered with cocoa beans. 'Your investment has paid off – we've harvested just over a ton of unique organic St Lucian Criollo cocoa.'

'You've done a fantastic job. Thank you.'

'As you see the cocoa needs just a few more days drying then we'll fill the sacks and load the trucks in readiness for your word to dispatch them to you. I've text you the GPS coordinates of the collection point.'

Dunstan checks his phone. 'Yes – I've got them.'

'I should tell you, Dunstan, it will be a miracle if the cocoa gets to you. Global Cocoa has the whole Caribbean teaming with people bribed to search all cargo ships for any cocoa they can acquire. And then there are the independent operators looking out for anything they can sell on the black market. I'm telling you – you don't need to go out to sea to be fleeced by pirates anymore. Of course if we do get the shipment onto a boat the oceans are teeming with pirate vessels – men and women armed to their sweet teeth. It's a dangerous time to be transporting cocoa.'

'All just part of the adventure, Ekow. You'll keep some cocoa for yourself.'

'As agreed.'

'Good.'

'Dunstan, I'm concerned that this might be our last crop. The drones are getting ever more inquisitive. We've blocked the tracks and if anyone does make it as far as the gates they'll think we are solely a rum distillery. But there are rumours about us. No one has been to this part of the forest for years. They'd forgotten about this plantation. But everyone is hunting for any cocoa trees they can find – especially the rare self-seeded naturally growing ones like these. It will not be long before the Global Cocoa militia arrive at our gates.'

'Understood – stay safe.'

'We will.'

DS Silky walks round the house of the literary academic a short distance from the university. Walls of books, inviting worn furniture, the scent of musk incense and wood smoke from, now cold, fires. In the bedroom a rail of his tweed suits. A house waiting to be a home when the occupants return. It even has a ghost. In each room is a different portrait of a woman spanning a decade of her life. The same woman in the photograph on Piper's desk. In the study there's a painting of her hanging on the wall from when the woman was in her early thirties. The scene swathes of colour describing a room of a Victorian house, its decor distressed twenty-first-century bohemian – this house. Lit by a nearby standard lamp, her fair hair loose around her gentle features and elegant neckline. She's wearing a blue dress that delicately veils her figure and curled, relaxing, in an old battered leather chair – the one in the living room. An open box of chocolates on the arm. She is smiling, her brown eyes looking up from her book at the viewer – the portrait depicting intelligence and happiness with love for the person the subject is looking at, and by whom, no doubt, the painting was commissioned. The painting is discreetly signed *K.Z.*

'Why do you look familiar?' DS Silky asks herself. It is then she gets a flashback to where she has seen this woman's face. It was as she flicked through Dorothea's research file – she is a victim of The Chocolate Poisoner, her name – Isidora Effra.

On the desk, waiting to be found, is Leonard Piper's will. It reveals that the man had no living relatives and his library is to be gifted to a shelter for impoverished writers along with the contents of his bank accounts.

'You wanted to die.'

The Chocolate Thieves are joined around a table in The Sleight Of Hand by Scarlett Vamp and landlord Stanley Oak.

'Midas is trying to secure a place in history as the last man to make chocolate,' says Savage.

Scarlett is angry. 'The heritage of the artisan chocolatiers is being soiled by his actions.'

Stanley Oak is the voice of experience. 'The villainy of which you speak is the history of chocolate.'

'Searching for and using Blood Cocoa is something every chocolatier who knew about it has never done,' says Scarlett. 'It's culturally too sensitive. Too…'

'…real,' finishes Dorothea.

'Yes,' says Scarlett. 'We've always known there's a price to pay, a trade-off between our values and the desire for the perfect chocolate but doing something so culturally disrespectful…'

Dunstan leans forwards, putting his chocolate stout down on the table. 'These people and their heritage, however cruel and bloody, only exist as a folk tale to add value to what is sold – there's always a price that will be paid.'

'Midas has the wealthiest clients who regard what they can buy, what they can own, with that wealth as the right of their ego,' adds Furness.

'So what are we going to do with these chocolates and the sacks of Blood Cocoa?' asks Kyoko.

'We give them to those who need them – it's the tradition of The Chocolate Thieves. The Blood Cocoa is an elixir. So we use it for what it's for – giving life,' says Afia.

'There's a woman I know, Mira, she runs an off-the-grid shelter here in Whitechapel for street children. Somewhere they can get food and sleep safely. If you would like I'll deliver them to her,' Oak tells them.

'Perfect – thank you,' says Afia as the rest of the table nods in agreement.

'And what of Midas and his network?' asks Scarlett.

'If this is what he's trading in now it really is time he was gone,' says Savage.

'But there's no evidence connecting him to Lullaby – there'll be no paperwork, no import trail,' points out Dorothea.

'We keep surveillance on his every movement to see what else he's getting his hands on and who he's selling it to,' says Dunstan. 'I'll keep my eyes on Midas. Scarlett, reach out to the artisan chocolatiers to find out what people are whispering.' She nods in agreement. 'Stanley, can you find out what cocoa is being traded through the usual underground routes?'

'Consider it done,' confirms Oak.

'Also, our cocoa will be ready to leave the plantation on Saturday night. These are the coordinates for the collection point.' Dunstan shows Oak the text from Ekow. As he does so a man with nondescript features sitting at the next table with fellow drinkers who has been eavesdropping on The Chocolate Thieves' conversation subtly cranes his neck to read the screen.

'*The Cocoa St Lucia* will be waiting for your cargo. Captain Martin can be trusted – he's spent a lifetime navigating the cocoa winds,' Oak tells them.

The Chocolate Poisoner file compiled by Dorothea includes a photograph of a colour-coded map, in her usual synaesthesia style, of the location of the victims – white for the 1960s, red for the 1970s, orange for the 1980s, teal for the 1990s and silver for the 2000s.

There are six deaths linked directly to TCP poisoning.

8 July 1967, Rosetta Carthy, 24 – sculptor. Part of the psychedelic movement, she collapsed after a Pink Floyd gig at Middle Earth in Covent Garden. The autopsy revealed Rosetta had consumed 5mg of TCP, smoked cannabis, drunk a bottle of wine and eaten a selection of Miss Eliza's Lavender Truffles. Primary cause of death – respiratory failure.

6 October 1977, Dryden Tulmach, 27 – guitarist with the band Planet Hunter. Found dead sprawled across the back seat of the band's tour bus. As part of the band's rider at the Town & Country Club the night before, Tulmach had consumed eight pints of vodka-laced lager, fish and chips, and numerous Constellation Confectionary chocolates including: Stardust, Supernova, Moon Rock and Asteroid. One of which was laced with 6mg of TCP. Primary cause of death – he choked on his own vomit.

14 February 1986, an unidentified homeless woman,

suggested age 18 years. Found dying in a state of terror in her shelter at Cardboard City near Waterloo Station. A half-eaten box of Dreamer's Love chocolates, including Love Heart, All Your Desires and Forget Me Not, clutched in her hand. She died in the ambulance on the way to hospital. The autopsy revealed sustained malnutrition, injuries consistent with living on the streets and a dosage of 7mg of TCP. Primary cause of death – drug misuse.

18 October 1993, Freyja, 20 – a Faroese model. Died on the catwalk at London Fashion Week. Witnesses reported that she tripped out on the catwalk halfway through her performance. Thinking it was part of the show, with the photographers snapping every spasm and twitch of her seizure, the audience applauded the daring death of a beauty in lingerie. The show had been called Deadly Beautiful designed by Lorence L. Lace. Freyja had consumed champagne and a selection of Deadly Beautiful chocolates made by the chocolatiers at Boutique Cocoa especially for the show. 8mg of TCP was found in her system along with 100mg of cocaine. Primary cause of death – epileptic seizure.

1 January 2000, Tyler Ptolemy, 44 – CEO of Ptolemy Artificial Intelligence LTD. Died plugged into his games console immersed in the alternative reality experience Ptolemy One. The host of a New Year's Eve millennium party, Ptolemy, a teetotaller, had been drinking apple juice all night and eaten from the party's buffet which included a selection of Millennium Chocolate Mints. 10mg of TCP was found in his system. Primary cause of death – stroke.

4 August 2009, Isidora Effra, 37 – publisher's reader. Isidora drowned during an Anonymous End of Capitalism barge party on the river Thames. All alcohol and food, including chocolates, on the barge had been looted and re-branded with the ubiquitous Anonymous mask logo. The

autopsy revealed Isidora had consumed enough alcohol, at least two bottles of wine, to keep her inhibitions at bay, a selection of picnic foods and chocolates – one of which was laced with 9mg of TCP. Primary cause of death – drowning.

A witness statement given by Leonard Piper states that Isidora had been politically enthused all day – leading the anti-capitalist chanting. But as the day went on she'd become, uncharacteristically, more intoxicated and erratic in her moods – swinging from kindness to rage. But the last thing she did was kiss him, tell him she loved him, and jump into the water to join others in a swim protest at Westminster. He'd stayed on the boat and never saw her alive again.

There are also a dozen reports over the decades, correlating with the TCP deaths, of people arriving at A&E suffering from severe hallucinations – these being ascribed to drug misuse and successfully treated by medical staff.

Having pinned all the historical cases from The Chocolate Poisoner file on a wall, along with the map of the poisonings and the Leonard Piper autopsy, DS Silky takes a step back and talks herself through the evidence. 'Their deaths are spread across the city by the cultural movement of that specific decade. Everything this person does is opportunism. It's about the chaos. Their intent is not to kill, just to randomly get someone high. The Chocolate Poisoner clearly goes where people gather at culturally significant events in history. But it's not history at the time – it's the zeitgeist. So where next? And how do they acquire the TCP? If they buy it – where and whom from? Or, if they make it themselves, what do they need to create the formula and where is their lab?'

Later the same night a hooded man, scarf wrapped around

face, makes his way across the roof of the buildings to a skylight in the roof of Vamp. Letting himself in he makes his way floor to floor down through the building, passing the sleeping-in-her-bed Scarlett, to the shop where, after disabling the alarm, he opens the door and lets in his three accomplices.

'The deviant's asleep upstairs,' he tells his friends.

They begin to fill their holdalls with chocolates as the lead looter finds his way to the tasting room.

Upstairs, awoken by the tasting room intruder alarm linked to her phone, Scarlett zips up her blue catsuit and slips on her pair of steel-tipped boots.

When the chocolatier walks into the centre of the shop there is a pause in the looting.

'Good evening, wankers,' Scarlett condemns the room.

The three men have the option of making a run for it, but overconfidence in their ability to take care of a single female chocolatier is their undoing. With grins they'll soon regret they drop their bags and launch themselves at her. Scarlett batters them – attacking their eyes, throats and genitals with poking fingers, chops, punches and kicks. They don't land a hand on her before they are a pile of broken men on the pavement in the street outside the shop.

The lead looter appears out of the tasting room, Scarlett's Book of Cocoa in his hand; he sees his friends outside crawling and staggering away in agony. He timidly hands the chocolatier her book. 'Sorry.'

Scarlett takes the book out of his trembling fingers and swiftly cracks the spine of it across the man's nose. He crumples to the floor, blood pouring out of his broken face.

'Fucking hell,' he pitifully cries.

Scarlett looks with utter contempt down at him kneeling, bleeding, at her feet. He looks up at her with a pathetic look of 'Please, no more' in his watery eyes.

Leaning forwards she picks him up by his testicles and holds him on tiptoes with a playful twist of his scrotum.

She meets his fear with a smile and gives his testicles another twist. 'Pleasure or pain?'

'What?' he squeaks.

'What you're feeling now. I'm curious.'

'Pain – definitely pain,' he squeaks again.

'Good. You were sent by his gold nibs?'

The man nods.

She tightens her grip – he howls. She holds the intruder there, laughing at him, watching his face contorted in a unique sketch of agony. After what seems to him to be an eternity of terror, Scarlett throws him out onto the street – where he crumples blooded, bruised and humiliated into the gutter.

She locks the door, resets the alarm and goes back to bed, eating a Scarlett Heart chocolate on the way. 'Oh, Midas – when I get my hands on you…'

News-streams exclaim that pure cocoa is now the most valuable food commodity on the planet at £1,000 a gram. The reports are illustrated with images of addicts across the world selling their houses and possessions for one last taste of chocolate.

With a shake of his head Savage looks away from the television back towards the task in hand. What he had intended to be a brief personal memoir has, with Dorothea's enthusiasm and drive, become a forensic examination of the lives of their ancestors. To this end the dining room of The Black Truffle Hotel is now a research hub for *The History of The Chocolate Thieves*. Full of every photograph and piece of family memorabilia Savage possesses along with his monographs and reference books on the history of cocoa and chocolate.

Across one wall is The Chocolate Thieves' family tree. A work in progress of all six family members' ancestries and every character they've had dealings with – all the generations of the city's chocolatiers, all the Stanley Oaks, all the art forgers, all their fellow rogues of every black market trade and every detective that has investigated them.

The names Savage, Furness and Dunstan stretch back into pre-Industrial Revolution London. Their trades over successive generations being: cobblers, furniture makers, candle makers, mudlarks, oyster traders, actors, ferrymen, clay pipe makers, tanners, brewers, gin distillers, drayman, coopers, ladder makers, seamstresses, felt makers, milliners and cooks.

Dorothea's ancestry goes north to Scotland via the lineage of both her parents – occupations including boat builders and police officers in their time. Afia's south to St Lucia courtesy of her grandparents – her Akan ancestors were cocoa plantation slaves. Then with freedom lived off fishing and rum distilling. Kyoko's east to Japan via her father – a family of writers and teachers.

All of Dorothea's work on chocolate crime is here too. The map visualising the history of The Chocolate Thieves' heists is pinned up – fascinating and bewildering the rest of the household in its obsessiveness.

Maps from every era of cocoa plantations and trade routes cover the other walls. The world's contemporary plantations are plotted on maps, including Ekow's plantation, with information about the owners and their ethical practices, their location, size and yield – and if they are still viable.

Savage, cup of tea in hand, surveys their work to date and the volume of work still to be done. 'I'm both fascinated by it and have a consuming urge to burn it all.'

'Really?' says a surprised Dorothea looking up from the box of photographs she is flicking through. 'This is your life's work. What are you suddenly trying to escape from?'

'We've created a future because of this history – it's served its purpose. Let's box it up and put it in the attic.'

'It's a story of real lives lived so let's be the ones to tell it.'

'Separating fact from fiction – is that possible?'

'Does it matter? Your family has created a brilliant, colourfully absurd and wonderful history. What they and you, Furness and Dunstan have achieved is to act as witnesses to the collective chocolate obsession of society.'

'Witnesses to our city's chocolate and cultural history. Sounds a bit self-important. Isn't everyone a witness?'

'The fact you see that makes the telling of the story more compelling. And as I said, you aren't just witnesses – you're creators of history.'

'You think so?'

'The history of The Chocolate Thieves is one of a family who have preserved their way of life while evolving through, and playing a part in, the cultural shifts of the last hundred years.'

'All this history just to create an ordinary life – a life worth living. It's just sometimes, well, isn't the past where it belongs? I don't know. But I'm thinking it's true despite my addiction and fascination for this history. For the first time in my life I'm living in the present in the life I always wanted. And I like it.'

Dorothea kisses him. 'Look at that family tree – just think about telling the story of all those characters.'

Savage smiles as he reads out a name. 'Quibble Quirk.'

'Who was he?'

'Quirk created the most extraordinary chocolate flavours branded as Quibble's Quirks. You could taste

Autumn Cobweb, Winter Cobble Stone, Coal Soot And Smog, Thames Water Porridge and many other weird and wonderfully unpleasant flavours extracted from the city. Apparently all his collected ingredients and recipes were genuine attempts at real-to-life flavours. Which, sadly, was the end of him. He died after contracting rat-bite fever having been bitten while licking a rat on a trip into the bowels of our city in his attempt to recreate the flavour of London sewer rat.'

'Bloody brilliant,' utters an astonished Dorothea at this story.

Having begun when the river police pulled Leonard Piper's body out of the water onto the foreshore at Westminster Bridge, DS Silky has traced, using all the available footage from street cameras, his last movements back through the city to his starting point.

Now she plays it forward in time.

Piper leaves the university at 5.06pm and, choosing not to take the Underground or a bus, walks at his natural pace past Russell Square, along Southampton Row, then turning east through Holborn directly to The Sleight Of Hand in Whitechapel – arriving at 6.10pm.

He leaves the public house at 8.16pm and staggers through the streets with no real aim of reaching a destination.

The city at night is a living hell swathed in flashing blue lights and the orange-red of dancing flames – everyone out on the streets gorging on violence and what chocolate they can find.

As well as the present dangers of the real world, from Piper's mannerisms what is also going on in his mind is clearly very disturbing. The exaggerated paranoid jerks of his head in all directions – obsessively looking out for perceived dangers and the tensing of his body in defence positions indicating that what is real and what is imaginary have become indistinguishable from each other.

The sound of something approaching from behind makes him spin round. He becomes frozen in fascination and fear. What DS Silky cannot see is from Piper's point of view a funeral cortège passes by – the grotesque melting faces of mourners leering at him with loud maniacal laughter.

Terrified, Piper takes shelter in a dark alley – cowering in the shadows – trembling hands to his sweating face. As he slowly gathers his senses to a place of understanding his name is spoken by a gentle, familiar, female voice. 'Leonard.'

He smiles through his fear. 'Isidora?'

Isidora beckons him to her.

DS Silky watches Piper re-emerge from the alley holding the hand of someone who isn't there.

It is now 8.32pm.

Isidora leads Leonard through The Chocolate Apocalypse. Enchanted by his once-lost lover he is now oblivious to the collapse of civilisation surrounding him.

From DS Silky's point of view it is now that Piper's progress takes on a purpose; he walks along Aldgate High Street, then Fenchurch Street, Cannon Street, Ludgate Hill, along Fleet Street to Waterloo Bridge, along the Embankment and down onto the foreshore at Westminster – a journey on foot of just over an hour.

It is now 9.36pm.

At the river there are shared adoring smiles, a kiss, then the two reunited lovers walk hand in hand into the cold, dark, brooding water of the Thames.

Kyoko watches as DI Gloom, with considerable relief and

trembling fingers, closes the gallery door – looking nervously out onto the street at the flurry of people and traffic. Pale and clammy, he is a man barely holding it together – a fascinating portrait of the effects of agoraphobia.

Kyoko pretends not to know who he is. 'Hello. Can I help you?'

DI Gloom, now safely inside the gallery, looks at her and smiles – the persona of a fragile confidence taking over his features. 'Yes, I hope so.'

'What are you looking for?'

'Actually I think I'll just browse a while.'

'Please do – take your time.'

Dunstan appears in the doorway at the back of the gallery; on seeing DI Gloom he steps back out of sight, sharing a mischievous smile with Kyoko as he does so.

Out of the corner of her eye, when dealing with another customer, Kyoko sees DI Gloom touch a number of paintings, lick his fingers and be disappointed at the taste of paint.

Having completed her sale Kyoko walks over to the Detective Inspector. 'Anything tantalise your palate?'

'It's all such wonderfully original work,' DI Gloom tells the artist in genuine appreciation.

'Thank you. But I'm still tiptoeing around the ankles of giants.'

DI Gloom gives her a 'Don't talk nonsense' frown. He looks around hoping they're alone. There are two other people in the gallery. So conspiratorially he quietly asks, 'Have you anything a bit different?'

Kyoko, at normal volume, replies, 'Different?'

DI Gloom is quieter still. 'Anything I could devour?'

Slightly louder than she would normally speak Kyoko replies, 'The nudes are often perceived as erotica.'

DI Gloom winces. 'I was thinking something more edible.'

'Female or male?'

'That depends on the provenance.'

'All the models are ethically sourced.'

Kyoko directs DI Gloom's attention to four film-noir-inspired chocolate paintings: a couple dancing in a room of mirrors; figures walking through a rainy night-time cityscape; a detective standing in the shadow of a doorway; a femme fatale sitting alone in a bar drinking a gin and tonic and smiling seductively at the viewer.

Ten minutes later DI Gloom leaves the gallery after paying £7,000 for the pleasure of having the femme fatale in his arms.

DS Silky makes her way through the drinkers to the bar where Stanley Oak is serving. As she reaches the bar Oak walks over to her, reading aloud what it says in her ID wallet, '*DS Silky*,' adding, 'also known as The Chocolate Thieves Detective – welcome to The Sleight Of Hand.'

On hearing her name the room goes silent for a moment and the drinkers at the bar edge away. DS Silky scowls – though impressed with the sleight of hand that had extracted her ID wallet from her pocket and passed it to Oak by the time she walked the short distance from door to bar.

Having sized up the detective the patrons continue their conversations – though slightly more hushed than before, as if each person is both talking and listening to DS Silky and Stanley Oak's conversation.

With a welcoming smile Oak hands back her ID. 'Never leave these premises without checking you've all about your person what you've entered with.' He watches the detective tuck her ID deeper into her jacket pocket. 'Now what brings you in here?'

DS Silky uses the eavesdropping of the patrons to her advantage by speaking so everyone can hear. 'I'm investigating the poisoning and death of Leonard Piper, who according to your menu,' she refers with a glance to the menu board on the wall near the bar, 'and his stomach drank and ate here two nights ago.'

There is a shiver of concern through the pub at the suspicious death of one of their own.

She reaches for her phone but it is not there. Oak produces it as if from thin air and holds it out to her. With an amused sigh she snatches it out of his hand and accesses a photograph of Piper and shows it to the landlord.

'We know who he is. A collector of stories – a kind man.'

'He'd indulged in what is nowadays an expensive amount of chocolate.'

Stanley Oak thinks for a moment – judging the level of truth he must divulge to appease both DS Silky and his customers. 'The Pick-Pocket's-Purse. That's what he ate – four of them if I recall correctly.'

'I'm sure you do. One of the chocolates he ate was laced with the hallucinogen TCP.'

DS Silky knows Oak doesn't want her to publicly ask him to show her the footage of the bar he secretly films with hidden cameras – they share a look of understanding of this truth.

'Why don't I introduce you to our chocolatier?'

DS Silky follows Stanley Oak through a door at the end of the bar. He takes her upstairs to an office and draws her attention to the monitor and the ten camera feeds from every room in The Sleight Of Hand streaming to it.

Pointing at the shot of the kitchen, where a small team

of chefs are busily cooking, Oak says, 'Everything we serve is prepared here from raw ingredients in this kitchen.'

'Who made the Pick-Pocket's-Purse served here two nights ago?'

'Greg.' A man in his early twenties is serving up two fantastic-looking slices of Whitechapel Gateau. 'I assure you, DS Silky, we playfully trick the people who come through our door, they expect it, but we certainly do not poison them. We are rogues not murderers.'

'Show me the footage of Leonard Piper.'

Stanley Oak plays the footage from that evening.

Piper enters The Sleight Of Hand at 6.10pm. It is bustling with after-work drinkers and diners. Orders his first drink and his food at the bar and then finds a private table where he reads the evening paper, drinks and eats. Not speaking to anyone but the staff. His chocolate stout replenished four times – each time with a purse-shaped chocolate delivered on a small silver tray. With each chocolate consumed he takes a moment to consider it and says something to the chocolate.

'What did he just say?' asks DS Silky.

Oak replays the footage. 'This time, please, for Isidora.' The detective gives Oak a quizzical look. 'After a lifetime working in a noisy pub you learn to lip read,' he tells her.

'He wanted to die the way she did.'

'Then it's suicide.'

'No. More death by poetic design. He was looking for the same poison that killed the love of his life. Replay each chocolate being delivered.'

They follow the journey of each chocolate from kitchen to Piper's mouth. Watching the delivery of the fourth chocolate. 'There!' shouts out DS Silky.

Oak stops, rewinds and scrolls through the footage

frame by frame. A slender figure of a man in a charcoal thigh-length coat, jeans and brogues with a navy silk scarf tied loosely around his neck and a flat cap pulled down over his eyes crosses the path of the waiter and swaps, with elegant sleight of hand, the chocolate on the tray with one hidden in his left hand, palming the chocolate he has taken.

'Very good,' admires Oak.

Tracing the poisoner's movements in the bar they see him lift a Pick-Pocket's-Purse off the table of another customer a few minutes before and slip it into the left pocket of his coat. Standing alone near the fireplace, drinking his cocoa rum, he awaits his opportunity – which comes when Piper orders his fourth chocolate. Having made the swap, The Chocolate Poisoner eats the chocolate he palmed as he walks out of the door.

'When did he poison the chocolate?' wonders Oak.

'Most likely he had a syringe in his pocket,' deduces DS Silky.

'It is the work of an artist,' says Oak.

'At no point is there a clear view of his face on camera,' points out DS Silky.

What they can see of the man's features is an unshaven angular cheekbone and a thin-lipped mouth. He also has straight, mousy shoulder-length hair.

'That's by design,' offers Oak.

'Someone here that night saw his face,' DS Silky tells him.

'No they didn't,' insists Oak.

'They must have,' the detective protests.

'You really think he let anyone see him? Look at the way he moves, he's anonymous, no one is looking at him. The waiting staff walk past him as if he isn't there. He talks to no one. He ordered his drink, a neat shot, at the busiest moment so no time was lingered on him. There are four people behind the bar – I'm one of them and I didn't see him. You think anyone else did? And this is a place where people observe and see what others don't – this is a place of opportunity. But it is also somewhere to hide – a place of secrets.'

'I need you to ask.'

'There's a code dating back hundreds of years – who and what you see in these walls is not to be told to another. I cannot go down there and ask anyone what they saw that night. It would be a betrayal of the values that have held this establishment as a sanctuary to those that work the streets of this city. Besides, as I have just pointed out, he's an expert at not being seen. Who does he look like? Describe him. He's everyone and no one – that's his sleight of hand.'

'He's a killer.'

'Everyone kills someone.'

DS Silky stares at Stanley Oak for a time but knows he'll not yield on this point and that he is right – The Chocolate Poisoner had not let himself be seen. She hands him her card. 'Please email me the footage.'

As she goes to leave, with a cheeky smile, Stanley Oak hands DS Silky her wallet. 'Don't leave without this.'

'Bloody hell!' Taking it back DS Silky checks the money and cards are still there, they are, and leaves the company of Stanley Oak and the secrets of The Sleight Of Hand.

Damon and Katla, the two waiting staff, are just about keeping a civilised order to the high turnover of desperate chocolate-addicted diners that is lunchtime at The Furness restaurant. Looking like they were hired straight from Comic-Con, in their self-designed Chocolate Thieves T-shirts, they are a new addition due to the sudden popularity of The Furness. Brought about by the rumour on the street that the restaurant is where The Chocolate Thieves hang out and more importantly by the fact it still has chocolate on the menu.

DI Gloom sees the queue of hopeful diners waiting for a table stretching along the street and gives up the idea of getting lunch. Instead he drives around to the rear of the building.

The 6 Music news on the radio in the kitchen reports the latest on The Chocolate Apocalypse. 'Global Cocoa is stockpiling the last of the cocoa harvest from every known commercial plantation in the world…'

Furness and Afia have just sent out the latest course of chocolate desserts cut from the row of cakes on the counter – 50% cocoa Dark Chocolate and Cherry with Ginseng Cake, 30% cocoa Milk Chocolate Laced Carrot Cake and White Chocolate Apple and Cinnamon Cake.

Afia takes the scan of the foetus growing inside her womb out of her pocket, kisses her fingers and touches the tiny forehead in the image.

Furness is cutting the first slice from his new recipe – a rich flavoured 70% cocoa Dark Chocolate and Blackcurrant Cake. 'This looks so good.'

Afia shows the foetus Furness. 'This is your rogue father.'

Furness carefully places the slice of cake on a plate. 'Who rescued your destitute mother from the gin-soaked streets of this cruel city.'

'He left the kitchen door unlocked and I took shelter from the winter rain.'

'She broke in to steal food.'

'He was making bacon sandwiches – what was a homeless and hungry young woman to do?'

'And she hasn't left yet.' He cuts and prongs a chunk of cake with a fork and eats it. 'Fuck – that's good.'

'I saved him from himself.'

Furness forks a piece of cake into Afia's mouth. 'We rescued each other by making an Easter egg out of the rarest of cocoa.'

Afia nods her approval at the cake. 'And spent the money on making his derelict house a home and on cousin Ekow's cocoa plantation.'

'So we can make more chocolate.'

'The finest chocolate in the world.'

'The last chocolate in the world.'

'And we've made you.'

They kiss.

Furness's face turns to panic. 'The world. It's going to hell. How many people are there on the planet? Seven billion and rising. How much cocoa is left? There's not enough cocoa left in the world. You can't bring up a child without chocolate.'

'This is so selfish of us,' says an equally panicking Afia. 'What life will she have in The Chocolate Apocalypse?'

'What life can we give her? Chocolate Thieves without any chocolate to steal.'

In a terrified panic they start stuffing each other's mouths with Chocolate and Blackcurrant Cake.

'It's orgasm time,' says Katla matter-of-factly as yet again the dining room becomes a loud chorus of sounds of delight. Damon nods in agreement as they listen to every diner groaning in sensual satisfaction at the chocolate flavours in their mouths.

In the kitchen Furness and Afia are now on the prep table pulling off each other's clothes.

'I love you,' she tells him.

'I love you too,' he tells her.

'Pregnant women get cravings, yes?'

'Yes.'

'Good.' Afia pushes Furness's head down between her legs and stuffs more of his orgasmic cake into her mouth.

It is now that DI Gloom creeps in through the kitchen door – tiptoeing around the sexually preoccupied Chocolate Thieves, he is able to sneak about the kitchen. There is none of Midas's stolen cocoa in sight, none in the storeroom, nor the cellar. Which leaves the question, 'How are they making chocolate without cocoa?' Not having an answer DI Gloom helps himself to a slice of the Chocolate and Blackcurrant Cake and slips back out of the kitchen door.

The Detective Inspector checks the outside bins – there are no empty cocoa sacks either. He looks at the back of the building. He's up the fire escape and looking through the window into the flat before he can stop himself. Just the detritus of shared staff accommodation. He tries the door – it is locked.

The city looms over him, leers and threatens him from all directions and he begins to sweat. DI Gloom bites into the slice of cake to distract himself from his uncontrollable environment and immediately goes into a chocolate high in the street. In full arousal, his knees buckling beneath him, he crawls into his car – collapsing in euphoria onto the back seat.

Sitting in the bar at Delilah's, Midas is impatiently drinking his second cocoa whisky. Unable to wait any longer for news he phones his unleashed detective inspector.

Still on the back seat of his car recovering from his cake orgasm DI Gloom takes the call. 'Yes.'

'Well?'

'Nothing.'

'Nothing?'

'No evidence of your cocoa at the gallery – nor the restaurant.'

'What about chocolate?'

'Oh yes, the most wonderful chocolate – sensually light, wild floral top notes underpinned with a naturally woody base note.'

'Not a bloody and soulful chocolate?'

'No, this is sun-kissed and wildly dreamy.'

'Bring me some to taste.'

'Too late.'

'Fucking hell!' Midas hangs up and downs his drink, snaps his fingers at the barman, points at his glass and phones someone else as his whisky is being replenished. 'I want you to close down The Furness restaurant.'

The Chocolate Apocalypse news-stream does not make for good viewing, with cocoa being declared extinct on the African continent and in Asia. And informing all viewers that Global Cocoa is now the only operational cocoa company left and that they are in sole control of the last remaining commercially viable plantations on the planet in South America and the Caribbean.

CEO of Global Cocoa Bill Whittaker is standing in front of the conglomerate's headquarters in central London issuing a statement to the gathered news-streams. 'We at Global Cocoa can assure every chocolate lover, on every continent, that we will ensure that all the cocoa left in the world will be distributed as fairly as possible. But due to the precarious nature of the political context and the environmental crisis our plantations are in we cannot guarantee that everyone on the planet will eat chocolate again.

'But while Global Cocoa are in control of the cocoa we

have left we will support the cultures that depend on its cultivation for economic stability and we will try to sate the palates of those markets with a long tradition of chocolate consumption.

'The last of the world's chocolate is safe in the hands of Global Cocoa.'

Dunstan switches off the television and says out loud what the rest of the world is thinking: 'So that's chocolate totally fucked.'

Having spent the afternoon trawling through security camera footage from the streets surrounding The Sleight Of Hand and discovering they have captured nothing of The Chocolate Poisoner's movements – the man disappears from view at the end of the street – DS Silky has turned her attention to the where and how he gets his supply of TCP.

'He's not the sort of character to get his hands dirty,' MacCarrion tells her.

'Why do you say that?'

'He didn't synthesise the TCP.'

'Go on.'

'The synthesis of street TCP is an odorous and dangerous practice.'

'So he'd need ventilation and secrecy. Not easy to find in London. But not impossible.'

'Indeed. But curious at the purity of the synthesis I did some detective work myself. My deduction is he buys or steals the tenocyclidine as a crystalline solid from a chemical supplier – somewhere like this.' MacCarrion hands her a single-sheet product information print-out. The River Chemicals logo flows across the top of the sheet in waves of blues. 'Based in Limehouse they are the only London supplier of industrially synthesised TCP. But he could be getting it delivered from a company in Cambridge or shipped from an overseas supplier.'

DS Silky reads out the salient product information. '*Tenocyclidine (hydrochloride) synonym TCP, C15,H23,NS.HC1, purity 98%, stability 2 years at -20°C, supplied as a crystalline solid. A stock solution can be made by dissolving the TCP in a solvent such as ethanol, DMSO and dimethylformamide (DMF) which should be purged with an inert gas.*'

'In short with the tenocyclidine as a crystalline solid your poisoner can synthesise liquid TCP with basic chemistry lab equipment,' adds MacCarrion.

'So we aren't going to find him through the creation of the drug,' acknowledges DS Silky.

The detective contacts River Chemicals and discovers they'd reported the disappearance of 100mg of their TCP stock and bottles of ethanol six months ago.

'You're fucking kidding me!' exclaims DS Silky as Dorothea tells her the home address of The Chocolate Thieves. 'But that's... I can see it from here,' she says looking out of the office window across the wrecked city beneath the cloudless blue morning sky.

'I know – brilliant, isn't it? All these years living hidden in this quiet street. Within sight of everyone looking for them. Now remember – you're sworn to secrecy.'

Sixteen minutes later Dorothea opens the front door of The Black Truffle Hotel and invites the detective inside.

'Wow!' is all that DS Silky can say as she surveys the recently renovated home of The Chocolate Thieves. Walking into the research room she expels a 'Bloody hell' as she surveys the piles of documents, the photographs and the maps on the walls.

'Welcome to *The History of The Chocolate Thieves* and

our home, DS Silky,' Savage warmly greets her as they shake hands.

'Hello, Savage.' She is drawn to the family tree. 'Here you all are – it's wonderful work.' She sees her own name with below it a list of her significant investigations. Her focus is drawn to The Westminster Library Book case – a dead spy, a parliamentary secretary and two political careers – one ended, one began. Her first piece of career-defining detective work – in the eyes of her superiors anyway.

'Have you done your family tree?' asks Dorothea as she pours each of them a cup of tea.

'An involuntary sharing of DNA is as close as I want my family to be.'

'Know the past, create a future – so it seems,' says Savage.

'That is why I need your help. What do you know about The Chocolate Poisoner – beside what's written in here?'

Dorothea takes the file. 'I didn't think dear old Uncle Gloom would do anything with it.'

'He knew you'd discovered a connection between the reported deaths and, well, it seems The Chocolate Poisoner is active once again. So here I am.'

'Crikey!' Dorothea reads the report on Leonard Piper's death. 'This is suicide.' She hands the file to Savage.

'That's for the coroner and courts to decide. Savage, who is The Chocolate Poisoner?'

The Chocolate Thief flicks through the file. 'I do not know.'

Dorothea offers DS Silky a homemade chocolate biscuit to go with her tea – which she readily accepts with an instant dunk and a delighted nibble. 'Looking at your history I find that hard to believe.'

'He's never had a name. And he always looks like he

should be where he is.'

'But you do know about him?'

'Yes – how could I not? He's a ghost story. An allegory. The chocolate lover's nemesis. Don't steal chocolate for fear of The Chocolate Poisoner's hand. But?'

'But?'

'Has he killed anyone?'

'You have there a file of dead people who have all eaten chocolates laced with a lethal dose of TCP.'

'There's no evidence they didn't consent to eating the drug,' points out Dorothea.

'So it's manslaughter,' concedes the detective. 'But unlikely in the case of the teetotal Ptolemy and it seems the homeless young woman was a victim of a cruelty that demands some kind of justice.'

'True,' says Savage, 'but how do you prove he laced the chocolates?'

DS Silky plays them the footage from The Sleight Of Hand on her phone.

'Bloody clever,' says Dorothea.

Savage has gone quiet so DS Silky prompts him. 'That's why I need to know what you know. He's been at this for fifty years. Your family must have come into contact with him – moved in the same cultural scenes over the decades.'

'The cultural scene is the key to catching him in the act,' Savage tells her. 'It's how he disguises himself – he's a situationist.'

'So what he is doing is political?'

'Yes and it's art. In the 1960s during the psychedelic movement, where he began, The Chocolate Poisoner, like everyone else, was experimenting with the boundaries of perception. If someone was dead in their bed in the morning, what of it – their corpse was part of the situation.'

'By the 1970s,' continues Dorothea, 'it was a statement about cultural decay – a decade of decadence and rage that saw the evolution of glam rock and punk. He left boxes of chocolates in the rubbish-filled streets for people to trip out on and as part of a band's rider just to see what anarchy would ensue.'

'In the 1980s,' picks up Savage, 'he commented on the rise of the individual as the personification of capitalism – the iconography of the self. So he fed TCP-laced chocolates to the homeless – society's discarded. Satirical art at its cruellest.'

'By the 1990s,' says Dorothea, 'society's deification of the supermodel epitomised the way the era defined itself as a celebration of the ego. So he drugged a world both beautiful and grotesque – its indulgence a poison in itself.'

'At the turn of the new millennium, lacing the chocolates of who he did on New Year's Eve – the creator of a virtual reality – was a reaction to the delusion of simulacra,' offers Savage, 'that the only hope for humanity is the creation and sanctuary of a false reality.'

'And 2008 speaks for itself,' says Dorothea, 'the financial crash, the end of capitalism depicted in the form of masked anonymous people, who, with the complicity of ignorance, enslaved themselves to the lies of the previous decades.'

'On a purely politically artistic level the man's work is brilliant,' concludes Savage, 'if you follow his personal logic that his victims are already dead.'

'Everyone kills someone,' muses DS Silky.

'What?' asks Dorothea.

'Something Stanley Oak said to me.'

Savage nods. 'There is a man who is no one's fool.'

'And now, in the rage of The Chocolate Apocalypse, the whole city is his situation,' states DS Silky.

'Everyone really is creating his art for him,' adds Dorothea.

'He's stalking the streets of our dystopia and he will be there at the end of chocolate,' says Savage gravely.

DS Silky draws their attention to a still in the crime file of The Chocolate Poisoner taken from The Sleight Of Hand footage. 'Is there a photograph anywhere in this archive that might be of him?'

There is lots of rummaging through boxes of photographs so DS Silky eats another chocolate biscuit and reads the story of chocolate on the walls of the room – the scale of the centuries of indulgence of people's cravings is staggering.

Savage eventually finds a photograph taken at a party in the 1960s. 'Yes – this could possibly be him. In the foreground are Dunstan of CHOC 3 and Aunt Lydia. That could possibly be The Chocolate Poisoner in profile, there, in the background – in conversation with the redheaded lady.'

DS Silky compares Savage's photograph with the image of the present day Chocolate Poisoner. Just over fifty years apart there is still a potential likeness. 'Where was this taken? Who's he talking to?'

Savage turns the photograph around in her fingers. Written on the back is *Delilah's New Year's Eve 1968/69*.

'Who's Delilah?'

'A friend lost to time,' Savage tells her.

Dorothea frowns at him but says nothing.

DS Silky's eyes flick over the family tree but she doesn't see Delilah written on it.

Savage interrupts her search. 'You do know it's very unlikely you'll apprehend him before all the chocolate is gone.'

The detective meets The Chocolate Thief's eyes. 'We

will see.'

Sitting at the window table in the Cocoa Tree Cafe, drinking a pot of tea and eating his second heavily buttered toasted teacake, Dunstan watches Midas's, closed to walk-in customers, boutique. All his staff were laid off as soon as The Chocolate Apocalypse hit – the chocolatier having no desire to unnecessarily share through the paying of wages what profits there were left to be made.

The Chocolate Apocalypse morning news, on the television bracketed high on the wall in a corner of the cafe, reports that chocolate addicts, having run out of shops and vending machines to loot, are now increasingly raiding the kitchen cupboards of friends and neighbours for a fix of chocolate. With the Home Secretary Robina Head describing the situation as 'Wide spread and out of control across the country.'

The 'ordinary' Kettle family of four from Walthamstow are interviewed – the parents comforting their teary-eyed daughters.

'We'd saved the cocoa for the twins' thirteenth birthday. I was making the cake – a double-choc triple-layer sponge with three fruit compote fillings of apricot, raspberry and blackberry, coated in a thick chocolate icing. I'd just taken the three sponges out of the oven and was letting them cool down as I made the chocolate icing. When in they burst through the kitchen door – three of them. The first punched me in the face and pinned me against the fridge – that's how I got this,' says Martha, the twins' bloody-nosed mother.

'I heard the crash of the back door and Martha's cries for help from in the living room where I was putting up the birthday decorations,' says John, the black-eyed father, adding, 'In the kitchen I got into a scrap with one of them.'

170

Martha continues the story. 'And you know what the third one did? She only went and finished making the cake. Assembled all three layers with compote and iced it in front of us as we fought for our chocolate lives.'

John ends the story. 'She then ran off with it – so the other two stopped fighting and gave chase for fear of not getting their share.'

The interviewer gets a word in. 'Did you recognise them?'

Martha doesn't hesitate. 'Oh yes…'

John interrupts his wife. 'They were wearing head-to-toe second-skin suits – orange, green and yellow. Their faces were completely covered.'

'But I know it was the Pawleys from Number 22 – can't bake to save her life.'

Just as Dunstan washes down the last of the teacake with a gulp of tea a black Global Cocoa van pulls into the mews alongside the boutique and Midas appears at the side entrance to greet Whittaker who is accompanied by four armed guards. Ten clearly labelled sacks of Forastero Cocoa from Sri Lanka are carried in through the kitchen door by two of the guards. The other two guards, with submachine guns in their hands, stand at the back of the van watching the entrance to the muse. Whittaker hands Midas legitimising paperwork for the cocoa and after a brief exchange he gets back into the van with his guards and drives away.

Midas locks himself inside the boutique.

Dunstan doesn't doubt for one minute that what is in the sacks, delivered in person by Whittaker, is not what is on the label. But what is the best course of action? The Chocolate Thieves could easily gain access and deprive the chocolatier of the sacks of cocoa. No. Patience is what is called for. Leave Midas to work his ego then do what The

Chocolate Thieves do best – liberate the man of his high-value chocolates. That will hurt him the most.

DI Gloom, his tongue to chocolate femme fatale, is shocked out of his reverie when DS Silky knocks twice, opens the door and walks into his office without being invited. He quickly fumbles the painting out of sight.

'We have to stop the selling of chocolate,' she demands.

'What chocolate?' he replies, licking the chocolate off his lips. 'We're running out – nearly all the city's chocolate shops are empty.'

'People are being poisoned by the chocolate that's left.'

'People are looting the chocolate that's left. We can't stop them eating chocolate – that's too cruel.'

'No one knows who The Chocolate Poisoner is – how am I supposed to stop him?'

'Don't.'

'What?'

'Look on the bright side.'

'What bright side?'

'Think it through. Even if we shut the remaining chocolate outlets the chocolatiers that are left with any cocoa will just sell their chocolates to affluent private clients and he'll simply break in and poison the stock. There is nothing you can do.'

'It's our duty to do what we can,' demands DS Silky.

'They'll keep selling chocolates, he'll keep poisoning the chocolates, people will keep buying, stealing and eating chocolate until there is no more chocolate to make, poison, buy, steal and eat. Which will be very soon. So end of poisonings and end of killings.'

'Then why do we turn up to work each day? To follow your logic we should let all killers kill until there are no people left to kill so every murder case doesn't need to get solved because we're all dead.'

'My point is in this scenario the dying will end soon because the murder weapon will no longer exist. And he doesn't intend to kill them – just get people high. Their death is just an unfortunate by-product of his actions – it's manslaughter.'

'The high dosage he laces the chocolates with – it's crossing the line. And what do you think people are going to become addicted to next to replace the absence of chocolate? We've already got coffee and tea, ice cream and doughnuts. Maybe fudge – it's sweet and filling. Yes, I give you The Fudge Poisoner. Trust me it won't be long before you have one of Dorothea's files with TFP written across the front of it.'

'Ah.'

'He's an artist. He will always need to create. To respond to the world he lives in. Although for what it's worth he may be described as a situationist but he's doing this for one simple reason – his own entertainment. And he's been allowed to get away with harming people for fifty fucking years. So I intend to stop him.'

'How?'

'Well, let me tell you…'

'Yes.'

'I'm going to do the bloody obvious…'

'Which is?'

'I'm going to work out the pattern of cocoa supply…'

'Which will lead you where?'

'I'll find out who's got cocoa and how much of it and who's going to run out of chocolate last. That's where he'll be – somewhere along the remaining chocolate supply line. So that is where I will catch him.'

'Good.'

'What?'

'Glad we got there in the end. My door is always open. Do close it behind you.'

DS Silky storms out, slamming the door behind her. 'Fucking hell!'

DI Gloom looks down at his chocolate femme fatale – he's nearly licked off the whole of the mise en scène surrounding her. How enigmatically she is looking at him. He gives her his best seductive smile, picks up the painting and gives her slender feet a lick.

Enjoying the post-evening-shift quiet of The Furness restaurant, Damon and Katla are in the kitchen eating hot dogs.

Damon admires his food. 'This is so good. Smoked venison and wild boar with red wine and herbs sausage in a fresh-out-of-the-oven roll drizzled with fiery chocolate sauce.'

'It's incredible how every distinct flavour of each ingredient cartwheels around the taste buds,' Katla excitedly replies.

'Such a great deal – money, free food and somewhere to live. All for waiting tables.'

'Indeed it is. What cake are you going to eat afterwards?'

'Once I've eaten two of these I'm going to follow them up with a very large slice of the newly created Chocolate and Blackcurrant.'

'I'm going for the very traditional White Chocolate Apple and Cinnamon.'

'Controversial.'

Suddenly, the kitchen door bursts open and two large thuggish men, with the classic features of low brows, fat necks, strong arms, solid chests and stomachs wrapped in bomber jackets, walk into the kitchen. On seeing the slight figures of Damon and Katla they take a moment to scoff at the task in hand.

The four of them stare at each other.

Damon decides to speak first. 'You know – I think they've come to steal our hot dogs and chocolate cakes.'

'Is this true? Have you come to steal our hot dogs and chocolate cakes?' enquires Katla.

Thug One looks at her quizzically. 'Yeah – that's why we're 'ere. And why you talkin' like that?'

'Yeah,' says the second thug, 'where you from?'

'Reykjavik.' Katla turns to Damon. 'You think I talk funny?'

'Not at all – he's being rude. I love your accent. You are my lyrical elf.'

'And you're a sexy-elf-fucker.' She wipes sauce off his chin and provocatively sucks it off her finger.

Thug One isn't impressed. 'Sexy! Look at 'im, he's a fuckin' anaemic troll.'

Thug Two snorts in agreement.

'Did you just refer to the man I love as a troll?'

'Yeah I did you elfing-troll-fucker.'

'You know if I didn't have a soft spot for trolls that could be offensive,' muses Damon.

'They're so cute when they're grumpy,' says Katla.

Damon and Katla playfully do impressions of grumpy trolls to each other.

'Fuck this – let's close these freaks down,' says Thug One and the two men advance.

'Wait,' commands Damon.

The Thugs stop.

Damon turns up 6 Music – 'Little Talks' by Of Monsters and Men has just come on.

'I love this song,' exclaims Katla.

The two men advance again. Unfortunately for them

their bulk is a hindrance more than an asset in the confines of the restaurant kitchen. Damon leans back out of the way of a punch and brings a frying pan across Thug One's nose. Katla ducks under Thug Two's fist and brings a copper pan up to connect with his chin. Both Thugs reel backwards.

The guardians of The Furness await the second advance of their assailants.

Tempers flaring, the Thugs throw themselves at Damon and Katla who simultaneously jump up and grab hold of the overhead utensil and pan rack, bring up their knees and kick both men in the face – crushing septums with the heels of their boots and sending the men flying backwards again.

Landing on his feet Damon grabs a blow torch, lights it and melts Thug One's right ear as the man lifts him off his feet in a bear hug and tries to crush his ribs – Thug One squeals in agony.

On her feet again Katla reaches up for a meat hook off the rack – avoiding Thug Two's pan-clanking fists she hooks him by the nose. 'Hello, Little Piggy.' She snorts and grunts at him as she wrenches him by his nostrils onto his fat toes.

'This is so cool,' says Damon above Thug One's screams. He is now also hitting the man's left ear with a meat tenderiser.

'So much fun.' Katla giggles, picking up a baking tray and repeatedly whacking the still-hooked Thug Two on the head with it.

The distraught, bloodied Thugs fall away from them and Damon and Katla step back a moment, casually resuming the eating of their hot dogs, giving the men the opportunity to leave.

The enraged Thugs, adrenalin keeping the full effect of

their pain at bay, refuse the opportunity to give up the fight – both reaching for carving knives. But before they can wield the knives Damon and Katla grab a rolling pin each and smash out the Thugs' front teeth with swift single swings. With kicks in the arse sending the Thugs out of the kitchen, the door is closed and locked on them.

A short time later, Midas, in the bar at Delilah's, is raging on the phone. 'Are you seriously telling me some daylight-dodging waitress and her splash-back waiter boyfriend did you over?'

A brutalised, gutter-dwelling Thug One pitifully growls in pain down the phone, 'She was more of a lyrical elf and both were as strong as trolls.'

Midas hangs up and takes a mouthful of cocoa whisky. 'How the fuck is this happening?'

In the kitchen of The Furness, without a scratch nor a bruise, Damon opens the window to remove the scent of seared human flesh and disinfects the blood spattered surfaces. 'Like The Chocolate Thieves would leave the premises unguarded – what was Midas thinking?'

Katla, with a cheeky chuckle, cuts two extra-large portions of their favourite cakes in celebration of a job well done. 'Fucking idiot.'

Over the next few days DS Silky marks on a map of the city and visits all the still-active chocolate locations that could be potential targets for The Chocolate Poisoner.

Chocolatier after chocolatier says, 'Of course I've heard of him,' but shakes their head at her when shown the 1968/69 photograph and the still from The Sleight Of Hand footage of The Chocolate Poisoner.

And one by one potential poisoning locations are crossed off her list as they run out of chocolate – Hoddinot, Featherlight, Reaper, Barge and Ealing all make their last batch of chocolates – refusing to pay the extortionate Global Cocoa prices for cocoa.

Rumours spread out of the self-denial of an addict's logic that chocolatiers are stockpiling their cocoa for their own consumption. This leads to cruel threats and farcical acts of violence as broken-into empty shops are not looted of anything.

'If they are, who can blame them,' says Furness as he, Afia and DS Silky stand talking in the kitchen of the restaurant, 'they've earned the right after years of chocolate-making.'

'So where are you getting your cocoa from?' the detective asks as she bites into a slice of Milk Chocolate Laced Carrot Cake and pulls a 'That's fucking sublime' expression.

Furness smiles at her as she appreciates his baking. 'A legitimate private source.'

'An insightful detective might suspect you of investing your Kew Gardens Easter Egg money in a secret cocoa planation in a certain person's ancestral home.'

'A detective would be bloody right too,' Afia informs her.

'So how are you getting the cocoa into the country? The Government have granted Global Cocoa all the import licences.'

'We have our best mind on that very problem,' teases Furness.

The 6 Music news on the radio catches their attention as it informs them that all Caribbean cocoa shipping routes have been completely cut off by pirates. The on-the-scene reporter dramatically describes how Global Cocoa have lost four ships sailing out of Grenada, St Vincent and the Grenadines, Barbados and St Lucia. 'The ships were intercepted just out to sea having attempted to secretly slip away with their highly prized cargo – each ship reportedly carrying 1,000 tonnes of cocoa. A ransom of £250,000,000 has been demanded by the pirates for the return of each ship and its precious cargo.'

DS Silky smiles at the two Chocolate Thieves. 'I shall be interested to see how Dunstan pulls it off.'

With their thirtieth-anniversary takeaway meal of sushi devoured, their glasses replenished with Chablis, Gillian Day looks expectantly at her husband, Daniel. 'Well? It was your year to buy our anniversary gift.'

Daniel, ever the one to build up the anticipation, slowly reaches beneath the table and picks up the gift bag from Vamp and puts it down in front of his wife.

Gillian's eyes go wide and she squeals in excitement. 'I so love you.' She reaches over and kisses him.

'I love you too.' He smiles. 'We may have to raid the pension pot if we want to go on a New Year skiing trip. I've spent two years' holiday money on these chocolates.'

'I don't mind, I really don't mind. Thank you.' Gillian opens the bag and carefully takes out the box of chocolates. Across the lid she reads, 'Vamp Nightshade.' She opens the box and inhales the seductive aroma of 70% cocoa, spices and nectars.

They read the chocolate menu together – Gillian selects a Peekaboo for Daniel, he selects an Oh You Naughty Girl for her.

'Could there be a more deliciously erotic anniversary present?' His wife laughs as he watches her enjoy the pulse-quickening flavours.

The TCP quickly begins to take effect on Gillian and she becomes detached from linear time. They drink several bottles of the wonderful wine. Enjoying the chocolates. Take it in turns to select their favourite music and dance into the night. To the strains of 'Do You Love Me?' by Nick Cave and The Bad Seeds finding their way to the bedroom they dissolve into each other in sensual and intense sex.

They sleep.

Now she wakes up into a strange grey-blue half-light. Daniel is a decayed corpse, dust and bones, lying next to her in bed. Her heart sinks into fear and loneliness. Walking through the cold house she leaves footprints in the dust and brushes away cobwebs. The air the scent of damp earth. All the photographs have faded – those of their children age to dying. The dinner table still set with the rotted remnants of their food and wine just as they left it after their last meal together. The remaining chocolates in their box. 'Oh You Naughty Girl,' she hears Daniel say as he put the chocolate into her mouth with that wickedly mischievous smile of his. In a mirror she sees reflected a very old woman decaying before her eyes – a face gouged with lines, skin paper-thin and liver-spotted, her once lovely hair now grey, dirty, matted and falling out, her eyes clouding over. She is terrified, but can't scream, can't make a sound, nor shed a tear. She is trapped in the cold, isolating, silence of death.

In the gentle light of the morning Daniel finds the woman he has loved since they were eighteen years old still standing in front of the mirror – staring beyond her reflection into a void.

Gillian collapses into his arms and dies.

DS Silky arrives to get Dr MacCarrion's autopsy report on Gillian Day's cause of death. MacCarrion pulls back the sheet covering the dead woman to reveal she has a melancholic expression the like of which the detective has never seen. It is a description of a terrible, devastating loss.

'She died of a heart attack brought on by 11mg of TCP,' MacCarrion tells her.

The detective silently, respectfully, angrily leaves the room.

'I'm telling you The Chocolate Poisoner hasn't come into the shop,' insists Scarlett Vamp having already said she doesn't recognise the man in the still from the The Sleight Of Hand footage shown to her by the detective.

And she is right. The man DS Silky is looking for does not appear on the screen as they view, on the chocolatier's iPad, the shop's security footage of the time leading up to Daniel Day's purchase.

They watch Daniel Day come into the shop and select chocolates under the chocolatier's advisement. The chocolates are boxed and gift-wrapped. Day pays for them and exits the shop through the door held open by Dunstan.

'Let it play as he walks away,' instructs the detective.

As Day steps out of the shop into the flow of pedestrians walking along the busy street it is now The Chocolate Poisoner, in the same coat, flat cap and scarf, walks past Vamp in the same direction as Day.

DS Silky sighs. 'Damn it.'

'You were hoping to see how he did it?'

'Yes. That man being where the last of the chocolate is being sold isn't enough evidence of his hand in the poisonings.' DS Silky looks around the shop. 'You've got plenty of stock?'

'Yes – but these are likely to be our last creations. Our supply of cocoa will soon be gone too.'

'Who else is left making chocolate now? I know The Chocolate Thieves are trying to import cocoa.'

'Just four of us, here, Furness, Midas and,' she takes a moment to smile, 'Delilah's.'

'Delilah's?' DS Silky takes the 1968/69 photograph of The Chocolate Poisoner out of her pocket.

Scarlett looks at the photograph with curiosity, trying to recognise the image. DS Silky flips it over, showing the writing on the back. Vamp reads it with fascination, then looks at the photograph again. 'Of course – there's the Cocoa Clock reflected in the mirror.'

'So it's a place not a person?'

'It's both, darling. Tradition has it that the proprietor is always referred to as Delilah. It's the oldest and most secretive chocolate house in the city. Where every illicit cocoa deal and chocolate vice has taken place for the last 300 years.'

'For days every chocolatier I've spoken to has denied knowing who or what Delilah's is. The Chocolate Thieves too. Why haven't I been told about it? I'm trying to stop a killer.'

'Because, sweetheart, no one on my side of the street, and certainly no one on your side of the street ranked above you, wants you, with your detective wits, anywhere near the place. But now The Chocolate Poisoner has violated my palace of sensuality, I'm telling you, he'll end up at Delilah's eventually.'

'But if he was there in 1968 he won't poison there again.'

'Darling, I've no doubt he's laced a few chocolates there, on request, guaranteed, but he's never poisoned anyone at Delilah's. And trust me, that it's the truth, when I tell you, it's going to be the place to be the night chocolate ends.'

'Where is it?' asks DS Silky angrily.

Scarlett tells her the location of the secretive chocolate house in St James, adding, 'Detective, the chocolatier with the last of the world's cocoa to make the last-ever chocolate is going to become very rich selling it or assassinated for that historically exclusive tongue orgasm.'

'Your point being?'

'If it's Midas and the situation is the latter – let it happen.'

Having collated what street footage DS Silky can of The Chocolate Poisoner she discovers that from Vamp he followed Day into Goodge Street Underground station. The footage from the train carriage revealing The Chocolate Poisoner standing next to Day on the packed train, right hand holding on to the rail, left hand pulled from his coat pocket and hanging, out of view, beside the Vamp gift bag – again no definitive view of the poisoning taking place. Both men alight the train at Waterloo Station and disappear in the melee of travellers.

Based on Scarlet Vamp's information on who is still making chocolate, DS Silky sets up covert surveillance cameras outside The Furness restaurant, Midas's boutique and Delilah's. And settles in for however many days and nights it takes in front of the three live streams coming from each of The Chocolate Poisoner's potential targets for her to spy her quarry.

The latest report on The Chocolate Apocalypse news-stream exclaims that the last of the South American cocoa plantations to be resisting witches' broom disease and owned by Global Cocoa are now in the hands of drug cartels.

DS Silky looks away from the television back to the live stream of the queue outside The Furness restaurant and sees The Chocolate Poisoner join the line of people.

DI Gloom pauses at the door of the police station with a worried look. The thought of going out into the violence of

The Chocolate Apocalypse that is the nightlife of the city terrifies him. 'Where's the back-up?'

DS Silky doesn't hesitate, grabbing him by the arm and pulling him out through the doors. 'Don't be ridiculous, we're in an apocalypse, there's rioting everywhere – there is no back-up.'

As they drive past the front of the restaurant they see The Chocolate Poisoner walking in through the door.

A minute later DS Silky and an anxious, sweating, DI Gloom rush in through the kitchen door.

'Good evening, Detectives,' Furness greets them as he and Afia busily plate up orders. 'This is Katla – she'll look after you.'

The two detectives and the waitress look through the kitchen door into the restaurant.

'That's him just being seated at the fourth table along the window,' says DS Silky.

'We can't observe him properly from here, we need to be in the room with him,' points out DI Gloom, his stomach rumbling.

'I'll take you to a table,' offers Katla.

'Sit us so we're not in his line of sight but so we can still see his hands,' instructs DS Silky, adding, 'treat him as a normal customer. If you see him injecting a chocolate or doing any sleight of hand let us know.'

When Damon distracts The Chocolate Poisoner by taking his order Katla shows the detectives to a just-vacated table.

Taking her seat DS Silky studies the man's face of old, pale skin hanging on square features decorated with a charming thin-lipped smile and bright teasing light-blue eyes – he could be described as mischievous, a comedic rake. But he's not either of these – he is a killer.

The main courses and the desserts come and go. The

Chocolate Poisoner orders the Venison in a Seductive Blackcurrant & Chocolate Sauce with Parsnip Mash and for dessert the Apple and Blackberry Crumble with White Chocolate Custard. DS Silky has the Fish Pie and for dessert two scoops of Sheep's Milk Ice Cream – Raspberry and 80% Cocoa Chocolate. DI Gloom has the Duck in Plum and Chocolate Sauce and for dessert the Cherry and Honey Crumble with White Chocolate Custard. Every mouthful of their dinner is like eating food for the first time – the flavours delightfully waltzing around their palates.

Now, The Chocolate Poisoner and the detectives are served coffee and 60% Criollo Cocoa Wild Elderberry and Port Liqueur chocolates.

Coffee and chocolates consumed The Chocolate Poisoner compliments the chef, pays his bill and leaves a large tip.

'Did you see him do anything?' enquires a puzzled DI Gloom.

DS Silky shakes her head. 'Nothing. Just him enjoying his food as much as we did. I'll follow him.'

Along the street he is twenty strides ahead of her, crossing the road into an alley. On entering the alley something is wrong – time feels like it is slipping away from her and comprehension of the scene is difficult. There is the sound of his footsteps and an elongated shadow of The Chocolate Poisoner on the buildings.

DS Silky steps out of the other end of the alley and finds herself pushed up against the wall – his hands on either side of her face as he looks into her eyes. Strangely she offers little resistance, merely gripping his arms in an attempt to hold him there and to steady herself. She is watching him speak, detached from herself, an observer of his lips moving.

'Yes. Wonderful chocolates,' says The Chocolate Poisoner – his voice gently oozing curiosity.

DS Silky pulls herself back into the moment. 'What?'

The Chocolate Poisoner speaks again. 'Detective, one of the liqueur chocolates you ate contained 4mg of TCP.'

'Oh no!' is her simple expression of realisation at his sleight of hand. How could she have been so careless?

DS Silky's mind rewinds back to the restaurant. Watching The Chocolate Poisoner at his table. She slows down the footage in her mind's eye searching for the moment he laced one of the chocolates on his plate. Was that it? When he picked up his coffee with his right hand and took a sip of it? Yes. His left hand, syringe palmed within it, reaches out to his plate of chocolates. That's when he delivered a quick injection of TCP.

And the swapping of the TCP-laced chocolate liqueur?

Katla stops alongside his table, distracted by a diner requesting their bill. Then another diner in between them stands up from her table, taking The Chocolate Poisoner out of DS Silky's line of sight for what seemed only a few seconds but giving him just enough time to pick up and palm a chocolate off the tray Katla is carrying as he drops the poisoned chocolate in its place. The waitress then walks over to her table and serves the detectives their coffee and chocolates.

'Just enough to get you to see the world you hide from yourself.' He smiles – the sycophantic reassurance of evil. DS Silky drifts again. 'Oh – yes. What beautiful blue eyes. What will you see?' He kisses her on her forehead as a father would a child at bedtime. 'Sweet dreams, Detective Sergeant Silky.'

He runs.

She pulls herself back to this reality once again and gives chase. She runs through the ever-shifting people – so many people in her way. The drug clawing at her trying to take full effect. Across roads through the cacophony of traffic. Swept along by the current in the coursing veins of light running through the city. Completely disassociated from the structures around her she is floating, heart rate up, blood pressure high, breathing laboured, her chest tightens and aches.

She finds herself in Piccadilly Circus. People become grotesques – talking and laughing loudly, too close to her face.

His voice is in her head. How?

He steps from behind her. 'Look at it. Can you see the beauty of it? The Chocolate Apocalypse – it's wonderful.'

DS Silky looks around her – kaleidoscope skyscrapers spiral up into the shooting stars, flaming buildings are laughing and dancing along the street, people scream in joy and terror as they are confronted by humanity's freak show of violence.

DS Silky searches for words but they are too elusive.

'You know I only exist because they do,' he tells her.

She tries to reach him but he repeatedly loses corporeal form.

'This is what he wants. Concentrate. Don't give him what he wants. Don't let him get away,' she tells herself, desperate to hold on to reality. 'Where is he?'

She clears her mind enough to see his silhouette head down into the Underground station. Goes to follow him but hands grab at her – a couple of primitive clowns – a man and a woman trying to rob her of money and clothes.

'Hit her – I want that jacket,' shouts the woman.

The man steps in front of her, his fist clenched ready to punch her in the face. The woman is behind her trying to pull off her jacket. DS Silky ducks and the man punches his girlfriend hard on the chin sending her onto her back.

Stunned at what he has done the man stares bewilderedly at the detective. DS Silky watches her fist, in slow motion, go through the man's face and punch out the back of his skull.

Both clowns are left crying in ridiculed pain as DS Silky continues her pursuit of The Chocolate Poisoner.

She jumps onto a train just as the doors close. The carriage is sparsely populated – fear of the streets leads to fear of the confinement of the Underground and the claustrophobia of train carriages. Nowhere is safe now. Time stretches to snapping point as she travels at the speed of light. All existence converges into one point of stillness. How long can she hold on to a sense of herself? The doors connecting the carriages are locked. An empty carriage between them. She watches him watching her. The train comes to a sudden halt and the detective stumbles onto the platform and sees her quarry head to the escalators. Is she running? She doesn't know. Nothing is real anymore. Nothing has surface tension. She is a ghost. Gliding upwards with the metal steps she reaches the top of the escalator where The Chocolate Poisoner is waiting for her.

'It's true – everyone kills someone,' he tells her. And his long arm reaches out a thin-skinned skeletal hand and a long bony finger pokes her in the chest and she falls backwards down the escalator. The Chocolate Poisoner's cruel cackle echoing around her as he walks away into the night.

And she falls.

She tumbles head over heels. Her head connects repeatedly with the biting edges of the steps, her legs twisted beneath her, she bounces off the metal side panels, tumbling over and over, she reaches out with her hands – fingers desperate to grip. But there is nothing to hold on to. There is no way to save herself. DS Silky falls for an eternity, becoming part of the screaming machine.

Afraid.

And she falls.

Alone.

And she falls.

Slipping out of time.

Until.

There is nowhere left to fall.

Her crumpled lifeless body ascends with the escalator.

Everything is red.

She can't breathe.

It's cold. Bloody hell – it's cold!

With the first cut comes her silent scream. She feels every incision of the autopsy of her cadaver. The cutting of skin and muscle, the slicing of nerves, the sawing of her rib cage, the pathologist's fingers lifting out her organs. Is it really possible to scream so loudly and not be heard?

Floating.

Weightless.

She is one of a series of forensic specimens preserved in jars of formaldehyde. In the other jars are all her past lovers and friends. 'Everyone kills someone.'

There is a flash of light along with the click of a camera shutter and she is a photograph being put into The Chocolate Poisoner case file – his latest victim.

The last thing she sees is the grieving face of DI Gloom as the case file is closed on her.

And she is in darkness – forever in solitude.

The in-flight Global Cocoa drones pick up the truck as it leaves the plantation and follow its progress along the narrow overgrown forest tracks. The truck struggles at a slow pace through the thick undergrowth. The track ahead is blocked by a fallen tree and the wheel of the truck gets stuck in a rut cut by the mountain rains as it is forced to stop. The men leap out and frantically cut away the tree's branches then push the truck free to the buzzing sound of the hovering drones and the growing ever-louder engines of the four-wheel-drive vehicles of the approaching Global Cocoa militia. Staying just ahead of their pursuers the plantation truck arrives at the cove in time to catch the tide.

Global Cocoa's militia spill out of the forest, guns aimed. Pulling back the tarpaulin to reveal the cocoa they've come to steal all they find are crates of rum and a sound system.

The driver of the truck leans out of his window. 'We're just here to party, man.'

Other vehicles filled with more partygoers arrive at the cove and the militia retreat back into the forest.

Once the decoy truck is out of sight and picked up by the drones, Ekow, with two of his men sitting alongside him, drives a Global Cocoa–branded black van, acquired through devious use of alcohol and loquacious distraction in the form of a find-the-cocoa-nib-under-the-cups wager down at the docks the previous evening, out of the plantation and heads along the main roads across the island to the airport. Where the security guards, seeing the Global Cocoa logo on the side of the van, wave Ekow through without considering to impede his progress. And he drives up to the private jet called *The Cocoa St Lucia*.

He gets out of the van and walks over to the pilot. 'Captain Martin, I presume?'

'At your service.' The tall, uniformed gentleman smiles.

'How will you fly?' asks Ekow.

'Upon chocolate winds,' the pilot answers correctly.

'That's good to hear.' The plantation owner grins.

Ekow opens the van and within no time at all the twenty-one sacks of cocoa are loaded onto the jet and Captain Martin has taken off into the night sky.

As he watches the plane fly away Ekow phones Dunstan who is sitting in the kitchen, at home with the rest of The Chocolate Thieves, awaiting his call. 'The cocoa is on its way to you.'

'You're a beautiful man,' Dunstan tells him.

'This is what I tell my wife every day.' Ekow laughs. 'Enjoy your chocolate, my friends.'

The Chocolate Thieves arrive at London City Airport to collect their cocoa in an unmarked black van acquired for them by Stanley Oak the previous evening through clandestine extraction.

Captain Martin is waiting for them with the plane in a hangar.

Dunstan walks up to the pilot. 'How did you fly?'

'Freely upon the chocolate wind.' The pilot smiles and Dunstan shakes his hand. 'Mind you, I landed on fumes – maximum distance possible on the tanks.'

Savage, Furness and Dunstan load the sacks of cocoa into the van – leaving one on the plane. 'Payment in cocoa,' Dunstan tells the pilot.

'Perfect,' Captain Martin replies. 'That's the pension sorted. There's a client list I fly around the world that will pay a fortune for a sack of chocolate gold.'

'Good luck and thank you,' says Dunstan just as two police vehicles, a patrol car and a van, screech into the hangar – six officers jump out of them and surround The Chocolate Thieves.

'Nobody move,' commands DI Gloom through the patrol car's public address system.

They don't.

So he decides it's safe to get out of the vehicle. One of the officers has drawn his firearm.

'What are you doing with that?' DI Gloom snaps at him. 'They're cocoa smugglers not armed robbers. This is England, we cosh them – not shoot them.'

The gun is put away.

The tip-off had come via a phone call an hour earlier. Waking DI Gloom who'd been safely and comfortably asleep in his office. The morning light yet to creep through the gaps in the blinds, the last thing he needed to see, on reluctantly opening his eyes, was the name Midas written across the screen of his phone. Followed, on answering, by hearing the arrogant tones of the man's voice.

'Get yourself and as many officers as you can to London City Airport and take ownership of a cargo of St Lucian cocoa,' demanded the chocolatier, adding, 'The plane will land in the next hour – this is your opportunity to arrest The Chocolate Thieves.'

DI Gloom inspects the sacks in the van. 'I've been informed that this cocoa, along with the plane, was stolen and flown directly here from St Lucia.'

Captain Martin steps forwards. 'With respect, sir, that's incorrect. The cocoa is not stolen. This is a routine privately chartered cargo flight authorised by our CEO Mr Whittaker.'

DI Gloom frowns. 'Paperwork?'

'In the cockpit.'

DI Gloom nods and Captain Martin retrieves the relevant flight and import paperwork.

'I think you'll find everything is in order, sir,' the pilot says as he hands the documents to DI Gloom with a raised eyebrow and half-smile to Dunstan.

'Yes, well, yes, these papers do appear to be in order,' the Detective Inspector stumbles, puzzled as to what to do next. He looks at The Chocolate Thieves. 'Then why are these men in balaclavas and gloves?'

'Well, I think you'll agree, there's a nip to the air this early in the morning,' offers the pilot.

'Yes – I suppose there is,' agrees DI Gloom. 'And the unmarked black van – where's the company logo?'

'Do you really expect us to drive through The Chocolate Apocalypse advertising the fact that we have cocoa in the back of the van?' asks Savage in his best incredulous tone.

'No – of course not,' replies the abashed DI Gloom. He mutters to himself, 'This is not going well.'

And it does not get any better for the Detective Inspector as a black Range Rover screeches into the hangar. Out of it get a gang of four black-boiler-suited balaclava-wearing individuals brandishing high-pressured paintball guns.

'Everybody on the floor – now!' comes the order from the gang leader. When the police officers fail to do this all six of them are laid flat with accurately fired blue paint balls.

Everyone still standing lies down.

The in-agony paint-splattered officer next to DI Gloom glares at his senior officer. 'Would you like me to cosh him, sir?'

'We are Chocolate For The People and we claim this cocoa for the people,' the gang leader informs them.

One member of the gang sprays the slogan *CHOCOLATE FOR THE PEOPLE* over the conglomerate's logo on the side of the plane and the police vehicles in chocolate-coloured paint. The patrol car parked in front of the van of cocoa is pushed out of the way before the tyres of both police vehicles are slashed. Two of the gang steal the van full of cocoa while the other two make their escape in the vehicle in which they arrived.

'Get that fucking cocoa back!' screams DI Gloom giving chase on foot out of the hangar, reluctantly followed by his stumbling injured officers.

'Well done, DI Gloom.' Dunstan sighs.

'He really is a bloody fine police officer,' adds Furness.

'A credit to the force.' Savage takes out his phone. 'We need a taxi please.'

The reporter is standing in the smoking ashes of a cocoa plantation in Peru. 'In an attempt to take back control of the last of their South American cocoa plantations from the drug cartels, Global Cocoa's privately deployed militia have simultaneously stormed their plantations in Peru, Ecuador, Brazil and Venezuela – only for all the plantations to be destroyed by fire having been deliberately or accidentally set alight. Neither side will take responsibility for the catastrophe, with a Global Cocoa spokesperson admitting that, "This is truly a disaster for the world's cocoa production. But, well, we could not have the last of the world's supply of chocolate controlled by organised crime." Which most people will think applies to Global Cocoa themselves. It seems that whichever side set the plantations alight it was a deliberate act to stop the other side having control of the most valuable crop in the world – a "well if we can't have it, neither can you" attitude.'

It's lunchtime in Delilah's and Midas and Whittaker are sitting in irritated silence.

But Whittaker cannot keep quiet for long. 'Just so I'm clear, for when I write my memoirs and I'm recounting my experiences of The Chocolate Apocalypse, just to get this absolutely clear in my mind. The fucking Chocolate Thieves secretly invested in a lost cocoa plantation hidden in a forest on St fucking Lucia which successfully cultivated over a tonne of very fucking rare organic Criollo cocoa with a chocolate market value of £100,000,000, which they have now harvested, not put on a truck that decoyed the Global Cocoa militia away to a fucking beach party under the pretence that this is where they were, according to your intelligence, smuggling it off the fucking island on a ship, away from the actual cocoa which was driven to the airport in a stolen van with our logo on the fucking side of it, put on *The Cocoa St Lucia* which you neglected to check with me wasn't the name of a fucking ship but the name of a Global Cocoa–owned private fucking jet, had the cocoa flown to London at our fucking expense which was then stolen out of the hands of both The Chocolate Thieves and your unleashed gloomy detective inspector by those anarchist fuckers Chocolate For The People.'

'Yes,' agrees Midas, 'that very eloquently sums up the chain of events.'

'Good – I just wanted to be sure you know I understand what a cocoaing fuck-up you've made of making me richer than I already am.'

A member of staff arrives at their table with a letter for Midas – in the envelope with the letter is a sample of cocoa.

It's a simple scenario. The St Lucia cocoa you desire is yours for £25,000,000 – Stanley Oak at The Sleight Of Hand is our intermediary. CFTP.

'Ah.' Midas passes the letter to Whittaker and inhales the scent of the cocoa.

'£25,000,000!' exhales Whittaker.

'As you just pointed out it's worth four times the investment. It seems some of our Chocolate For The People revolutionaries are true capitalists at heart after all

– it must have been your words of wisdom on television.'

Whittaker looks around him at the chocolate house in all its fading decadent glory, in two minds as to what to do. He could easily retire from this life, he tells himself. Spend his days hunting and fishing. He doesn't need the money, doesn't need any more houses, ex-wives or children. But…

'We don't have to use our own money,' Midas assures his friend. 'I have an elite client list. You know that – you're one of them.'

Whittaker watches a man of similar age and neglected physique to himself pop a gold-flaked truffle into the mouth of a woman half his age and avarice wins out. 'Whose money did you have in mind?'

Midas smiles that Midas smile and sniffs the cocoa again. 'The scent of the divine.'

DS Silky opens her eyes. A tear roles down her cheek that she quickly wipes away. She is lying in a hospital bed, attached to a vital signs monitor, and she has a saline drip in her arm. She is alone in the room. Flowers and a card from DI Gloom and colleagues are on the bedside cabinet. She checks her body for injuries – she has all the expected cuts and bruises. It is when she reaches forwards for her chart she yells out in pain – clearly she has bruised every rib. She reads her chart. Generally she is in a stable condition with a concussion – which explains the pounding headache and wooziness. Or is the drug still in her system? Maybe – but most likely it has been flushed out. Depends. What's the date? The chart tells her she's been unconscious for two days. How the hell is nothing broken? She unplugs herself from the monitor and pulls out the saline drip. And with impressive determination, accompanied with another cry out of pain, the detective gets out of bed, walks with more pain to the window and looks out across the city – The Chocolate Apocalypse is still on the wind. Which means she still has a poisoner to catch.

An hour later DS Silky walks into DI Gloom's office without knocking, startling her detective inspector out of his melancholy by her sudden arrival. 'Bloody hell, they said you'd be out for a week.' He gets up to help her into the chair opposite him. 'How the hell you didn't break your neck…'

'Strong bones.'

'Have you seen the footage of your fall? It's all over the internet.'

'I lived it – I don't need to see it.' DS Silky smiles a painful smile at him and carefully takes the offered seat.

From a jug on a side table DI Gloom pours and hands his, thankfully still breathing, detective a glass of water.

She uses it to take some painkillers. 'You're worried.'

'I am,' he replies, retaking his usual sedentary position. 'Have you looked into a reflective surface today?'

DS Silky spots The Chocolate Poisoner file on DI Gloom's desk and painfully reaches for it. She is the latest entry. DS Silky holds out her hand and the Detective Inspector hands her his pen. She writes *Alive* at the bottom of the report.

'No. It's something else. I can see it in your eyes. And you're definitely trembly. What have you done?'

Her DI hesitates but he needs his best detective's help. 'I've gotten involved with Midas.'

'How?'

'He promised me some chocolates along with the handing-over of a short film.'

'A short film depicting what?'

'There was a party at Delilah's a year ago – I met a very

197

seductive Latvian young lady with the most exquisite truffles…'

'You fucking idiot.'

Russian oligarch Andrei Egorov is sampling chocolates in Midas's office. He is not a healthy man. He is forty-nine years old and a sweating twenty-six stone. In fact any shift upwards in blood pressure could be the end of him according to every cardiologist he's paid for an opinion to ignore. Never missing an opportunity to quote them, he says, '"Get healthy, Mr Egorov", "Change your diet, Mr Egorov", "Your days are numbered, Andrei Egorov". They've been telling me this for years – and it's still beating.' He laughs as he pounds his chest with his fist.

Such is his defiance of death it is thought that he actually never uses his heart – he is, after all, a man who lacks any empathy for the suffering of others. It is what made him an expert SFB interrogator and latterly businessman trading in 'Capitalism's dark secrets – our last taboos', as he says at any inquisition of his activities as he taps a fat forefinger against his snout.

Today he is doing one of his favourite things – showing off. 'Ecuadorian – Nacional cocoa with ginger and an exquisite marmalade liquor.'

'That is one incredible chocolate palate you have, Andrei,' compliments Midas, needlessly.

'Wealth has indulged it.'

Egorov samples another chocolate. 'Sri Lankan – a wild Criollo with a brutal chase of Pays d'Auge Calvados.'

'Marvellous. You know you are the last person in the world to taste these cocoas.'

'It is a pity it is to end.'

'But not just yet.'

'No. Indeed not. £25,000,000 of cocoa into

£100,000,000 of chocolate. Okay, alchemist, I'm in. I'll transfer the money now.'

Midas smiles that Midas smile.

Having used his phone to transfer the £25,000,000 from one of his untraceable offshore accounts into an untraceable offshore account used for Global Cocoa's illicit deals, Egorov throws another chocolate into his mouth, sucks the flavours out of it – a Black Russian cocktail in a casing of 60% Columbian Criollo cocoa – swallows, inhales sharply, pulls an expression of surprise as he realises this is to be his last-ever breath, exhales with a grunt and drops dead face down onto the desk.

DS Silky walks into the boutique through the side door to find Midas, who, with great effort, has dragged Egorov into the kitchen, with a cleaver in one hand, the dead man's arm in the other.

There's a shared expression of surprise that he'd left the door unlocked while attempting to butcher a corpse, before the detective speaks. 'This doesn't look good, Midas.'

Midas continues to look at her – now with fascination. 'I'd heard you were dead – look at the state of you. Did they perform an autopsy on you while you were still alive?'

'Is that Andrei Egorov? Political blackmailer, money launderer, black market arms dealer, sanction-breaking oil trader, sex-slave-trafficker, chocolate connoisseur…'

'The very man.'

'You should cut out his tongue and have it embalmed.'

'Andrei was a friend and one of my most appreciative clients. You were supposed to catch the bloody Chocolate Poisoner. Now look at what he's done.'

'What was your plan – conch him into a chocolate and gold-flaked oligarch caviar and champagne truffle?'

'I can't have people dying here – it's bad for business.'

'That man dying here is bad for your life. Where's his security?'

'He cared not for lackeys.'

'And what business? There's no chocolate left.'

'There will always be cocoa to be found, however rare, and chocolate to be made and sold.'

'No, Midas, your time really is coming to an end.' They look at each other in an impasse, then with a sigh the detective says, 'Hand over your film of DI Gloom's Latvian adventure and I'll call in the cleaners. No one will know Andrei Egorov died here.'

Midas considers this for a fraction of a second. 'Deal,' he says, dropping the Russian's arm that he is still holding back down beside the corpulent corpse.

An hour later Andrei Egorov has been loaded into a mortuary van, all forensic evidence of the Russian dying at the boutique has been cleaned away and DS Silky has retrieved all evidence of DI Gloom's indiscretion from the chocolatier.

'You know there's a fate ahead of you way worse than you can imagine,' the detective tells Midas with an unnerving smile as she walks out of the boutique.

There is silence in every home for the solemn, trembling-voiced announcement by the journalist on The Chocolate Apocalypse news-stream. 'The last of the world's commercially viable cocoa plantations in the Caribbean have been destroyed in a tropical storm.'

This news is backed up by images of the wild 180-mile-an-hour winds of storm Cortes reaping total environmental devastation across the Caribbean. The islands being blown clean of people's homes, cars tumbling along roads, the yachts in the marinas stacked on the quays, and out to sea boats are skimmed across the waves like pebbles on a pond. The most heartbreaking sight for the watching chocolate addicts is seeing the cocoa trees in the plantations ripped out of the ground and scattered like twigs.

The journalist adds, 'With all the world's plantations destroyed, Global Cocoa has stockpiled the last supplies of cocoa in its warehouses around the globe and is selling to the highest bidders on that continent – the world's richest of the rich will be the last people to taste chocolate.'

DS Silky takes the call from Scarlett Vamp.

'Delilah's End Of Chocolate Party is happening on Friday – everyone will be there,' the chocolatier tells her with revengeful relish.

Two days.

'It takes years of practice, patience and skill,' Oak informs the detective having guided her into the Rogues Gallery at The Sleight Of Hand for their discreet conversation.

'I only need to pick his pocket once.'

'Okay. What's he going to be wearing to this party?'

'You know about it?'

'Of course I know about it – I've been invited.'

'Who are you going with?'

'You of course.'

'Are you?'

'How else are you going to get in without an invitation?'

'Good thinking. What are you going to wear?'

'Concentrate.'

DS Silky takes a moment to picture The Chocolate Poisoner at a party. 'He'll celebrate his youth – he'll be dressed in a blue velvet frock coat, paisley shirt, pinstripe waist coat and trousers, navy cravat and black boots.'

'Wait here.'

Oak returns a few minutes later wearing a black velvet frock coat. And says in response to the detective's querying look, 'It was my father's.'

'Cool.' DS Silky hands him a small syringe. 'He's left handed.'

Oak puts the syringe into the outside left-hand pocket of the coat and turns away from her. 'Now – pick my pocket.' The moment her fingers touch the lip of the pocket he grabs her wrist. 'Don't hesitate. Take what you want as if you already own it.'

She tries again with the same result. And again, and again. Repeatedly she gets her fingers no further than the lip of the pocket. 'This isn't working – you're expecting me to pick your pocket.'

'So is he,' Oak growls at her, his eyes fiercely alive. 'He's been expecting you for over fifty years. That's how he nearly killed you.' DS Silky feels strangely vulnerable. 'Good,' says Oak, seeing the fear in her eyes flick to defiance. 'Why isn't this working? What are you not doing?'

'Owning what you own.'

'And?'

'Controlling the scene,' she realises.

Oak smiles. 'Distraction is key to successfully pickpocketing anyone. Either you draw their attention away from their possessions – a pull on the elbow to get past them in a busy street and your hand goes into their pocket. Or if face to face walk directly at them so you both turn sideways to pass each other and your hand goes in their pocket. Or you lift when they have distracted themselves in conversation or browsing in a bookshop or like you when you walked in here today. You were looking for me to get you to some future place in time. Look in your wallet.'

DS Silky takes out her wallet from the same right-hand pocket of her trousers she always puts it in and finds it empty of money and all cards.

Oak pulls the contents of her wallet out of her left inside jacket pocket and hands them back to her. 'You're alert, despite the bang on the head, intelligent and streetwise – yet you were still too focused on what you were looking for, not in the moment of what was actually happening. I used your dedication to catching your quarry to my advantage. If you want to stop this man you have to exist in the time and place where he exists.'

'Context. His last situation. He'll be celebrating The Chocolate Apocalypse. Distracted by success he'll embrace the dark romance of the dystopia. That's where I will need to be to catch him.'

'Good. But how are you going to get to that point in time? Hand me your ID.' DS Silky reluctantly hands it over. 'You've two days to get this back off me so you can arrest The Chocolate Poisoner.'

After days of trying and anxious waiting, Ekow is on the line from St Lucia. The Chocolate Thieves gather round the phone. Afia watching keenly at Dunstan's shoulder to see how her cousin is faring.

Ekow is standing in the midst of his destroyed home and plantation – his family and friends around him sorting through the destruction. 'Dunstan, Afia – we're alive. All of us. We've been in the storm shelter for days.'

'Thank fuck for that,' express The Chocolate Thieves.

'But the plantation is devastated.' Ekow pans the phone round to show them the level of destruction. 'The storm took the house and the distillery. The whole island is destroyed.'

'So sorry to hear that,' says Afia.

'And all your cocoa trees are gone,' Ekow tells them.

'That is a concern for another time,' replies Dunstan.

'How can we help you?' Afia asks her cousin.

'We're going to be okay,' Ekow manages a teared smile, 'we're going to rebuild our lives…'

The line cuts out.

Dunstan calls again but there is no longer a signal through to the Caribbean.

Outside the open doors of an empty Global Cocoa warehouse at the Port of Tilbury in London the journalist, with inappropriate glee, delivers her latest report on The Chocolate Apocalypse. 'In a simultaneous act of political defiance and self-serving cultural addiction, across the world, every Global Cocoa warehouse has been looted. All the commercial stockpiles of cocoa across the world are now in the hands of black marketeers and chocolate addicts. The company's share price has collapsed and Global Cocoa has ceased all commercial trading.'

In the lock-up at The Sleight Of Hand, Midas and Whittaker check the quality of the sacks of St Lucian Criollo cocoa under the watchful eye of Stanley Oak.

Midas scoops up the mahogany-coloured beans in his hands and rubs them gently together. 'Such a seductive aroma – quite wonderful.' He tastes one of the beans, bitter as they still are, the desired organic chocolate flavours enthuse the palate. 'Truly unique.'

Whittaker checks that each sack is full of cocoa beans.

Satisfied at the authenticity of the merchandise the two men follow Stanley Oak into the Rogues Gallery.

Sitting across the table from Midas and Whittaker, who are now unable to hide how desperate they are to secure their future wealth by doing this deal, are three black-boiler-suited, balaclava-and-glove-wearing, cool-to-freezing-point members of Chocolate For The People.

All smarm, Whittaker leans forwards and tests the mood of the room. 'You could cut a deal where we share the profits of the chocolate we make.'

The CFTP member sitting in the centre of the three leans forwards to meet the gaze of the CEO of Global Cocoa. 'You're asking me to trust you? You're the fat, arrogant boor from the TV debate – you should be hanging naked in a butcher's shop.'

'Transfer the money into this account,' the CFTP member to the left slides a piece of paper with bank account details written on it across the table to Whittaker, 'and the van with the cocoa in it is yours to drive away.'

Neither Whittaker nor Midas reach for the piece of paper.

The third member of CFTP, to the right, joins the conversation. 'Do you know the history of The Sleight Of Hand? The people who have walked through its door in the last three centuries – real people, true of character, dangerous people. It's very brave of the likes of you to walk in here. Or is it the arrogance of cowards who believe they can buy their way out of any life-ending situation?'

The centre member of CFTP takes up the thread. 'Stanley makes a mean meat pie. Don't you Stanley?' Oak smiles. 'Two juicy capitalist swine like you would chop up nicely and cook well-seasoned and encased in his divine hot-water crust pastry – *Cocoa Capitalist Pig Pie* he'll write on the menu.'

Whittaker is completely unnerved by the intimidation coming from beneath the balaclavas and the sudden isolation of his surroundings. All authority gone, he sweats and looks at Midas to hurry him along so they can escape the anarchy into which they've walked.

But Midas wants to play a little longer. 'You will double your money.'

'We know how much we want,' says the second CFTP member, '£25,000,000.'

'I think £15,000,000 will be enough,' patronises Midas.

This suggestion is met with silence.

'How about £18,000,000?' offers Whittaker.

Silence.

'£20,000,000 – final offer,' says Midas with surly arrogance.

The three CFTP members stand up and move as one to leave the meeting.

'£22,500,000?' Whittaker looks at Midas, desperate for his help to conclude the deal.

Midas watches them reach the door – they really are going to leave the room. 'Wait!' he shouts. He can't lose out on this deal. 'Okay – we'll pay you £25,000,000.'

The three CFTP members return to their seats at the table – staring into the fear-filled eyes of their quarry.

Whittaker transfers the money via the banking app on his phone. The CFTP member to the left checks receipt of it into their account on their phone and nods to say that it is there.

'The cocoa is yours.' The centre CFTP member nods to Oak who hands Midas the keys to the van.

Without hesitation, tripping over each other, escorted by Stanley Oak, the two greedily grinning men hurriedly leave The Sleight Of Hand.

Into the Rogues Gallery walk Savage, Furness and Dunstan and sit down at the Chocolate For The People table where Dorothea, Afia and Kyoko pull off their balaclavas to reveal the broadest of smiles across their faces.

The Chocolate Thieves immediately distribute their profits from the Midas-Whittaker con between the different NGOs working in devastated cocoa regions across the globe.

Delilah's delightfully decadent chocolate proposition had been The End Of Chocolate Party. With the twelfth chime of the Cocoa Clock at midnight marking the official end of the world's chocolate. History will record the last chocolate to be eaten was at Delilah's Chocolate House – a place synonymous with the greatest of cocoa-enriched lives – an icon of the decadence of capitalist wealth and human endeavour in self-gratification.

The theme of the party is every era of Delilah's – suits and dresses to be worn as costumes for seduction, masks for the perceived illusion of secrecy.

DS Silky arrives at Delilah's looking disarmingly beautiful in a contemporary cut sapphire silk dress – face adorned with a mask of black crow feathers tipped with sapphire and silver.

Over the last two days the detective has been introduced to the art of the one-handed palming, vanishing, injecting and swapping of chocolates while constantly trying to retrieve her ID.

The friendlier rogues at The Sleight Of Hand, though still wary of the detective, knowing what she is trying to achieve with her newly learned skills, advise and offer encouragement.

But time after time she fails to retrieve her ID.

She has worked out that he feels the weight of her hand on the coat, sees her reflection in the glass of picture frames, in glasses on tables and in hands, and in bottles of beer and wine. He also seems to possess an uncanny ability to sense her presence through the change in the light and the air around him as she moves towards him. Every time, his strong hands grip her wrist as soon as her fingers touch the pocket with her ID in it. Then he infuriatingly smiles sweetly as if to a playful child, shakes his head and walks away.

Stanley Oak is dressed immaculately in tailored black tie evening wear and a long-eared owl mask. 'You are stunning – the tantalising undercover detective.'

'Thank you. And look at you – the sophisticated rogue.' The detective triumphantly holds up her ID.

Forty-eight hours after her first attempt she finally retrieves, with expertly dipped fingers, her ID out of Oak's jacket pocket – his attraction towards her distracting him into letting his guard down.

'Very good.' Oak smiles, impressed by her opportunism. 'You are a quick learner. Now – where are you going to keep it?'

It's true she has no bag and nowhere on her person in this dress to secure her ID. 'Damn it.' She hands it back to him and he returns it to the jacket pocket from whence it came.

On entering the party they are each served a Delilah Cocktail from a silver tray by a Cocoa Nymph – it is a delicious mix of cocoa rum, milk and vodka in iced flute glasses.

Exploring the party they discover the bar, lounge, library and dining room are a bacchanalian orgy of chocolate. There are silver ladles and cups from which to indulge in the exotic provenance of the last of the world's chocolate flowing out of the chocolate fountain. In the bar the Cocoa Clock ticks down to the end of its time. In the dining room the tables and chairs have been pulled aside to make room for dancing – 'Gimme Shelter' is being played to its full dystopian potential by the darkly comical apocalyptic cabaret band.

Standing in the eye of the storm of The Chocolate Apocalypse, DS Silky feels the most unimpressed she has ever felt. 'Why is everyone involved in chocolate so fucking eccentric?'

'How can you be serious when your whole life is dedicated to getting high on cocoa?' replies Oak.

DS Silky catches a glimpse of her quarry in the shifting, flailing forms of the dancers. Where has he gone? That was him – she's sure of it. And suddenly there he is – The Chocolate Poisoner. He is dancing in the centre of the floor, surrounded by the self-obsessed writhing bodies of the beautiful, the sexy, the rich and the for-sale. His unmistakable wiry frame twisting in time to the music. She was correct in every detail of his costume, even when informed it was a masked affair, with the addition of a plague doctor's beaked mask – a parody of sophistication, a simulacra of a truth.

DS Silky joins the dancers, gradually moving across the room, lifting a Delilah's Last Dance 70% cocoa English Red Rose Champagne Truffle off a silver tray on her way. She is now dancing behind The Chocolate Poisoner. The man is swinging with the music – his coat pocket moving away from and back towards his hip. She moves her body in rhythm with his movements, anticipates the swing of his coat as it moves away from him again, takes a confident step forwards; now alongside him she reaches out with her right hand, pushes it down into the pocket and retrieves the syringe in a swift, decisive movement.

She moves around him, catching his eye as she passes in front of him – she remains enigmatic. The syringe has 10mg of TCP in it, she'd expected more – he may have laced a few chocolates already. With sleight of hand she injects the chocolate in her hand with all of the remaining

TCP.

She dances mask to mask with The Chocolate Poisoner, her hands cutting through the air, hips gyrating, the poisoned chocolate now palmed in her left hand. He watches the temptress performing for him. She reveals the chocolate between her fingers. His eyes fill with craving. Palming the chocolate she crosses and uncrosses her hands in time with the music; hands behind her, she swaps the chocolate palm to palm. Moving around him again – using his lustful curiosity to draw him in closer to her.

Facing him again, DS Silky holds out her crossed hands. He looks into her expectant eyes, taking what he thinks is a seductive moment to choose which hand holds the chocolate. He slowly reaches out the long bony fingers of his left hand and taps the top of her right hand.

DS Silky slowly opens it to reveal the chocolate.

Closing her hand before he can take it, she steps forwards and whispers in his ear, 'I know how to get into The Black Room.'

He looks at her in disbelief.

Stepping back, away from him, she lets the dancers envelope her.

The Black Room – a place of sensory deprivation.

Legend has it that it is the only place on earth where your perception is concentrated so intensely to your sense of smell and taste that you truly experience, in whatever chocolate you eat, the taste of the Origin Chocolate – the fruit of the first cocoa tree – the purest of Criollo that is still the root flavour in all descendent chocolate.

Only the highest in Delilah's hierarchy – those who have proven their skill at cocoa deals and amassing vast cocoa wealths – those that have truly subjugated themselves to the will of the cocoa gods – are invited to enter this room of pure sensual delight and truly taste chocolate.

The Chocolate Poisoner follows her through the revellers, up the wide, elegant stairs, along the landings, past room after room, through Polaroids of history on a labyrinthine journey. The people they pass are animated ancestors of those whose portraits hang upon the walls – courtesans entice courtiers into gilded dens, poet lords pull wenches onto luxurious chaise lounges and gentlemen explorers escort coy ladies into their empires. When all eyes are looking elsewhere the temptress slips through a hidden door in the wall of floating gold flock. She has lit a candle and beckons him along the secret passage behind the rooms of solicited desires.

They ascend a secret staircase.

She flickers in and out of vision.

Where are they?

In the very heart of the building she disappears through a black door.

He reaches out his hand for the door handle, opens the door and steps willingly inside.

There are no walls to see, nor ceiling, nor floor – such is the blackness. By her single candle flame he sees she is standing beside a gold sculpture of a cocoa tree. On one of its leaves is the chocolate. He pulls off his mask – his face in a place of wonder. He picks up the Delilah's Last Dance.

And she blows out the candle.

Silence.

And darkness.

He lets his senses calm.

Slowly he puts the chocolate into his mouth. He chews, releasing the delightfully delicate flavours of the truffle. And he waits for his isolated senses to take him on a journey back through the millennia of cocoa flavours.

But before he can travel anywhere the candle flickers back to life and DS Silky pulls off her mask to reveal her identity to the apothecary.

'Detective – you're still alive.'

She does not reply.

'What a fall you took down that escalator. Over and over you went. I thought for certain you were dead. But look at you. So beautiful. Here at The End Of Chocolate Party. Tell me, what did you see?'

'A place of peace.'

'Now – why don't I believe you?'

'What you've done is cruel.'

'What I've done is art – a mirror to the damned.'

'Have you ever looked into the mirror yourself?'

'Every day.'

'And do you see the lie?'

'A lie is itself a truth.'

'Did you enjoy that chocolate you ate?'

He gives her a quizzical look.

She glances down at the empty syringe lying on the leaf where the chocolate had been.

His left hand goes to the empty pocket it should be in before he gives an ironic smile. 'Very clever, Detective.' He looks towards the door where the imposing figure of Stanley Oak blocks any thought of escape.

Once again the candle is blown out.

Her footsteps walk away.

The door opens and swooshes closed and a key is turned in the lock.

The blackness is total.

All around him The End Of Chocolate Party revels in hedonism.

But here in this room is silence.

In here is sightlessness.

In here he is out of time.

The Chocolate Thieves, having cautiously made their way through The Chocolate Apocalypse, drive CHOC 2, 3 and 4 into the mews alongside the Midas Boutique.

Using the sounds of the city in chaos as cover they forget about subtlety and use a battering ram to open the side door to make entrance into the boutique.

The cellar door has a digital key code lock. With a wry smile Furness hands Dunstan some cocoa powder that he blows onto the lock – it sticks to six of the ten keys.

'One, four, zero, two, one, nine, eight, two,' instructs Savage.

Dunstan inputs the numbers and the door unlocks.

'It's the date of his birth – obvious when seeing the numbers used,' Savage informs the 'how did you know that?' expressions on the faces of his fellow rogues.

The cellar is a treasure trove of the world's rarest Criollo cocoa's, including their yet-to-be-used sacks of St Lucian cocoa, and chocolates from London's finest chocolatiers: there are boxes of Hoddinot's, Reaper's, Lullaby's, Featherlight's, Barge's and Ealing's.

'He looted their last creations,' observes Dunstan.

'He's been acquiring the best of the best,' comments Furness.

'Knowing it was all coming to an end,' says Savage.

'So shall we take them all?' asks Afia.

'It would be wrong not to.' Dorothea grins. 'Taking into account what a complete cocoa cock he is and all that.'

'And we know he didn't acquire these to enjoy the art of these chocolate-makers – the contents of this room would create a truly Midas profit,' points out Kyoko.

The sound of the street reaches them in the cellar – Covent Garden is now a total free-for-all.

'We need to get a move on,' Dunstan tells them.

Cocoa sack after cocoa sack is passed along the line of Chocolate Thieves and loaded into each taxi followed by the boxes of the city's finest artisan chocolates.

In the bar at Delilah's the tall beauty in a mirror-sequinned mini dress and peacock-feathered mask beckons the highwayman-costumed Midas to follow her. He leaves his fellow highwayman Whittaker feeding Iced Lime Infused Gin and Tonic Chocolate Tear Drops to two giggling Trampy Fairies.

The tall beauty leads the chocolatier up to the second floor and into the room of mirrors. Once inside she locks the door behind them and, without him seeing, slips the key discreetly into her glove.

The walls, ceiling and floor are mirrored glass. The lighting a bright crystal chandelier. The furniture is a bed of white silk sheets and a white upholstered chair with a white occasional table on which is a dish of white chocolate blood-warming allspice Delilah Delights and a single flute of white chocolate champagne.

She takes a lingering sip of the champagne, watching Midas smile that Midas smile as he admires his own reflection.

She approaches him and removes his mask, slowly, deliberately stripping him of his costume.

Stepping away she takes another sip of champagne.

Hanging on the back of the chair is a whip – she picks it up and uncoils it.

Midas looks towards her, ready for sex.

The enigmatic beauty pulls off her mask – it is Scarlett Vamp.

'Oh fuck!' crawls over his lips.

Making eye contact with him, expression and voice at

its smokiest, she says, 'Oh yes – it's really me.'

Swish! Crack!

The whip lashes across his face. He falls to the floor and bleeds into his reflection.

He looks back towards her. 'You fucking…'

Swish! Crack!

'Scarlett – please. Stop!'

Midas gets up to run at her.

Swish! Crack!

His blood sprays across the mirrored walls as he spins away from her. 'Why?'

'Do you really not understand? Think harder.'

Swish! Crack!

Midas yells in anger at the pain and tries to open the door – but he cannot escape. He turns back towards her, shaking with fear. 'Wait, I know, I know. It's about the Blood Cocoa – you're here to avenge the slaves.'

Swish! Crack!

He screams louder.

'I don't have the right to do that. I know nothing of their suffering. But the chocolate gods have given me this opportunity to punish you, so, while I'm here – this is for them.'

Swish! Crack!

He screams louder still – truly terrified his life is coming to an end.

'I'm here to avenge every artisan chocolatier you've debased over the decades. I know it was you who looted them of their last-ever chocolates. And the fact that like all cowards you sent thugs to do your dirty work for you. To break into my shop to steal my life's work – my cocoa bible. And my chocolates of pure sensuality.'

Swish! Crack!

He hears his screams echo around the room – repeating

to fade.

'And simply for the pleasure of whipping you.'

Rage shimmers through him and he tries to lunge at her again – she steps back so he lands face down at her feet.

Sprawled on the floor Midas looks up at Scarlett and sees his subjugated form reflected in her dress.

Slowly he gets to his feet, determined to regain his dignity. 'I am Midas – the greatest living chocolatier. I have the right to do whatever I want, whenever I chose, with the gift the chocolate gods have given me. It is the price the world has to pay.'

Swish! Crack!

He falls back onto the bed. Impotent. Staring at himself reflected in the ceiling – every bloodied wound viciously stinging. 'This really isn't how I thought this evening would go.'

'And just in case you're wondering, I chose the mirror room to see you watch yourself bleed.'

Swish! Crack!

Across his genitals.

Scarlett takes a moment to enjoy another sip of her champagne.

She watches the limp Midas roll off the bed and slump onto the floor against the wall as if trying to disappear into his reflection. Staring at himself in the blood-sprayed mirror he quietly, pitifully repeats, 'I'm sorry, I'm sorry, I'm sorry, I'm sorry.'

Scarlett slinks towards him. 'Now – where were we? Oh – yes.'

Swish! Crack!

In a room down the hallway from Midas's whipping one of the Trampy Fairies slowly hovers a candle flame around the nipples of the naked-and-tied-to-a-vertical-rack

Whittaker – the scent of his singeing chest hair filling his nostrils as he sweats with fear.

Her companion standing beside her accesses Global Cocoa's offshore trading account via her phone. 'We're going to need your password.'

His gag is pulled from his mouth.

He shakes his head. 'Fuck you – you fucking bitches.'

He is re-gagged.

'How rude,' comments the Trampy Fairy with the phone.

The candle flame lingers so to sear the skin.

'It smells like pork crackling.' The Trampy Fairy holding the candle giggles.

The buildings all around them are now ablaze. With the sound of shattering glass the front of the Midas Boutique gives way to looters destructively searching for chocolate. The locked door between the shop and the rear of the building is being kicked in. Furness and Afia find what they can to barricade the door – up ending prep tables and building a pile of conching machines and juicers as the others keep loading the taxis. Their progress halted, the looters set the empty shop on fire. Thankfully the rioting chocolate addicts have so far neglected to enter the mews where they would find what they are looking for. The fire rapidly takes hold above Savage and Dorothea's heads as they pass the chocolates out of the cellar.

'Get out of there,' Dunstan shouts down to them.

'There's more to come,' calls back Dorothea.

Dunstan doesn't argue nor hesitate to run down the cellar steps and drag Dorothea out of the now dangerously smoke-filled on-fire cellar, passing her to Kyoko who pulls her up and out of the building, instructing her to get behind the wheel of CHOC 4. The air is now thick with acrid smoke laced with the tragic scent of melting chocolate. Savage is choking and struggling to find his way out. And Dunstan's held breath is rapidly running out as he grabs Savage by the lapels and pulls him to the cellar steps just as the fire-eaten ceiling collapses into the cellar. Furness pulls them up the steps and out of the building – throws the just-about-breathing Savage into the back of CHOC 4 then gets into the back of CHOC 3 where Afia waits in the driver's seat; Kyoko pushes the choking Dunstan into the back of CHOC 2 and takes the wheel.

The three drivers start their engines, switch on their headlights and wheelspin out of the mews into the dystopian street, scattering startled rioters. But they are soon swamped by people trying to open the doors.

A Molotov cocktail explodes on the bonnet of CHOC 2 – the flaming fuel licking up the windscreen – but Kyoko keeps her nerve and her foot firmly on the accelerator, weaving through the volley of burning missiles.

CHOC 3 is covered with bodies clawing at the vehicle like raging zombies so Afia sends the taxi into a spin – the tyres billowing smoke and screeching like a banshee – sending bodies flying across the market.

A burning wheelie bin is pushed in front of CHOC 4 and Dorothea is forced to swerve and speed away in the opposite direction to CHOC 2 and 3. A silhouetted figure descends from the sky, landing on the roof. Surfing the taxi through the streets the man cheers and whoops with maniacal glee until Dorothea connects him with a low-hanging sign of a bespoke tailor's shop.

Separated, the taxis speed through the burning streets. Their escape repeatedly diverted by the looters' desperate attempts to halt their progress and claim their cargo.

Eventually they converge, line astern, upon Shaftesbury Avenue where the theatre costume stores have been raided

– the street full of drunks performing a surrealist dance of death. On seeing the black cortège, the players remove their hats and bow their heads in remorseful pose. Travelling at a crawl through the actors the three taxis become a ghostly line of hearses in their performance.

And from the inferno's ringleader comes a eulogy. 'Out, out, brief candle! Life's but a walking shadow, a poor player that struts and frets his hour upon the stage and then is heard no more. It is a tale told by an idiot, full of sound and fury, signifying nothing.'

As one they floor their accelerators.

Swinging around the British Museum, having successfully travelled through the carnival of delights that is The Chocolate Apocalypse, they arrive safely back at The Black Truffle Hotel.

The Chocolate Poisoner stares into the void, waiting for the effects of the TCP to take hold.

But what is there in this environment to see?

To feel separated from?

Where is he physically?

There is only the self.

He feels his heart rate and breathing increase.

He is sweating nervously.

But where are the hallucinations?

He feels himself smile and hears himself give a short knowing laugh – just before the panic and the stomach-wrenching terror grips him.

He can barely breathe.

'Stay calm,' he repeats to himself. But this is the cruellest of tortures for a man of illusion.

He tries to let his imagination wander but the darkness stops him.

The silence of the situation unnerves him too.

Where is he?

Where is the party?

Where is the city?

With its glorious distractions – its scents, its colours, its sounds, its life, its joy, its cruelty, its farce – its death.

Frozen to the spot in the darkness he doesn't know who he is without the disguise of his illusion – his personal dystopia.

His performance is over.

His mask discarded.

He disintegrates in this desolate void.

Into his isolation.

He calls for help and beats his fists against the walls and the floor.

But no one hears him.

No one comes to help him.

To rescue him from himself.

Fear.

The realisation of failure.

The terror of the exposure of who he really is.

But most of all it is the truth of this dark room – a place that will, he knows, never leave his consciousness however hard he tries to transcend it.

It is a place of one reality.

A place where he cannot perform.

A place where no one can witness his art – his manifesto of the satire of reality.

His mirror on the damned.

Where she has put him has no reflection – so he no longer exists.

He convulses onto his knees.

And with the syringe held between shaking, fumbling, fingers he blindly scratches his name into the black floor.

As the Cocoa Clock strikes the twelve chimes of midnight on 30th September 2020 – the official historical date and time of the end of chocolate – Delilah speaks to her guests. 'Ladies and gentlemen, here tonight in Delilah's – the most beautiful, the most decadent and definitely the most notorious of London's chocolate houses – will be the last chocolate you ever taste.'

There is a respectful silence as each guest selects from silver trays carried amongst them a 100% Cocoa Extinction Chocolate Bean.

And as the Cocoa Clock strikes its twelfth and last chime, as one, they put the chocolate in their mouths.

Delilah looks at the gathered masked faces of her world. 'Chocolate is extinct.'

On the 1st October 2020 Nicholas Culpeper, sixty-nine, from Spitalfields, aka The Chocolate Poisoner, is arrested on suspicion of murder.

But it will not be possible to secure a conviction of beyond reasonable doubt – all the evidence of his actions is circumstantial to the crimes.

His house gives little away – it is the spotlessly clean home of a single man still living in sixties' modernist interior design. His lab equipment washed up and neatly stacked to dry – there is no trace of TCP.

The consolation for the detective who stopped him is the knowledge that with his identity now made public all prestige is gone. An illusionist whose one trick is exposed. His disguise obsolete. His face now familiar.

DI Gloom sits in his office looking out of the window watching the city finally fall silent for the first time in months, having rioted itself out of the oxygen needed for self-destruction. Knowing that slowly the city will return to its familiar ebb and flow, he takes a last lick of the femme fatale's enigmatic smile and she is gone.

It is a beautiful sunny autumn day at The Black Truffle Hotel where The Chocolate Thieves, joined by Scarlett Vamp, Stanley Oak, DS Silky, Damon and Katla, are enjoying an afternoon-tea buffet of the last of the city's artisan chocolates.

All the guests admire the newly renovated house.

Oak and Scarlett trade stories on the names of chocolatiers lost to history.

DS Silky watches, with satisfaction, Savage add The Chocolate Poisoner and his real name to the list of solved cases beneath her own name on the family tree. 'Why didn't you just tell me about Delilah's?'.

'We had plans of our own and we didn't want to trip over you as we went about our endeavours. As events transpired we were able to complement each other's aims. Besides, we both know the truth of the matter is that you would find the chocolate house through your own detective work when the time was right.'

'Thereby protecting your reputation of inscrutability.'

'Precisely. And you still got your man. Quite poetically – if I may compliment you.'

'You may. Though it would not have been possible without the assistance of Mr Oak – the man with the architectural plans of Delilah's.'

In the garden, as the sun bathes them in the last of its seasonal warmth, there is something to make known.

'Family and friends,' says Furness, 'Afia and I would like to announce that…'

'We are having a baby.' Afia excitedly holds up the scan of her womb.

Congratulations come from everyone.

Savage studies the scan. 'The first member of the next generation of The Chocolate Thieves – how wonderful.'

Dunstan tops up every glass with The Chocolate Thieves cocktail. 'Ladies and gentlemen, as we mourn the end of chocolate – let's raise our glasses to the beginning of a new life.'

PART THREE

THE LAST CHOCOLATE TREES

Winter is still bitter to the touch and The Chocolate Thieves are warming themselves for the day ahead with a full-octane Furness and Afia cooked breakfast. The fire stoked alive in the kitchen hearth completes the homely scene.

The 6 Music news broadcast on the kitchen's radio does not bring news they want to hear. 'After months of heated debate and behind-the-scenes wrangling over trade deals and aid packages for deprived cocoa countries the United Nations have agreed to award Global Cocoa the universal rights to the world's cocoa recultivation. The company will use cocoa plant material in cryopreservation stored at the Linnaeus Cocoa Laboratory in London to start the recultivation process. The licence gives Global Cocoa full plant rights to all commercially grown cocoa on the planet for the next one hundred years in an attempt to secure chocolate for future generations.

'The British prime minister has hailed the agreement as an important opportunity for Great Britain, saying, "In the hands of Global Cocoa, using world-beating British-based scientific expertise, we have the most realistic opportunity to recultivate chocolate for all of humanity."

'Vocal critics of the plan are Chocolate For The People, their spokesperson Seb Lilburne saying, "The cultivation of a mono-culture cocoa will have a devastating effect on the diversity of unique ecosystems and cocoa cultures wherever the hybridised strain is exploited for the sole purpose of high yields and profits."

'A claim dismissed by Global Cocoa as "blatant scaremongering".'

A collective sigh fills the room and is summed up in two simple words from Dunstan: 'Fucking idiots.'

As The Chocolate Thieves digest the news they've just heard they become aware of the sound of a phone ringing somewhere in the house. They all instinctively take out their mobile phones – it is not any of them. This is a phone with a very old bell ringtone.

Realising the ringing is coming from another part of the house they appear as one at the kitchen door and slowly move along the hall towards the front of the house.

The ringing is getting louder.

They look around them, confused as to where the sound is coming from.

Furness heads up the stairs but the ringing immediately quietens. 'Not up here,' he says shaking his head as he descends.

Dunstan steps into the lounge. 'Not from in here,' he says stepping back into the hall.

Dorothea is in the dining room. 'Nor from in here,' she says rejoining the others.

Kyoko and Afia are searching behind the photographs and pictures hanging on the walls of the hall – both finding nothing.

Savage is standing staring at the coats hanging just inside the door. He knows none of the coats would have the kind of phone in them that would make the bright shrill emanating from their direction. The others gather at his shoulder.

Still the phone persistently rings.

Savage parts the coats to reveal the oak-panelled wall behind. The ring is in the wall. Running his fingers around the edge of a panel he presses lightly and the panel swings open to reveal a small cupboard housing a black, 1920s telephone. 'I had entirely forgotten that this was here,' he says with fascination in his voice at the sight of the ringing museum piece.

'Did I ever know it was?' asks Furness.

'No – I didn't either,' replies Dunstan.

'Listen to it – a genuine hundred-year-old telephone bell ring,' says an excited Dorothea.

'Yes – listen to it, persistently ringing,' says an irritated, seven-months-pregnant Afia.

'Are you going to answer it?' asks Kyoko, both curious and suspicious of why this very old telephone is ringing at this point in time.

Savage reaches out a hand and tentatively picks up the handset off its cradle and puts it to his ear. 'Hello?'

'Who's that?' asks the husky female voice down the crackling line.

'Savage.'

'Good – very good. This is Mabel Arber.

'Mabel Arber?'

'Yes – that's what I heard myself say.'

'Blood hell, really – you're alive?'

'No, this is a voice from the afterlife. The only way of contacting you is through this phone – the device I last used to speak with your father.'

'What?'

'In other words, my dear Savage – evidently I'm still bloody alive. What's wrong with the world? No one ever believes I could still be kicking about.'

'Well, yes, of course, I suppose…'

'Oh – is this still a secure line?'

'I've really no idea. We've only just realised, when you rang it, it was still connected – in fact, that there was still a phone in the wall.'

'I see. Yes. Why would you. No need for it these days, I suppose. Anyway – I want to see you. I need your help. The Chocolate Thieves, that is. You're my only hope of getting done what needs to be done.'

'And what is it that needs to be done?'

'The resurrection of real chocolate, of course.'

Standing in front of the family tree pinned to the wall in the dining room, Savage points to Mabel Arber's name. 'There she is branching off CHOC 2, *Mabel Arber (Aunt by friendship), 1920–?, SOE operative and chocolate scientist at Chocolate Tree Farm.* According to the history of The Chocolate Thieves I received from my father, Aunt Mabel is a brilliant botanist. She was studying at Oxford when the war broke out so joined SOE. Helped repatriate CHOC 2 after their plane was shot down over France and thanks to them she became addicted to the science of chocolate. And, well, by the telling of it, at three points in time, she could have been all our fathers' mother. And who can blame them – there was a war on after all.'

'She's a hundred years old,' says Dorothea in wonderment.

'She sounded half that age,' Savage tells them.

'A chocolate scientist. What is she up to?' ponders Furness.

'Growing a natural alternative to the genetically engineered strain of chocolate being cultivated by Global Cocoa?' offers Afia.

'What was SOE?' asks Kyoko.

'Special Operations Executive. They were the bravest of spies. Men and women who were experts in espionage. Highly trained saboteurs working behind the enemy lines of World War Two,' explains Dunstan.

'I'm sure there's a photograph of her with our grandparents.' Savage searches out a photograph from the 1940s section of their archive. 'I have the faintest essence of a memory of her being in this house when I was a small child. Discussing the growing of cocoa trees. She gave me a bag of chocolate bombs. You two were still babies. Never seen, nor heard from her, since.'

'Where do we find her?' enquires Dorothea, seriously eager to meet this woman.

'We are to arrive at the coordinates she insisted I not write down and await further instructions,' Savage tells them. 'Here she is.'

The photograph depicts everything you'd want from a spy – a glamorous woman in her early twenties, with wavy dark shoulder-length hair, high cheekbones, dark secretive eyes and an enigmatic smile. Dressed in the clothes of the day – trench coat, silk floral scarf and leather gloves. A woman determined to do want she can to aid the fight and survive. Who has stopped for the briefest of moments to have her photograph taken in their garden.

'Aunt Mabel is a chocolate spy. Bloody brilliant.' Dunstan smiles, adding, 'I've got a very good feeling about this.'

The whole of The Chocolate Thieves household, ready to leave, comes to a standstill when cocoa botanist Dr Rikard Linnaeus is featured on the rolling cocoa news-stream on the television in the lounge.

Dr Linnaeus is talking live from his laboratory. 'To cultivate a new strain of cocoa is going to be not without risk of failure. And we only have one opportunity of success. But I am hopeful that we can do it. The germplasm we are using to cultivate the new strain of cocoa is collected tissue cultures from a high-yielding variety of cocoa tree. It's all we have left after the world's gene banks, including this one, were raided during The Chocolate Apocalypse riots by chocolate addicts for our cocoa plantlets and the budwood we use for cultivation. Ignorant individuals thinking they'll be able to grow their own chocolate – they won't. Thus destroying any opportunity of a controlled systematic and diverse recultivation of cocoa.

'To put the cocoa cultivation as simply as possible – the in-vitro process begins with sterile tissue cultures we have stored in cryopreservation,' he rests his hand on a 4.5 litre stainless steel thermo-flask on the bench next to him, 'that have been placed in a cryoprotectant of glucose and frozen in a flask of liquid nitrogen at -196 degrees to bring to a virtual standstill their metabolic processes and biological deterioration. These tissues, once thawed, will be cultivated in an agar growth medium.

'Once the plantlets have grown they will be transplanted into a cocoa-friendly compost and cultivated in an ex-situ context to ensure the plant regeneration goes according to plan without the threat of disease and human interference. This will take place in a safe environment here at the Linnaeus Cocoa Laboratory in England.

'When at the correct growth phase the cocoa trees will be exported to plantations across the world to grow in-situ in carefully selected cocoa-friendly environments so the trees can grow to their full fruiting potential. The variety of cocoa we are cultivating is RLC-2021 – a fast-growing, high-yielding, disease-resistant Forastero hybrid variety.

'The whole process from sterile tissue culture to chocolate will take two to three years. And is our last chance of cultivating a sustainable global cocoa crop for future generations.'

Piled into CHOC 4 with their six overnight bags and Afia's ubiquitous birthing bag, with Savage at the wheel, The Chocolate Thieves head off in search of The Chocolate Spy.

The coordinates Aunt Mabel has given Savage lead them south out of London. An hour later they arrive, as instructed, at the Oak Tree crossroads just as Savage's phone rings. All six look around for any sign of an old lady.

'Bloody spooky,' says Dorothea – observing out loud what everyone is thinking.

'I need a pee,' states Afia and she climbs out of the car and heads behind a hedge to relieve herself. Which starts a chain reaction of the others joining her in relieving themselves. Savage answers his phone and takes his next instructions.

Turning right, half an hour later, after travelling a further twenty-five miles, they are at White Willow Pond. Savage's phone rings again. 'In a mile take the next left and drive for a further ten miles,' commands Aunt Mabel.

'We're travelling southwest across the South Downs,' Dunstan tells them.

Twelve minutes later Savage stops CHOC 4 in Foxglove Lane just as his phone rings again.

'Two miles straight ahead. You won't see it until you're on top of it. But the entrance is there on the left,' the spy tells him.

The passengers in CHOC 4 look on alarmed as Savage pulls into the hedge – the optical illusion swallowing CHOC 4 into a very narrow lane that leads them to Chocolate Tree Farm – an exquisite Elizabethan red brick, oak-framed, farmhouse.

Aunt Mabel comes out of the front door of the house to greet them – a hundred-year-old woman with the energy of someone half her age. Her youthful features looking disarmingly like it was but a short time since she posed for Savage's photograph, not the seventy-seven years ago it was.

'You're unmistakable,' she declares on meeting them. 'Extraordinary DNA – the absolute images of your fathers and grandfathers. And how beautiful you three are – Dorothea, Afia and Kyoko. Welcome, all of you, to Chocolate Tree Farm.'

'How do you know us?' asks Kyoko.

Aunt Mabel smiles warmly. 'You're infamous – the lot of you rogues. I still take a drink at The Sleight Of Hand to keep up with the news off the chocolate street whenever I'm in town. Stanley Oak told me all about the three women who saved The Chocolate Thieves from themselves. Now come on in and I'll get the kettle on.'

'What a home,' approves Savage.

The whole interior is a museum to a well-travelled life. There are artefacts from every cocoa-growing region and beyond – from as far east and south as you can travel before you are in the west and the north again.

Aunt Mabel leads them along an oak-panelled hallway into a parlour at the back of the house. 'Afia, you'll find the downstairs facilities are on through the kitchen. When's it due?'

'Late April,' calls back Afia as she makes a dash for the toilet.

'Wonderful.'

The aroma of the house is wood smoke and fresh cocoa. Nostalgia flickers across the eyes of Savage, Furness and Dunstan as their olfactory senses stir forgotten and still-just-out-of-reach memories of being here in their very early childhood.

'Once you're refreshed I'll take you on a tour,' she tells

them.

'And the name?' enquires Dunstan.

'All in due course.' Aunt Mabel enigmatically smiles.

Aunt Mabel places a large pot of tea with cups, a jug of milk and a tin of homemade chocolate biscuits on the table in front of them. Six hands eagerly take a biscuit, each at the same time, and they bite into them with the groans of an addict's appreciation. She smiles at their faces of pleasure – like six children visiting their favourite aunt.

'You really know how to make biscuits,' Afia tells her.

'Thank you. I've been doing it for ninety-seven years. My mother's recipe – first thing she taught me to do in the kitchen.'

'Perfect balance of 75% Ecuadorian Criollo cocoa with organic flour, walnuts and honey,' deduces Furness. 'Delicious.'

'Now that's a palate worthy of the reputation,' responds Aunt Mabel with delight.

Six more biscuits leave the tin for their mouths. Followed by slurps of tea.

'Look at you. Brilliant, all of you. Possibly the most extraordinary generation so far. Each generation of Chocolate Thieves has been the people best suited to survive their time. But you are doing more than that – you're redefining your time. You're an inspiration to the world. Despite being, well, actually, because you are rogues. What you've done this last year – incredible. Savage and Dorothea the cultural historians with eyes on the future through understanding the past. Furness and Afia the chocolatiers creating wondrous recipes. Truly understanding the beauty in celebrating the flavours of the treasure that is cocoa. Dunstan and Kyoko, the deal-maker and the artist. The one connecting us to each other. The other quietly seeing humanity's soul. Both holding up a mirror to ourselves. What wonderful people you are. What better company to die in.'

Savage splutters tea for all of them. 'What?'

Aunt Mabel smiles. 'You think we're all going to get through this unscathed by the truth of war?'

'Yes,' asserts Furness.

'Well – we will see soon enough,' Aunt Mabel gently replies and sips her tea.

'What's going on? What war?' asks a concerned Afia holding her womb.

Aunt Mabel raises an eyebrow. 'Dunstan?'

'Aunt Mabel is still SOE,' Dunstan informs them. 'And she has a very dangerous mission for us behind enemy lines.'

The centenarian spy smiles with delight at their collected expressions of curiosity. 'More of that later,' she says, and she dunks a biscuit.

'There's a hundred and twenty acres in total,' Aunt Mabel tells them as they walk out of the kitchen door into the south-facing wild meadow garden stretching away from the farmhouse up to the dense wood. 'Half of which is native woodland. It's where the hives are along with the deer. Behind that line of trees is the fish pond – trout mainly. I've a few cows in the western meadows. The horses are in the eastern meadows. The chickens are that way too. There's the orchards of apples, cherries and plums to the north.'

Parked in one of the barns are an iconic 1946 Ferguson TE20 tractor, two 1944 WDH16 Norton motorcycles and a British racing green 1948 Aston Martin DB1 sports car. Littering the back of the barn are the necessary spare parts to keep all the vehicles working.

The walled vegetable garden is ready for this season's planting and home to the groves of blackcurrant and raspberry bushes. On the other side of the walled garden and full of flourishing cocoa trees are the greenhouses. There are eight in total, dating from the early 1900s.

'Each greenhouse grows a specific variety by nationality – brought here as budwood from their native countries to cultivate and study. There are trees from the root stock of Mesoamerican cocoa, Colombian and Ecuadorian Criollo, Peruvian White Nacional, Forastero from Brazil and so on. You'll know this one – it's from St Lucia. Acquired just after you invested in the plantation. The trees are so healthy because the greenhouses perfectly emulate the cocoa's growing environment of ten degrees north and ten degrees south of the equator. Creating an average atmosphere of twenty-eight degrees Celsius with 90% humidity. There's an automated rain system. The soil has PH range of 5 to 7.5 and is anionic and cationic balanced with a total nitrogen and total phosphorous ratio of around 1.5. You'll find a high organic matter of 3.5% in the topsoil with a 1.5 metre depth of soil with good drainage. Try not to kill too many of the midges, annoying as they are, they're necessary for natural pollination.'

The Chocolate Thieves are shell-shocked – literally speechless. Aunt Mabel lets them wander in wide-eyed wonder until Savage finds some words. 'The last chocolate trees.'

'They're all fruiting,' points out Furness.

'The only cultivated cocoa in the world,' states Dunstan.

'How are you keeping the farm a secret?' asks Kyoko.

Aunt Mabel smiles. 'Usual routine. Hiding in plain sight. To the casual observer I'm an eccentric old lady living on a crumbling, sprawling smallholding. What is hidden is the secret at its centre. My life's work. Check your phone signal.' They do – there is none. 'A digital faraday cage. Keeps phones and the low-flying drones from transmitting this location. The whole farm is as blind or as visible to modernity as I want it to be. There's also a glaring of feral cats roaming around the farm keeping the mice and rats, and most importantly, human intruders at bay. All the power comes from solar energy. The water supply is from the farm's own spring.'

'Drones?' enquires Dorothea.

'Someone knows that I'm somewhere around here. Before and during the war it was a government-run agricultural and scientific research facility. Which included work with SOE. I fell in love with the place the first time I came here. So bought the farm… well, I say bought – your grandfathers helped me acquire the deeds after the war. Completely off the grid. Has never officially existed on a map or piece of ministry paper after 1930. But somewhere in Defra or the old spy network someone has remembered the rumours of Chocolate Tree Farm and I've been monitoring increased surveillance in the area ever since The Chocolate Apocalypse began.'

They step out of the sixth greenhouse.

'The point is there are enough cocoa trees here to repopulate the planet with the key varieties of cocoa that make chocolate taste like chocolate. Not that generic-tasting product Dr Rikard Linnaeus finds himself creating in a lab. I'm not saying RLC-2021 isn't needed – it will have its uses. But do we really want Global Cocoa to own the rights to all cocoa for a hundred years when we don't need to let them,' proffers Aunt Mabel.

'You want us to acquire the Global Cocoa tissue cultures,' Dunstan correctly deduces.

'Yes I do,' confirms Aunt Mabel.

'And that's what the empty greenhouse over there is

for,' observes Furness.

'Indeed.' Aunt Mabel smiles, delighted that they are as sharp as their reputation suggests.

'And Dr Rikard Linnaeus?' enquires Savage.

'Oh yes, him too – we're going to need his expertise.'

'Here we go again,' says Afia with an amused shake of her head.

They hear Kyoko laughing behind them. 'Brilliant.'

They join her. There are only three saplings in this greenhouse, labelled *Savage*, *Furness* and *Dunstan* – the trees they'd returned to Kew Gardens.

'Well, I had to rescue them from The Chocolate Apocalypse – didn't I,' explains Aunt Mabel.

Dorothea insists that the three men stand next to their respective sapling for a photograph.

Back in the parlour, having spent the rest of the afternoon exploring the farm, Dorothea and Kyoko lift Afia's swollen and aching feet up onto a footstool and relax back either side of her on the sofa in front of the roaring wood burner being stoked by Aunt Mabel.

'Look at you three – how did they catch such gorgeous creatures?' she asks, straightening up from the fire and looking at the three young women with an impressed smile as she warms herself.

'I was homeless and smelt Furness cooking bacon sandwiches. He caught me stealing one and has had me washing up and waiting tables ever since,' Afia tells her, adding, 'and now look at me.'

'Stockholm syndrome,' reveals Kyoko. 'Dunstan locked me in my studio when I was a penniless artist and forced me to paint forgeries. Then I seduced him – it's been terrible.'

'I went in search of Savage. Couldn't find him

anywhere. Just a trail of chocolate heists. Then one day he turned up at my stall and bought a teapot from me,' confesses Dorothea.

'Bloody brilliant.' The botanist laughs.

'What about you, Aunt Mabel?' asks Dorothea.

'You're beautiful,' says Kyoko.

'A well sexy centenarian,' adds Afia.

'Me?' Aunt Mabel blushes. 'There's been some wonderful lovers. But I don't want one here constantly under my feet. I've important work to do. And, they lacked the vitality I require, if you get my drift – kept dying. I think I might have actually fucked a few of them to death. No, I've had no time for husbands and children. Which is now a pity as I've no grandchildren nor great-grandchildren.'

Furness and Dunstan come into the room, having taken their bags upstairs, followed by Savage carrying a tray of tea and chocolate biscuits.

With a cup of tea and a biscuit Aunt Mabel settles into her favourite chair. 'With the cocoa trees in the greenhouses it will be possible to recultivate original strains of the world's cocoa in their native soil. But to ensure their safety we have to eliminate the threat of Global Cocoa, the British Government and the United Nations.'

'If their planting succeeds,' offers Furness.

'It will. Dr Rikard Linnaeus is a bloody genius when it comes to cocoa cultivation.'

'Not a descendant of the father of modern taxonomy, Carl Linnaeus?' wonders Savage.

'Yes, he's the tenth generation grandson of the very man.'

'Blimey,' says a concerned Dorothea.

That evening Furness cooks a sublime meal, with ingredients sourced from the farm, of venison in a blackcurrant wine sauce with roasted winter vegetables followed by apple and blackberry crumble with farmhouse ice cream.

Elbows on table, Aunt Mabel cups her hands round her hot chocolate and tells them what's on her mind. 'The cryopreserved Linnaeus cocoa is a hybrid variety, its preservation and cultivation funded by the British Government, notionally publicly owned but very much in the hands of corporate Britain. As you know they are the last known commercially viable cocoa tissue cultures on the planet. But no doubt Global Cocoa and others are secretly developing artificially created chocolate in their labs. Of course there will always be wild cocoa growing in small pockets of their native countries but they're for the cocoa hunters and those with deep enough pockets to pay for expeditions.

'The loss of cocoa is a significant ecological and cultural change – brought about by our greed. If we are to make amends it is not by giving the likes of Global Cocoa the sole rights to cultivate and exploit cocoa as they see fit. This United Nations licence will perpetuate more ecological disaster. Cultivating and harvesting the yield of a mono-crop cocoa is further environmental vandalism. I've no doubt we will end up back where we are now in another four generations – the earth will only take so much.

'The new chocolate made from genetically homogenised high crop yielders will be diluted of all flavour and character. Chocolate will be sterilised. And in the long term devoid of any essence of organic cultivation. Global Cocoa is fighting a war against nature for short-term personal gain and long-term cultural hierarchy. Yes, of course they'll keep the rare special original varieties for the elite palate of Midas's clients. But for everyone else, well, we've let them create the world we find ourselves in – it's time to stop enslaving ourselves to their ideology.

'By controlling the fate of the Linnaeus cocoa we can control the fate of real cocoa chocolate for future generations. Let's give our descendants a chocolate that is the most natural they've ever tasted. The truly wonderful gift given to us by the earth.'

'It takes up to five years for a naturally grown cocoa tree to produce its first fruit,' says Furness, wanting to make sure everyone understands the time frame they are in. 'With the planting of the budwood from your most vigorous trees, maybe three years to create a yielding plantation.'

'We'll offset the natural cocoa yield time with the Linnaeus cocoa,' instructs Aunt Mabel.

'We'll have to rebuild the cocoa communities,' offers Savage.

'We have the contacts to do that,' reassures Aunt Mabel.

'First we have to acquire Dr Rikard Linnaeus and his cocoa,' Dunstan reminds them.

Savage, Furness and Dunstan think over the situation for a few moments – then do their smile.

'What did I miss?' asks a puzzled Aunt Mabel.

'Nothing and everything,' Dorothea reassures her. 'They always do this – it's a hive mind of roguishness.'

'It's bloody irritating,' says Afia rubbing her very full belly.

Kyoko smiles. 'I like the mystery.'

'Wonderful.' Aunt Mabel grins excitedly.

Savage and Dorothea will be sleeping in the green room that looks out over the wild meadow garden at the rear of the house. Like all the bedrooms it is home to a wonderful oak bed piled with feather pillows and wrapped in inviting warm blankets.

Stepping away from the window Dorothea ponders a question. 'Why did your parents never bring you here?'

Savage, hanging up his suit, thinks for a moment. 'Actually – I think they may have done. When we were very young. On walking in for what I thought was the first time, earlier today, there was an unreachable memory. I'm sure Furness and Dunstan felt it too. But I suppose she was the past – we do need to find out more about her.'

In Furness and Afia's ochre room, lying in bed, they watch the bats flicker about in the walled garden and around the green houses.

'The cocoa she grows – it really is like your palate is travelling from cocoa country to cocoa country,' Afia thinks aloud. 'She's a fucking genius.'

'Her secret is a simple one – she lets nature do what nature does,' replies Furness, adding with a hint of disappointment and in wonderment, 'What we could have learned visiting here all these years.'

Dunstan and Kyoko are in the yellow room looking out at the star-filled sky over the orchards.

Kyoko has been observing how time is depicted in the natural light at the farm without the intense artificial light pollution of the city. 'It's the most truthful and peaceful of places. No wonder she fell in love with living here.'

Dunstan is equally intrigued by the idea of living by nature's time. 'It's the same life values – lived differently. Our family survived living off what the capital's streets provided and here she was surviving by living directly off what the land gives her. The air here is incredible – so clean.'

In his office, serious of features, DI Gloom hands DS Silky a traditionally-constructed-from-newsprint ransom note. It reads, *For the safe return of Lovisa Linnaeus hand over the Global Cocoa tissue cultures outside Tate Modern at 4pm today.* The ransom note is signed *Liberation Of Chocolate For The People.* Included with the note is a Polaroid photograph of a fair-haired woman in her mid-thirties curled up on the floor of a kitchen – she is gagged and chained to water pipes.

'It arrived this morning. Handed by a scarf-faced cyclist to the postman as he delivered the post to the Linnaeus Cocoa Laboratory. As you've no doubt deduced they are a direct-action splinter group of the political lobbyists. Dr Lovisa Linnaeus is the wife of cocoa scientist Dr Rikard Linnaeus. Taken yesterday evening while stargazing with the local astronomical group in Richmond Park. A herd of deer were stampeded by two stolen deerhounds towards the group. Her Global Cocoa security detail was taken out by the deer and in the chaos of trampled telescopes and stargazers she was thrown, according to a single witness from the group, by two unidentified assailants into the back of an unmarked dark in colour, blue they think, van. We've had no luck yet in tracking the van with the available traffic cameras. And there's no fingerprints on the paper or the photograph.'

DS Silky hands the note back to DI Gloom. 'Give them what they want.'

'I agree. The Government doesn't. Too much invested politically and financially in the future of Global Cocoa.'

'Do the kidnappers know what they're taking receipt of?'

'You mean con them.'

'Yes.'

'No need to.'

'The Government would really sacrifice Lovisa Linnaeus for chocolate?'

'Of course they will, and so will the people. I dare you, do an online survey, click "Like" if the wife should die to save chocolate.'

'What do you think? You're a chocolate addict.'

'I'm not that kind of addict. The Government's concern is that Dr Linnaeus will do what the kidnappers want.'

'What caring person wouldn't.'

'Precisely. To stop him doing that, through the use of Global Cocoa security, they are keeping an even tighter guard on the good doctor's movements until you find his wife.'

'Just me.'

'Just you.'

'Then we leak that she's been taken.'

'Do you want to keep on being a detective?'

'We can't go along with this. And there's no point in doing so, Rikard Linnaeus will social media it – "Have you seen my wife", etc.'

DI Gloom shakes his head.

DS Silky realises what's happening. 'They've slapped a D-notice on it and told him that they need to control the flow of information for Lovisa's safety.'

DI Gloom nods.

'Is Dr Rikard Linnaeus really going to cultivate cocoa while his wife is missing?'

'There are other cocoa scientists – what ego doesn't want their name attached to the resurrection of chocolate. And if he's been assured Lovisa will be returned safely...'

DS Silky runs, in her mind's eye, through the different scenarios for the kidnapped woman – they all end with her being abandoned by the state in favour of chocolate.

'It's down to you, DS Silky. Use your chocolate world

contacts to find Lovisa to avoid the situation where Rikard Linnaeus is faced with the reality of how much the life of his wife is worth to the united nations of billions of chocolate addicts.'

'If the Government is controlling this, why are you giving me this investigation? They could easily fabricate looking for Lovisa.'

'Because the powers that be do not want there to be an absence of evidence of there being a real investigation. They just don't care if you succeed.'

At her desk DS Silky reads up on Dr Rikard Linnaeus – specialist in cultivating disease-resistant cocoa varieties through selected cross-breeding. Set up the Linnaeus Cocoa Laboratory, Richmond, in 2010. Married to Dr Lovisa Linnaeus – an astrophysicist, specialising in the search for earth-like planets, who lectures at UCL. No children. Both Swedish – photographs of the Linnaeuses revealing their native Scandinavian features.

At the Chocolate For The People offices, their public face, Seb Lilburne, is insisting that what DS Silky has been told is true is not true. 'There is no organisation called Liberation Of Chocolate For The People. I'm in constant contact with all the leading chocolate activists in the city, and on the planet, I assure you – these people do not exist.'

'You're suggesting it's a badge of convenience not a movement.'

'Yes.'

DS Silky looks around her, taking in the chocolate addicts in the activists' headquarters. They fall into two categories – overweight with serious dentistry and lean, fit, healthy eco-warriors. Could it be any of these people?

Lilburne reads her mind. 'They all have alibis – a

strategy meeting was taking place in this office at the time Dr Lovisa Linnaeus was taken.'

'You have a list of names of those attending I can compare against membership details?'

'Those details are confidential.'

'What of those members more inclined towards direct action?'

'We're libertarians – we don't keep track of our supporters.'

'I'm sure you know all the key activists by name and their preferred activities.'

'So you can trust my word when I tell you they were all here, or accounted for, and none are inclined to kidnap.'

DS Silky goes to leave when he stops her with a politically leading question. 'How many police officers are searching for Lovisa?'

'You're looking at her.'

'I thought that might be the case.'

Back out on the street DS Silky phones Dorothea – the antiquarian's phone is unavailable.

The Dunstan Gallery is closed, with no sign of life – she tries calling Dunstan but gets no answer.

The Furness restaurant is closed too – Katla and Damon are still living in the flat but haven't seen Furness and Afia for days.

DS Silky knocks on the door of The Black Truffle Hotel – no one opens the door. She phones Dorothea again – there's still no answer. 'This really is getting suspicious. Where are you?'

The detective picks the lock and lets herself in. The house is as empty as it sounded from the outside. She searches every room and the garden for signs of life, or death, but to no avail. 'No chocolate – no Chocolate

Thieves.'

Standing in the dining room she scans the family tree – her eyes coming to rest on the name *Mabel Arber*.

Her phone buzzes in her pocket.

It is a *Watch this now* text with a YouTube link attached to it, from DI Gloom. *Why hasn't this been on the news – who is this kidnapped woman?* reads the tagline beneath the footage of the stampeding deer in Richmond Park and the abduction of Lovisa Linnaeus. The motion-activated night-vision camera filming the stampede of the startled deer, the swallowing up in their wake of the security detail, the dash for their lives of the twelve stargazers, the trashing of their telescopes, the arrival of the van, the getting out of the back of it of two hooded junkie-physiqued masked figures, their searching, spotting and shining of a torch beam into the face of Lovisa Linnaeus, the tasering of her, the stumbling dragging of her limp body into the back of the van, the closing of the van doors by a third slight, hooded and masked person, who, having done this, jumps into the passenger seat and the driving away of the van by an unseen fourth person. The footage was posted by *DeerParkNature* whose other eighty-four videos are of the animals and plant life living in the park.

The idiots in power thought they could D-notice the internet.

It takes but digital moments for viewers of the footage to name Dr Lovisa Linnaeus and – more importantly to the wider chocolate-bereft world – identify her as the wife of the chocolate scientist Dr Rikard Linnaeus. *What does this mean for chocolate?* is the primary topic discussed in the comments below the footage.

Re-watching the events of the previous evening it is clear to see none of the potential witnesses has their eyes on the abduction for any length of time – fleeing as they all are in different directions.

DS Silky switches on the television in the lounge.

The virtual dust has barely settled before there comes the duplicitous appeal from the Prime Minister James Hind standing in front of 10 Downing Street before the world's media. The PM speaks with rehearsed precision. 'I assure you that my Government, with the assistance of Global Cocoa, are doing everything necessary to secure the future of chocolate and the safe return of Lovisa Linnaeus. To the kidnappers I say this: there is only one way to secure the future of chocolate and that is with the laboratory-controlled cultivation of the cocoa tissue cultures Dr Rikard Linnaeus has at his disposal. Holding his wife captive will not alter his resolve to save chocolate for the world. Please return Lovisa safely and avoid all prosecution for the mistake you have made in believing your chocolate ideology is the correct one. Believe me – it is not.'

DS Silky looks at her phone, knowing it's about to ring, answering DI Gloom's call as soon as it does. 'I take it the circus has come to town.'

'Indeed it fucking has.' DI Gloom looks out of his office at the gaggle of senior uniforms heading his way, determined to be seen actively overseeing his policing of the kidnap investigation in an attempt to control the impending wave of media and public scrutiny. 'But their performance won't have changed – it'll be the same tired Machiavellian routine.'

'They will lie with every word they speak.'

'Yes they fucking well will. Now you really do have to find Lovisa before they abandon her to her fate of "Circumstances beyond our control" and that "Despite our best efforts we sadly failed to find her in time. But fear not, your chocolate is safe in our hands."'

247

'I was always going to.'

'I know. I'll applaud the high wire walkers here – you stay out there on the street.'

'Try not to get fired out of a cannon by the clowns.'

DS Silky, not for the first time that winter, texts Stanley Oak from his bedroom on the second floor of The Sleight Of Hand. *I'm waiting – join me…*

A minute later Stanley Oak is walking through the bedroom door. 'How are you getting in here without being seen? And shouldn't you be…'

DS Silky steps, naked, out of the blue silk robe she is wearing towards Oak, puts her fingers to his lips and undresses him. Throwing him onto his back on the bed she straddles him. He's still wearing a quizzical expression when she slides onto him. But all becomes clear very quickly after a few moments of anticipation and gentle movements to get him fully aroused. At the point of his submission to his increasing pleasure she playfully tightens the muscles in her vagina around his penis and holds him viced at her mercy.

'Ow – fucking hell!' He tries to tell her to stop but he is laughing at the pain. 'Silky!' he finally gasps.

She relaxes, 'Well?' She enquires.

'We had a deal.'

She tightens her grip again.

He's locked in the pulsating pain of her hold on him and the increasing desire of ejaculation. 'Oh, bloody hell!'

'Why do you always laugh at pain?'

'Because it's ridiculous,' he replies, his voice rising a full octave.

She nods her understanding of his rationale as she holds him there in the ecstasy of pure pain. Eyes wide he grips the sheets, finger tips digging into the mattress to dissuade the driving excruciating sensation for the need of release.

'Someone has taken a women hostage just to get some fucking chocolate.'

'I know – and you know if I can help her I will.'

'So who are the LOCFTP?'

'I've been trying to find out. And you know I will. I just need time.'

'Something Lovisa may not have.'

'I understand that.'

'Good.' She relaxes and concentrates on their mutual pleasure. But her thoughts quickly return to the case. 'What will happen to her?'

'Bloody hell – nothing.'

'How can you know that?'

'The footage of the kidnapping reveals them to be opportunist amateurs who got lucky with successfully taking their target. They're trying to pull off a con - pretending to give a fuck about saving chocolate. But once they have the tissue cultures they'll sell them to the highest bidder. So they'll return her for the cocoa - they won't have the stomach to hurt her. At worst they'll drug her and dump her somewhere in the city.'

'Just another lost and vulnerable person.'

Stanley Oaks nods, 'But not for long – she's too recognisable.'

'No – too easily someone else will take the opportunity to make a profit from her.'

'You know I will do what I can to stop that from happening.'

She grins at him and tightens her grip again. 'Where are The Chocolate Thieves?'

'Ow!'

'Stop laughing.'

He grabs her breasts and twists her nipples – she just

groans with disarming pleasure. 'Enough with the interrogation.'

Relaxing her grip she leans forwards and kisses him. 'Okay.'

Then without warning DS Silky jumps off Oak leaving him bruised and throbbing red, 'Silky!'

Pulling on her clothes DS Silky shrugs, 'We've a kidnapping to end – we haven't time for this.'

'You bloody witch.'

'You know how to finish yourself off.'

'Nobody likes you,' he shouts after her as she goes through the door.

'Yes you do.'

He looks down at his forlornly quivering self, 'Yes I do.'

It is 3.30pm. DS Silky sits on a bench outside Tate Modern. Beside her is a black holdall in which resides a silver flask acquired from Dr MacCarrion. Numerous plain-clothed officers, borrowed from other investigations for an hour, controlled through earpieces by the detective, mingle with the visitors to the gallery.

They wait.

At 4pm a silver-flask-carrying man wearing a Global Cocoa security bomber jacket walks past her. A black-clad cyclist, face wrapped in a scarf, comes from the opposite direction and stops in front of the man and holds up a phone with a picture of Lovisa on it. The flask is handed over and the cyclist rides away as fast as they can – quickly disappearing from view.

The expected 'What the hell is going on?' comes through her earpiece from her colleagues. 'Everyone stand down,' DS Silky instructs them. They could stop the cyclist further along the river bank but being uninformed about this exchange means detaining the kidnapper would possibly be putting Lovisa at risk. And clearly some sort of negotiation for her release is taking place – the detective hopes.

DS Silky walks over to the man and shows him her ID. 'Explain?'

His smile is a successful combination of being arrogant and patronising as he holds up his corporate ID. It reads *Karl Dance, Global Cocoa Head of Security Operations.* 'Following orders.'

'What was in the flask?'

'What do you think was in it?'

'When's Lovisa Linnaeus being returned?'

Karl Dance shrugs and walks away.

Clearly he's been instructed to say as little as possible to her. DS Silky calls DI Gloom and relates to him what has just happened and asks, 'What the fuck was handed over?'

'That information has not been communicated in my direction. I can only assume they've decided to attempt a pay-off.'

'Yes – but to what end?'

A day later, having returned to London, The Chocolate Thieves have set about planning the acquisition of the cocoa tissue cultures from behind Global Cocoa's wall of security at the Linnaeus Cocoa Laboratory. A task made more sensitive by the media storm surrounding the missing Dr Lovisa Linnaeus.

Sitting next to the fire in The Sleight Of Hand, drinking bottles of stout, Savage draws Furness and Dunstan's attention to the map on the screen of his phone. 'The Linnaeus Cocoa Laboratory is situated on the south bank of the river to the west of Richmond Park. As you see there are multiple road routes in and out in all directions – the key one being the A307 running north and south. There is also the option of the river.'

Dunstan in turn scans through the photographs of the laboratory he has on his phone. 'The security is at a level of a full-scale counter-terrorism operation. There's a shoot-to-kill armed guard every two metres surrounding the building, on the roof and inside. Everyone is strip-searched as they arrive and leave – including the guards.'

'Where's the weak point?' enquires Furness.

'It's already been utilised,' Dunstan informs him.

'Lovisa,' says Savage.

Dunstan nods in agreement of this truth.

Furness shakes his head. 'I just don't see how we can justify taking the tissue cultures when they're needed to trade for the man's wife.'

The other two agree. With Dunstan adding the caveat, 'If he is allowed to trade the cultures for Lovisa.'

'You think Global Cocoa and the Government will stop him?' asks Savage.

'I do,' is Dunstan's well-observed cynical reply. 'We can't take them yet because I've no doubt that Rikard Linnaeus is willing to hand over the cocoa tissue cultures in a blink of an eye to get his wife back in one piece. But if you were Global Cocoa or the Government would you let him make that trade? Just look at the security. That's just as likely to be there to control Rikard Linnaeus's activities for fear of him paying the ransom.'

'So you are about to suggest we find the abducted Dr Lovisa Linnaeus and reunite her with Dr Rikard Linnaeus in the hope of persuading him to work with us, not his pay masters,' deduces Furness.

'That is exactly what I'm suggesting we do,' says Dunstan.

'You think we can get him to see the reality of the opportunity we offer?' enquires Savage.

'I'm counting on him having already realised his life is no longer his own,' says Dunstan, 'and that he and Lovisa are expendable in the eyes of our Government's favourite conglomerate.'

Walking awkwardly and sitting with care, a genitally bruised Stanley Oak joins them at their table. 'Good afternoon, gentlemen.'

'Good afternoon,' they reply.

'A certain detective wants me to see if I can ascertain and inform her where a disappeared certain doctor of astrophysics is being held. I've agreed to do this for the obvious reasons – simultaneously self-centred and altruistic.'

'Understood,' Savage reassures him.

'So I suggest you have a conversation with the woman nervously drinking a fortifying neat gin at the bar.'

The three of them look towards the withered-faced, sunless-skinned, scrawny-limbed woman who still carries hints of her true age of thirty-two years but looks more like she's creeping towards a decade older.

'Your reason being?' asks Dunstan.

'Her shopping bag,' answers Furness.

Savage and Dunstan look at the bulging bag at the woman's feet.

'Word is she lives with an occasional lover and a cat. I've only ever known her buy food for the cat,' Oak informs them.

'And cats generally, as a rule, do not eat pesto chicken pasta bake ready meals for two and garlic bread washed down with a bottle of claret,' points out Furness.

'Wouldn't the kidnappers just feed Lovisa takeaways?' asks Dunstan, adding, 'It's what I'd do.'

'No, what you'd do is get me to cook for her,' offers Furness to which Savage and Dunstan nod in agreement.

'It's a case of the alcoholic's delusions of grandeur – distorted and trapped in their own unhappy upbringing,' observes Oak.

'So who is she?' asks Savage.

'Her name is Lorna Tower – keeps the company of the pickpocket John Wall and drinks with the short-con artists Denise Wills and Nathan Hackney.'

'She hasn't the strength to kidnap a fully grown adult,' suggests Furness.

'But she could close a van door on those that do,' points out Dunstan.

'Don't be fooled by her demeanour, she's a scratcher and has had the strength of will to survive this long – all of them have.'

'Seriously – just on the evidence of her shopping you suspect her?' questions Savage.

'No – of course not. Wall and Hackney were seen stealing a blue van not two streets away just after drinking in here when the talk was of nothing else but the news of the Linnaeus cocoa trees. And, along with Wills, have since gone to ground.'

'Are they smart enough to work a plan so quickly?'

'They are certainly cunningly opportunistic and connected – Wall's sister is a cleaner at the Global Cocoa Headquarters. She could easily overhear a discussion on how they intend to monitor the Linnaeuses' movements. And there's the fact that our dipsomaniac Lorna keeps mumbling to herself with every mouthful of gin, and telling anyone within ear shot that, "I've got to cook my friend a proper meal – she's visiting for a few days. Educated ain't she – so she eats properly."'

There is no point in trying to follow Lorna – she'd spot them as soon as they stepped out the door after her. Experienced a pickpocket as she is she'll have nothing about her person to identify her or reveal her address should she be caught. Seeing the vulnerability written through the woman – years of physical and psychological self-abuse and from a neglectful mother, would-be fathers, brothers and lovers – the solution is a simple one.

Dunstan makes a call – they will use the female touch.

Lorna's throat takes what body weight she has, restricting the air she needs to relieve the ache in her tar-filled lungs, lifted as she is by the gloved right hand of the balaclava-wearing woman. Her feet trying to tiptoe on the alley's cobbles hoping to gain some purchase. Drunken panic and the fear of the pain she's experienced too often in her life flickers in her watering eyes.

Kyoko keeps her voice calm. 'Where are you holding Lovisa?'

Lorna's eyes flit to either end of the alley where silhouetted figures stand reducing any chance of escape to zero – but she'll try anyway. Why give these bastards what they want. The Lovisa woman's going to be her friend. She'd always wanted a descent and kind friend – for once she'd have some genuine affection in her life. Who are these people to take that away from her? For the second time she goes for Kyoko's eyes with her dirty, chewed nails. And like the first time she'd tried it they're simply knocked away with either hand like they are irritating flies. The hand that holds her by the throat swapped with such speed that her pedalling feet don't hit the ground so to run away. She is in pain, angry, frightened and trapped.

Kyoko calmly repeats, 'Where is Lovisa?'

Dr Rikard Linnaeus is a very worried man. The platitudes delivered in their false tone of gravitas by the Home Secretary Robina Head and the Commissioner of Police

Jack Bellingham are not reassuring.

'We are doing all we can to bring your wife home,' she lies.

'We have leads – let us do our job as you continue to do yours,' he instructs.

'We'll keep you informed of any progress,' she lies again.

'I assure you, experience tells us that in these situations they will not harm your wife – they need her alive to achieve their aims,' he wants him to believe.

And the message in Bill Whittaker's unreassuring smile is clear. 'The chocolate comes first.'

'What leads?' asks Rikard.

'We're questioning every known member of Chocolate For The People about their associates in this group of chocolate anarchists,' misleads the Commissioner of Police.

'Then why is Seb Lilburne being interviewed on the news as you stand here lying to me?' asks Rikard turning up the sound on the television in the corner of the living room to hear what Lilburne is saying.

Standing outside CFTP's offices, looking straight down the lens of the camera, Lilburne doesn't hold back. 'The activities of every active member of CFTP have been looked into – it's not one of us. We're cooperating fully with DS Silky's investigation, who, by the way, seems to be the only detective working on the case. Trust me when I tell you, there is no such group as the Liberation Of Chocolate For The People. And I don't doubt for one minute that the British Government and Global Cocoa are behind the abduction of Dr Lovisa Linnaeus as a way of keeping Dr Rikard Linnaeus compliant in the cultivation of the cocoa trees they have the plant rights to. This is how our democracy works. But it's not too late to change it –

for the sake of all our lives.'

'What nonsense.' The Home Secretary squirms. 'Unfortunately we can't just arrest people without evidence – however ridiculous their conspiracy theories.'

'And I assure you we've more than one detective searching for your wife,' lies the Commissioner of Police.

'Bring Lovisa home now, you vile halfwits!' Rikard instructs the self-aggrandising trio patronising him. 'Or,' he unequivocally informs them, 'there will be no chocolate.'

'Oh there'll be chocolate, Dr Linnaeus,' threatens Whittaker, 'with or without the world's leading cocoa scientist.' The CEO steps towards Rikard, all pretence of reassurance gone. 'You'll see your dear wifey Lovisa when I see chocolate trees.'

At this last comment the Commissioner of Police and the Home Secretary's expressions join Whittaker's in being undeniably ones of 'This is your new reality.'

The one-bedroom flat in Southwark is a squalid place. Home to a self-deluding lifestyle of the cheapest available stimulants that can be drunk and smoked. It has an aroma of cat piss blended with the odour of too many unwashed bodies continuously in too small a space.

The sprawled-on-the-sofa, alcohol-and-cannabis-induced dozing, shambolic, unwashed individual, John Wall, had not risen at the sound of the turn of the key in the door lock. Now through his half-open eyes he sees there is something wrong with the figure standing in front of him. 'He has no face. Ah – it's a balaclava,' he dreamily thinks. Then he realises. 'Oh fuck! It's The Chocolate Thieves!' And now his eyes are wide open and he is as wide awake as he can be considering what's in his blood stream.

A leather-gloved finger is raised to indicate he should quietly stay where he is seated. 'Coward or evil bastard?' Furness asks him.

Wall sees the whimpering bound and gagged Lorna at his feet. A gulp then a whispered reply, 'Coward.'

'Good.'

Wall glances up to the left at the second figure looking down at him – it's that DS Silky. And now he really knows that his situation is not a good one.

To Wall's left on the grubby red carpet stands the open flask he'd picked up from Global Cocoa's Karl Dance. On the coffee table a small collection of diamonds spill out of a brown envelope.

Furness passes the note that came with them to DS Silky who reads it aloud. '*You don't want the chocolate – it's more trouble than it's worth. We have a more lucrative proposition for you – hold on to Lovisa Linnaeus until instructed otherwise. Here's a down payment for your trouble, GC.*'

In the bedroom the inebriated Denise Wills and Nathan Hackney aren't impressed by the arrival of Dunstan and Kyoko during their afternoon rancid-sheeted sex session. But any expletives barely have time to leave their lips before two gloved fists land in their faces rendering them quivers of rotten humanity.

Kidnappers silenced – where is Lovisa?

DS Silky walks into the kitchen – there she is, as depicted in the Polaroid, curled up on the floor in the corner of the kitchen, chained to the water pipes. Next to her a bin vomits empty fast-food wrappers, gin bottles and beer cans. The detective holds up her ID to reassure the woman. 'I'm here with The Chocolate Thieves – we're here to take you home.'

Lovisa doesn't react and tries to warn the detective why

258

with a glance to her left. At which point what does react is a mangy cat that has been sitting as guard of the captive – it leaps from its cosy place on a cushion on a stool, extending its claws as it travels through the air with a hellish-sounding screech.

DS Silky puts her arms up to cover her face. The cat doesn't reach her. Kyoko grins at the detective having caught the cat in mid-leap by the scruff of its neck – its claws frantically scratching the air.

Thinking he has a chance of making his escape, in the distraction of the cat attack, Wall makes to stand up and throw a fist at Furness. He doesn't. Furness's brogue pins the man to his seat by his groin. Wall cries pathetic tears of self-pity. 'Not fair – it's really not fair.'

Kyoko throws the cat into the bedroom with the naked Wills and Hackney – the sound of bodies tumbling about and blood-drawn shrieks ensue through the closed and locked door.

Using a burner phone, having already taken photographs of the four kidnappers, Dunstan photographs the chained-up Lovisa before releasing her with the keys found in Wall's trouser pocket thrown to him by Furness. The diamonds and note are photographed too before handing the phone to the detective. Wall and Tower are chained up together where they'd kept the astrophysicist – who in an act of revenge picks up the taser left on the kitchen counter and shocks both of them unconscious.

And DS Silky walks the freed Lovisa out to the waiting Savage in CHOC 4.

Surrounded by a scuffle of news reporters and cameras Savage pulls up outside the Linnaeuses home. The door of the house opens and Rikard pushes past the gun-raised security detail and pulls Lovisa into his arms in a suffocating embrace of love and relief as she steps out of CHOC 4.

Inside the house Karl Dance is unimpressed when DS Silky removes all the hidden cameras and microphones installed by Global Cocoa. 'The contract signed by Dr Linnaeus gives us the authority to take what measures necessary to protect our asset.'

'I'm sure it does give you the right to protect the Linnaeuses,' agrees DS Silky, 'but not spy on them twenty-four seven. You've seen the house – the only street access away from here is through the front door that your personnel can observe from the van you've parked outside. So unless you want me to arrest you on the grounds of forced imprisonment, good night.'

The head of security and his four armed security personnel reluctantly retreat from the house.

Once they have gone DS Silky speaks to the Linnaeuses. 'That has bought you some privacy, for now, but don't expect it to last. Global Cocoa will have their lawyers enforcing that full surveillance clause in no time. And the Government will agree to it until your work is completed. You are now effectively under house arrest.'

The detective hands Rikard the burner phone acquired from Dunstan. 'Look through the photographs.' He does – naturally appalled at what he sees. 'These are the type of people Global Cocoa get to do their dirty work. They initially kidnapped Lovisa for personal financial gain. The liberation of the cocoa tissue cultures you have in your possession was a front. Their intention being to sell them to the highest bidder on the cocoa black market. Until…'

'Global Cocoa and the Government saw an opportunity to control me and my work,' Rikard finishes the detective's sentence. 'Whittaker didn't hide it from me.' Turning to his wife, he says, 'I'm sorry I caused this to happen to you.'

'It wasn't your fault,' Lovisa tells her husband, excitedly adding, 'The Chocolate Thieves rescued me along with DS Silky.'

'Really – is this true?' asks Rikard.

'Yes,' says DS Silky. 'I've come to realise that any official police action, and station, would not be a safe place for Lovisa – not out of the glare of political opportunity. So, on securing her freedom with their help, we brought her straight home.'

'Thank you, DS Silky, for your integrity in the face of what I can only imagine has been a lot of political pressure,' says Rikard.

'Dr Linnaeus, the people you are working for have no interest in your well-being. My superior, DI Gloom, expressed it accurately when he set me the task of finding Lovisa: "Click 'Like' if the wife should die to save chocolate." The public, the Government and certainly not Global Cocoa are to be trusted with the well-being of either of your lives.'

Rikard looks exhausted by the situation and at a loss as to what to do. 'I just wanted to save cocoa.'

'Trust me when I tell you a solution to your predicament is going to present itself very soon,' the detective tells him. 'For now, lock the front door securely behind me.'

The solution to the Linnaeuses' predicament comes in the form of the video call app ringing on the burner phone.

'Answer it,' Lovisa tells her husband.

Rikard cautiously answers the phone, 'Hello?'

'Dr Rikard Linnaeus – I presume?' asks the female with the husky voice.

'Yes.'

'Good.'

'This is my wife, Lovisa.'

'Pleasure. So would you like rescuing?'

'Yes – but from here to where?'

'Excellent question. My name is Mabel Arber.'

'The Mabel Arber? You're a bloody cocoa legend.'

'Yes I am. And you, Dr Rikard Linnaeus, are a cocoa genius – so we'll make a good team.'

'But you must be… well…'

'Yes, I'm a hundred years old. Why is everyone so surprised? I live off the purest of cocoa – it's life-giving. Ask Lovisa about the biscuits I sent to hasten her recovery from her ordeal.'

Lovisa reluctantly produces a chocolate biscuit out of her pocket that she'd been saving for eating in bed with a cuppa later that night.

'Go on – taste it,' Aunt Mabel instructs him.

He does and there is the expected delightful sensation of the purest of cocoa chocolate flavours transmitted through his taste receptors.

'Good – eh?'

'Incredible,' is Rikard's response.

'Now, I have enough of that cocoa to resurrect chocolate outside of the grubby hands of Global Cocoa and their political puppets. Do you want to know more?'

Twenty minutes later after a quick tour of Chocolate Tree Farm's greenhouses Lovisa has one question.

'How safe will it be?'

'Are you safe where you are now?' They all know the answer is no. So Aunt Mabel adds, 'This is a very secure location, I assure you, but we will no doubt, once found, come under physical threat. But you will not be prisoners and your safety will be a priority – we've got chocolate to grow after all.'

The following morning Rikard Linnaeus is standing on the doorsteps of his home facing the gathered media, the Home Secretary and the Commissioner of Police all smiles either side of him. 'I am relieved to tell you that Lovisa is safely back at home, unharmed, but angered and very frightened by her ordeal. Thank you to DS Silky and The Chocolate Thieves for rescuing her from the kidnappers. It was down to their determination to do what is right that Lovisa has been returned.'

'The kidnappers are in custody,' interrupts the Home Secretary. 'Now it is time to grow some chocolate.'

She curtails any questions from the journalists by escorting Rikard to the car waiting to take him to his laboratory.

The small fleet of taxis coming along the hidden lane announces the arrival of The Chocolate Thieves to Chocolate Tree Farm. Cases and boxes of everything they need for an extended stay are quickly unloaded and they are soon settled into their new home.

Having brought with them the first draft of *The History of The Chocolate Thieves*, immediately upon arrival Savage and Dorothea inhabit the library to set about their first edit of the manuscript. Which means spending the first few days distracting themselves with scouring every book on the floor-to-ceiling shelves of the bookcases lining the walls for new knowledge.

Whole shelves are given over to Aunt Mabel's cocoa research. It is a study of the cultivation of naturally disease-resistant rootstock using the DNA of pure native varieties of cocoa and the husbandry of the trees through their environmental requirements. Primarily arguing for flavour over yield but also proving the case for selected hybridisation of naturally compatible varieties that retain optimum flavour while producing higher yields to satisfy the ever-increasing global population of chocolate addicts. Nowhere is she imperialistic – her manifesto is purely an excitement at the conservation of native varieties and the exploration of new flavour hybrids rather than an industrial-scale cultivation of a simulacra of cocoa.

'This really does have to be the final chapter,' points out Savage as he types across the top of a blank page on the laptop. 'What do you think of "Resurrecting Chocolate" as a title?'

'It's good. But there's more than a final chapter to write, isn't there? We've an opportunity to tell in clearer detail about how CHOC 2 and Aunt Mabel met during the war.'

'True.'

'To which end, look at what I've found.' Dorothea shows Savage a manuscript with the title *The Chocolate Spy*, authored by Mabel Arber, copyright dated 1946. Written as a fiction it is an account of her wartime adventures as an SOE agent.

They scan through the opening chapters detailing the character's modest upbringing in North London, university life in Oxford, recruitment to SOE and training until they find what they are looking for…

On the 30th June 1942, having checked the flight paths of that evening's sorties over enemy territories, with the confidence of her training, she walks over to the crew of the Wellington bomber named CHOC 2-AIR and introduces herself to Savage the Pilot, Furness the Second Pilot/Air Gunner, Dunstan the Observer/Navigator, Stanley Oak the Wireless Operator/Air Gunner and one George Midas, Air Gunner.

'Good evening, gentlemen. Violette Begue. Any chance of a lift? You seem to be flying to where I want to be. Don't

worry I've brought my own parachute,' she says, disarming them with a mischievous smile.

The night is cloudy enough to make it across the Channel without any problems but arriving over Normandy into a clear moonlit sky the flak from the anti-aircraft defence is ferocious and on target. And the German air defence in the form of the Luftwaffe in their Messerschmitt Bf 109s are in feisty mood as well. Despite Savage's expert defensive flying and the best efforts of Furness, Oak and Midas at their guns – hitting their targets and sending the enemy spiralling to the ground – CHOC 2-AIR's time, after a hundred sorties, is up. When both engines burst into flames, Savage reluctantly gives the order for the crew and their passenger to bale out. Violette points to her map and tells the crew to meet her at an ancient yew tree in a stone circle four miles due south of Bayeux. The last to jump, Savage puts the plane onto a specific crash course – the fuel depot they were intending to bomb.

Parachuting to the ground, CHOC 2-AIR's crew and one passenger watch as the plane hits her target of the fuel depot two miles east of the town of Bayeux and the 4,500 pounds of bombs in her bomb-bay do their job – igniting the stored fuel at the depot. And the night sky is set on fire.

An hour later the cold barrels of the three rifles quietly touch the back of Savage, Furness and Dunstan's necks – freezing them to the spot with raised hands.

Keeping out of the moonlight they'd walked into what appeared to be a deserted ancient stone circle in the centre of which is the beautiful hundreds-of-years-old yew tree. Clearly it wasn't deserted.

There are unnerving moments of silence.

Then out from behind the yew tree steps Violette. 'Now that was one hell of a flight.' She speaks in French to the man beside her and he gives a short nod to his compatriots who lower their guns. 'This is Andre Jourdin – he's the leader of the local Resistance. And our host for the time of our stay.'

A mile away, Stanley Oak, crouched behind a fallen rotting tree trunk in a field, watches the German officer's Mercedes-Benz car pull to a halt in the road just ahead of the nonchalantly strolling Midas. Is he really going to brazen it out? A soldier gets out of the passenger seat and points his gun at the young airman. There follows a short inaudible exchange in German. Midas speaks fluent German? Although not able to speak the language himself, Oak can understand the surprise and curiosity in the voice coming from the back seat of the car. The commanding officer leans into the moonlight to look at Midas, smiles, then invites him to get into the rear of the car next to him – which the airman does without resistance and is driven away.

Oak makes his way to the yew tree to rendezvous with the rest of his crew – informing them of what he had just witnessed.

Violette radios SOE headquarters to arrange an extraction for the crew of CHOC 2-AIR and gets them to a safe place of hiding – the loft of the Jourdin family's Bayeux town house, while she goes about her own mission.

Operation Tapestry is the assassination of General Karl Guderian – the man in overall command of the Bayeux region – acquiring the German military plans for the area and the coordination of the Resistance in the disruption of German military operations.

With the help of Andre and his people she is able, over the next few days, to schedule the clockwork-like movements of Guderian.

'Interestingly, he's taken up residence in a suite at Bayeux Chocolat, a factory that does seem, according to Andre's inside contact, to produce nothing but chocolate. I need to get into the labs to find out what else is being developed there,' Violette informs the airmen over supper on the fourth night.

'You'll find it's nothing but chocolate flavour trials,' says Savage.

'What makes you so sure?' questions Violette.

'We know chocolate and the people who are addicted to it. I believe General Guderian is one of the purveyors of Berlin's finest luxury cocoa delights,' offers Furness.

'And he has Midas, suggesting on the face of it that Midas is in cahoots with the Germans, which despite his family history of opportunism in the extreme, I think not on this occasion,' says Dunstan.

Furness's expression says he doesn't agree with this analysis.

'Why not?' asks Violette.

'Because he is proudly British,' says Oak. 'He won't let anyone harm his country if he can stop it. And the fact that his father's chocolate factory was bombed by the Luftwaffe a few weeks ago.'

'No, what General Karl Guderian has Midas doing is making English chocolate,' states Dunstan.

'Oh, bloody hell!' exclaims Violette.

'Indeed,' says Savage. 'They're going to lace the chocolate, drop it into our cities and poison anyone who eats it.'

'With sweet rationing it will be an indulgence of uncontrollable temptation with a grotesque outcome,' adds Furness.

'It's genocide by chocolate,' says Violette.

'You're going to need our help – we know how to steal

chocolate,' Dunstan tells the spy.

'Who are you people?' demands Violette.

'Between you and us,' says Savage, indicating to Furness and Dunstan, 'we're The Chocolate Thieves.'

Violette looks at Stanley Oak. He confirms they are telling the truth with a smile and a nod. 'I just lend a sleight of hand when it's needed.'

The SOE agent grins at them. 'Perfect.'

In the morning Andre and Violette join Monsieur Begue, the owner of Bayeux Chocolat, at his table in The Liberte Cafe in the town square. The chocolatier listens to what they have to say and wistfully tells them, 'I knew this day would come. And if the reasons you say are true – then it is the right thing to do. I will draw up a detailed plan of the factory indicating where the explosives will have the most effect.'

It is at this moment they are unexpectedly joined at their table by General Guderian. 'Good morning, Monsieur Begue.'

'Good morning, General,' replies the chocolatier.

'And who do we have here?'

'Well, I'm sure you know Andre Jourdin, the history teacher in our school.'

'Of course, good morning.' His eyes are quickly on Violette. 'But you I have not met.'

'I'm Violette Begue, just arrived in town to steal some of my uncle's chocolates,' she says with a smile.

'A charming idea, Mademoiselle Begue. And I'm sure with that disarming smile you could simply walk out of the gates of the factory, arms full of your uncle's exquisite creations. But alas I cannot let you do such a thing.'

'How disappointing.'

'Not without first inviting you to an evening of tasting

the sophisticated chocolate inspirations of my homeland.'

The following evening at 7pm, Violette Begue walks into the General's suite at Bayeux Chocolat. And finds herself plied with champagne and a selection of 'Specially handmade for the evening' Cabaret Chocolates: The Foxtrot, The Tango and The Waltz.

'German decadence of 65% Sao Tome cocoa chocolates made with the sophisticated expertise of your Bayeux chocolatiers.'

She indulges the General in tasting his confectionary – disappointingly, it is as good a chocolate as he believes it to be – drinks his champagne and listens to the decadence of his life story as a pre-war chocolatier in Berlin.

Violette turns up the music as loud as it will play on the gramophone and entreats the General to dance with her.

At 8pm twenty men and women of the French Resistance take on 160 German soldiers across the town.

And the town is alive with explosions, bursts of machine-gun fire, single-round shots, the shouts of commanding officers, the screams of the dying and the ricochet of bullets echoing along the streets.

Bodies litter the pavements and cafes.

Very calmly, Andre Jourdin, The Chocolate Thieves, Stanley Oak and five Resistance fighters step out of the shadows of a nearby street and make their way across the road, walk through the left-open-for-them factory gates, releasing bursts of rapid fire from their Sten guns as required and set about laying charges and seeking out Midas.

With the loud music the sound of the war outside has yet to breach the romance of the suite. Thinking he has seduced Violette's consent for sex, General Guderian is making his move. As he holds her in his arms, his nimble fingers unbutton her dress – ready for him, like it or not. Violette turns away from him and lets his lips caress her neck. His smooth, strong hands running over her. She leans forwards pushing herself against him, exciting him to complete distraction, and reaches with her right hand for the Browning HP pistol she has strapped to the inside of her left thigh.

Gun in hand, she spins round to face the German – violently pushing him off her as she does so.

Now the war comes to his ears.

The startled and afraid General Karl Guderian calculates the distance to his own gun hanging on the back of a chair and the time needed to reach it. In the fraction of a moment this all takes, Violette, as trained, releases two rapid shots into Guderian's chest and he drops to the floor dead.

The SOE agent searches for and quickly finds the General's troop movements and armament plans for the area. Heading out of the apartment and down the stairs she shoots and kills the soldiers who have just shot dead Monsieur Begue and his wife in their apartment on the floor below.

Dunstan pulls aside the dead soldier and opens the door to the laboratory. Finding Midas inside, preparing to burn papers indicating his complicity.

'There's no need for that,' Dunstan tells him and sets the timers of the explosives he places around the lab for one minute.

Furness walks over to the young chocolatier. 'What have you been doing here?'

'They wanted English chocolate laced with cyanide – I've been using pure almond extract to fool them.'

Furness picks up a vessel and sniffs the clear liquid inside – it smells of almonds. 'Taste it.'

'You have serious trust issues, Furness. I'm not my father.'

'One day you might be tempted to be.'

Midas drinks from the vessel. He doesn't die.

Dunstan is at the door. 'Gentlemen, I suggest we leave now.'

In the yard Savage jumps behind the wheel of a truck laden with chocolates; a man of his word, Monsieur Begue has left four trucks loaded with chocolate with the keys in the ignition as if ready for an early-morning delivery. Savage starts the engine. In the passenger-door mirror he sees a Resistance fighter shot dead by a soldier as he goes to climb into the passenger seat alongside him. Under fire from Stanley Oak the soldier takes cover around the back of the truck. Savage slips it into reverse gear and crushes the soldier against the wall behind him.

Oak gets into the truck next to Savage's and starts the engine.

Furness, Dunstan and Midas shoot their way to the other two trucks and Violette jumps in alongside Savage. With Andre and his Resistance fighters clinging to the side of the trucks, continuously firing, in convoy they roar out of the factory under a hail of bullets.

And then the bombs go off – razing Bayeux Chocolat to the ground.

Four miles south of the town the makeshift runway receives the extraction plane – dropping much-needed weaponry for the Resistance and carrying the crew of CHOC 2-AIR back to their squadron. Violette entrusting The Chocolate Thieves with delivery of the German military plans to SOE headquarters before she and Andre, along with the surviving Resistance members, disappear into the night with their booty of chocolates to continue their fight.

The mist of theobromine and valerian synthesised by Aunt Mabel and Rikard Linnaeus creeps slowly from the river towards the Linnaeus Cocoa Laboratory, shrouding the building – seeping in through air vents to fill the corridors.

One by one the security guards begin to relax, some sit down, their guns placed on the ground at their feet, others lean against walls, their guns dropped by their sides. As the mist thickens to a dense fog they all begin to drift into a peaceful daze.

Rikard Linnaeus had insisted that he needed to establish the new cocoa tissue cultures' viability in laboratory conditions – getting the trees past the in-vitro stage to the growth level of plantlets to ensure their chance of ex-situ survival before any escape plan could be enacted.

Streamed live, the growth of the cocoa trees is watched across the world – a three-year Global Cocoa clock counting down to the first new chocolate embedded in the footage.

At 9pm the electricity to the building is cut. Alone in his sealed laboratory, air conditioning off – so no risk of mist inhalation – Rikard Linnaeus has seconds to wait before the back-up generator kicks in – but it doesn't. Good. He readies himself to leave. Having paced out the steps to the cocoa plantlets and across the laboratory to the door repeatedly over the previous weeks he finds his way easily in the dark.

There are four small humidity trays – a hundred plantlets in total to carry. Stacking them on top of each other he makes it to the laboratory door. There is the sound of the slumping to the ground of the guards on the other side.

Then the door opens and the gas-masked figure of Dunstan, with Furness beside him, shines a torch onto him and says, 'Taxi for Chocolate Tree Farm.'

Dunstan puts a gas mask on the scientist – who nods that he can breathe – and splitting the trays of plantlets between them the three men walk swiftly through the mist-filled building. Reaching the lobby they find CHOC 4 waiting for them, having been reversed through the locked glass doors. The three men get into the taxi and Savage drives them away.

Once they are a street away everyone pulls off their gas masks, The Chocolate Thieves wearing balaclavas, and Rikard Linnaeus realises he still doesn't know what who he is entrusting his and Lovisa's lives to look like. But he sees the friendly smiles in his rescuers' eyes.

'Now let's go pick up your wife,' says Savage.

Lovisa Linnaeus runs. Having jumped out of the bathroom window into the garden – all the doors and windows on the ground floor to the garden and street being locked and keys removed by her guards. She runs faster than she has ever run. A determined sprint across the wet grass. She has to make it the whole length of their garden. She knows she can make the twenty metre run-up. It's the jump she's not sure about. And now she's at that point where she has to step onto the garden bench and launch herself off it up into the tree.

The security detail, having burst through the front door, have now reached the garden.

They shout at her to stop.

Don't look back, she thinks, they've got night-vision eyes and carry guns – which she knows are pointing at her.

One of them fires a warning shot over her head.

She ignores it.

On pure survival instinct Lovisa steps onto the bench, it falls away from her feet as she reaches up to the lowest hanging branch and pulls herself up. More gunfire. After frantically climbing up through the branches, she jumps over the wall into the neighbour's garden and into the arms of Rikard.

As the security detail spill over the garden wall after her it is a dash the length of this garden, through the sleeping house, out to the street and into the back of the waiting taxi.

Savage floors the accelerator and they rip through the streets of Richmond pursued by a Global Cocoa drone.

Under the cover of trees in Richmond cemetery, Savage emergency stops CHOC 4 alongside CHOC 3 with Dorothea at the wheel. Plantlets in their arms the Linnaeuses jump across to the other taxi.

Once again Savage floors the accelerator, emerging from beneath the trees, travelling at full throttle through the gravestones and out into the street. CHOC 4 heads north into central London, the drone hawking above, the Global Cocoa security van now on their tail.

At Putney Bridge DS Silky lets the taxi across and then closes the north and south end of the bridge with police vehicles.

Trapped, the Global Cocoa van screeches to a halt.

Stanley Oak and his crew disguised as armed police officers pull the unimpressed security detail out of the van and demand the drone be grounded.

In the early hours of the next day, having taken the necessary circuitous route to evade detection, CHOC 3, followed a short time later by CHOC 4, arrives at Chocolate Tree Farm and deposits Rikard and Lovisa Linnaeus and the cocoa tree plantlets at a place of sanctuary.

Aunt Mabel plies them with mugs of hot chocolate and shows them to their room – they can talk and explore their new home after breakfast.

Their first day at Chocolate Tree Farm is full of rain and wonderment. Full introductions are made without balaclavas masking identities.

'We are in your debt,' Rikard tells The Chocolate Thieves, 'for rescuing Lovisa and bringing us here.'

'Please, think nothing of it,' Savage tells him.

'It was the right thing to do,' says Furness.

'And without you, Dr Linnaeus, Aunt Mabel tells us we cannot resurrect chocolate,' adds Dunstan.

Aunt Mabel gives her new house guests a tour of the farm – Rikard, open-mouthed, is barely able to speak at the sight of such beautifully cultivated cocoa trees.

Seeing the trees through the eyes of a fellow cocoa scientist, especially one as esteemed as Dr Rikard Linnaeus, Aunt Mabel realises how pleased she is with her endeavours and how little she gives herself credit for her life's work.

'And here is a dedicated greenhouse for your plantlets,' she tells him.

Rikard's mind is whirling with the cocoa-cultivation possibilities before him. 'Light, temperature, humidity, soil – it's a perfect ecosystem,' he gasps.

'Good,' says Aunt Mabel. 'Now, Lovisa, I have something to show you.' The two women leave Rikard to his new-found cocoa tree paradise and walk across the meadow to the east of the house where Aunt Mabel gives Lovisa the key to her observatory housing a fifteen-inch Newtonian telescope. 'There's little to no light pollution so the constellations are exquisite.'

The astrophysicist's face contorts into a cute smile of curiosity and excitement. 'Thank you.'

Heading back to the house Aunt Mabel laughs, a light pleased laugh – the Linnaeuses will do just fine here.

Back in DI Gloom's office DS Silky listens with resigned irritation as the Commissioner of Police paces up and down the room in pristine media-friendly authoritarian uniform. 'This anarchy has to stop. You are to find The Chocolate Thieves and return Dr Linnaeus and the chocolate trees. Our reputations depend upon it. The law and order of our society depends upon it. The chocolate world is depending on it. Damn it! Every wide-eyed chocolate junkie is watching our every move.'

DS Silky glares at DI Gloom – who simply shrugs. It's his fault: if he hadn't handed her that bloody file a year ago she'd still be happily tracking down murderers. Not searching for confectionary. 'Can we not just accept that chocolate is finished and, I don't know, eat an apple instead?' she suggests.

'No we bloody well cannot,' blurts out the astounded Commissioner of Police. 'How dare you even suggest such a thing. You can't replace chocolate with fruit – what is wrong with you?'

'It could be the end of obesity and diabetes if we just accept that chocolate is extinct,' goads DS Silky.

'This is our best detective?' The senior officer raises a mocking, sceptical, eyebrow at DI Gloom.

'You know she is, sir,' defends DI Gloom with a barely suppressed smile. 'The case of The Late Horologist is my favourite – never get tired of reading that one.'

'Which suggests she is deliberately ignoring the cliff edge of the ecological disaster the world is standing on,' points out their senior officer.

'It's true, Commissioner, I don't have shares in Global Cocoa,' impertinently responds DS Silky.

'It took us a hundred years to get close to The Chocolate Thieves a second time,' interjects DI Gloom. 'They know how to disappear.'

'Which is what I suggest you do immediately, Detective. Use all your chocolate world contacts and go detect.' And with that the Commissioner of Police exits the office with the air of someone who believes they are going to get the outcome they desire.

'They know how to live off-grid without leaving a trace of their existence. How are you going to find them?' DI Gloom asks his detective.

'You've answered your own question,' DS Silky informs him. But DI Gloom just looks at her with his usual querying brow. 'I shall seek them where no one lives.' She enigmatically smiles.

All news channels are excitedly reporting the disappearance of Dr Rikard Linnaeus and the cocoa tissue cultures. Reporters tripping over their words at 'What a catastrophe for the chocolate-craving world this is.'

What is interesting is the suppression of the fact that Global Cocoa and the Government know it can be no one else but The Chocolate Thieves that rescued the Linnaeuses and stole the cocoa plantlets – a deliberate act of starving the anti–Global Cocoa chocolate liberationists cause of oxygen.

It is also reported that, 'An emergency session of the United Nations has been called to discuss the latest developments in The Chocolate Apocalypse.'

'Here we go.' Savage sighs as, all gathered in the lounge, they watch the latest hysterical news report.

The Home Secretary is being interviewed along with Seb Lilburne of Chocolate For The People.

'Home Secretary, this wasn't part of the plan, was it?' asks the journalist.

'Well, no, clearly not. Let me just say to the people who have perpetrated this crime,' she looks directly into the camera, 'what do you hope to gain? Where is the profit in what you are doing? Don't you like chocolate?'

Lilburne simply says, 'It wasn't us. Chocolate For The People want to see chocolate returned to the people – we can't do that if there isn't any cocoa from which to make chocolate.'

'So you agree with the Home Secretary that there is no profit in this action?'

'I try not to use the words "profit" and "chocolate" in the same breath. Our first concern is the welfare of the Linnaeuses – their and the cocoa's security was clearly a farce.'

'So you think heads should roll?' provokes the journalist.

'The head of every member of this self-serving socially neglectful Government should roll – a cultural revolution is long overdue in this country. Don't you think the Home Secretary's head would look pretty on a spike at the Tower of London?'

'Anarchy is not going to solve any of life's problems,' rebukes the Home Secretary.

'Yes – but it's fun to imagine it could.' Lilburne pulls on the Home Secretary's collar and examines her neck, sizing up a cutting point.

'Get off!' Ruffled, she brushes his hand away. 'We're getting off the point – where are our bloody chocolate trees?'

'Do you think there is much hope of seeing the cocoa trees again?' enquires the journalist.

'Let me assure you and everyone watching this broadcast,' the Home Secretary now glares down the lens of the camera, 'this Government will stop at nothing to retrieve our chocolate trees.'

'Which means they'll be letting the Global Cocoa

militia find us and deal with us with lethal force,' comments Dunstan.

The report turns its attention to the conspiracy theorists who have ignited the social-networking sites stating that a secret world order known as the Obscuranti now control cocoa with the intention of cultivating a super-cocoa genetically engineered to enslave all the world's people through addiction to do the bidding of an elite 1%.

'I thought they'd done that already with absolutely everything we consume,' muses Kyoko.

'It's time to talk security,' Aunt Mabel tells her house guests having gathered them in the library. And presses a hidden button on the bookcase to the left of the fireplace. There is the clanking sound of the unlocking of a door and the bookcase opens out into the room to reveal a secret staircase taking them down into a basement control room beneath the library. Which, judging by its furnishings, was set up during World War Two. Large-scale maps of the farm and the surrounding area hang on the walls. With the later addition of a bank of monitors revealing that the whole farm and the roads leading to it are covered by security cameras.

'From this bunker we can observe and control all access to and movement within the farm,' says Aunt Mabel. 'The cameras are fully controllable.' She zooms in on a deer grazing at the edge of the wood. 'You know about the digital faraday cage – no phone or drone signal and no person-to-person radio signal. That console there controls the areas it is deployed in. At present it's set to everywhere.

'They can't attack with heavy armaments for fear of destroying the cocoa trees. But there are plenty of ways they can eliminate us so we need to be able to actively defend ourselves. This switch here,' she points to an innocuous brass toggle, 'operates the electric moat: a series of conducting cables, charged by the solar panels on the barns, laid on the ground surrounding the farm buildings and the greenhouses – a line of defence of alternating current with up to 2,000 volts and 20 amps running through it.' She draws their attention to one of the maps. 'It runs just the other side of the observatory to the east, along the tree line of the wood to the south around the greenhouses and the barns to the west and just inside the orchards and across the lane to the north.' Pointing at a monitor where a rabbit is grazing, she says, 'We can go from a light jolt, little more than a static shock, to warn the little fellows off.' She adjusts the dial and switches on the moat. In their heads they can hear the rabbit squeal as it leaps into the air, ears and hair sticking up on end, at the jolt of electricity. 'To a killer shock.' Aunt Mabel turns the switch to max and sends a second jolt of electricity. This time the rabbit comically shivers and falls over. 'And supper is caught.' The room is in stunned silence. 'It is, as you see, a potentially lethal security measure that will be permanently switched on at medium disabling pain and embarrassing defecation level. So memorise where it is for fear of getting zapped. And from now on one of us will be down here, in shifts, monitoring for any unwanted activity. We don't know when Global Cocoa will arrive but be assured they will come for their cocoa.'

Dunstan finds himself inspecting the armoury lining the wall behind them. A selection of lethal weaponry dating from World War Two – a rack of Sten guns, Browning pistols, and Bren light machine guns. With boxes of ammunition. There is also a collection of sheathed Fairbairn–Sykes double-edged fighting knifes.

'Don't worry, we shan't be using the killing stuff –

they're here as museum pieces. You don't need to kill to win battles – you just need to disarm your enemy. To which end we have nature on our side.' Aunt Mabel issues everyone with a gas mask. 'To be carried with you at all times.'

'What is that red button for?' asks Kyoko pointing at the large key-locked button on the right side of the console.

'That, my dear, destroys the greenhouses,' is Aunt Mabel's blunt answer. 'The unlocking and pressing of it creates an explosive chain reaction that will burn all the trees to ashes.' They are horrified at the thought of this scenario. 'If it comes to it, have no doubt, it is a decision I'm willing to take to stop any state or conglomerate with nefarious intentions getting their glutinous fingers on my life's work.'

In her minimalist one-bedroom Islington flat, all white walls and just enough furniture to be comfortable and hint at being a home, DS Silky removes every camera and bug installed in her absence by Karl Dance and his team – destroying them in the microwave.

She then prints off the photograph she took of The Chocolate Thieves family tree and studies it, circling the name *Mabel Arber* – chocolate scientist at Chocolate Tree Farm.

Switching off her phone and iPad she puts both in the safe behind the painting of the woman sitting in an armchair reading a book and eating chocolates hanging in the living room.

Changing into black combat gear she packs a rucksack of survival essentials.

Having blinded Global Cocoa to her activities in her apartment, she has to now get out of the building undetected or at the very least not be followed once she is outside. Looking out of the living-room window she sees the presence of the Global Cocoa security detail – a man and woman sitting in the SUV across the street that had followed her home from Scotland Yard. In the sky above the building a drone hovers. Out of the bedroom window she sees the second security detail, another man and a woman in another SUV, watching her route down the fire escape at the back of the building. No doubt they are monitoring the CCTV on the landings and in the stairwells as well.

Putting on an outer layer of black waterproof trousers and jacket, with hood up, she walks out of the front door of the building into the road, pulls up a manhole cover and climbs down into the sewers. Pulling the cover back into place just as a bus stops over the top of it to drop off passengers.

Half a mile into her subterranean journey DS Silky sees a shaft of daylight appear just ahead of her as a manhole cover is lifted. A Global Cocoa security operative steps onto the metal rung ladder and descends into the sewer. The detective advances on the woman. Hearing the echo of running footsteps she looks about her just as DS Silky grabs hold of her, pulls her off the ladder and throws her into the brick wall lining the sewer – decisive blows crumple the operative unconscious to the floor.

Another half a mile later, pausing to check her route on her map, she hears approaching footsteps. Extinguishing her head torch and stepping out of sight into a side tunnel she watches a second Global Cocoa security operative walk past her. Stealthily, she catches up with him – a kick to the back of the knee buckles him, a baton to his right ear disorientates him, and lifting him up she shoves him head first, waist deep, into a nearby fatberg.

A mile on the detective stops and turns to look at the

third security operative to follow her into the sewers. The female operative stops and stares at her – none of them have the remit to approach, or attack. Their orders are to simply follow the detective to wherever she goes and report on her interactions. So she waits. DS Silky is just standing there looking at her. Listening. The detective smiles at the sound of the swirl and low rumble of water. Too late the operative looks up and realises she is beneath an inflow pipe – the shower of effluence taking her off balance, flushing her along the tunnel, soaking and stinking her to the bone.

Laughing, DS Silky steps into a side tunnel continuing her journey through the brick-lined maze.

Another half a mile and the sound of another manhole cover being lifted, then the splashing of footsteps coming in her direction tell her she is still being followed. She stops. Where is she? Just below Shoreditch High Street. How do they know which direction she is walking in? The detective checks her pockets and the seams of her clothes. Nothing. She searches her rucksack. There it is – a tracking device pushed into the seam of the left outside pocket. She pulls it out and walks along to the next intersection of tunnels. The sound of footsteps grows closer to her. She embeds the tracker in a lump of floating faeces, sails it away from her and sets off in the opposite direction.

Twenty minutes later she emerges into a dark, forgotten corner of the cellar of The Sleight Of Hand, pulls off her waterproofs, grabs a bottle of beer and makes her way upstairs. She opens the door to the bar just enough for Stanley Oak to see her face and he follows her upstairs to his living quarters.

DS Silky shows him the print-out of The Chocolate

Thieves family tree with Mabel Arber's name circled. 'They are with her at this location, aren't they?'

Stanley Oak nods. 'Most likely.' He tells her what he knows about Mabel Arber but does not know where the farm is.

'Do you have her phone number?'

'No. She calls you – never leaving a traceable number.'

Sitting down at Oak's computer and accessing the National Library of Scotland's online archive of UK maps, the detective scans map after map radiating out from central London to a distance of a taxi ride away – looking for a location possible to get to before being spotted by drones and drive to by avoiding the main road arteries. Somewhere where cocoa trees will grow.

Era by era, map after map, from the late 1800s to the present day, looking for Chocolate Tree Farm – it does not exist on any of them. But what she does begin to see is the disappearance of farms that existed in the 1920s but vanish off the maps drawn leading up to World War Two. Then she sees that these farms reappear on maps drawn after the war – but not all of them. Long Acre Farm, Ash Tree Farm, Wild Lane Farm, Dragonfly Pond Farm, Windmill Farm and Tawny Owl Farm have all disappeared.

DS Silky maps out a route to each of the locations where the farms should be. 'I've got to get to them before Global Cocoa raises their militia and causes more harm than good.'

'What level of harm?' enquires Oak.

'I have no doubt that under their UN-sanctioned cocoa plant rights they are going to kill whoever they find at the farm. Claiming legal rights to any cocoa they find there in the name of corporate chocolate resurrection.'

'And the world will let it happen.'

'There will be short-term outcry but the members of the

Government with shares in Global Cocoa will weather historical criticism for this lifetime's chocolate profits.'

'What are you going to do?'

'Get in the way.'

'A dangerous and possibly futile thing to do.'

'You only die once – might as well make it ridiculous.'

'There's no need to die alone.'

'Let me find out what The Chocolate Thieves set-up is first. For now I need you here on the street and DI Gloom at the Yard as my eyes and ears of what's happening in the city.'

Oak provides her with a burner phone, cash and the key to his Range Rover. And with a concerned smile of 'Good luck' and a kiss he watches her drive away into the night.

Seb Lilburne doesn't hesitate to post the film emailed to him by The Chocolate Thieves on the Chocolate For The People website of Rikard and Lovisa Linnaeus explaining why they had to escape from Global Cocoa's incarceration – including all the evidence of the company's complicity in the kidnapping of Lovisa. And that the cocoa plantlets are being cultivated in a secret location. Included in the film is hacked footage from Global Cocoa's security cameras in the Linnaeus home of the threat to Lovisa's life if Rikard doesn't cultivate the RLC-2021 cocoa by Bill Whittaker as the Home Secretary and Commissioner of Police look on.

It has the atomic bomb effect all concerned had intended. By lunchtime the following day Global Cocoa's share price is washed into the gutter and flowing straight into the stock market sewer. The Home Secretary has resigned in an attempt to save the Government and the Commissioner of Police is clearing his desk.

On the international political stage the Portuguese

General Secretary of the United Nations, Abriana Magellan, calls an emergency session to discuss the cocoa recultivation crisis.

And with perfect timing The Chocolate Thieves release a second film, this time presented by Aunt Mabel from inside the Chocolate Tree Farm greenhouses.

'My name is Mabel Arber, I am a hundred years old – thanks to the wonderful life-giving properties of cocoa. And I am an SOE agent. I tell you this as a point of reference but also as a fact to reinforce in your minds that I talk to you from first-hand experience and knowledge of the tyranny of totalitarianism. But most importantly I am a cocoa scientist – all my research papers are in the British Library and posted online for you to read.

'And these are my cocoa trees – a variety from every cocoa-growing region of the world. As you can see they are healthy, high-yielding trees.' She takes a bite of one of her chocolate biscuits. 'The chocolate is bloody delicious too.

'I would like to point out that these trees are under the protection of The Chocolate Thieves – so I advise anyone who would think of taking ownership of them not to try.

'Theobroma means "food of the gods". Chocolate is certainly a beautiful food of nature – a gift we have forgotten the true taste of due to the flavour-extracting industrialisation and commercialisation of chocolate. And nature has done what nature does – taken advantage of our weakness, our greed, and so these are the only commercially viable cocoa trees left in the world. The immune system of these trees is strong enough to survive the diseases they will encounter if grown naturally in their true environment and not exploited beyond nature's yield. We have enough budwood to begin the recultivation of cocoa for the population of the world. If you let us.

'So this is what I propose. Budwood from these trees will be sent to their region of origin in Central and South American countries to be recultivated by native cocoa experts with the primary intention of resurrecting a naturally grown sustainable cocoa crop for the generations to come. This will take time – up to five years.

'As for the plantlets Dr Rikard Linnaeus has cultivated from his tissue cultures,' Aunt Mabel walks into Linnaeus's greenhouse where he is busily documenting the growth of the plantlets, the scientist smiles reassuringly at the camera, 'these will be planted in-situ in non-naturally growing cocoa countries that have expertise in these genetic vanguard varieties. I speak, of course, of the African continent and of Indonesia.'

Aunt Mabel concludes with, 'If the United Nations let us do this we will resurrect chocolate sustainably with fair trade practices for all of us living today and for the generations that follow us. It is up to you – the chocolate-loving people of the world.'

The noise of support in response to this film from all continents of the world is politically deafening. Aunt Mabel's war record is extracted from The National Archives and verified, her cocoa expertise analysed and proven to be without peer but for Dr Rikard Linnaeus. Her life as an SOE agent and the fact that she disappeared after the war to dedicate her life to cocoa is romanticised across every news channel and in every film producer's billion-dollar-box-office imagination.

The General Secretary of the United Nations walks out of the self-serving, flag-waving, table-thumping, jingoistic-wrangling-over-ownership-of-cocoa meeting and issues a statement live on television that leaves the government of each country a choice – defy the will of the majority of their people or capitulate. 'We agree to work with Mabel Arber, Dr Rikard Linnaeus and The Chocolate Thieves to recultivate chocolate. To which end, the plant rights granted to Global Cocoa by the United Nations are rescinded and transferred, rightfully, to the people of the world.'

And so the global search for the secret location of the last chocolate trees begins.

'Now they really are going to come for us,' says Savage, as The Chocolate Thieves watch the latest news coverage of The Chocolate Apocalypse. 'History tells us we must be prepared for a fight.'

'But who will arrive first – the British Government, the United Nations or Global Cocoa?' asks Furness.

'It will definitely be Global Cocoa – they have a militia, they are stateless and lawless. And they've lost everything,' says Dunstan.

Aunt Mabel appears at the door to the lounge. 'Right, ten minutes, I want everyone outside for combat training.'

'Cool.' Dorothea grins and mock punches Savage in the stomach. Who in return flicks her left ear.

Kyoko gives Dunstan a malicious smile. 'I'm so going to beat you up.' Dunstan gives her forearm a burning twist. 'Ow! You are a mean man.'

'Oh, how I'm going to hurt you, Furness,' says Afia, 'now help me up – I've sunk into the cushions.' Furness just tuts and pulls her up.

'Bloody children.' Aunt Mabel laughs.

Across the lawn are placed four straw-stuffed mannequins. The Chocolate Thieves and Linnaeuses are dressed in padded blue overalls. Aunt Mabel has the tone of an instructor addressing new recruits. 'The heel of your hand goes up onto the end of the nose of your assailant with enough force as if you are trying to make contact with the back of their skull. Chop with the edge of your hand to the throat or side or back of the neck as if you are trying to decapitate them. Your knee goes into their groin as if sending their genitals into their stomach – a punch will do this too.'

All take to the mannequins with disturbingly brutal relish, leaving the straw figures crumpled and defeated.

Next comes throwing. Dorothea brings her foot down across Savage's shin and twists him onto his knees by his right arm. Afia spins out of Furness's grip, grabs his shirt at the chest and trips him over her heel. Kyoko doubles over and throws Dunstan over her shoulder, pinning him to the ground by his throat. Lovisa stamps on Rikard's toe and wrenches him to the floor by his lapels as he hops about.

'Wonderful,' exclaims Aunt Mabel.

In reverse, Savage knocks away Dorothea's fists, spins her around, grabs her by the back of her trousers and collar, picks her up and lays her flat on her front. Furness dances around the pregnant Afia as she tries to get at him, suddenly grabbing her by each cheek and kissing her on the lips, holding her trapped there trying to push him away. Dunstan moves with such speed that Kyoko hasn't time to react, as she is turned upside down, swung round and slammed down onto her back – her limbs flopping defencelessly next to her. Rikard shows his wife no quarter either – grabbing her by the shoulders he falls backwards away from her punch, launching her over the top of him onto her back, jumps up and restrains her in a chokehold.

'I've never seen such enthusiastic fake killing,' utters a bewildered Aunt Mabel. 'Well, you're all clearly naturals at this. Amazing what having something to fight for reveals in people.'

Long Acre Farm and Ash Tree Farm are private houses –
the land long ago sold off. Wild Lane Farm is a
wonderfully creepy derelict cluster of buildings down, as
described, a lane reclaimed by nature. Dragonfly Pond
Farm is a nature reserve and Windmill Farm is a windmill
in a field with no sign of farming.

At sunset, now at Tawny Owl Farm, from her position
on the road to the east of the farm buildings, DS Silky,
standing on the roof of the Range Rover, looks through her
field glasses over the top of the hedge, observing the
smoke tendrils curling out of the farmhouse's chimneys –
someone lives and farms here.

As she scans the landscape the peculiar sight of a rabbit
leaping into the air and falling dead to the ground, as if
electrocuted by some invisible means of current, draws her
attention.

Focusing back on the house she sees the figure of
Savage, cocoa gin and tonic in hand, walk out into the
evening sunlight. 'So this is Chocolate Tree Farm.'

But where is the entrance?

Having sussed out the electric moat – what other
security have they in place? And how does she get through
it to reach The Chocolate Thieves?

Picking out the nearest security camera, the detective
takes out her torch and sends a Morse code message into
its lens: dash dot dot, dot dot dot, dot dot dot, dot dash,
dash, dash dot dash dash, dash dash dash, dot dot dash, dot
dash dot, dot dot dot, dot, dot dash dot, dot dot dot dash,
dot dot, dash dot dash dot, dot.

As Furness is serving up rabbit stew Aunt Mabel comes
up from the control room with the words, 'She's here. I
knew she'd find us. You'll need to set another place for

dinner,' and walks out of the front door.

'Who is here from where?' is expressed across the faces of the hungry household.

Standing at the front door, Mabel sends her own Morse code message by torch light: dot dash dash, dot, dot dash dot dot, dash dot dash dot, dash dash dash, dash dash, dot. Then she draws a line with the torch beam to the detective's right picking out the secret lane.

Five minutes later into the warmth of the parlour walks a roguishly smiling DS Silky. 'Good evening.'

Over dinner the detective brings them up to date on the events in the capital and the reality of the actions being taken by all political and commercially interested parties.

'According to my contacts in Special Branch, Westminster and MI5, the Government has washed their hands of the situation. You'll hear them make the correct political sounds in cautious support of the UN Secretary General's pronouncement – but they've personally too much invested. They sent me to find you because they knew I would.'

DS Silky describes how she discarded the security detail assigned to follow her every move and how, using the digital archive of old maps, she drew up a list of possible locations for Chocolate Tree Farm – impressing all around the table, particularly Aunt Mabel, with her ingenuity.

But the detective is quick to warn them of an inevitability. 'Someone within MI5 or Special Branch will do the same search. As far as Number 10 is concerned you're to be regarded as cocoa terrorists. They won't dream of sending in official forces – too politically unsound. The loudest voices of the people are on your side. They are politically constipated by the fear of it being an act leading to a civil war that would destabilise the economy. As long as they are in power they have a chance of turning a profit. But to do that they need your cocoa. So, by feeding Global Cocoa your location they get their desired end result.'

'What is the strength of Global Cocoa's militia?' asks Dunstan.

'According to my and DI Gloom's contacts in MI5 and Stanley Oak's sources within Global Cocoa, at last count, they have up to 200 well-trained ex-military men and women of multiple nationalities signed up. They're being flown in from all the company's territories. They aren't going to lay siege to you. They will attack quickly and brutally before the world can stop them.'

At sunrise DS Silky is taken on a tour of the farm by Aunt Mabel. 'It's a real pleasure to meet you, DS Silky – it's good to have you on side.'

'Thank you. It's good to be here,' she says fussing a friendly horse that has wandered over to them to say hello. 'I've read your SOE record – you're an inspiration.'

'Thank you, that is kind, but I am a dangerous one I fear,' replies Aunt Mabel looking back to the farmhouse, hearing The Chocolate Thieves chatting and laughing together as they make breakfast.

DS Silky reads the concern on the woman's face. 'They love the romance of what they do. And doing it with you, here, at least they can succeed. What would a retired Chocolate Thief do with themselves but try to resurrect chocolate so they can steal it again.'

'Very true. Idle hands, etc. But it's important that they understand the reality of what is happening. The potential cost of our actions. Something that is hard to do when we dream of perfect worlds. So it's good to have your voice with us.'

'I'll bring Oak and DI Gloom up to speed and between

us we should be able to have some effect on how many of the militia arrive at your door.'

'You're damaging your career.'

'No, I'm doing as ordered in finding you. I will not be telling them where you are – but I will be upholding the law in helping prevent civil war.'

'You know I've followed your cases, The Dancing Spy is my favourite – the way you decoded that cipher was inspired work.'

'I am a bloody good detective.'

'Ah, ha! Wonderful. You really are one of us.'

After breakfast, having received a security of Chocolate Tree Farm briefing from Aunt Mabel, and agreeing her plan of action for the coming days with The Chocolate Thieves, the detective, with a pocket of fortifying chocolate biscuits, sets out to get in the way of the Global Cocoa militia.

Afia looks at her reflection in the bedroom mirror and recites a mantra from a birthing book. 'Breathe. You'll be ready when the time comes.' She frowns. 'Do people really believe that rubbish? How can anyone be ready to give birth?'

Furness appears behind her and puts his arms around her. 'You will be. You trust in nature, don't you?'

'I trust in chocolate.'

'Chocolate is life.'

They both laugh at how ridiculous they sound.

'She will be here so soon.' Afia cradles her womb.

'I know – but could there be a healthier, more natural place to give birth?'

'You mean with the impending arrival of a fully armed militia intending to kill us.'

'I was thinking more romantically. And practically of

you pushing her out in one of the stables. So much easier to clean up the mess.'

'Fuck off. If it happens here it happens in that ridiculously comfortable bed.' Afia looks out of the window at the inviting warmth of the early spring sun; the breeze ruffling the meadow grass; a buzzard circling, hunting; the cows grazing in the meadows beyond the greenhouses; hearing the birdsong on the air – and sees in her mind's eye flashes of its destruction. 'I think we should stay safe in this room forever.'

'Just let the world happen around us.'

'I'm sure the others would fetch and carry cake for us.'

'How fat would we get?'

'Very fat.'

'I'll still love you.'

'Liar – I wouldn't.'

'Talking of food – we've work to do.'

Down in the kitchen they go through the cupboards, the stone-shelved larder and the produce sheds, calculating how long the food supplies will last now they are living in self-imposed exile from the world. Coming out of the winter into spring Aunt Mabel's stores from last year's harvest are, as expected, depleted but still enough to feed everyone for the time being. There are sacks of potatoes, boxes of parsnips, carrots, cabbages and swedes, hangings of onions and garlic, boxes of apples, jars of chutneys, pickles, jams and honey. In the freezers are bags of peas, broad beans, blackcurrants, blackberries, cherries, plums and raspberries. In the butchery they find two of the four freezers empty, the other two crammed with boar, venison and rabbits.

By Furness and Afia's calculations, with nine mouths to feed, they've just enough stored food to last a month.

'Long enough to establish the cocoa tissue cultures and

294

harvest the budwood from my trees ready for export,' insists Aunt Mabel.

As for the cocoa, a whole barn is given over to the scientific study of the fermentation, drying and storing in sacks of every variety grown on the farm.

And most exciting of all is the discovery Furness and Afia make of Aunt Mabel's research into the origin varieties of cocoa grown by the ancient Mesoamerican civilisations and the wild cocoa harvested from the forests of the upper Amazon – with their mysterious flavours that time-travel the palate and the imagination to thousands of years before the present.

There is the sound of the motorbikes being kick-started in the vehicle barn. And out ride Dunstan and Kyoko setting out on reconnaissance to get a human eye view of the contours of the land and routes of potential encroachment.

Out past the greenhouses and around the pond they ride through the cattle-grazing meadows. Running through a line of trees is the natural defence of a small full-flowing river marking the boundary of the farm to the west. They stop to consult the map Aunt Mabel has given them – they are now southwest of the farmhouse with the wood lying due south. The B road beyond marking the southern boundary of the farm. A rook caws above them and they watch its progress through the clear sky. Following it they find themselves confronted by a rookery in a clump of trees teeming with the cacophony of at least a thousand birds – the horror film reference is not lost on either of them.

Into the cool light-dappling wood they follow the animal tracks. Startling the grazing red deer and avoiding a lively family of wild boar as they ride down to the southern edge of the farm where for the most part dense undergrowth obstructs access from the road beyond – but there are enough incursion points and tracks to use by the militia to stealthily make their way through the wood to the farmhouse and the cocoa tree greenhouses.

Riding on they pass through the bright sunlit glades that are home to the beehives. In the wild heart of the wood they stop to drink their bottles of homemade ginger beer and it's not long before they are naked and fucking against a tree.

Leaving the wood to the east they encounter a field littered with rabbits hopping and darting in all directions into warrens as the two motorbikes come out of the trees. Riding through this meadow and the next, where the horses casually graze, takes them alongside the road upon which they drove to the farm, across the secret lane leading up to the house and through the orchards to the north where there are more beehives. The two-metre-thick bramble hedges, acting as nature's razor wire, running around these fields and the orchards also have within them, completely obscured, racks of rusting metal spikes strong enough to deter vehicles and do serious injury to infantry. They ride back around the farm buildings and into the vehicle barn.

The next few days are full of defence preparations. Twenty-four mannequins are made of straw, dressed in blue overalls and positioned, standing and crouching with fake wooden guns, as a false line of defence in the garden meadow and along the electric moat. Canisters of theobromine, valerian and liberty cap gas are created and strategically placed throughout the garden meadow, at the edge of and in the wood and around the greenhouses. Pouches of rosehip with a small explosive charge are attached to trip wires and laid in the wood. Cocoa is roasted and liquefied to make urns of boiling hot chocolate and attached to two paintball cannons in the observatory. Lights and public address system speakers are attached to trees ready to illuminate and broadcast throughout the wood.

On the afternoon of the 4th April 2021 a blue and white Dauphin 2 helicopter, a favourite of special forces units, makes a reconnaissance flight over Chocolate Tree Farm. Circling the boundary then hovering over the greenhouses for a short time before flying away to the north.

At the Global Cocoa warehouse at the Port of Tilbury the gathered militia comprising of 175 international mercenaries is preparing to move out.

DS Silky looks on from the driver's seat of the Range Rover – there are fewer of them than she anticipated but still too many. She calls DI Gloom. 'They're loading trucks and helicopters with enough crates of armaments to start an incursion violent enough to overthrow a third-world country's democratically elected government.'

'There is not the political motivation to stop them.'

'And what about the law?'

'There's no will from above to prosecute it.'

'Then it is solely in our hands.'

'It would seem so – good luck.'

An SUV pulls up alongside her. In it is a team of CFTP activists disguised as immigration officials. With a nod from the detective they begin to check the validity of the paperwork each mercenary is carrying – all of them conveniently have diplomatic passports.

DS Silky walks over to Karl Dance, observing the circled location on the map he has laid out on the table before him – it is Chocolate Tree Farm. 'A weekend training exercise on the South Downs.'

'These are dangerous times, Detective,' he retorts, adding, 'You'll find my operatives all have diplomatic immunity.'

'Your militia can still be detained if they are deemed to be in danger of doing harm to others or themselves. Or are suspected of committing a grave crime. And that immunity only applies to those nationals with whom the UK have a consular convention.'

'No one is going to let you get in our way,' he confidently informs her and goes to walk away.

As he passes her DS Silky pulls his sidearm from its holster and points it at his head. He keeps his composure. Those around them pause – hands to weapons.

DS Silky smiles. 'Last chance to save yourself from the consequences of your actions, Mr Dance.'

'Where's the fun in staying at home?'

The detective drops the gun. 'Don't have a safe trip.'

He arrogantly saunters away.

DS Silky sends a live feed via her phone to the CFTP website of the heavily armed Global Cocoa militia departing in trucks and helicopters.

As the militia drive out of the city Stanley Oak blocks Queen Elizabeth Bridge over the Thames with burning vehicles and CFTP eco-warriors on bikes slash the tyres of the pulled-up-to-a-standstill trucks and spray paint their windscreens to obscure the drivers' views. They successfully hinder the convoy's progress but the pointing of guns, warning shots and threats of serious harm allow the vehicles to continue on their journey.

Battering the trucks off the M25 at speed with appropriated armoured police vans proves effective at ending some of the militia's travel plans – but still too many of the vehicles get to their destination.

That evening from the top of the meadow above the rookery Dunstan, Kyoko and Aunt Mabel watch, through field glasses, the gathering of the Global Cocoa militia to the south – the distance to the farm approximately two miles through the dense wood.

A hundred men and women of multiple nationalities with their trucks of armaments arrive via the B road and by air in three helicopters – all no doubt paid well for the pleasure of what they are about to do.

Dunstan picks out the two familiar figures of Whittaker and Midas studying a map and observing the landscape – discussing with Karl Dance the layout of the farm and how best to secure the greenhouses. Dance is clearly instructed that none of his people are to put the greenhouses at risk through military action.

'The pipers are here to lead their rats,' states Dunstan.

'They will never cease,' observes Kyoko.

'We will stop them,' bristles Aunt Mabel in a lethal icy tone.

Back at the farm Dunstan sends Seb Lilburne footage of the gathering militia with instructions for its immediate broadcast.

An hour after sunset seventy members of the militia cross the road and enter the wood.

At the farm The Chocolate Thieves take up their positions in the greenhouses – flasks of hot chocolate and a supply of chocolate biscuits to hand. And Rikard and Lovisa head over to the observatory.

All the lights at the farm are switched off.

Locked in the control room Aunt Mabel turns up the electric moat to 1,600 volts with 10 amps, and zones the digital faraday cage allowing earpiece communication between The Chocolate Thieves, the Linnaeuses and herself.

'Communication check, Mabel to observatory?'

'Here,' comes Rikard and Lovisa's reply.

'Mabel to greenhouses.'

'In position,' from the six Chocolate Thieves.

'Remember, we have the advantage,' Aunt Mabel informs them.

She pours herself a cup of hot chocolate and takes a moment to dunk a biscuit and enjoy its rich chocolate flavours. Her eyes keenly on the bank of monitors displaying a direct feed from every security camera at the farm. The cameras film in night vision – their footage broadcast on the Chocolate For The People website.

Aunt Mabel's tone is serious as, zooming the camera in on the red button, she informs the watching world, 'I have to turn the key anti-clockwise two clicks, the first to counter my first impulse, the second only if I am absolutely sure it is the right decision, and then I punch the red button down as hard as I can. I promise you it is not an idle threat to destroy the cocoa trees if Global Cocoa win the night.'

She lets silence fill the airwaves – so to give this information time to sink into the minds of those watching across the world.

'Good – now let's freak out these fuckers,' and with these words Aunt Mabel releases the hallucinogenic gas into the wood.

It is not long before there are the screams of the first causalities of the tripwires – hands to inflamed and watering blinded eyes and burning itching faces they stumble back out of the wood.

Ten militia down – the advance temporarily stalled.

Cocooned in greenhouse three Furness takes a break

from recipe planning and looks about him. 'I spy with my little eye something beginning with C.'

As quick as a flash, 'Cocoa pod,' shouts Afia through everyone's earpiece from greenhouse four, where, with her eyes on her womb, she senses the baby inside her is telling her she is ready to come into the world. 'Really – at this point in time?'

'I was about to say that,' complains Dorothea from greenhouse two.

'Too slow, chocolate tongue,' teases Afia. 'I too spy with my little eye something beginning with C.'

'Chocolate biscuit,' shouts Savage from greenhouse one through a mouth full of chocolate biscuit.

'Correct,' replies Afia.

'Damn it! Too slow – again,' complains Dorothea.

In greenhouse six Kyoko laughs and shakes her head at this ridiculous exchange.

From greenhouse five Dunstan interrupts the game. 'If you'd all like to log on to the CFTP website on your phones you can watch the live stream of what is happening in the wood.'

They all do.

When the militia continue their advance into the heart of the wood the shout goes out, 'Gas!' Fingers fumble as they rapidly pull on their gas masks – but not soon enough. And the disorientating, perception-bending, gas ensures nature is now a weapon in the claustrophobic darkness of the wood.

Time elongates and the haunting calls of tawny owls send shivers down spines. Then the night birds in eerie silence, with black deathly glares, swoop through the trees, talons gripping collars and carrying away members of the militia to feed to their chicks. Sabre-toothed badgers clench jaws on legs as their dens are stumbled into. Boars with ever-elongating tusks gouge abdomens of anyone crossing their path. Stags with spears for antlers rut the too slow to retreat. But how can they retreat with the trees running in all directions, knocking them over. And all they just want to do, to a man and a woman, is curl up in the undergrowth on a bed of moss and fall asleep – but the seizure-inducing strobe lighting and the shrill sound of the screaming trees amplified a thousand times in their heads won't let them.

Brutalised, eventually finding their way back out of the wood the way they came, the militia await the dawn and the hangover of recovery before trying again.

Another twenty-five seriously injured militia are permanently out of the fight.

In the observatory Lovisa is locating the telescope, searching out a celestial body to show Rikard. 'There it is – Asteroid 9 Metis. Have a look.' Rikard looks through the telescope. 'Discovered by the astronomer Andrew Graham in 1848, it's one of the main-belt asteroids, with a diameter close to 200km and composed of silicates and metallic nickel-iron.'

Rikard studies the celestial object with fascination. 'It has the shape of a cocoa seed.'

'No, it doesn't. Seriously – only you could look into the night sky and see what you see in your hand every day. It's now at its closest to us,' continues Lovisa, 'passing through opposition – the sun, earth and the asteroid now being aligned.'

'What does Metis mean?'

'Metis was a mythical Titaness – in Greek philosophy she was the mother of "wisdom" and "deep thought", although her name originally suggested "magical cunning". The Stoic commentators interpreted Metis as the embodiment of "wise counsel", which is what she was for the Renaissance.'

Rikard straightens up from the telescope. 'Thank you – it's wonderful.'

'Yes it is,' says Lovisa having another look at the asteroid.

'Wise counsel, magical cunning – sounds like you're describing Mabel Arber.'

'With what she has planned it's a true description. Can you imagine what it must feel like to be a hundred years old? How many times will she see humanity try to end itself?'

Rikard pours them each a cup of hot chocolate and quietly ponders, 'The following generation's inheritance is the Anthropocene extinction.'

Lovisa sadly shakes her head. 'It's so ridiculous what is happening. People believe we are going to survive by living off-world. Travel to an earth-like exoplanet as if they are in some sci-fi utopia. There isn't the time to create an off-world future.'

'Or that extra-terrestrials will make first contact and rescue us from ourselves.'

'If they notice we are here. The distances needed to travel by other intelligent life to reach us, well, by the time the radio waves we broadcast get their attention we will be nothing but particles of dust.'

Rikard nods in agreement. 'In just ten thousand years humans have evolved from primitive farmers to an advanced civilisation beyond our true comprehension – and into a species that is killing the environment we live in.'

'It's absurd.'

They thoughtfully sip their hot chocolate.

'With the intelligence we do have we know the wonderful opportunities that will unfold in our future lives,' points out Rikard.

'You think there could be a future life?'

'Can we change human behaviour? We have to be optimistic.'

'Is it too late? Unless we succeed on this night, doing this one simple act of protecting these cocoa trees and the liberty of the ideology they represent, then we will truly surrender all our futures to the land of the blind and the one-eyed opportunists.'

Sunrise. Gas masks on, with heads feeling like they've been hit by wrecking balls, the militia cautiously return to the wood. And two helicopters full of militia take to the air.

Aunt Mabel watches them rise up from beyond the camp and whistles four staccato notes into a microphone – the sound of whistles comes out of a speaker in the rookery. And with the terrorising cries of demons the birds take to the air, divide into two flocks and dive at the helicopters and in through the open doors – beaks tear at exposed flesh and eyes, talons slice through veins. In the confined space of the helicopters the men and women inside can do little to defend themselves and so take the option to jump. Birds still upon them as they land with bone-breaking crunches into the trees. The pilots lose control of their flying machines, spinning away from the field of battle, both baling out at the last minute, and the helicopters crash into the Global Cocoa camp destroying munitions in balls of flames. And another twenty-four militia are out of the fight.

Aunt Mabel smiles to herself. 'I've lived here for over seventy years – time enough to train some feisty birds.'

She presses a button on the control desk and an agitating, peace-disrupting, vibroacoustic signal is sent through to every beehive in the clearings in the wood. A million angry bees swarm out of the hives and vent their distress upon the creeping militia. A smile ripples across the faces of everyone at the farm as they watch on their screens the panic and fear accompanied with the sounds of the screams of pain as the militia crash through the trees away from the bee attack.

'Everyone, gas masks on,' commands Aunt Mabel and she releases the gas in the garden meadow, around the farmhouse and in and around the greenhouses.

Twenty-five militia simultaneously run, firing, out of the wood into the gas-filled meadow. Greeted by the sound effect of return gunfire from the silhouetted mannequins they dive into the long grass and onto the electric moat. The air is filled with the sound of electric static and arcing jagged blue streaks of electricity – the screaming militia performing a hysterical danse macabre of defecating souls.

The third helicopter flies into the fray attempting to rope drop a dozen militia within the electric moat. This is Karl Dance with his elite team of handpicked militia – the twelve men and women with the reputation of being the most proficient killers.

Lovisa and Rikard open the observatory shutters and unleash a volley of anti-aircraft hot chocolate from their paint ball cannons connected to electrically heated kettles. Machine-gun fire cracks the air and bullets rattle off the observatory but they keep firing, successfully drenching the aircraft – scalding the militia inside and impeding the helicopter pilot's vision, forcing him to make an emergency landing in the walled garden.

Alighting the helicopter the chocolate-covered militia are immediately set upon by the glaring of feral farm cats, their claws lacerating flesh, their teeth biting to the bone – seriously bloodied, the militia who can flee.

There is a pause in the battle.

An eerie silence.

The militia who have survived the bee attack and the crossing of the electric moat, over the flailing bodies of their comrades, nervously move through the fog of gas towards the farm.

There is a sound. What is it? Yes – it's the galloping of hoofs – getting louder.

DS Silky's horse ploughs through two of the militia, her baton swiftly sending another unconscious to the ground as she charges down a fourth forcing the militiawoman to fall back onto the moat as she takes aim to fire at the detective – her electrocuted screams send shivers of terror through those still standing.

Stanley Oak as good as decapitates a militiaman with his baton, charging down a militiawoman and trampling her into the ground just as she was thinking, 'How fucking surreal the last twelve hours have been.'

The militiaman reels in terror at the sight of the white horse rearing up in front of him, not so stupefied he doesn't go to fire his gun, but Scarlett Vamp is too quick for him and brings her baton down upon the militiaman knocking out his teeth with a jaw-breaking whack. She brings the horse round and another of the militia gets her steel-heeled boot down on his head.

Katla whacks a militiawoman towards Damon who whacks a militiaman towards her, his girlfriend in turn whacks his militiaman back to him as he whacks her militiawoman back to her – all the man and woman want to do is fall unconscious to the ground but Katla and Damon are having too much fun.

Karl Dance and the five members of his team who

survived the hell of the helicopter ride and landing have now stealthily reached the greenhouses. Once they secure the cocoa trees the battle is won. Walking through the swirling fog of the gas along the path in front of the greenhouses they are surprised to meet no resistance.

Aunt Mabel, glancing towards the red button, reaches out with her right hand, and turns the key – once.

In unison the six militia open a door to a greenhouse and step inside – the trees, the humidity and the fog create a still and eerie, claustrophobic, time-displacing atmosphere.

The Chocolate Thieves take the advantage, stepping silently out of the cover of the trees and ripping off each of the militia's gas mask. The lungs of the militia fill with the hallucinogen and they know they have but a short time to secure the greenhouses before the full effect of the gas overcomes them.

Savage wrestles the machine gun out of the militiaman's hands – bullets spraying through the glass panels of the roof of the greenhouse. Relieved of his machine gun the militiaman reaches for his pistol but this too is snatched from his hand and thrown to the ground. The militiaman pulls out his combat knife and goes to fling it at the ever-increasing-in-size Chocolate Thief. But the giant raises a finger to stop his attack. He then picks up his barrel of hot chocolate and with a sigh the giant throws the scalding, sweet, delicious-smelling drink into the militiaman's face. Savage calmly steps forwards, grabs hold of the militiaman's knife-holding hand, swings the blade away from him and brings the heel of his very large right hand into the militiaman's face – connecting with his nose with a satisfyingly sickening crack. He is sent onto his back, out cold.

Dorothea throws her militiaman over her shoulder. He

lands into a role back onto his feet pulling out a sidearm as he does so, she ducks behind a tree, giving him nothing to fire at as he turns back towards her. He looks around him – where is she? He takes two cautious steps along the greenhouse. The air particles are dancing colours. Reaching around the tree Dorothea pulls him against the trunk in a chokehold with her right arm while trying to control the gun in his left hand. The gun is fired; thankfully it's his foot that the bullet goes through. Still holding him in a chokehold, Dorothea drags the militiaman out of the greenhouse and throws him onto the electric moat to finish him off.

Furness recoils from a slash of the militiawoman's blade, grabs her arm to twist it but she is ready for him and he finds himself on the ground with the knife coming at his chest. In her eyes The Chocolate Thief's gas-masked face distractedly begins to melt into a puddle of dark chocolate. Furness grabs the wrist of the hand holding the knife and with his free hand reaches out for the small plant pot to his right – taking hold of it he brings it up and smashes it against the side of the militiawoman's head, knocking her away from him. Getting to his feet he still has hold of her knife wrist and pinning her to the ground with the heel of his shoe on her neck he twists her arm to breaking point. But she resists the pain with a raging scream and kicks his legs from beneath him. She is quickly on him again with the knife aimed at his throat but he is quick enough to bring his knees up and kicks her over his head onto her back. Spinning round he rolls her onto her front and with her own knife he pins both her hands together behind her back.

Stepping into view Afia, with decisive brutality, shoves a luminous yellow cocoa pod into the militiawoman's young, pretty face and quickly relieves her of all her weaponry. Blood pouring out of her nose, feeling queasy from the gas and rapid blood loss she pulls a bewildered expression on seeing Afia is pregnant. Not only that but the baby in her womb is laughing and waving at her. She backs away from The Chocolate Thief. Now a luminous red cocoa pod leaves Afia's hand and travels through her forehead, passing completing through her skull, wiping away all reason to be there in a shower of fireworks and baby-faced cocoa seeds. Turning away she stumbles to the door. Afia throws another two cocoa pods after her, striking the militiawoman on the head, sending her flying out of the greenhouse door with a cry of pain. At which point Afia's water breaks. 'Bloody hell – here we go.'

Breaking all the laws of physics with his rapidity of movement Dunstan brings the side of his shoe down on the militiaman's shin and breaks the hold he has on his arms by bringing his head back into the militiaman's face. Turning round Dunstan lands a series of punches keeping the militiaman on his heels – sending him backwards out of the door. Now time is suspended as he hangs in the air – slowly falling to the ground. Time jolts back into reality. Onto his feet the militiaman comes back in through the door blocking the next two punches and landing a couple himself. He is back in the fight and drawing his knife towards The Chocolate Thief. Dunstan just dodges serious injury from the slash of the blade. He grabs the militiaman's knife hand and they grapple into the cocoa trees – both landing body blows. The militiaman has his weight on Dunstan's throat. Time lingers again. He still has to hold off the blade in the militiaman's right hand. His head being pushed into the soil of one of the pots releases some of the pressure on his windpipe and he wrenches himself out of the militiaman's grip. Time jolts back to the present. The militiaman lurches forwards, his head going through a pane of glass in the side of the greenhouse. Dunstan pulls him back in and throws him face down onto the ground. Lifting the militiaman's knife hand he twists the arm as far as it will go and stamps on his elbow, shattering the joint. A second stamp on the face and the militiaman is unconscious.

Kyoko delivers two rapid punches into Karl Dance's eyes, followed by a series of kicks to his body. Disassociated from the pain, he's had enough of her attitude. He blocks Kyoko's next high kick to his head and lands successive stomach punches with extreme force. Moving with controlled aggression he picks her up above his head and throws her along the greenhouse. Crumpled on the ground she hears his footsteps approaching. Grabbing his foot to stop his follow-up stamp on her head Kyoko regains her feet – aggressively twisting him around and off balance. It works and as he spins for eternity on the spot Kyoko delivers rapid and vicious kidney punches. But he is resilient enough to take them and reaching out of the vortex he grabs her by the hair and draws his pistol to shoot her in the head. Kyoko grabs hold of the gun, lifts up her feet and plants them in Dance's face. Whiplashing his head back, she backflips out of his grip onto her feet and breaks his knees with two vicious kicks. Next she twists his gun arm out of its socket. He watches her take the just-drawn knife out of his last good hand and with fascination sees her dislocate this arm too. Global Cocoa's Head of Security Operations lies on the ground unable to move – laid out like a dissected skeleton.

Aunt Mabel reaches out with her right hand and unturns the key in the red button.

Over the next few hours the defeated Global Cocoa militia are forced to carry each other off Chocolate Tree Farm into the waiting police vehicles, summoned by DS

Silky, and taken into custody and to hospital.

'Well done, everyone!' exclaims Aunt Mabel walking into the parlour, where they've all gathered for a shot of cocoa gin. 'How exciting that was – don't you think?' The Chocolate Spy's words are greeted with wry smiles. 'And we're all still alive.'

Afia is lying in her ridiculously comfortable bed, knees raised, legs apart, with no choice but to give birth. She grips Furness's hand and her eyes, as they meet his, tell a story of love, fear, helplessness and rage at this situation and then they both begin to laugh.

'Oh fucking hell – you utter bastard.'

'Breathe – I love you.'

'Fuck off – I love you.'

And then, with a push and a scream of effort, she is in the world. Their small beautiful daughter. Quickly scooped into her mother's arms – both cradled by Furness – the parents weeping with joy.

The rest of The Chocolate Thieves arrive in the room to be introduced to the new addition to their family – expressing involuntary 'Oohs' and 'Aahs' at the delicate little child and the loving scene of her with her mother and father.

'Her name is Serene Cocoa Furness,' Afia tells them.

At last there is a real sense of peace and a feeling of happiness to their world.

Aunt Mabel walks into the bedroom full of smiling and tearful people. 'Look at the three of you. Wonderful – simply wonderful.'

In that split second a spray of bullets comes through the window, hitting the wall just over mother and daughter's heads. Furness covers Afia and Serene with his body.

Dunstan looks out of the window. 'Midas.'

Aunt Mabel is the first outside, pistol raised, ready to shoot the chocolatier where he arrogantly stands.

Having discarded his spent machine gun Midas now has a pistol in his hand. 'We are here to claim our chocolate.'

'You're just like every Midas before you.'

'We are men of ambition.'

'Men of low cunning and of little chocolate talent.'

The chocolatier bristles with rage, his finger ready to pull the trigger. 'I am the most successful artisan chocolatier in the world.'

'You know, Midas, after so many lessons in humility I'd have thought you would have learned something about yourself. But still you don't see how mistaken you are in every action you take. You'll always be a rancid, egotistic maker of very average chocolate,' Aunt Mabel calmly replies.

'Just kill the old witch for fuck's sake and let's take what is rightfully ours.' Whittaker grins sleazily as he steps forward to stand beside his friend.

At which moment Lovisa, taser in hand, darts out of the house past Aunt Mabel and, before he can react to protect himself, shocks the glutenous CEO of Global Cocoa in his testicles – just enough of a shock to cause a lot of pain and keep him conscious to feel it. Whittaker screams like a scalded swine and drops to his knees, clutching his tortured parts.

'You fat bastard – that's for abandoning me to the mercy of those kidnappers,' Lovisa shouts at him.

Rikard arrives on the scene and lays into him with punches and kicks. 'How dare you try and steal our chocolate.'

'Get them the fuck off me,' demands the defeated bully.

It takes both Stanley Oak and Scarlett Vamp to pull the seriously riled Rikard and Lovisa off Whittaker.

Laughing at his friend's pain, Midas turns back towards Aunt Mabel. He is now surrounded by The Chocolate Thieves. But with a gun in his hand Midas is predictably dangerous.

So Aunt Mabel will not lower her weapon. 'What good company to die in,' she had said to them on that first day. And she had meant it.

'We're taking control of the cocoa trees,' snarls Midas. 'I've seen your fighting techniques – very entertaining. But you're not killers and that is what you will have to be to stop us.'

'I am – when it is time,' is Aunt Mabel's chilling reply.

Like two duellists the SOE agent and the chocolatier take aim with their pistols.

They fire simultaneously.

In the explosion of sound is the crack and whistle of ricochet as the two bullets collide in the air between the duellists.

Everyone stands in silence.

Nothing in the world has changed.

But it is now the end of the battle.

A startled Midas goes to fire again only for his gun to be snatched out of his hand by DS Silky.

'Detective!' exclaims a now-vulnerable Midas.

Savage rests his hand over Aunt Mabel's still-aimed gun. And she lowers it. The Chocolate Thieves and their friends step menacingly towards the vile chocolatier.

'Ah.' Midas takes a nervous step backwards. 'Gentlemen? Ladies? All is fair in cocoa love and war – is it not?'

Furness literally punches Midas off his feet, sending him out cold to the ground.

Within a day the footage of *The Battle For Chocolate Tree*

Farm is edited together from all the different camera angles of the broadcast feeds into a single feature-length film and is rapidly becoming the highest-viewed online film in history.

The brilliance of the use of nature as a defensive weapon to defeat a stronger foe quickly becomes a contemporary allegory for the cause of defiance against political and cultural injustice.

The Secretary General of the United Nations arrives at Chocolate Tree Farm to agree a plan of action for the in-situ recultivation of cocoa. And a UN protection force is posted at the farm to guard the work of Aunt Mabel and Dr Linnaeus.

Within a month the first of the cocoa budwood and plantlets are distributed to the cocoa-growing regions of the world to be grown by native cocoa farmers under the guidance of Rikard Linnaeus and his handpicked team of cocoa scientists. Seb Lilburne acts as a civilian observer and Chocolate For The People obtain the fair trading licence for the global distribution of all the newly grown cocoa.

…And so the world waits for the return of chocolate.

The three grooms in their best suits and the three brides in exquisite floral summer dresses and carrying bouquets of delicate cocoa flowers are gathered in the kitchen of The Black Truffle Hotel.

Dunstan pours each of them a shot of Chocolate Tree Farm Cocoa Gin. 'A hundred and one years of The Chocolate Thieves.'

'How will our descendants judge their history?' asks Dorothea.

'We see our ancestors through the world they leave

behind,' answers Kyoko.

'So we teach them our different way of living. Show them some of us wanted to leave them a better world than the one we lived in,' says Afia.

'CHOC 4 – the generation that resurrected chocolate,' adds Furness.

Savage's smile is the broadest of the six of them. 'We really are living legends.'

'To the family we've created,' they say together with light laughs and down their fortifying shots.

The three couples walk out of the kitchen into the late-August-sunshine-filled garden to 'The Ballad Of The Chocolate Thieves' played by Stanley Oak on his fiddle and the applause and cheers of their invited guests – Aunt Mabel, Scarlett Vamp, DS Silky, DI Gloom, Damon and Katla, Seb Lilburne, Rikard and Lovisa Linnaeus.

Afia takes Serene off DS Silky into her arms.

And Aunt Mabel stands before them. 'I am delighted to have the honour of officiating your vows in the presence of your ancestors and your friends on such a lovely day in the beautiful wild flower garden of your wonderful home.

'The history of The Chocolate Thieves is one of whimsical brilliance, of the struggle and determination to survive, of farcical acts and feats of daring-do, of life's tragedies and of its joys. Most importantly it is a history of the loyalty of friendship and lives full of love. And the six of you exceptional rogues, the fourth generation of this family, are fully deserving of that love.'

The three couples exchange rings and speak with true hearts.

'Dorothea, I give myself to your curiosity.'

'Savage, I give myself to your intellect.'

'Afia, I give myself to your spirit.'

'Furness, I give myself to your gentleness.'

'Kyoko, I give myself to your inspiration.'

'Dunstan, I give myself to your imagination.'

And say together, 'For all the time of our days to come.'

Traditional photographs are taken, in showers of cocoa petals, as couples, a family and with guests. And they feast on the produce of Chocolate Tree Farm – a buffet of dressed trout, game pie and organic walled-garden summer vegetables washed down with a specially brewed barrel of Sleight Of Hand Chocolate Stout. At the centre of the table is a three tier 80% Wild Amazonian Criollo cocoa chocolate wedding cake filled and decorated with summer fruits – on top a London taxi with the registration CHOC 4 and six Chocolate Thieves dressed for a heist.

And the toast – the guests stand and raise their glasses. 'The Chocolate Thieves.'